Doris Lessing was born in Persia in 1919 but moved to Southern Rhodesia, where her father went to farm, at the age of five. In 1949 she came to London, where she still lives.

Her first novel, *The Grass Is Singing*, was published in 1950, and she made her début as an accomplished writer of short stories with *This Was the Old Chief's Country* in 1951. 1956 saw her last visit to the country where she grew up and which provides the setting for so much of her fiction (the Southern Rhodesian authorities declared her a Prohibited Immigrant after her return to England). Her experiences there produced *Going Home*, a bitter, prophetic and often bleakly funny account of white settler society and its victims. Between 1952 and 1969 her famous novel-sequence, *Children of Violence*, appeared, and in 1962 what is perhaps her most well known and haunting work, *The Golden Notebook*, was published.

Doris Lessing has been honoured with the Society of Authors' Somerset Maugham Award and is also a winner of the Prix Medici. As a novelist, she ranks among the most distinguished writing in English today, and, in an age when the short story seems to be in sad decline, she is one of the few authors whose writings in this form find both critical acclaim and popular success.

D0226642

Also by Doris Lessing

NOVELS
The Grass Is Singing
The Summer Before the Dark
The Golden Notebook
Briefing for a Descent into Hell
Memoirs of a Survivor

In the novel-sequence 'Children of Violence'
Martha Quest
A Proper Marriage
A Ripple from the Storm
Landlocked
The Four-Gated City

NON-FICTION
In Pursuit of the English
Particularly Cats
Going Home

SHORT STORIES
This Was the Old Chief's Country
Five
The Habit of Loving
A Man and Two Women
African Stories
The Story of a Non-Marrying Man and Other Stories
Winter in July
The Black Madonna
This Was the Old Chief's Country (Collected African
    Stories Vol. 1)
The Sun Between Their Feet (Collected African Stories Vol. 2)
The Temptation of Jack Orkney (Collected Stories Vol. 2)

PLAYS
Play with a Tiger

Doris Lessing

To Room Nineteen

VOLUME ONE of Doris Lessing's Collected Stories

TRIAD PANTHER

Published in 1979 by Triad/Panther Books
Frogmore, St Albans, Herts AL2 2NF

ISBN 0 586 04595 3

Triad Paperbacks Ltd is an imprint of
Chatto, Bodley Head & Jonathan Cape Ltd
and Granada Publishing Ltd

First published in Great Britain by
Jonathan Cape Ltd 1978
Copyright © Doris Lessing, 1958, 1962, 1963, 1964,
1968, 1969, 1971, 1972
This edition copyright © Doris Lessing 1978

Set, printed and bound in Great Britain by
Cox & Wyman Ltd, Reading
Set in Intertype Plantin

BIBLIOGRAPHICAL NOTE

'The Other Woman' was first published in *Lilliput*; 'Through the Tunnel' in *John Bull*; 'The Habit of Loving', 'Pleasure', 'The Day Stalin Died', 'Wine', 'He' and 'The Eye of God in Paradise' in *The Habit of Loving*; and 'One off the Short List', 'A Woman on a Roof', 'How I Finally Lost My Heart', 'A Man and Two Women', 'A Room', 'England versus England', 'Two Potters', 'Between Men' and 'To Room Nineteen' appeared in *A Man and Two Women*.

These stories have appeared previously in paperback in the following editions: 'The Habit of Loving', 'The Woman', 'Through the Tunnel', 'Pleasure', 'The Day Stalin Died', 'Wine', 'He' and 'The Eye of God in Paradise' in *The Habit of Loving*; 'The Other Woman' in *Five*. The rest of the stories appear in *A Man and Two Women*. These collections are all published in Panther Books.

CONTENTS

THE HABIT OF LOVING

In 1947 George wrote again to Myra, saying that now the war
was well over she should come home and marry him. She wrote
back from Australia, where she had gone with her two children
in 1943 because there were relations there, saying she felt they
had drifted apart; she was no longer sure she wanted to marry
George. He did not allow himself to collapse. He cabled her the
air fare and asked her to come over and see him. She came, for
two weeks, being unable to leave the children for longer. She
said she liked Australia; she liked the climate; she did not like
the English climate any longer; she thought England was, very
probably, played out; and she had become used to missing
London. Also, presumably, to missing George Talbot.

For George this was a very painful fortnight. He believed it
was painful for Myra, too. They had met in 1938, had lived
together for five years, and had exchanged for four years the
letters of lovers separated by fate. Myra was certainly the love
of his life. He had believed he was of hers until now. Myra, an
attractive woman made beautiful by the suns and beaches of
Australia, waved goodbye at the airport, and her eyes were
filled with tears.

George's eyes, as he drove away from the airport, were dry.
If one person has loved another truly and wholly, then it is
more than love that collapses when one side of the indissoluble
partnership turns away with a tearful goodbye. George dismissed the taxi early and walked through St James's Park.
Then it seemed too small for him, and he went to Green Park.
Then he walked into Hyde Park and through to Kensington
Gardens. When the dark came and they closed the great gates
of the park he took a taxi home. He lived in a block of flats near
Marble Arch. For five years Myra had lived with him there,
and it was here he had expected to live with her again. Now he
moved into a new flat near Covent Garden. Soon after that he

wrote Myra a very painful letter. It occurred to him that he had often received such letters, but had never written one before. It occurred to him that he had entirely underestimated the amount of suffering he must have caused in his life. But Myra wrote him a sensible letter back, and George Talbot told himself that now he must finally stop thinking about Myra.

Therefore he became rather less of a dilettante in his work than he had been recently, and he agreed to produce a new play written by a friend of his. George Talbot was a man of the theatre. He had not acted in it for many years now; but he wrote articles, he sometimes produced a play, he made speeches on important occasions and was known by everyone. When he went into a restaurant people tried to catch his eye, and he often did not know who they were. During the four years since Myra had left, he had had a number of affairs with young women round and about the theatre, for he had been lonely. He had written quite frankly to Myra about these affairs, but she had never mentioned them in her letters. Now he was very busy for some months and was seldom at home; he earned quite a lot of money, and he had a few affairs with women who were pleased to be seen in public with him. He thought about Myra a great deal, but he did not write to her again, nor she to him, although they had agreed they would always be great friends.

One evening in the foyer of a theatre he saw an old friend of his he had always admired, and he told the young woman he was with that that man had been the most irresistible man of his generation – no woman had been able to resist him. The young woman stared briefly across the foyer and said, 'Not really?'

When George Talbot got home that night he was alone, and he looked at himself with honesty in the mirror. He was sixty, but he did not look it. Whatever had attracted women to him in the past had never been his looks, and he was not much changed: a stoutish man, holding himself erect, grey-haired, carefully brushed, well dressed. He had not paid much attention to his face since those days many years ago when he had been an actor; but now he had an uncharacteristic fit of vanity and remembered that Myra had admired his mouth, while his wife had loved his eyes. He took to taking glances at himself in foyers and restaurants where there were mirrors, and he saw himself as unchanged. He was becoming conscious, though, of a discrepancy between that suave exterior and what he felt. Beneath his ribs his heart had become swollen and soft and painful, a monstrous area of sympathy playing enemy to what he had been. When people made jokes he was often unable to laugh; and his manner of talking, which was light and allusive and dry, must have changed, because more than once old friends asked him if he were depressed, and they no longer smiled appreciatively as he told his stories. He gathered he was not being good company. He understood he might be ill, and he went to the doctor. The doctor said there was nothing wrong with his heart, he had thirty years of life in him yet – luckily, he added respectfully, for the British theatre.

George came to understand that the word 'heartache' meant that a person could carry a heart that ached around with him day and night for, in his case, months. Nearly a year now. He would wake in the night, because of the pressure of pain in his chest; in the morning he woke under a weight of grief. There seemed to be no end to it; and this thought jolted him into two actions. First, he wrote to Myra, a tender, carefully phrased letter, recalling the years of their love. To this he got, in due course, a tender and careful reply. Then he went to see his wife. With her he was, and had been for many years, good friends. They saw each other often, but not so often now the children were grown-up; perhaps once or twice a year, and they never quarrelled.

His wife had married again after they divorced, and now she was a widow. Her second husband had been a member of Parliament, and she worked for the Labour Party, and she was on a Hospital Advisory Committee and on the Board of Directors of a progressive school. She was fifty, but did not look it. On this afternoon she was wearing a slim grey suit and grey shoes, and her grey hair had a wave of white across the front which made her look distinguished. She was animated, and very happy to see George; and she talked about some deadhead on her hospital committee who did not see eye to eye with the progressive minority about some reform or other. They had always had their politics in common, a position somewhere left of centre in the Labour Party. She had sympathized with his being a pacifist in the First World War – he had been for a time in prison because of it; he had sympathized with her militant feminism. Both had helped the strikers in 1926. In the thirties, after they were divorced, she had helped with money when he went on tour with a company acting Shakespeare to people on the dole, or hunger-marching.

Myra had not been at all interested in politics, only in her children. And in George, of course.

George asked his first wife to marry him again, and she was so startled that she let the sugar tongs drop and crack a saucer. She asked what had happened to Myra, and George said: 'Well, dear, I think Myra forgot about me during those years in Australia. At any rate, she doesn't want me now.' When he heard his voice saying this it sounded pathetic, and he was frightened, for he could not remember ever having to appeal to a woman. Except to Myra.

His wife examined him and said briskly: 'You're lonely, George. Well, we're none of us getting any younger.'

'You don't think you'd be less lonely if you had me around?'

She got up from her chair in order that she could attend to something with her back to him, and she said that she intended to marry again quite soon. She was marrying a man considerably younger than herself, a doctor who was in the progressive minority at her hospital. From her voice George understood that she was both proud and ashamed of this marriage, and that was why she was hiding her face from him. He congratulated her and asked her if there wasn't perhaps a chance for him yet? 'After all, dear, we were happy together, weren't we? I've never really understood why that marriage ever broke up. It was you who wanted to break it up.'

'I don't see any point in raking over that old business,' she said, with finality, and returned to her seat opposite him. He envied her very much, looking young with her pink and scarcely lined face under that brave lock of deliberately whitened hair.

'But dear, I wish you'd tell me. It doesn't do any harm now, does it? And I always wondered ... I've often thought about it and wondered.' He could hear the pathetic note in his voice again, but he did not know how to alter it.

'You wondered,' she said, 'when you weren't occupied with Myra.'

'But I didn't know Myra when we got divorced.'

'You knew Phillipa and Georgina and Janet and lord knows who else.'

'But I didn't care about them.'

She sat with her competent hands in her lap and on her face was a look he remembered seeing when she told him she would divorce him. It was bitter and full of hurt. 'You didn't care about me either,' she said.

'But we were happy. Well, I was happy . . .' he trailed off, being pathetic against all his knowledge of women. For, as he sat there, his old rake's heart was telling him that if only he could find them, there must be the right words, the right tone. But whatever he said came out in this hopeless, old dog's voice, and he knew that this voice could never defeat the gallant and crusading young doctor. 'And I did care about you. Sometimes I think you were the only woman in my life.'

At this she laughed. 'Oh, George, don't get maudlin now, please.'

'Well, dear, there was Myra. But when you threw me over there was bound to be Myra, wasn't there? There were two women, you and then Myra. And I've never never understood why you broke it all up when we seemed to be so happy.'

'You didn't care for me,' she said again. 'If you had, you would never have come home from Phillipa, Georgina, Janet *et al* and said calmly, just as if it didn't matter to me in the least, that you had been with them in Brighton or wherever it was.'

'But if I had cared about them I would never have told you.'

She was regarding him incredulously, and her face was flushed. With what? Anger? George did not know.

'I remember being so proud,' he said pathetically, 'that we had solved this business of marriage and all that sort of thing. We had such a good marriage that it didn't matter, the little flirtations. And I always thought one should be able to tell the truth. I always told you the truth, didn't I?'

'Very romantic of you, dear George,' she said dryly; and soon he got up, kissed her fondly on the cheek, and went away.

He walked for a long time through the parks, hands behind his erect back, and he could feel his heart swollen and painful in his side. When the gates shut, he walked through the lighted streets he had lived in for fifty years of his life, and he was remembering Myra and Molly, as if they were one woman, merging into each other, a shape of warm easy intimacy, a shape of happiness walking beside him. He went into a little restaurant he knew well, and there was a girl sitting there who knew him because she had heard him lecture once on the state of the British theatre. He tried hard to see Myra and Molly in her face, but he failed; and he paid for her coffee and his own and went home by himself. But his flat was unbearably empty, and he left it and walked down by the Embankment for a couple of hours to tire himself, and there must have been a colder wind blowing than he knew, for next day he woke with a pain in his chest which he could not mistake for heartache.

He had flu and a bad cough, and he stayed in bed by himself and did not ring up the doctor until the fourth day, when he was getting lightheaded. The doctor said it must be the hospital at once.

But he would not go to the hospital. So the doctor said he must have day and night nurses. This he submitted to until the cheerful friendliness of the nurses saddened him beyond bearing, and he asked the doctor to ring up his wife, who would find someone to look after him and would be sympathetic. He was hoping that Molly would come herself to nurse him, but when she arrived he did not mention it, for she was busy with preparations for her new marriage. She promised to find him someone who would not wear a uniform and make jokes. They naturally had many friends in common; and she rang up an old flame of his in the theatre who said she knew of a girl who was looking for a secretary's job to tide her over a patch of not working, but who didn't really mind what she did for a few weeks.

So Bobby Tippett sent away the nurses and made up a bed for herself in his study. On the first day she sat by George's bed sewing. She wore a full dark skirt and a demure printed blouse

with short frills at the wrist, and George watched her sewing
and already felt much better. She was a small, thin, dark girl,
probably Jewish, with sad black eyes. She had a way of letting
her sewing lie loose in her lap, her hands limp over it; and her
eyes fixed themselves, and a bloom of dark introspection came
over them. She sat very still at these moments like a small china
figure of a girl sewing. When she was nursing George, or letting
in his many visitors, she put on a manner of cool and even
languid charm; it was the extreme good manners of heart-
lessness, and at first George was chilled: but then he saw
through the pose; for whatever world Bobby Tippett had been
born into he did not think it was the English class to which
these manners belonged. She replied with a 'yes' or a 'no' to
questions about herself; he gathered that her parents were dead,
but there was a married sister she saw sometimes; and for the
rest she had lived around and about London, mostly by herself,
for ten or more years. When he asked her if she had not been
lonely, so much by herself, she drawled, 'Why, not at all, I don't
mind being alone.' But he saw her as a small, brave child, a waif
against London, and was moved.

He did not want to be the big man of the theatre; he was
afraid of evoking the impersonal admiration he was only too
accustomed to; but soon he was asking her questions about her
career, hoping that this might be the point of her enthusiasm.
But she spoke lightly of small parts, odd jobs, scene painting
and understudying, in a jolly good-little-trouper's voice; and he
could not see that he had come any closer to her at all. So at last
he did what he had tried to avoid, and sitting up against his
pillows like a judge or an impresario, he said: 'Do something
for me, dear. Let me see you.' She went next door like an
obedient child, and came back in tight black trousers, but still
in her demure little blouse, and stood on the carpet before him,
and went into a little song-and-dance act. It wasn't bad. He had
seen a hundred worse. But he was very moved; he saw her now
above all as the little urchin, the gamin, boy-girl and helpless.
And utterly touching. 'Actually,' she said, 'this is half of an act.
I always have someone else.'

There was a big mirror that nearly filled the end wall of the large, dark room. George saw himself in it, an elderly man sitting propped up on pillows watching the small doll-like figure standing before him on the carpet. He saw her turn her head towards her reflection in the darkened mirror, study it, and then she began to dance with her own reflection, dance against it, as it were. There were two small, light figures dancing in George's room; there was something uncanny in it. She began singing, a little broken song in stage cockney, and George felt that she was expecting the other figure in the mirror to sing with her; she was singing at the mirror as if she expected an answer.

'That's very good, dear,' he broke in quickly, for he was upset, though he did not know why. 'Very good indeed.' He was relieved when she broke off and came away from the mirror, so that the uncanny shadow of her went away.

'Would you like me to speak to someone for you, dear? It might help. You know how things are in the theatre,' he suggested apologetically.

'I don't maind if I dew,' she said in the stage cockney of her act; and for a moment her face flashed into a mocking, reckless, gamin-like charm. 'Perhaps I'd better change back into my skirt?' she suggested. 'More natural-like for a nurse, ain't it?'

But he said he liked her in her tight black trousers, and now she always wore them, and her neat little shirts; and she moved about the flat as a charming feminine boy, chattering to him about the plays she had had small parts in and about the big actors and producers she had spoken to, who were, of course, George's friends or, at least, equals. George sat up against his pillows and listened and watched, and his heart ached. He remained in bed longer than there was need, because he did not want her to go. When he transferred himself to a big chair, he said: 'You mustn't think you're bound to stay here, dear, if there's somewhere else you'd rather go.' To which she replied, with a wide flash of her black eyes, 'But I'm resting, darling, resting. I've nothing better to do with myself.' And then: 'Oh aren't I aw*ful*, the things wot I sy?'

'But you do like being here? You don't mind being here with me, dear?' he insisted.

There was the briefest pause. She said: 'Yes, oddly enough I do like it.' The 'oddly enough' was accompanied by a quick, half-laughing, almost flirtatious glance; and for the first time in many months the pressure of loneliness eased around George's heart.

Now it was a happiness to him because when the distinguished ladies and gentlemen of the theatre or of letters came to see him, Bobby became a cool, silky little hostess; and the instant they had gone she relapsed into urchin charm. It was proof of their intimacy. Sometimes he took her out to dinner or to the theatre. When she dressed up she wore bold, fashionable clothes and moved with the insolence of a mannequin; and George moved beside her, smiling fondly, waiting for the moment when the black, reckless, freebooting eyes would flash up out of the languid stare of the woman presenting herself for admiration, exchanging with him amusement at the world; promising him that soon, when they got back to the apartment, by themselves, she would again become the dear little girl or the gallant, charming waif.

Sometimes, sitting in the dim room at night, he would let his hand close over the thin point of her shoulder; sometimes, when they said good night, he bent to kiss her, and she lowered her head, so that his lips encountered her demure, willing forehead.

George told himself that she was unawakened. It was a phrase that had been the prelude to a dozen warm discoveries in the past. He told himself that she knew nothing of what she might be. She had been married, it seemed – she dropped this information once, in the course of an anecdote about the theatre; but George had known women in plenty who after years of marriage had been unawakened. George asked her to marry him; and she lifted her small sleek head with an animal's startled turn and said: 'Why do you want to marry me?'

'Because I like being with you, dear. I love being with you.'

'Well, I like being with you.' It had a questioning sound. She was questioning herself? 'Strange,' she said in cockney, laughing. 'Strainge but trew.'

The wedding was to be a small one, but there was a lot about it in the papers. Recently several men of George's generation

had married young women. One of them had fathered a son at
the age of seventy. George was flattered by the newspapers, and
told Bobby a good deal about his life that had not come up
before. He remarked for instance that he thought his generation
had been altogether more successful about this business of love
and sex than the modern generation. He said, 'Take my son, for
instance. At his age I had had a lot of affairs and knew about
women; but there he is, nearly thirty, and when he stayed here
once with a girl he was thinking of marrying I know for a fact
they shared the same bed for a week and nothing ever happened. She told me so. Very odd it all seems to me. But it
didn't seem odd to her. And now he lives with another young
man and listens to that long-playing record thing of his, and
he's engaged to a girl he takes out twice a week, like a schoolboy. And there's my daughter, she came to me a year after she
was married, and she was in an awful mess, really awful . . . it
seems to me your generation are very frightened of it all. I
don't know why.'

'Why my generation?' she asked, turning her head with that
quick listening movement. 'It's not my generation.'

'But you're nothing but a child,' he said fondly.

He could not decipher what lay behind the black, full stare of
her sad eyes as she looked at him now; she was sitting cross-
legged in her black glossy trousers before the fire, like a small
doll. But a spring of alarm had been touched in him and he
didn't say any more.

'At thirty-five, I'm the youngest child alive,' she sang, with a
swift sardonic glance at him over her shoulder. But it sounded gay.

He did not talk to her again about the achievements of his
generation.

After the wedding he took her to a village in Normandy
where he had been once, many years ago, with a girl called Eve.
He did not tell her he had been there before.

It was spring, and the cherry trees were in flower. The first
evening he walked with her in the last sunlight under the white-
flowering branches, his arm around her thin waist, and it
seemed to him that he was about to walk back through the gates
of a lost happiness.

They had a large comfortable room with windows which overlooked the cherry trees and there was a double bed. Madame Cruchot, the farmer's wife, showed them the room with shrewd, non-commenting eyes, said she was always happy to shelter honeymoon couples, and wished them a good night.

George made love to Bobby, and she shut her eyes, and he found she was not at all awkward. When they had finished, he gathered her in his arms, and it was then that he returned simply, with an incredulous awed easing of the heart, to a happiness which – and now it seemed to him fantastically ungrateful that he could have done – he had taken for granted for so many years of his life. It was not possible, he thought, holding her compliant body in his arms, that he could have been by himself, alone, for so long. It had been intolerable. He held her silent breathing body, and he stroked her back and thighs, and his hands remembered the emotions of nearly fifty years of loving. He could feel the memoried emotions of his life flooding through his body, and his heart swelled with a joy it seemed to him he had never known, for it was a compound of a dozen loves.

He was about to take final possession of his memories when she turned sharply away, sat up, and said: 'I want a fag. How about yew?'

'Why, yes, dear, if you want.'

They smoked. The cigarettes finished, she lay down on her back, arms folded across her chest, and said, 'I'm sleepy.' She closed her eyes. When he was sure she was asleep, he lifted himself on his elbow and watched her. The light still burned, and the curve of her cheek was full and soft, like a child's. He touched it with the side of his palm, and she shrank away in her sleep, but clenched up, like a fist; and her hand, which was white and unformed, like a child's hand, was clenched in a fist on the pillow before her face.

George tried to gather her in his arms, and she turned away from him to the extreme edge of the bed. She was deeply asleep, and her sleep was unsharable. George could not endure it. He got out of bed and stood by the window in the cold spring night air, and saw the white cherry trees standing under the white moon, and thought of the cold girl asleep in her bed. He was there in the chill moonlight until the dawn came; in the morning he had a very bad cough and could not get up. Bobby was charming, devoted, and gay. 'Just like old times, me nursing you,' she commented, with a deliberate roll of her black eyes. She asked Madame Cruchot for another bed, which she placed in the corner of the room, and George thought it was quite reasonable she should not want to catch his cold; for he did not allow himself to remember the times in his past when quite serious illness had been no obstacle to the sharing of the dark; he decided to forget the sensualities of tiredness, or of fever, or of the extremes of sleeplessness. He was even beginning to feel ashamed.

For a fortnight the Frenchwoman brought up magnificent meals, twice a day, and George and Bobby drank a great deal of red wine and of calvados and made jokes with Madame Cruchot about getting ill on honeymoons. They returned from Normandy rather earlier than had been arranged. It would be better for George, Bobby said, at home, where his friends could drop in to see him. Besides, it was sad to be shut indoors in springtime, and they were both eating too much.

On the first night back in the flat, George waited to see if she would go into the study to sleep, but she came to bed in her pyjamas, and for the second time, he held her in his arms for the space of the act, and then she smoked, sitting up in bed and looking rather tired and small and, George thought, terribly young and pathetic. He did not sleep that night. He did not dare move out of bed for fear of disturbing her, and he was afraid to drop off to sleep for fear his limbs remembered the habits of a lifetime and searched for hers. In the morning she woke smiling, and he put his arms around her, but she kissed him with small gentle kisses and jumped out of bed.

That day she said she must go and see her sister. She saw her sister often during the next few weeks and kept suggesting that George should have his friends around more than he did. George asked why didn't the sister come to see her here, in the flat? So one afternoon she came to tea. George had seen her briefly at the wedding and disliked her, but now for the first time he had a spell of revulsion against the marriage itself. The sister was awful – a commonplace, middle-aged female from some suburb. She had a sharp, dark face that poked itself inquisitively into the corners of the flat, pricing the furniture, and a thin acquisitive nose bent to one side. She sat, on her best behaviour, for two hours over the teacups, in a mannish navy blue suit, a severe black hat, her brogued feet set firmly side by side before her; and her thin nose seemed to be carrying on a silent, satirical conversation with her sister about George. Bobby was being cool and well mannered, as it were deliberately tired of life, as she always was when guests were there, but George was sure this was simply on his account. When the sister had gone, George was rather querulous about her; but Bobby said, laughing, that of course she had known George wouldn't like Rosa; she *was* rather ghastly; but then who had suggested inviting her? So Rosa came no more, and Bobby went to meet her for a visit to the pictures, or for shopping. Meanwhile, George sat alone and thought uneasily about Bobby, or visited his old friends. A few months after they returned from Normandy, someone suggested to George that perhaps he was ill. This made George think about it, and he realized he was not far from being ill. It was because he could not sleep. Night after night he lay beside Bobby, after her cheerfully affectionate submission to him; and he saw the soft curve of her cheek on the pillow, the long dark lashes lying close and flat. Never in his life had anything moved him so deeply as that childish cheek, the shadow of those lashes. A small crease in one cheek seemed to him the signature of emotion; and the lock of black glossy hair falling across her forehead filled his throat with tears. His nights were long vigils of locked tenderness.

Then one night she woke and saw him watching her.

'What's the matter?' she asked, startled. 'Can't you sleep?'

'I'm only watching you, dear,' he said hopelessly.

She lay curled up beside him, her fist beside her on the pillow, between him and her. 'Why aren't you happy?' she asked suddenly; and as George laughed with a sudden bitter irony, she sat up, arms around her knees, prepared to consider this problem practically.

'This isn't marriage; this isn't love,' he announced. He sat up beside her. He did not know that he had never used that tone to her before. A portly man, his elderly face flushed with sorrow, he had forgotten her for the moment, and he was speaking across her from his past, resurrected in her, to his past. He was dignified with responsible experience and the warmth of a lifetime's responses. His eyes were heavy, satirical, and condemning. She rolled herself up against him and said with a small sad smile, 'Then show me, George.'

'Show you?' he said, almost stammering. 'Show you?' But he held her, the obedient child, his cheek against hers, until she slept; then a too close pressure of his shoulder on hers caused her to shrink and recoil from him away to the edge of the bed.

In the morning she looked at him oddly, with an odd sad little respect, and said, 'You know what, George. You've just got into the habit of loving.'

'What do you mean, dear?'

She rolled out of bed and stood beside it, a waif in her white pyjamas, her black hair ruffled. She slid her eyes at him and smiled. 'You just want something in your arms, that's all. What do you do when you're alone? Wrap yourself around a pillow?'

He said nothing; he was cut to the heart.

'My husband was the same,' she remarked gaily. 'Funny thing is, he didn't care anything about me.' She stood considering him, smiling mockingly. 'Strange, ain't it?' she commented and went off to the bathroom. That was the second time she had mentioned her husband.

That phrase, the habit of loving, made a revolution in George. It was true, he thought. He was shocked out of himself, out of the instinctive response to the movement of skin against his, the pressure of a breast. It seemed to him that he was seeing Bobby quite newly. He had not really known her before. The delightful little girl had vanished, and he saw a young woman toughened and wary because of defeats and failures he had never stopped to think of. He saw that the sadness that lay behind the black eyes was not at all impersonal; he saw the first sheen of grey lying on her smooth hair; he saw that the full curve of her cheek was the beginning of the softening into middle age. He was appalled at his egotism. Now, he thought, he would really know her, and she would begin to love him in response to it.

Suddenly, George discovered in himself a boy whose existence he had totally forgotten. He had been returned to his adolescence. The accidental touch of her hand delighted him; the swing of her skirt could make him shut his eyes with happiness. He looked at her through the jealous eyes of a boy and began questioning her about her past, feeling that he was slowly taking possession of her. He waited for a hint of emotion in the drop of her voice, or a confession in the wrinkling of the skin by the full, dark, comradely eyes. At night, a boy again, reverence shut him into ineptitude. The body of George's sensuality had been killed stone dead. A month ago he had been a man vigorous with the skilled harbouring of memory; the long use of his body. Now he lay awake beside this woman, longing – not for the past, for that past had dropped away from him, but dreaming of the future. And when he questioned her, like a jealous boy, and she evaded him, he could see it only as the locked virginity of the girl who would wake in answer to the worshipping boy he had become.

But still she slept in a citadel, one fist before her face.

Then one night she woke again, roused by some movement of his. 'What's the matter *now*, George?' she asked, exasperated.

In the silence that followed, the resurrected boy in George died painfully.

'Nothing,' he said. 'Nothing at all.' He turned away from her, defeated.

It was he who moved out of the big bed into the narrow bed in the study. She said with a sharp, sad smile, 'Fed up with me, George? Well I can't help it, you know. I didn't ever like sleeping beside someone very much.'

George, who had dropped out of his work lately, undertook to produce another play, and was very busy again; and he became drama critic for one of the big papers and was in the swim and at all the first nights. Sometimes Bobby was with him, in her startling, smart clothes, being amused with him at the whole business of being fashionable. Sometimes she stayed at home. She had the capacity for being by herself for hours, apparently doing nothing. George would come home from some crowd of people, some party, and find her sitting cross-legged before the fire in her tight trousers, chin in hand, gone off by herself into some place where he was now afraid to try and follow. He could not bear it again, putting himself in a position where he might hear the cold, sharp words that showed she had never had an inkling of what he felt, because it was not in her nature to feel it. He would come in late, and she would make them both some tea; and they would sit hand in hand before the fire, his flesh and memories quiet. Dead, he thought. But his heart ached. He had become so used to the heavy load of loneliness in his chest that when, briefly, talking to an old friend, he became the George Talbot who had never known Bobby, and his heart lightened and his oppression went, he would look about him, startled, as if he had lost something. He felt almost lightheaded without the pain of loneliness.

He asked Bobby if she weren't bored, with so little to do, month after month after month, while he was so busy. She said no, she was quite happy doing nothing. She wouldn't like to take up her old work again?

'I wasn't ever much good, was I?' she said.

'If you'd enjoy it, dear, I could speak to someone for you.'

She frowned at the fire but said nothing. Later he suggested it again, and she sparked up with a grin and: 'Well, I don't maind if I dew . . .'

So he spoke to an old friend, and Bobby returned to the theatre, to a small act in a little intimate revue. She had found somebody, she said, to be the other half of her act. George was very busy with a production of *Romeo and Juliet*, and did not have time to see her at rehearsal, but he was there on the night *The Offbeat Revue* opened. He was rather late and stood at the back of the gimcrack little theatre, packed tight with fragile little chairs. Everything was so small that the well-dressed audience looked too big, like over-size people crammed in a box. The tiny stage was left bare, with a few black and white posters stuck here and there, and there was one piano. The pianist was good, a young man with black hair falling limp over his face, playing as if he were bored with the whole thing. But he played very well. George, the man of the theatre, listened to the first number, so as to catch the mood, and thought, Oh Lord, not again. It was one of the songs from the First World War, and he could not stand the flood of easy emotion it aroused. He refused to feel. Then he realized that the emotion was, in any case, blocked; the piano was mocking the song; 'There's a Long, Long Trail' was being played like a five-finger exercise; and 'Keep the Home Fires Burning' and 'Tipperary' followed in the same style, as if the piano were bored. People were beginning to chuckle, they had caught the mood. A young blond man with a moustache and wearing the uniform of 1914 came in and sang fragments of the songs, like a corpse singing; and then George understood he was supposed to be one of the dead of that war singing. George felt all his responses blocked, first because he could not allow himself to feel any emotion from that time at all – it was too painful; and then because of the five-finger-exercise style, which contradicted everything, all pain or protest, leaving nothing, an emptiness. The show went on; through the twenties, with bits of popular songs from that time, a number about the General Strike, which reduced the whole thing to the scale of marionettes without passion, and then on to the thirties. George saw it was a sort of potted history, as it were – Noël Coward's falsely heroic view of his time parodied. But it wasn't even that. There was no emotion, nothing. George did not know what he was supposed to feel. He looked curiously at the faces of the people around him and saw that the older people looked puzzled, affronted, as if the show were an insult to them. But the younger people were in the mood of the thing. But what mood? It was the parody of a parody. When the Second World War was evoked by 'Run Rabbit Run' played like *Lohengrin*, while the soldiers in the uniforms of the time mocked their own understated heroism from the other side of death, then George could not stand it. He did not look at the stage at all. He was waiting for Bobby to come on, so he could say that he had seen her. Meanwhile he

smoked and watched the face of a very young man near him; it
was a pale, heavy, flaccid face, but it was responding, it seemed
from a habit of rancour, to everything that went on on the stage.
Suddenly, the young face lit into sarcastic delight, and George
looked at the stage. On it were two urchins, identical it seemed,
in tight black glossy trousers, tight crisp white shirts. Both had
short black hair, neat little feet placed side by side. They were
standing together, hands crossed loosely before them at the
waist, waiting for the music to start. The man at the piano,
who had a cigarette in the corner of his mouth, began playing
something very sentimental. He broke off and looked with sardonic inquiry at the urchins. They had not moved. They
shrugged and rolled their eyes at him. He played a marching
song, very loud and pompous. The urchins twitched a little and
stayed still. Then the piano broke fast and sudden into a rage of
jazz. The two puppets on the stage began a furious movement,
their limbs clashing with each other and with the music, until
they fell into poses of helpless despair while the music grew
louder and more desperate. They tried again, whirling themselves into a frenzied attempt to keep up with the music. Then,
two waifs, they turned their two small white sad faces at each
other, and, with a formal nod, each took a phrase of music from
the fast flood of sound that had already swept by them, held it,
and began to sing. Bobby sang her bad stage-cockney phrases,
meaningless, jumbled up, flat, hopeless; the other urchin sang
drawling languid phrases from the upperclass jargon of the
moment. They looked at each other, offering the phrases as it
were, to see if they would be accepted. Meanwhile, the hard,
cruel, hurtful music went on. Again the two went limp and
helpless, unwanted, unaccepted. George, outraged and hurt,
asked himself again: What am I feeling? What am I supposed
to be feeling? For that insane nihilistic music demanded some
opposition, some statement of affirmation, but the two urchins,
half-boy, half-girl, as alike as twins (George had to watch
Bobby carefully so as not to confuse her with 'the other half of
her act') were not even trying to resist the music. Then, after a
long, sad immobility, they changed roles. Bobby took the
languid jaw-writhing part of a limp young man, and the other

waif sang false-cockney phrases in a cruel copy of a woman's voice. It was the parody of a parody of a parody. George stood tense, waiting for a resolution. His nature demanded that now, and quickly, for the limp sadness of the turn was unbearable, the two false urchins should flash out in some sort of rebellion. But there was nothing. The jazz went on like hammers; the whole room shook – stage, walls, ceiling – and it seemed the people in the room jigged lightly and helplessly. The two children on the stage twisted their limbs into the wilful mockery of a stage convention, and finally stood side by side, hands hanging limp, heads lowered meekly, twitching a little while the music rose into a final crashing discord and the lights went out. George could not applaud. He saw the damp-faced young man next to him was clapping wildly, while his lank hair fell all over his face. George saw that the older people were all, like himself, bewildered and insulted.

When the show was over, George went backstage to fetch Bobby. She was with 'the other half of the act', a rather good-looking boy of about twenty, who was being deferential to the impressive husband of Bobby. George said to her: 'You were very good, dear, very good indeed.' She looked smilingly at him, half-mocking, but he did not know what it was she was mocking now. And she had been good. But he never wanted to see it again.

The revue was a success and ran for some months before it was moved to a bigger theatre. George finished his production of *Romeo and Juliet* which, so the critics said, was the best London had seen for many years, and refused other offers of work. He did not need the money for the time being, and besides, he had not seen very much of Bobby lately.

But of course now she was working. She was at rehearsals several times a week, and away from the flat every evening. But George never went to her theatre. He did not want to see the sad, unresisting children twitching to the cruel music.

It seemed Bobby was happy. The various little parts she had played with him – the urchin, the cool hostess, the dear child – had all been absorbed into the hard-working female who cooked him his meals, looked after him, and went out to her theatre giving him a friendly kiss on the cheek. Their relationship was most pleasant and amiable. George lived beside this good friend, his wife Bobby, who was doing him so much credit in every way, and ached permanently with loneliness.

One day he was walking down the Charing Cross Road, looking into the windows of bookshops, when he saw Bobby strolling up the other side with Jackie, the other half of her act. She looked as he had never seen her: her dark face was alive with animation, and Jackie was looking into her face and laughing. George thought the boy very handsome. He had a warm gloss of youth on his hair and in his eyes; he had the lithe, quick look of a young animal.

He was not jealous at all. When Bobby came in at night, gay and vivacious, he knew he owed this to Jackie and did not mind. He was even grateful to him. The warmth Bobby had for 'the other half of the act' overflowed towards him; and for some months Myra and his wife were present in his mind, he saw and felt them, two loving presences, young women who loved George, brought into being by the feeling between Jackie and Bobby. Whatever that feeling was.

The Offbeat Revue ran for nearly a year, and then it was coming off, and Bobby and Jackie were working out another act. George did not know what it was. He thought Bobby needed a rest, but he did not like to say so. She had been tired recently, and when she came in at night there was strain beneath her gaiety. Once, at night, he woke to see her beside his bed. 'Hold me for a little, George,' she asked. He opened his arms and she came into them. He lay holding her, quite still. He had opened his arms to the sad waif, but it was an unhappy woman lying in his arms. He could feel the movement of her lashes on his shoulder, and the wetness of tears.

He had not lain beside her for a long time, years it seemed. She did not come to him again.

'You don't think you're working too hard, dear?' he asked once, looking at her strained face; but she said briskly, 'No, I've got to have something to do, can't stand doing nothing.'

One night it was raining hard, and Bobby had been feeling sick that day, and she did not come home at her usual time.

George became worried and took a taxi to the theatre and asked the doorman if she was still there. It seemed she had left some time before. 'She didn't look too well to me, sir,' volunteered the doorman, and George sat for a time in the taxi, trying not to worry. Then he gave the driver Jackie's address; he meant to ask him if he knew where Bobby was. He sat limp in the back of the taxi, feeling the heaviness of his limbs, thinking of Bobby ill.

The place was in a mews, and he left the taxi and walked over rough cobbles to a door which had been the door of stables. He rang, and a young man he didn't know let him in, saying yes, Jackie Dickson was in. George climbed narrow, steep, wooden stairs slowly, feeling the weight of his body, while his heart pounded. He stood at the top of the stairs to get his breath, in a dark which smelled of canvas and oil and turpentine. There was a streak of light under a door; he went towards it, knocked, heard no answer, and opened it. The scene was a high, bare, studio sort of place, badly lighted, full of pictures, frames, junk of various kinds. Jackie, the dark, glistening youth, was seated cross-legged before the fire, grinning as he lifted his face to say something to Bobby, who sat in a chair, looking down at him. She was wearing a formal dark dress and jewellery, and her arms and neck were bare and white. She looked beautiful, George thought, glancing once, briefly, at her face, and then away; for he could see on it an emotion he did not want to recognize. The scene held for a moment before they realized he was there and turned their heads with the same lithe movement of disturbed animals, to see him standing there in the doorway. Both faces froze. Bobby looked quickly at the young man, and it was in some kind of fear. Jackie looked sulky and angry.

'I've come to look for you, dear,' said George to his wife. 'It was raining and the doorman said you seemed ill.'

'It's very sweet of you,' she said and rose from the chair, giving her hand formally to Jackie, who nodded with bad grace at George.

The taxi stood in the dark, gleaming rain, and George and Bobby got into it and sat side by side, while it splashed off into the street.

'Was that the wrong thing to do, dear?' asked George, when she said nothing.

'No,' she said.

'I really did think you might be ill.'

She laughed. 'Perhaps I am.'

'What's the matter, my darling? What is it? He was angry, wasn't he? Because I came?'

'He thinks you're jealous,' she said shortly.

'Well, perhaps I am rather,' said George.

She did not speak.

'I'm sorry, dear, I really am. I didn't mean to spoil anything for you.'

'Well, that's certainly *that*,' she remarked, and she sounded impersonally angry.

'Why? But why should it be?'

'He doesn't like – having things asked of him,' she said, and he remained silent while they drove home.

Up in the warmed, comfortable old flat, she stood before the fire, while he brought her a drink. She smoked fast and angrily, looking into the fire.

'Please forgive me, dear,' he said at last. 'What is it? Do you love him? Do you want to leave me? If you do, of course you must. Young people should be together.'

She turned and stared at him, a black strange stare he knew well.

'George,' she said, 'I'm nearly forty.'

'But darling, you're a child still. At least, to me.'

'And he,' she went on, 'will be twenty-two next month. I'm old enough to be his mother.' She laughed, painfully. 'Very painful, maternal love . . . or so it seems . . . but then how should I know?' She held out her bare arm and looked at it. Then, with the fingers of one hand she creased down the skin of that bare arm towards the wrist, so that the ageing skin lay in creases and folds. Then, setting down her glass, her cigarette held between tight, amused, angry lips, she wriggled her shoulders out of her dress, so that it slipped to her waist, and she looked down at her two small, limp, unused breasts. 'Very painful, dear George,' she said, and shrugged her dress up quickly, becoming again the formal woman dressed for the world. 'He does not love me. He does not love me at all. Why should he?' She began singing:

> He does not love me
> With a love that is trew . . .

Then she said in stage cockney, 'Repeat; I could 'ave bin 'is muvver, see?' And with the old rolling derisive black flash of her eyes she smiled at George.

George was thinking only that this girl, his darling, was suffering now what he had suffered, and he could not stand it. She had been going through this for how long now? But she had been working with that boy for nearly two years. She had been living beside him, George, and he had had no idea at all of her unhappiness. He went over to her, put his arms around her, and she stood with her head on his shoulder and wept. For the first time, George thought, they were together. They sat by the fire a long time that night, drinking, smoking and her head was on his knee and he stroked it, and thought that now, at last, she had been admitted into the world of emotion and they would learn to be really together. He could feel his strength stirring along his limbs for her. He was still a man, after all.

Next day she said she would not go on with the new show. She would tell Jackie he must get another partner. And besides, the new act wasn't really any good. 'I've had one little act all my life,' she said, laughing. 'And sometimes it's fitted in, and sometimes it hasn't.'

'What was the new act? What's it about?' he asked her.

She did not look at him. 'Oh, nothing very much. It was Jackie's idea, really . . .' Then she laughed. 'It's quite good really, I suppose . . .'

'But what is it?'

'Well, you see . . .' Again he had the impression she did not want to look at him. 'It's a pair of lovers. We make fun . . . it's hard to explain, without doing it.'

'You make fun of love?' he asked.

'Well, you know, all the attitudes . . . the things people say. It's a man and a woman – with music of course. All the music you'd expect, played offbeat. We wear the same costume as for the other act. And then we go through all the motions . . . It's rather funny, really . . .' she trailed off, breathless, seeing George's face. 'Well,' she said, suddenly very savage, 'if it isn't all bloody funny, what is it?' She turned away to take a cigarette.

'Perhaps you'd like to go on with it after all?' he asked ironically.

'No. I can't. I really can't stand it. I can't stand it any longer, George,' she said, and from her voice he understood she had nothing to learn from him of pain.

He suggested they both needed a holiday, so they went to Italy. They travelled from place to place, never stopping anywhere longer than a day, for George knew she was running away from any place around which emotion could gather. At night he made love to her, but she closed her eyes and thought of the other half of the act; and George knew it and did not care. But what he was feeling was too powerful for his old body; he could feel a lifetime's emotions beating through his limbs, making his brain throb.

Again they curtailed their holiday, to return to the comfortable old flat in London.

On the first morning after their return, she said: 'George, you know you're getting too old for this sort of thing – it's not good for you; you look ghastly.'

'But, darling, why? What else am I still alive for?'

'People'll say I'm killing you,' she said, with a sharp, half angry, half amused, black glance.

'But, my darling, believe me . . .'

He could see them both in the mirror; he, an old pursy man, head lowered in sullen obstinacy; she . . . but he could not read her face.

'And perhaps *I'm* getting too old?' she remarked suddenly.

For a few days she was gay, mocking, then suddenly tender. She was provocative, teasing him with her eyes; then she would deliberately yawn and say, 'I'm going to sleep. Good night, George.'

'Well, of course, my darling, if you're tired.'

One morning she announced she was going to have a birthday party; it would be her fortieth birthday soon. The way she said it made George feel uneasy.

On the morning of her birthday she came into his study where he had been sleeping, carrying his breakfast tray. He raised himself on his elbow and gazed at her, appalled. For a moment he had imagined it must be another woman. She had put on a severe navy blue suit, cut like a man's; heavy black-laced shoes; and she had taken the wisps of black hair back off her face and pinned them into a sort of clumsy knot. She was suddenly a middle-aged woman.

'But, my darling,' he said, 'my darling, what have you done to yourself?'

'I'm forty,' she said. 'Time to grow up.'

'But, my darling. I do so love you in your nice clothes. I do so love you being beautiful in your lovely clothes.'

She laughed, and left the breakfast tray beside his bed, and went clumping out on her heavy shoes.

That morning she stood in the kitchen beside a very large cake, on which she was carefully placing forty small pink candles. But it seemed only the sister had been asked to the party, for that afternoon the three of them sat around the cake and looked at one another. George looked at Rosa, the sister, in her ugly straight, thick suit, and at his darling Bobby, all her grace and charm submerged into heavy tweed, her hair dragged back, without make-up. They were two middle-aged women, talking about food and buying.

George said nothing. His whole body throbbed with loss.

The dreadful Rosa was looking with her sharp eyes around the expensive flat, and then at George and then at her sister.

'You've let yourself go, haven't you, Bobby?' she commented at last. She sounded pleased about it.

Bobby glanced defiantly at George. 'I haven't got time for all this nonsense any more,' she said. 'I simply haven't got time. We're all getting on now, aren't we?'

George saw the two women looking at him. He thought they had the same black, hard, inquisitive stare over sharp-bladed noses. He could not speak. His tongue was thick. The blood was beating through his body. His heart seemed to be swelling and filling his whole body, an enormous soft growth of pain. He could not hear for the tolling of the blood through his ears. The blood was beating up into his eyes, but he shut them so as not to see the two women.

THE WOMAN

The two elderly gentlemen emerged on to the hotel terrace at the same moment. They stopped, and checked movements that suggested they wished to retreat. Their first involuntary glances had been startled, even troubled. Now they allowed their eyes to exchange a long, formal glare of hate, before turning deliberately away from each other.

They surveyed the terrace. A problem! Only one of the tables still remained in sunlight. They stiffly marched towards it, pulled out chairs, seated themselves. At once they opened newspapers and lifted them up like screens.

A pretty waitress came sauntering across to take the orders. The two newspapers remained stationary. Around the edge of one Herr Scholtz ordered warmed wine; from the shelter of the other Captain Forster from England demanded tea – with milk.

When she returned with these fluids, neatly disposed on similar metal trays, both walls of print slightly lowered themselves. Captain Forster, with an aggressive flicker of uneasy blue eyes towards his opponent, suggested that it was a fine evening. Herr Scholtz remarked with warm freemasonry that it was a shame such a pretty girl should not be free to enjoy herself on such an evening. Herr Scholtz appeared to consider that he had triumphed, for his look towards the Englishman was boastful. To both remarks, however, Rosa responded with an amiable but equally perfunctory smile. She strolled away to the balustrade where she leaned indolently, her back to them.

Stirring sugar into tea, sipping wine, was difficult with those stiff papers in the way. First Herr Scholtz, then the Captain, folded his and placed it on the table. Avoiding each other's eyes, they looked away towards the mountains, which, however, were partly blocked by Rosa.

She wore a white blouse, low on the shoulders; a black skirt, with a tiny white apron; smart red shoes. It was at her shoulders that the gentlemen gazed. They coughed, tapped on the table with their fingers, narrowed their eyes in sentimental appreciation at the mountains, looked at Rosa again. From time to time their eyes almost met but quickly slid away. Since they could not fight, civilization demanded they should speak. Yes, conversation appeared imminent.

A week earlier they had arrived on the same morning and were given rooms opposite each other at the end of a long corridor. The season was nearly over, the hotel half empty. Rosa therefore had plenty of time to devote to Herr Scholtz, who demanded it: he wanted bigger towels, different pillows, a glass of water. But soon the bell pealed from the other side of the corridor, and she excused herself and hastened over to Captain Forster who was also dissatisfied with the existing arrangements for his comfort. Before she had finished with him, Herr Scholtz's bell rang again. Between the two of them Rosa was kept busy until the midday meal, and not once did she suggest by her manner that she had any other desire in this world than to readjust Captain Forster's reading light or bring Herr Scholtz cigarettes and newspapers.

That afternoon Captain Forster happened to open his door; and he found he had a clear view into the room opposite, where Rosa stood at the window smiling, in what seemed to him charming surrender, at Herr Scholtz, who was reaching out a hand towards her elbow. The hand dropped. Herr Scholtz scowled, walked across, indignantly closed his door as if it were the Captain's fault it had been left open . . . Almost at once the Captain's painful jealousy was eased, for Rosa emerged from that door, smiling with perfect indifference, and wished him good day.

That night, very late, quick footsteps sounded on the floor of the corridor. The two doors gently opened at the same moment; and Rosa, midway between them, smiled placidly at first Herr Scholtz, then the Captain, who gave each other contemptuous looks after she had passed. They both slammed their doors.

Next day Herr Scholtz asked her if she would care to come with him up the funicular on her afternoon off, but unfortunately she was engaged. The day after Captain Forster made the same suggestion.

Finally, there was a repetition of that earlier incident. Rosa was passing along the corridor late at night on her way to her own bed, when those two doors cautiously opened and the two urgent faces appeared. This time she stopped, smiled politely, wished them a very good night. Then she yawned. It was a slight gesture, but perfectly timed. Both gentlemen solaced themselves with the thought that it must have been earned by his rival; for Herr Scholtz considered the Captain ridiculously gauche, while the Captain thought Herr Scholtz's attitude towards Rosa disgustingly self-assured and complacent. They were therefore able to retire to their beds with philosophy.

Since then Herr Scholtz had been observed in conversation with a well-preserved widow of fifty who unfortunately was obliged to retire to her own room every evening at nine o'clock for reasons of health and was, therefore, unable to go dancing with him, as he longed to do. Captain Forster took his tea every afternoon in a café where there was a charming waitress who might have been Rosa's sister.

The two gentlemen looked through each other in the dining room, and each crossed the street if he saw the other approaching. There was a look about them which suggested that they might be thinking Switzerland – at any rate, so late in the season – was not all that it had been.

Gallant, however, they both continued to be; and they might continually be observed observing the social scene of flirtations and failures and successes with the calm authority of those well qualified by long familiarity with it to assess and make judgments. Men of weight, they were; men of substance; men who expected deference.

And yet ... here they were seated on opposite sides of that table in the last sunlight, the mountains rising above them, all mottled white and brown and green with melting spring, the warm sun folding delicious but uncertain arms around them – and surely they were entitled to feel aggrieved? Captain Forster – a lean, tall, military man, carefully suntanned, spruced, brushed – was handsome still, no doubt of it. And Herr Scholtz

– large, rotund, genial, with infinite resources of experience – was certainly worth more than the teatime confidences of a widow of fifty?

Unjust to be sixty on such a spring evening; particularly hard with Rosa not ten paces away, shrugging her shoulders in a low-cut embroidered blouse.

And almost as if she were taking a pleasure in the cruelty, she suddenly stopped humming and leaned forward over the balustrade. With what animation did she wave and call down the street, while a very handsome young man below waved and called back. Rosa watched him stride away, and then she sighed and turned, smiling dreamily.

There sat Herr Scholtz and Captain Forster gazing at her with hungry resentful appreciation.

Rosa narrowed her blue eyes with anger and her mouth went thin and cold, in disastrous contrast with her tenderness of a moment before. She shot bitter looks from one gentleman to the other, and then she yawned again. This time it was a large, contemptuous, prolonged yawn; and she tapped the back of her hand against her mouth for emphasis and let out her breath in a long descending note, which, however, was cut off short as if to say that she really had no time to waste even on this small demonstration. She then swung past them in a crackle of starched print, her heels tapping. She went inside.

The terrace was empty. Gay painted tables, striped chairs, flowery sun umbrellas – all were in cold shadow, save for the small corner where the gentlemen sat. At the same moment, from the same impulse, they rose and pushed the table forward into the last well of golden sunlight. And now they looked at each other straight and frankly laughed.

'Will you have a drink?' inquired Herr Scholtz in English, and his jolly smile was tightened by a consciously regretful stoicism. After a moment's uncertainty, during which Captain Forster appeared to be thinking that the stoicism was too early an admission of defeat, he said, 'Yes – yes. Thanks, I will.'

Herr Scholtz raised his voice sharply, and Rosa appeared from indoors, ready to be partly defensive. But now Herr Scholtz was no longer a suppliant. Master to servant, a man

who habitually employed labour, he ordered wine without looking at her once. And Captain Forster was the picture of a silky
gentleman.

When she reappeared with the wine they were so deep in
good fellowship they might have been saying aloud how foolish
it was to allow the sound companionship of men to be spoiled,
even for a week, on account of the silly charm of women. They
were roaring with laughter at some joke. Or rather, Herr
Scholtz was roaring, a good stomach laugh from depths of lusty
enjoyment. Captain Forster's laugh was slightly nervous, emitted from the back of his throat, and suggested that Herr
Scholtz's warm Bavarian geniality was all very well, but that
there were always reservations in any relationship.

It soon transpired that during the war – the First War, be it
understood – they had been enemies on the same sector of the
front at the same time. Herr Scholtz had been wounded in his
arm. He bared it now, holding it forward under the Captain's
nose to show the long white scar. Who knew but that it was the
Captain who had dealt that blow – indirectly, of course –
thirty-five years before? Nor was this all. During the Second
War Captain Forster had very nearly been sent to North
Africa, where he would certainly have had the pleasure of
fighting Herr, then Oberst-leutnant, Scholtz. As it happened,
the fortunes of war had sent him to India instead. While these
happy coincidences were being established, it was with the
greatest amity on both sides; and if the Captain's laugh tended
to follow Herr Scholtz's just a moment late, it could easily be
accounted for by those unavoidable differences of temperament. Before half an hour was out, Rosa was dispatched for a
second flask of the deep crimson wine.

When she returned with it, she placed the glasses so, the
flasks so, and was about to turn away when she glanced at the
Captain and was arrested. The look on his face certainly invited comment. Herr Scholtz was just remarking, with that
familiar smiling geniality, how much he regretted that the 'accidents of history' – a phrase that caused the Captain's face to
tighten very slightly – had made it necessary for them to be
enemies in the past. In the future, he hoped, they would fight

side by side, comrades in arms against the only possible foe for either . . . But now Herr Scholtz stopped, glanced swiftly at the Captain, and after the briefest possible pause, and without a change of tone, went on to say that as for himself he was a man of peace, a man of creation: he caused innumerable tubes of toothpaste to reach the bathrooms of his country, and he demanded nothing more of life than to be allowed to continue to do so. Besides, had he not dropped his war title, the Oberstleutnant, in proof of his fundamentally civilian character?

Here, as Rosa still remained before them, contemplating them with a look that can only be described as ambiguous, Herr Scholtz blandly inquired what she wanted. But Rosa wanted nothing. Having inquired if that was all she could do for the gentlemen, she passed to the end of the terrace and leaned against the balustrade there, looking down into the street where the handsome young man might pass.

Now there was a pause. The eyes of both men were drawn painfully towards her. Equally painful was the effort to withdraw them. Then, as if reminded that any personal differences were far more dangerous than the national ones, they plunged determinedly into gallant reminiscences. How pleasant, said that hearty masculine laughter – how pleasant to sit here in snug happy little Switzerland, comfortable in easy friendship, and after such fighting, such obviously meaningless hostilities! Citizens of the world they were, no less, human beings enjoying civilized friendship on equal terms. And each time Herr Scholtz or the Captain succumbed to that fatal attraction and glanced towards the end of the terrace, he as quickly withdrew his eyes and, as it were, set his teeth to offer another gauge of friendship across the table.

But fate did not intend this harmony to continue.

Cruelly, the knife was turned again. The young man appeared at the bottom of the street and, smiling, waved towards Rosa. Rosa leaned forward, arms on the balustrade, the picture of bashful coquetry, rocking one heel up and down behind her and shaking her hair forward to conceal the frankness of her response.

There she stood, even after he had gone, humming lightly to

herself, looking after him. The crisp white napkin over her arm shone in the sunlight; her bright white apron shone; her mass of rough fair curls glowed. She stood there in the last sunlight and looked away into her own thoughts, singing softly as if she were quite alone.

Certainly she had completely forgotten the existence of Herr Scholtz and Captain Forster.

The Captain and the ex-Oberst-leutnant had apparently come to the end of their sharable memories. One cleared his throat; the other, Herr Scholtz, tapped his signet ring irritatingly on the table.

The Captain shivered. 'It's getting cold,' he said, for now they were in the blue evening shadow. He made a movement, as if ready to rise.

'Yes,' said Herr Scholtz. But he did not move. For a while he tapped his ring on the table, and the Captain set his teeth against the noise. Herr Scholtz was smiling. It was a smile that announced a new trend in the drama. Obviously. And obviously the Captain disapproved of it in advance. A blatant fellow, he was thinking, altogether too noisy and vulgar. He glanced impatiently towards the inside room, which would be warm and quiet.

Herr Scholtz remarked, 'I always enjoy coming to this place. I always come here.'

'Indeed?' asked the Captain, taking his cue in spite of himself. He wondered why Herr Scholtz was suddenly speaking German. Herr Scholtz spoke excellent English, learned while he was interned in England during the latter part of the Second World War. Captain Forster had already complimented him on it. His German was not nearly so fluent, no.

But Herr Scholtz, for reasons of his own, was speaking his own language, and rather too loudly, one might have thought. Captain Forster looked at him, wondering, and was attentive.

'It is particularly pleasant for me to come to this resort,' remarked Herr Scholtz in that loud voice, as if to an inner listener, who was rather deaf, 'because of the happy memories I have of it.'

'Really?' inquired Captain Forster, listening with nervous

attention. Herr Scholtz, however, was speaking very slowly, as if out of consideration for him.

'Yes,' said Herr Scholtz. 'Of course during the war it was out of bounds for both of us, but now . . .'

The Captain suddenly interrupted: 'Actually I'm very fond of it myself. I come here every year it is possible.'

Herr Scholtz inclined his head, admitting that Captain Forster's equal right to it was incontestable, and continued, 'I associate with it the most charming of my memories – perhaps you would care to . . .'

'But certainly,' agreed Captain Forster hastily. He glanced involuntarily towards Rosa – Herr Scholtz was speaking with his eyes on Rosa's back. Rosa was no longer humming. Captain Forster took in the situation and immediately coloured. He glanced protestingly towards Herr Scholtz. But it was too late.

'I was eighteen,' said Herr Scholtz very loudly. 'Eighteen.' He paused, and for a moment it was possible to resurrect, in the light of his rueful reminiscent smile, the delightful, ingenuous bouncing youth he had certainly been at eighteen. 'My parents allowed me, for the first time, to go alone for a vacation. It was against my mother's wishes; but my father on the other hand . . .'

Here Captain Forster necessarily smiled, in acknowledgment of that international phenomenon, the sweet jealousy of mothers.

'And here I was, for a ten days' vacation, all by myself – imagine it!'

Captain Forster obligingly imagined it, but almost at once interrupted: 'Odd, but I had the same experience. Only I was twenty-five.'

Herr Scholtz exclaimed: 'Twenty-five!' He cut himself short, covered his surprise, and shrugged as if to say: Well, one must make allowances. He at once continued to Rosa's listening back. 'I was in this very hotel. Winter. A winter vacation. There was a woman . . .' He paused, smiling, 'How can I describe her?'

But the Captain, it seemed, was not prepared to assist. He

was frowning uncomfortably towards Rosa. His expression said quite clearly: Really, *must* you?

Herr Scholtz appeared not to notice it. 'I was, even in those days, not backward – you understand?' The Captain made a movement of his shoulders which suggested that to be forward at eighteen was not a matter for congratulation, whereas at twenty-five . . .

'She was beautiful – beautiful,' continued Herr Scholtz with enthusiasm. 'And she was obviously rich, a woman of the world; and her clothes . . .'

'Quite,' said the Captain.

'She was alone. She told me she was here for her health. Her husband unfortunately could not get away, for reasons of business. And I, too, was alone.'

'Quite,' said the Captain.

'Even at that age I was not too surprised at the turn of events. A woman of thirty . . . a husband so much older than herself . . . and she was beautiful . . . and intelligent . . . Ah, but she was magnificent!' He almost shouted this, and drained his glass reminiscently towards Rosa's back. 'Ah . . .' he breathed gustily. 'And now I must tell you. All that was good enough, but now there is even better. Listen. A week passed. And what a week! I loved her as I never loved anyone . . .'

'Quite,' said the Captain, fidgeting.

But Herr Scholtz swept on. 'And then one morning I wake, and I am alone.' Herr Scholtz shrugged and groaned.

The Captain observed that Herr Scholtz was being carried away by the spirit of his own enjoyment. This tale was by now only half for the benefit of Rosa. That rich dramatic groan – Herr Scholtz might as well be in the theatre, thought the Captain uncomfortably.

'But there was a letter, and when I read it . . .'

'A letter?' interrupted the Captain suddenly.

'Yes, a letter. She thanked me so that the tears came into my eyes. I wept.'

One could have sworn that the sentimental German eyes swam with tears, and Captain Forster looked away. With eyes averted he asked nervously, 'What was in the letter?'

'She said how much she hated her husband. She had married him against her will – to please her parents. In those days, this thing happened. And she had sworn a vow to herself never to have his child. But she wanted a child . . .'

'*What?*' exclaimed the Captain. He was leaning forward over the table now, intent on every syllable.

This emotion seemed unwelcome to Herr Scholtz, who said blandly, 'Yes, that was how it was. That was my good fortune, my friend.'

'*When* was that?' inquired the Captain hungrily.

'I beg your pardon?'

'When was it? What year?'

'What year? Does it matter? She told me she had arranged this little holiday on grounds of her bad health, so that she might come by herself to find the man she wanted as the father of her child. She had chosen me. I was her choice. And now she thanked me and was returning to her husband.' Herr Scholtz stopped, in triumph, and looked at Rosa. Rosa did not move. She could not possibly have failed to hear every word. Then he looked at the Captain. But the Captain's face was scarlet, and very agitated.

'What was her name?' barked the Captain.

'Her name?' Herr Scholtz paused. 'Well, she would clearly have used a false name?' he inquired. As the Captain did not respond, he said firmly: 'That is surely obvious, my friend. And I did not know her address.' Herr Scholtz took a slow sip of his wine, then another. He regarded the Captain for a moment thoughtfully, as if wondering whether he could be trusted to behave according to the rules, and then continued: 'I ran to the hotel manager – no, there was no information. The lady had left unexpectedly, early that morning. No address. I was frantic. You can imagine. I wanted to rush after her, find her, kill her husband, marry her!' Herr Scholtz laughed in amused, regretful indulgence at the follies of youth.

'You *must* remember the year,' urged the Captain.

'But my friend . . .' began Herr Scholtz after a pause, very annoyed. 'What can it matter, after all?'

Captain Forster glanced stiffly at Rosa and spoke in English, 'As it happened, the same thing happened to me.'

'Here?' inquired Herr Scholtz politely.

'Here.'

'In this valley?'

'In this hotel.'

'Well,' shrugged Herr Scholtz, raising his voice even more, 'well, women – women you know. At eighteen, of course – and perhaps even at twenty-five–' Here he nodded indulgently towards his opponent – 'Even at twenty-five perhaps one takes such things as miracles that happen only to oneself. But at our age . . .?'

He paused, as if hoping against hope that the Captain might recover his composure.

But the Captain was speechless.

'I tell you, my friend,' continued Herr Scholtz, good-humouredly relishing the tale, 'I tell you, I was crazy; I thought I would go mad. I wanted to shoot myself; I rushed around the streets of every city I happened to be in, looking into every face. I looked at photographs in the papers – actresses, society women; I used to follow a woman I had glimpsed in the street, thinking that perhaps this was she at last. But no,' said Herr Scholtz dramatically, bringing down his hand on the table, so that his ring clicked again, 'no, never, never was I successful!'

'What did she look like?' asked the Captain agitatedly in English, his anxious eyes searching the by now very irritated eyes of Herr Scholtz.

Herr Scholtz moved his chair back slightly, looked towards Rosa, and said loudly in German: 'Well, she was beautiful, as I have told you.' He paused, for thought. 'And she was an aristocrat.'

'Yes, yes,' said the Captain impatiently.

'She was tall, very slim, with a beautiful body – beautiful! She had that black hair, you know, black, black! And black eyes, and beautiful teeth.' He added loudly and spitefully towards Rosa: 'She was not the country bumpkin type, not at all. One has some taste.'

With extreme discomfort the Captain glanced towards the plump village Rosa. He said, pointedly using English even at this late stage, 'Mine was fair. Tall and fair. A lovely girl. Lovely!' he insisted with a glare. 'Might have been an English girl.'

'Which was entirely to her credit,' suggested Herr Scholtz, with a smile.

'That was in 1913,' said the Captain insistently, and then: 'You say she had *black* hair?'

'Certainly, black hair. On that occasion – but that was not the last time it happened to me.' He laughed. 'I had three children by my wife, a fine woman – she is now dead, unfortunately.' Again, there was no doubt tears filled his eyes. At the sight, the Captain's indignation soared. But Herr Scholtz had recovered and was speaking: 'But I ask myself, how many children in addition to the three? Sometimes I look at a young man in the streets who has a certain resemblance, and I ask myself: Perhaps he is my son? Yes, yes, my friend, this is a question that every man must ask himself, sometimes, is it not?' He put back his head and laughed wholeheartedly, though with an undertone of rich regret.

The Captain did not speak for a moment. Then he said in English, 'It's all very well, but it did happen to me – it *did*.' He sounded like a defiant schoolboy, and Herr Scholtz shrugged.

'It happened to me, here. In this hotel.'

Herr Scholtz controlled his irritation, glanced at Rosa, and, for the first time since the beginning of this regrettable incident, he lowered his voice to a reasonable tone and spoke English. 'Well,' he said, in frank irony, smiling gently, with a quiet shrug, 'well, perhaps if we are honest we must say that this is a thing that has happened to every man? Or rather, if it did not exist, it was necessary to invent it?'

And now – said his look towards the Captain – and now, for heaven's sake! For the sake of decency, masculine solidarity, for the sake of our dignity in the eyes of that girl over there, who has so wounded us both – pull yourself together, my friend, and consider what you are saying!

But the Captain was oblivious in memories. 'No,' he insisted.

'No. Speak for yourself. It *did* happen. Here.' He paused, and then brought out, with difficulty, 'I never married.'

Herr Scholtz shrugged, at last, and was silent. Then he called out, 'Fräulein, Fräulein – may I pay?' It was time to put an end to it.

Rosa did not immediately turn around. She patted her hair at the back. She straightened her apron. She took her napkin from one forearm and arranged it prettily on the other. Then she turned and came, smiling, towards them. It could at once be seen that she intended her smile to be noticed.

'You wish to pay?' she asked Herr Scholtz. She spoke calmly and deliberately in English, and the Captain started and looked extremely uncomfortable. But Herr Scholtz immediately adjusted himself and said in English, 'Yes, I am paying.'

She took the note he held out and counted out the change from the small satchel under her apron. Having laid the last necessary coin on the table, she stood squarely in front of them, smiling down equally at both, her hands folded in front of her. At last, when they had had the full benefit of her amused, maternal smile, she suggested in English: 'Perhaps the lady changed the colour of her hair to suit what you both like best?' Then she laughed. She put back her head and laughed a full, wholehearted laugh.

Herr Scholtz, accepting the defeat with equanimity, smiled a rueful, appreciative smile.

The Captain sat stiffly in his chair, regarding them both with hot hostility, clinging tight to his own, authentic, memories.

But Rosa laughed at him, until with a final swish of her dress she clicked past them both and away off the terrace.

THROUGH THE TUNNEL

Going to the shore on the first morning of the holiday, the young English boy stopped at a turning of the path and looked down at a wild and rocky bay, and then over to the crowded beach he knew so well from other years. His mother walked on in front of him, carrying a bright striped bag in one hand. Her other arm, swinging loose, was very white in the sun. The boy watched that white, naked arm, and turned his eyes, which had a frown behind them, towards the bay and back again to his mother. When she felt he was not with her, she swung around. 'Oh, there you are, Jerry!' she said. She looked impatient, then smiled. 'Why, darling, would you rather not come with me? Would you rather—' She frowned, conscientiously worrying over what amusements he might secretly be longing for, which she had been too busy or too careless to imagine. He was very familiar with that anxious, apologetic smile. Contrition sent him running after her. And yet, as he ran, he looked back over his shoulder at the wild bay; and all morning, as he played on the safe beach, he was thinking of it.

Next morning, when it was time for the routine of swimming and sunbathing, his mother said, 'Are you tired of the usual beach, Jerry? Would you like to go somewhere else?'

'Oh, no!' he said quickly, smiling at her out of that unfailing impulse of contrition – a sort of chivalry. Yet, walking down the path with her, he blurted out, 'I'd like to go and have a look at those rocks down there.'

She gave the idea her attention. It was a wild-looking place, and there was no one there; but she said, 'Of course, Jerry. When you've had enough, come to the big beach. Or just go straight back to the villa, if you like.' She walked away, that bare arm, now slightly reddened from yesterday's sun, swinging. And he almost ran after her again, feeling it unbearable that she should go by herself, but he did not.

She was thinking, Of course he's old enough to be safe without me. Have I been keeping him too close? He mustn't feel he ought to be with me. I must be careful.

He was an only child, eleven years old. She was a widow. She was determined to be neither possessive nor lacking in devotion. She went worrying off to her beach.

As for Jerry, once he saw that his mother had gained her beach, he began the steep descent to the bay. From where he was, high up among red-brown rocks, it was a scoop of moving bluish green fringed with white. As he went lower, he saw that it spread among small promontories and inlets of rough, sharp rock, and the crisping, lapping surface showed stains of purple and darker blue. Finally, as he ran sliding and scraping down the last few yards, he saw an edge of white surf and the shallow, luminous movement of water over white sand, and, beyond that, a solid heavy blue.

He ran straight into the water and began swimming. He was a good swimmer. He went out fast over the gleaming sand, over a middle region where rocks lay like discoloured monsters under the surface and then he was in the real sea – a warm sea where irregular cold currents from the deep water shocked his limbs.

When he was so far out that he could look back not only on the little bay but past the promontory that was between it and the big beach, he floated on the buoyant surface and looked for his mother. There she was, a speck of yellow under an umbrella that looked like a slice of orange peel. He swam back to shore, relieved at being sure she was there, but all at once very lonely.

On the edge of a small cape that marked the side of the bay away from the promontory was a loose scatter of rocks. Above them, some boys were stripping off their clothes. They came running, naked, down to the rocks. The English boy swam towards them, but kept his distance at a stone's throw. They were of that coast; all of them were burned smooth dark brown and speaking a language he did not understand. To be with them, of them, was a craving that filled his whole body. He swam a little closer; they turned and watched him with narrowed, alert dark eyes. Then one smiled and waved. It was enough. In a minute, he had swum in and was on the rocks beside them, smiling with a desperate, nervous supplication. They shouted cheerful greetings at him; and then, as he preserved his nervous, uncomprehending smile, they understood that he was a foreigner strayed from his own beach, and they proceeded to forget him. But he was happy. He was with them.

They began diving again and again from a high point into a well of blue sea between rough, pointed rocks. After they had dived and come up, they swam around, hauled themselves up, and waited their turn to dive again. They were big boys – men, to Jerry. He dived, and they watched him; and when he swam around to take his place, they made way for him. He felt he was accepted and he dived again, carefully, proud of himself.

Soon the biggest of the boys poised himself, shot down into the water, and did not come up. The others stood about, watching. Jerry, after waiting for the sleek brown head to appear, let out a yell of warning; they looked at him idly and turned their eyes back towards the water. After a long time, the boy came up on the other side of a big dark rock, letting the air out of his lungs in a sputtering gasp and a shout of triumph. Immediately the rest of them dived in. One moment, the morning seemed full of chattering boys; the next, the air and the surface of the water were empty. But through the heavy blue, dark shapes could be seen moving and groping.

Jerry dived, shot past the school of underwater swimmers, saw a black wall of rock looming at him, touched it, and bobbed up at once to the surface, where the wall was a low barrier he could see across. There was no one visible; under him, in the water, the dim shapes of the swimmers had disappeared. Then one, and then another of the boys came up on the far side of the barrier of rock, and he understood that they had swum through some gap or hole in it. He plunged down again. He could see nothing through the stinging salt water but the blank rock. When he came up the boys were all on the diving rock, preparing to attempt the feat again. And now, in a panic of failure, he yelled up, in English, 'Look at me! Look!' and he began splashing and kicking in the water like a foolish dog.

They looked down gravely, frowning. He knew the frown. At moments of failure, when he clowned to claim his mother's attention, it was with just this grave, embarrassed inspection that she rewarded him. Through his hot shame, feeling the pleading grin on his face like a scar that he could never remove, he looked up at the group of big brown boys on the rock and shouted, '*Bonjour! Merci! Au revoir! Monsieur, monsieur!*' while he hooked his fingers round his ears and waggled them.

Water surged into his mouth; he choked, sank, came up. The rock, lately weighted with boys, seemed to rear up out of the water as their weight was removed. They were flying down past him now, into the water; the air was full of falling bodies. Then the rock was empty in the hot sunlight. He counted one, two, three . . .

At fifty, he was terrified. They must all be drowning beneath him, in the watery caves of the rock. At a hundred, he stared around him at the empty hillside, wondering if he should yell for help. He counted faster, faster, to hurry them up, to bring them to the surface quickly, to drown them quickly – anything rather than the terror of counting on and on into the blue emptiness of the morning. And then, at a hundred and sixty, the water beyond the rock was full of boys blowing like brown whales. They swam back to the shore without a look at him.

He climbed back to the diving rock and sat down, feeling the hot roughness of it under his thighs. The boys were gathering up their bits of clothing and running off along the shore to another promontory. They were leaving to get away from him. He cried openly, fists in his eyes. There was no one to see him, and he cried himself out.

It seemed to him that a long time had passed, and he swam out to where he could see his mother. Yes, she was still there, a yellow spot under an orange umbrella. He swam back to the big rock, climbed up, and dived into the blue pool among the fanged and angry boulders. Down he went, until he touched the wall of rock again. But the salt was so painful in his eyes that he could not see.

He came to the surface, swam to shore and went back to the villa to wait for his mother. Soon she walked slowly up the path, swinging her striped bag, the flushed, naked arm dangling beside her. 'I want some swimming goggles,' he panted, defiant and beseeching.

She gave him a patient, inquisitive look as she said casually, 'Well, of course, darling.'

But now, now, now! He must have them this minute, and no other time. He nagged and pestered until she went with him to a shop. As soon as she had bought the goggles, he grabbed them from her hand as if she were going to claim them for herself, and was off, running down the steep path to the bay.

Jerry swam out to the big barrier rock, adjusted the goggles, and dived. The impact of the water broke the rubber-enclosed vacuum, and the goggles came loose. He understood that he must swim down to the base of the rock from the surface of the water. He fixed the goggles tight and firm, filled his lungs, and floated, face down, on the water. Now, he could see. It was as if he had eyes of a different kind – fish eyes that showed everything clear and delicate and wavering in the bright water.

Under him, six or seven feet down, was a floor of perfectly clean, shining white sand, rippled firm and hard by the tides. Two greyish shapes steered there, like long, rounded pieces of wood or slate. They were fish. He saw them nose towards each other, poise motionless, make a dart forward, swerve off, and come around again. It was like a water dance. A few inches above them the water sparkled as if sequins were dropping through it. Fish again – myriads of minute fish, the length of his fingernail, were drifting through the water, and in a moment he could feel the innumerable tiny touches of them against his limbs. It was like swimming in flaked silver. The great rock the big boys had swum through rose sheer out of the white sand – black, tufted lightly with greenish weed. He could see no gap in it. He swam down to its base.

Again and again he rose, took a big chestful of air, and went down again. Again and again he groped over the surface of the rock, feeling it, almost hugging it in the desperate need to find the entrance. And then, once, while he was clinging to the black wall, his knees came up and he shot his feet out forward and they met no obstacle. He had found the hole.

He gained the surface, clambered about the stones that littered the barrier rock until he found a big one, and, with this in his arms, let himself down over the side of the rock. He dropped, with the weight, straight to the sandy floor. Clinging tight to the anchor of stone, he lay on his side and looked in under the dark shelf at the place where his feet had gone. He could see the hole. It was an irregular, dark gap but he could not see deep into it. He let go of his anchor, clung with his hands to the edges of the hole, and tried to push himself in.

He got his head in, found his shoulders jammed, moved them in sideways, and was inside as far as his waist. He could see nothing ahead. Something soft and clammy touched his mouth; he saw a dark frond moving against the greyish rock, and panic filled him. He thought of octopuses, of clinging weed. He pushed himself out backwards and caught a glimpse, as he retreated, of a harmless tentacle of seaweed drifting in the mouth of the tunnel. But it was enough. He reached the sunlight, swam to shore, and lay on the diving rock. He looked down into the blue well of water. He knew he must find his way through that cave, or hole, or tunnel, and out the other side.

First, he thought, he must learn to control his breathing. He let himself down into the water with another big stone in his arms, so that he could lie effortlessly on the bottom of the sea. He counted. One, two, three. He counted steadily. He could hear the movement of blood in his chest. Fifty-one, fifty-two . . . His chest was hurting. He let go of the rock and went up into the air. He saw the sun was low. He rushed to the villa and found his mother at her supper. She said only, 'Did you enjoy yourself?' and he said, 'Yes.'

All night the boy dreamed of the water-filled cave in the rock, and as soon as breakfast was over he went to the bay.

That night, his nose bled badly. For hours he had been underwater, learning to hold his breath, and now he felt weak and dizzy. His mother said, 'I shouldn't overdo things, darling, if I were you.'

That day and the next, Jerry exercised his lungs as if everything, the whole of his life, all that he would become, depended upon it. Again his nose bled at night, and his mother insisted on his coming with her the next day. It was a torment to him to waste a day of his careful self-training, but he stayed with her on that other beach, which now seemed a place for small children, a place where his mother might lie safe in the sun. It was not his beach.

He did not ask for permission, on the following day, to go to his beach. He went, before his mother could consider the complicated rights and wrongs of the matter. A day's rest, he discovered, had improved his count by ten. The big boys had made the passage while he counted a hundred and sixty. He had been counting fast, in his fright. Probably now, if he tried, he could get through that long tunnel, but he was not going to try yet. A curious, most unchildlike persistence, a controlled impatience, made him wait. In the meantime, he lay under water on the white sand, littered now by stones he had brought down from the upper air, and studied the entrance to the tunnel. He knew every jut and corner of it, as far as it was possible to see. It was as if he already felt its sharpness about his shoulders.

He sat by the clock in the villa, when his mother was not near, and checked his time. He was incredulous and then proud to find he could hold his breath without strain for two minutes. The words 'two minutes', authorized by the clock, brought close the adventure that was so necessary to him.

In another four days, his mother said casually one morning, they must go home. On the day before they left, he would do it. He would do it if it killed him, he said defiantly to himself. But two days before they were to leave – a day of triumph when he increased his count by fifteen – his nose bled so badly that he turned dizzy and had to lie limply over the big rock like a bit of seaweed, watching the thick red blood flow on to the rock and trickle slowly down to the sea. He was frightened. Supposing he turned dizzy in the tunnel? Supposing he died there, trapped? Supposing – his head went around, in the hot sun, and he almost gave up. He thought he would return to the house and lie down, and next summer, perhaps, when he had another year's growth in him – *then* he would go through the hole.

But even after he had made the decision, or thought he had, he found himself sitting up on the rock and looking down into the water; and he knew that now, this moment, when his nose had only just stopped bleeding, when his head was still sore and throbbing – this was the moment when he would try. If he did not do it now, he never would. He was trembling with fear that he would not go; and he was trembling with horror at that long, long tunnel under the rock, under the sea. Even in the open sunlight, the barrier rock seemed very wide and very heavy; tons of rock pressed down on where he would go. If he died there, he would lie until one day – perhaps not before next year – those big boys would swim into it and find it blocked.

He put on his goggles, fitted them tight, tested the vacuum. His hands were shaking. Then he chose the biggest stone he could carry and slipped over the edge of the rock until half of him was in the cool, enclosing water and half in the hot sun. He looked up once at the empty sky, filled his lungs once, twice, and then sank fast to the bottom with the stone. He let it go and began to count. He took the edges of the hole in his hands and drew himself into it, wriggling his shoulders in sideways as he remembered he must, kicking himself along with his feet.

Soon he was clear inside. He was in a small rock-bound hole filled with yellowish-grey water. The water was pushing him up against the roof. The roof was sharp and pained his back. He pulled himself along with his hands – fast, fast – and used his legs as levers. His head knocked against something; a sharp pain dizzied him. Fifty, fifty-one, fifty-two . . . He was without light, and the water seemed to press upon him with the weight of rock. Seventy-one, seventy-two . . . There was no strain on his lungs. He felt like an inflated balloon, his lungs were so light and easy, but his head was pulsing.

He was being continually pressed against the sharp roof, which felt slimy as well as sharp. Again he thought of octopuses, and wondered if the tunnel might be filled with weed that could tangle him. He gave himself a panicky, convulsive kick forward, ducked his head, and swam. His feet and hands moved freely, as if in open water. The hole must have widened out. He thought he must be swimming fast, and he was frightened of banging his head if the tunnel narrowed.

A hundred, a hundred and one . . . The water paled. Victory filled him. His lungs were beginning to hurt. A few more strokes and he would be out. He was counting wildly; he said a hundred and fifteen, and then, a long time later, a hundred and fifteen again. The water was a clear jewel-green all around him. Then he saw, above his head, a crack running up through the rock. Sunlight was falling through it, showing the clean, dark rock of the tunnel, a single mussel shell, and darkness ahead.

He was at the end of what he could do. He looked up at the crack as if it were filled with air and not water, as if he could put his mouth to it and draw in air. A hundred and fifteen, he heard himself say inside his head – but he had said that long ago. He must go on into the blackness ahead, or he would drown. His head was swelling, his lungs cracking. A hundred and fifteen, a hundred and fifteen pounded through his head, and he feebly clutched at rocks in the dark, pulling himself forward, leaving the brief space of sunlit water behind. He felt he was dying. He was no longer quite conscious. He struggled on in the darkness between lapses into unconsciousness. An immense, swelling pain filled his head, and then the darkness cracked with an explosion of green light. His hands, groping forward, met nothing; and his feet, kicking back, propelled him out into the open sea.

He drifted to the surface, his face turned up to the air. He was gasping like a fish. He felt he would sink now and drown; he could not swim the few feet back to the rock. Then he was clutching it and pulling himself up on to it. He lay face down, gasping. He could see nothing but a red-veined, clotted dark. His eyes must have burst, he thought; they were full of blood. He tore off his goggles and a gout of blood went into the sea. His nose was bleeding, and the blood had filled the goggles.

He scooped up handfuls of water from the cool, salty sea, to splash on his face, and did not know whether it was blood or salt water he tasted. After a time, his heart quietened, his eyes cleared, and he sat up. He could see the local boys diving and playing half a mile away. He did not want them. He wanted nothing but to get back home and lie down.

In a short while, Jerry swam to shore and climbed slowly up the path to the villa. He flung himself on his bed and slept, waking at the sound of feet on the path outside. His mother was coming back. He rushed to the bathroom, thinking she must not see his face with bloodstains, or tearstains, on it. He came out of the bathroom and met her as she walked into the villa, smiling, her eyes lighting up.

'Have a nice morning?' she asked, laying her hand on his warm brown shoulder a moment.

'Oh yes, thank you,' he said.

'You look a bit pale.' And then, sharp and anxious, 'How did you bang your head?'

'Oh, just banged it,' he told her.

She looked at him closely. He was strained; his eyes were glazed-looking. She was worried. And then she said to herself, Oh, don't fuss! Nothing can happen. He can swim like a fish.

They sat down to lunch together.

'Mummy,' he said, 'I can stay under water for two minutes – three minutes, at least.' It came bursting out of him.

'Can you, darling?' she said. 'Well, I shouldn't overdo it. I don't think you ought to swim any more today.'

She was ready for a battle of wills, but he gave in at once. It was no longer of the least importance to go to the bay.

PLEASURE

There were two great feasts, or turning points, in Mary Rogers's year. She began preparing for the second as soon as the Christmas decorations were down. This year, she was leafing through a fashion magazine when her husband said, 'Dreaming of the sun, old girl?'

'I don't see why not,' she said, rather injured. 'After all, it's been four years.'

'I really don't see how we can afford it.'

On her face he saw a look that he recognized.

Her friend Mrs Baxter, the manager's wife, also saw the magazine, and said, 'You'll be off to the south of France again, this year, I suppose, now that your daughter won't be needing you.' She added those words which in themselves were justification for everything: 'We'll stay faithful to Brighton, I expect.'

And Mary Rogers said, as she always did: 'I can't imagine why anyone takes a holiday in Britain when the same money'd take them to the Continent.'

For four years she had gone with her daughter and the grandchildren to Cornwall. It sounded a sacrifice on the altar of the family, the way she put it to her friends. But this year the daughter was going to the other grandmother in Scotland, and everyone knew it. Everyone. That is, Mrs Baxter, Mrs Justin-Smith, and Mrs Jones.

Mary Rogers bought gay cottons and spread them over the living room. Outside, a particularly grim February held the little Midlands town in a steady shiver. Rain swept the windowpanes. Tommy Rogers saw the cottons and said not a word. But a week later she was fitting a white linen sunsuit before the mirror when he said, 'I say, old girl, that shows quite a bit of leg, you know . . .'

At that moment it was acknowledged that they should go.

Also, that the four years had made a difference in various ways. Mary Rogers secretly examined her thighs and shoulders before the glass, and thought they might very well be exposed. But the clothes she made were of the sensible but smart variety. She sewed at them steadily through the evenings of March, April, May, June. She was a good needlewoman. Also, for a few happy months before she married, she had studied fashion designing in London. That had been a different world. In speaking of it now, to the women of her circle – Mrs Baxter, Mrs Justin-Smith, and Mrs Jones – her voice conveyed the degree of difference. And Mrs Baxter would say, kindly as always, 'Ah well, we none of us know what's in store for us when we're young.'

They were to leave towards the end of July. A week before, Tommy Rogers produced a piece of paper on which were set out certain figures. They were much lower figures than ever before. 'Oh, we'll manage,' said Mary vaguely. Her mind was already moving among scenes of blue sea, blue sky.

'Perhaps we'd better book at the Plaza.'

'Oh, surely no need. They know us there.'

The evening before they left there was a bridge party in the Baxters' house for the jaunting couple. Tommy Rogers was seen to give his wife an uneasy glance as she said, 'With air travel as cheap as it is now, I really can't understand why . . .'

For they had booked by train, of course, as usual.

They successfully negotiated the Channel, a night in a Paris hotel, and the catching of the correct train.

In a few hours they would see the little village on the sea where they had first come twenty-five years ago on their honeymoon. They had chosen it because Mary Hill had met, in those artistic circles which she had enjoyed for, alas, so short a time, a certain well-known stage decorator who had a villa there. During that month of honeymoon, they had spent a happy afternoon at the villa.

As the train approached, she was looking to see the villa, alone on its hill above the sea. But the hill was now thick with little white villas, green-shuttered, red-roofed in the warm southern green.

'The place seems to have grown quite a bit,' said Tommy. The station had grown, too. There was a long platform now, and a proper station building. And gazing down towards the sea, they saw a cluster of shops and casinos and cafés. Even four years before, there had been only a single shop, a restaurant, and a couple of hotels.

'Well,' said Mary bitterly, 'if the place is full of tourists now, it won't be the same at all.'

But the sun was shining, the sea tossed and sparkled, and the palm trees stood along the white beach. They carried their suitcases down the slope of the road to the Plaza, feeling at home.

Outside the Plaza, they looked at each other. What had been a modest building was now an imposing one, surrounded by gay awnings and striped umbrellas. 'Old Jacques is spreading himself,' said Tommy, and they walked up the neat gravel path to the foyer, looking for Jacques who had welcomed them so often.

At the office, Mary inquired in her stiff, correct French for Monsieur Jacques. The clerk smiled and regretted that Monsieur Jacques had left them three years before. 'He knew us well,' said Mary, her voice coming aggrieved and shrill. 'He always had room for us here.'

But certainly there was a room for Madame. Most certainly. At once attendants came hurrying for the suitcases.

'Hold your horses a minute,' said Tommy. 'Wait. Ask what it costs now.'

Mary inquired, casually enough, what the rates now were. She received the information with a lengthening of her heavy jaw, and rapidly transmitted it to Tommy. He glanced, embarrassed, at the clerk, who, recognizing a situation, turned tactfully to a ledger and prepared to occupy himself so that the elderly English couple could confer.

They did, in rapid, angry undertones.

'We can't, Mary. It's no good. We'd have to go back at the end of a week.'

'But we've always stayed here . . .'

At last she turned towards the clerk, who was immediately attentive, and said with a stiff smile: 'I'm afraid the currency regulations make things difficult for us.' She had spoken in English, such was her upset; and it was in English that he replied pleasantly, 'I understand perfectly, Madame. Perhaps you would care to try the Belle Vue across the street. There are many English people there.'

The Rogerses left, carrying their two suitcases igno-miniously down the neat gravelled path, among the gay tables where people already sat at dinner. The sun had gone down. Opposite, the Belle Vue was a glow of lights. Tommy Rogers was not surprised when Mary walked past it without a look. For years, staying at the Plaza, they had felt superior to the Belle Vue. Also, had that clerk not said it was full of English people?

Since this was France, and the season, the Agency was of course open. An attractive mademoiselle deplored that they had not booked rooms earlier.

'We've been here every year for twenty-five years,' said Mary, pardonably overlooking the last four, and another stretch of five when the child had been small. 'We've never had to book before.'

Alas, alas, suggested the mademoiselle with her shoulders and her pretty eyes, what a pity that St Nichole had become so popular, so attractive. There was no fact she regretted more. She suggested the Belle Vue.

The Rogerses walked the hundred yards back to the Belle Vue, feeling they were making a final concession to fate, only to find it fully booked up. Returning to the Agency, they were informed that there was, happily, one room vacant in a villa on the hillside. They were escorted to it. And now it was the turn of the pretty mademoiselle to occupy herself, not with a ledger but in examining the view of brilliant stars and the riding lights of ships across the bay, while the Rogerses conferred. Their voices were now not only angry, but high with exasperation. For this room – an extremely small one, at the bottom of a big villa, stone-floored, uncarpeted; with a single large bed of the sort Mary always thought of as French; a wardrobe that was no wardrobe, since it had been filled with shelves; a sink and a small gas stove – they were asked to pay a sum which filled them with disbelief. If they desired hot water, as the English so often do, they would have to heat it in a saucepan on the stove.

But, as the mademoiselle pointed out, turning from her appreciative examination of the exotic night scene, it would be such an advantage to do one's own cooking.

'I suggest we go back to the Plaza. Better one week of comfort than three of this,' said Mary. They returned to the Plaza to find that the room had been taken, and none were available.

It was now nearly ten in the evening, and the infinitely obliging mademoiselle returned them to the little room in the villa, for which they agreed to pay more than they had done four years before for comfort, good food, and hot water in the Plaza. Also, they had to pay a deposit of over ten pounds in case they might escape in the night with the bed, wardrobe, or the tin spoons, or in case they refused to pay the bills for electricity, gas, and water.

The Rogerses went to bed immediately, worn out with travelling and disappointment.

In the morning Mary announced that she had no intention of cooking on a holiday, and they took *petit-déjeuner* at a café, paid the equivalent of twelve shillings for two small cups of coffee and two rolls, and changed their minds. They would have to cook in the room.

Preserving their good humour with an effort, they bought cold food for lunch, left it in the room, and prepared themselves for enjoyment. For the sea was blue, blue and sparkling. And the sunshine was hot and golden. And after all, this was the south of France, the prettiest place in Europe, as they had always agreed. And in England now, said the *Daily Telegraph*, it was pouring rain.

On the beach they had another bad moment. Umbrellas stretched six deep, edge to edge, for half a mile along the silvery beach. Bodies lay stretched out, baking in the sun, hundreds to the acre, a perfect bed of heated brown flesh.

'They've ruined the place, ruined it,' cried Mary, as she surveyed the untidy scene. But she stepped heavily down into the sand and unbuttoned her dress. She was revealed to be wearing a heavy black bathing suit; and she did not miss the relieved glance her husband gave her. She felt it to be unfair. There he stood, a tall, very thin, fair man, quite presentable in an absurd bathing slip that consisted of six inches of material held on by a string round his hips. And there *she* was, a heavy firm woman, with clear white flesh – but middle-aged, and in a black bathing suit.

She looked about. Two feet away was a mess of tangled brown limbs belonging to half a dozen boys and girls, the girls wearing nothing but coloured cotton brassières and panties. She saw Tommy looking at them, too. Then she noticed, eighteen inches to the other side, a vast, grey-haired lady, bulging weary pallid flesh out of a white cotton playsuit. Mary gave her a look of happy superiority and lay down flat on the sand, congratulating herself.

All the morning the English couple lay there, turning over and over on the sand like a pair of grilling herrings, for they felt their skins to be a shame and a disgrace. When they returned to their room for lunch, it was to find that swarms of small black ants had infested their cold meats. They were unable to mind very much, as it became evident they had overdone the sunbathing. Both were bright scarlet, and their eyes ached. They lay down in the cool of the darkened room, feeling foolish to be such amateurs – they, who should have known better! They kept to their beds that afternoon, and the next day ... several days passed. Sometimes, when hunger overcame them, Mary winced down to the village to buy cold food – impossible to keep supplies in the room because of the ants. After eating, she hastily washed up in the sink where they also washed. Twice a day, Tommy went reluctantly outside, while she washed herself inch by inch in water heated in the saucepan. Then she went outside while he did the same. After these indispensable measures of hygiene, they retired to the much-too-narrow bed, shrinking away from any chance of contact with each other.

At last the discomfort of the room, as much as their healing flesh, drove them forth again, more cautiously clothed, to the beach. Skin was ripping off them both in long shreds. At the end of a week, however, they had become brown and shining, able to take their places without shame among the other brown and glistening bodies that littered the beach like so many stranded fish.

Day after day the Rogerses descended the steep path to the beach, after having eaten a hearty English breakfast of ham and eggs, and stayed there all morning. All morning they lay, and then all afternoon, but at a good distance from a colony of English, which kept itself to itself some hundreds of yards away.

They watched the children screaming and laughing in the unvarying blue waves. They watched the groups of French adolescents flirt and roll each other over on the sand in a way that Mary, at least, thought appallingly free. Thank heavens her daughter had married young and was safely out of harm's way! Nothing could have persuaded Mary Rogers of the extreme respectability of these youngsters. She suspected them all of shocking and complicated vices. Incredible that, in so few years, they would be sorted by some powerful and comforting social process into these decent, well-fed French couples, each so anxiously absorbed in the welfare of one, or perhaps two small children.

They watched also, with admiration, the more hardened swimmers cleave out through the small waves into the sea beyond the breakwater with their masks, their airtubes, their frog's feet.

They were content.

This is what they had come for. This is what all these hundreds of thousands of people along the coast had come for – to lie on the sand and receive the sun on their heating bodies; to receive, too, in small doses, the hot blue water which dried so stickily on them. The sea was very salty and warm-smelling – smelling of a little more than salt and weed, for beyond the breakwater the town's sewers spilled into the sea, washing back into the inner bay rich deposits which dried on the perfumed oiled bodies of the happy bathers.

This is what they had come for.

Yet, there was no doubt that in the Plaza things had been quite different. There, one rose late; lingered over coffee and rolls; descended, or did not descend, to the beach for a couple of hours' sun worship; returned to a lengthy lunch; slept, bathed again, enjoyed an even more lengthy dinner. That, too, was called a seaside vacation. Now, the beach was really the only place to go. From nine until one, from two until seven, the Rogerses were on it. It was a seaside holiday with a vengeance.

About the tenth day, they realized that half of their time had gone; and Tommy showed his restlessness, his feeling that there should be more to it than this, by diving into one of the new and so terribly expensive shops and emerging with a mask, frog's feet, and airtube. With an apology to Mary for leaving her, he plunged out into the bay, looking like – or so she rather tartly remarked – a spaceman in a children's comic. He did not return for some hours.

'This is better than anything, old girl, you should try it,' he said, wading out of the sea with an absorbed excited look. That afternoon she spent on the beach alone, straining her eyes to make out which of the bobbing periscopes in the water was his.

Thus engaged, she heard herself addressed in English: 'I always say I am an undersea widow, too.' She turned to see a slight girl, clearly English, with pretty fair curls, a neat blue bathing suit, pretty blue eyes, good legs stretched out in the warm sand. An English girl. But her voice was, so Mary decided, passable, in spite of a rather irritating giggle. She relented and, though it was her principle that one did not go to France to consort with the English, said: 'Is your husband out there?'

'Oh, I never see him between meals,' said the girl cheerfully and lay back on the sand.

Mary thought that this girl was very similar to herself at that age – only, of course, *she* had known how to make the best of herself. They talked, in voices drugged by sea and sun, until first Tommy Rogers, and then the girl's husband, rose out of the sea. The young man was carrying a large fish speared through the back by a sort of trident. The excitement of this led the four of them to share a square yard of sand for a few minutes, making cautious overtures.

The next day, Tommy Rogers insisted that his wife should don mask and flippers and try the new sport. She was taken out

c

into the bay, like a ship under escort, by the two men and young Betty Clarke. Mary Rogers did not like the suffocating feeling of the mask pressing against her nose. The speed the frog feet lent her made her nervous, for she was not a strong swimmer. But she was not going to appear a coward with that young girl sporting along so easily just in front.

Out in the bay a small island, a mere cluster of warm, red-brown rock, rose from a surf of frisking white. Around the island, a couple of feet below the surface, submerged rocks lay; and all over them floated the new race of frog-people, face down, tridents poised, observing the fish that darted there. As Mary looked back through her goggles to the shore, it seemed very far, and rather commonplace, with the striped umbrellas, the lolling browned bodies, the paddling children. That was the other sea. This was something different indeed. Here were the adventurers and explorers of the sea, who disdained the safe beaches.

Mary lay loose on the surface of the water and looked down. Enormous, this undersea world, with great valleys and boulders, all wavering green in the sun-dappled water. On a dazzling patch of white sand – twenty feet down, it seemed – sprouted green grass as fresh and bright as if it grew on the shore in sunlight. By reaching down her hand she could almost touch it. Farther away, long fronds of weed rocked and swayed, a forest of them. Mary floated over them, feeling with repugnance how they reached up to her knees and shoulders with their soft, dragging touch. Underneath her, now, a floor of rock, covered with thick growth. Pale grey-green shapes, swelling like balloons, or waving like streamers; delicate whitey-brown flowers and stars, bubbled silver with air; soft swelling udders or bladders of fine white film, all rocking and drifting in the slow undersea movement. Mary was fascinated – a new world, this was. But also repelled. In her ears there was nothing but a splash and crash of surf, and, through it, voices that sounded a long way off. The rocks were now very close below. Suddenly, immediately below her, a thin brown arm reached down, groped in a dark gulf of rock, and pulled out a writhing tangle of grey-dappled flesh. Mary floundered up, slipping painfully on the rocks. She had drifted unknowingly close to the islet; and on the rocks above her stood a group of half-naked bronzed boys, yelling and screaming with excitement as they killed the octopus they had caught by smashing it repeatedly against a great boulder. They would eat it – so Mary heard – for supper. No, it was too much. She was in a panic. The loathsome thing must have been six inches below her – she might have touched it! She climbed on to a rock and looked for Tommy, who was lying on a rock fifty feet off, pointing down at something under it, while Francis Clarke dived for it, and then again. She saw him emerge with a small striped fish, while Tommy and Betty Clarke yelled their excitement.

But she looked at the octopus, which was now lying draped over a rock like a limp, fringed, grey rag; she called her husband, handed over the goggles, the flippers and the tube, and swam slowly back to shore.

There she stayed. Nothing would tempt her out again.

That day Tommy bought an underwater fish gun. Mary found herself thinking, first, that it was all very well to spend over five pounds on this bizarre equipment; and then, that they weren't going to have much fun at Christmas if they went on like this.

A couple of days passed. Mary was alone all day. Betty Clarke, apparently, was only a beach widow when it suited her, for she much preferred the red-rock island to staying with Mary. Nevertheless, she did sometimes spend half an hour making conversation, and then, with a flurry of apology, darted off through the blue waves to rejoin the men.

Quite soon, Mary was able to say casually to Tommy, 'Only three days to go.'

'If only I'd tried this equipment earlier,' he said. 'Next year I'll know better.'

But for some reason the thought of next year did not enchant Mary. 'I don't think we ought to come here again,' she said. 'It's quite spoiled now it's so fashionable.'

'Oh, well – anywhere, provided there's rocks and fish.'

On that next day, the two men and Betty Clarke were on the rock island from seven in the morning until lunchtime, to which meal they grudgingly allowed ten minutes, because it was dangerous to swim on a full stomach. Then they departed again until the darkness fell across the sea. All this time Mary Rogers lay on her towel on the beach, turning over and over in the sun. She was now a warm red-gold all over. She imagined how Mrs Baxter would say: 'You've got yourself a fine tan!' And then, inevitably, 'You won't keep it long here, will you?' Mary found herself unaccountably close to tears. What did Tommy see in these people? she asked herself. As for that young man, Francis – she had never heard him make any remark that was not connected with the weights, the varieties, or the vagaries of fish!

That night, Tommy said he had asked the young couple to dinner at the Plaza.

'A bit rash, aren't you?'

'Oh, well, let's have a proper meal, for once. Only another two days.'

Mary let that 'proper meal' pass. But she said, 'I shouldn't have thought they were the sort of people to make friends of.'

A cloud of irritation dulled his face. 'What's the matter with them?'

'In England, I don't think . . .'

'Oh come off it, Mary!'

In the big garden of the Plaza, where four years ago they had eaten three times a day by right, they found themselves around a small table just over the sea. There was an orchestra and more waiters than guests, or so it seemed. Betty Clarke, seen for the first time out of a bathing suit, was revealed to be a remarkably pretty girl. Her thin brown shoulders emerged from a full white frock, which Mary Rogers conceded to be not bad at all and her wide blue eyes were bright in her brown face. Again Mary thought: If I were twenty – well, twenty-five, years younger, they'd take us for sisters.

As for Tommy, he looked as young as the young couple – it simply wasn't fair, thought Mary. She sat and listened while they talked of judging distances underwater and the advantages of various types of equipment.

They tried to draw her in but there she sat, silent and dignified. Francis Clarke, she had decided, looked stiff and commonplace in his suit, not at all the handsome young sea god of the beaches. As for the girl, her giggle was irritating Mary.

They began to feel uncomfortable. Betty mentioned London, and the three conscientiously talked about London, while Mary said yes and no.

The young couple lived in Clapham, apparently; and they went into town for a show once a month.

'There's ever such a nice show running now,' said Betty. 'The one at the Princess.'

'We never get to a show these days,' said Tommy. 'It's five hours by train. Anyway, it's not in my line.'

'Speak for yourself,' said Mary.

'Oh I know you work in a matinée when you can.'

At the irritation in the look she gave him, the Clarkes involuntarily exchanged a glance; and Betty said tactfully, 'I like going to the theatre; it gives you something to talk about.'

Mary remained silent.

'My wife,' said Tommy, 'knows a lot about the theatre. She used to be in a theatre set – all that sort of thing.'

'Oh, how interesting!' said Betty eagerly.

Mary struggled with temptation, then fell. 'The man who did the décor for the show at the Princess used to have a villa here. We visited him quite a bit.'

Tommy gave his wife an alarmed and warning look, and said, 'I wish to God they wouldn't use so much garlic.'

'It's not much use coming to France,' said Mary, 'if you're going to be insular about food.'

'You never cook French at home,' said Tommy suddenly. 'Why not, if you like it so much?'

'How can I? If I do, you say you don't like your food messed up.'

'I don't like garlic either,' said Betty, with the air of one confessing a crime. 'I must say I'm pleased to be back home where you can get a bit of good plain food.'

Tommy now looked in anxious appeal at his wife, but she inquired, 'Why don't you go to Brighton or somewhere like that?'

'Give me Brighton any time,' said Francis Clarke. 'Or Cornwall. You can get damned good fishing off Cornwall. But Betty drags me here. France is overrated, that's what I say.'

'It would really seem to be better if you stayed at home.'

But he was not going to be snubbed by Mary Rogers. 'As for the French,' he said aggressively, 'they think of nothing but their stomachs. If they're not eating, they're talking about it. If they spent half the time they spend on eating on something worthwhile, they could make something of themselves, that's what I say.'

'Such as – catching fish?'

'Well, what's wrong with that? Or . . . for instance . . .' Here he gave the matter his earnest consideration. 'Well, there's that government of theirs for instance. They could do something about that.'

Betty, who was now flushed under her tan, rolled her blue eyes, and let out a high, confused laugh. 'Oh well, you've got to consider what people say. France is so much the rage.'

A silence. It was to be hoped the awkward moment was over. But no; for Francis Clarke seemed to think matters needed clarifying. He said, with a sort of rallying gallantry towards his wife, 'She's got a bee in her bonnet about getting on.'

'Well,' cried Betty, 'it makes a good impression, you must admit that. And when Mr Beaker – Mr Beaker is his boss,' she explained to Mary, 'when you said to Mr Beaker at the whist drive you were going to the south of France, he was impressed, you can say what you like.'

Tommy offered his wife an entirely disloyal, sarcastic grin.

'A woman should think of her husband's career,' said Betty. 'It's true, isn't it? And I know I've helped Francie a lot. I'm sure he wouldn't have got that raise if it weren't for making a good impression. Besides you meet such nice people. Last year, we made friends well, acquaintance, if you like – with some people who live at Ealing. We wouldn't have, otherwise. He's in the films.'

'He's a cameraman,' said Francis, being accurate.

'Well, that's films, isn't it? And they asked us to a party. And who do you think was there?'

'Mr Beaker?' inquired Mary finely.

'How did you guess? Well, they could see, couldn't they? And I wouldn't be surprised if Francis couldn't be buyer, now they know he's used to foreigners. He should learn French, I tell him.'

'Can't speak a word,' said Francis. 'Can't stand it anyway – gabble, gabble, gabble.'

'Oh, but Mrs Rogers speaks it so beautifully,' cried Betty.

'She's cracked,' said Francis, good-humouredly, nodding to indicate his wife. 'She spends half the year making clothes for three weeks' holiday at the sea. Then the other half making Christmas presents out of bits and pieces. That's all she ever does.'

'Oh, but it's so nice to give people presents with that individual touch,' said Betty.

'If you want to waste your time I'm not stopping you,' said Francis. 'I'm not stopping you. It's your funeral.'

'They're not grateful for what we do for them,' said Betty, wrestling with tears, trying to claim the older woman as an ally. 'If I didn't work hard, we couldn't afford the friends we got . . .'

But Mary Rogers had risen from her place. 'I think I'm ready for bed,' she said. 'Good night, Mrs Clarke. Good night, Mr Clarke.' Without looking at her husband, she walked away.

Tommy Rogers hastily got up, paid the bill, bade the young couple an embarrassed good night, and hurried after his wife. He caught her up at the turning of the steep road up to the villa. The stars were brilliant overhead; the palms waved seductively in the soft breeze. 'I say,' he said angrily, 'that wasn't very nice of you.'

'I haven't any patience with that sort of thing,' said Mary. Her voice was high and full of tears. He looked at her in astonishment and held his peace.

But next day he went off fishing. For Mary, the holiday was over. She was packing and did not go to the beach.

That evening he said, 'They've asked us back to dinner.'

'You go. I'm tired.'

'I shall go,' he said defiantly, and went. He did not return until very late.

They had to catch the train early next morning. At the little station, they stood with their suitcases in a crowd of people who regretted the holiday was over. But Mary was regretting nothing. As soon as the train came, she got in and left Tommy shaking hands with crowds of English people whom, apparently, he had met the night before. At the last minute, the young Clarkes came running up in bathing suits to say goodbye. She nodded stiffly out of the train window and went on arranging the baggage. Then the train started and her husband came in.

The compartment was full and there was an excuse not to talk. The silence persisted, however. Soon Tommy was watching her anxiously and making remarks about the weather, which worsened steadily as they went north.

In Paris there were five hours to fill in.

They were walking beside the river, by the open-air market, when she stopped before a stall selling earthenware.

'That big bowl,' she exclaimed, her voice newly alive, 'that big red one, there – it would be just right for the Christmas tree.'

'So it would. Go ahead and buy it, old girl,' he agreed at once, with infinite relief.

THE DAY STALIN DIED

That day began badly for me with a letter from my aunt in Bournemouth. She reminded me that I had promised to take my cousin Jessie to be photographed at four that afternoon. So I had; and had forgotten all about it. Having arranged to meet Bill at four, I had to telephone him to put it off. Bill was a film writer from the United States who, having had some trouble with an un-American Activities Committee, was blacklisted, could no longer earn his living, and was trying to get a permit to live in Britain. He was looking for someone to be a secretary to him. His wife had always been his secretary but he was divorcing her after twenty years of marriage on the grounds that they had nothing in common. I planned to introduce him to Beatrice.

Beatrice was an old friend from South Africa whose passport had expired. Having been named as a communist, she knew that once she went back she would not get out again, and she wanted to stay another six months in Britain. But she had no money. She needed a job. I imagined that Bill and Beatrice might have a good deal in common but later it turned out that they disapproved of each other. Beatrice said that Bill was corrupt, because he wrote sexy comedies for TV under another name and acted in bad films. She did not think his justification, namely, that a guy has to eat, had anything in its favour. Bill, for his part, had never been able to stand political women. But I was not to know about the incompatibility of my two dear friends and I spent an hour following Bill through one switchboard after another, until at last I got him in some studio where he was rehearsing for a film about Lady Hamilton. He said it was quite all right, because he had forgotten about the appointment in any case. Beatrice did not have a telephone, so I sent her a telegram.

That left the afternoon free for Cousin Jessie. I was just

settling down to work when comrade Jean rang up to say she wanted to see me during lunch hour. Jean was for many years my self-appointed guide or mentor towards a correct political viewpoint. Perhaps it would be more accurate to say she was one of several self-appointed guides. It was Jean who, the day after I had my first volume of short stories published, took the morning off work to come and see me, in order to explain that one of the stories, I forget which, gave an incorrect analysis of the class struggle. I remember thinking at the time that there was a good deal in what she said.

When she arrived that day at lunchtime, she had her sandwiches with her in a paper bag, but she accepted some coffee, and said she hoped I didn't mind her disturbing me, but she had been very upset by something she had been told I had said.

It appeared that a week before, at a meeting, I had remarked that there seemed to be evidence for supposing that a certain amount of dirty work must be going on in the Soviet Union. I would be the first to admit that this remark savoured of flippancy.

Jean was a small brisk woman with glasses, the daughter of a Bishop, whose devotion to the working class was proved by thirty years of work in the Party. Her manner towards me was always patient and kindly. 'Comrade,' she said, 'intellectuals like yourself are under greater pressure from the forces of capitalist corruption than any other type of Party cadre. It is not your fault. But you must be on your guard.'

I said I thought I had been on my guard; but nevertheless I could not help feeling that there were times when the capitalist press, no doubt inadvertently, spoke the truth.

Jean tidily finished the sandwich she had begun, adjusted her spectacles, and gave me a short lecture about the necessity for unremitting vigilance on the part of the working class. She then said she must go, because she had to be at her office at two. She said that the only way an intellectual with my background could hope to attain to a correct working-class viewpoint was to work harder in the Party; to mix continually with the working class; and in this way my writing would gradually become a real weapon in the class struggle. She said, further, that she would send me the verbatim record of the Trials in the thirties, and if I read this, I would find my present vacillating attitude towards Soviet justice much improved. I said I had read the verbatim records a long time ago; and I always did think they sounded unconvincing. She said that I wasn't to worry; a really sound working-class attitude would develop with time.

With this she left me. I remember that, for one reason and another, I was rather depressed.

I was just settling down to work again when the telephone rang. It was Cousin Jessie, to say she could not come to my flat as arranged, because she was buying a dress to be photographed in. Could I meet her outside the dress shop in twenty minutes? I therefore abandoned work for the afternoon and took a taxi.

On the way the taxi man and I discussed the cost of living, the conduct of the government, and discovered that we had everything in common. Then he began telling me about his only daughter, aged eighteen, who wanted to marry his best friend, aged forty-five. He did not hold with this; had said so; and thereby lost daughter and friend at one blow. What made it worse was that he had just read an article on psychology in the woman's magazine his wife took, from which he had suddenly gathered that his daughter was father-fixated. 'I felt real bad when I read that,' he said. 'It's a terrible thing to come on suddenlike, a thing like that.' He drew up smartly outside the dress shop and I got out.

'I don't see why you should take it to heart,' I said. 'I wouldn't be at all surprised if we weren't all father-fixated.'

'That's not the way to talk,' he said, holding out his hand for the fare. He was a small, bitter-looking man, with a head like a lemon or like a peanut, and his small blue eyes were brooding and bitter. 'My old woman's been saying to me for years that I favoured our Hazel too much. What gets me is, she might have been in the right of it.'

'Well,' I said, 'look at it this way. It's better to love a child too much than too little.'

'Love?' he said. 'Love, is it? Precious little love or anything else these days if you ask me, and Hazel left home three months ago with my mate George and not so much as a postcard to say where or how.'

'Life's pretty difficult for everyone,' I said, 'what with one thing and another.'

'You can say that,' he said.

This conversation might have gone on for some time, but I saw my cousin Jessie standing on the pavement watching us. I said goodbye to the taxi man and turned, with some apprehension, to face her.

'I saw you,' she said. 'I saw you arguing with him. It's the only thing to do. They're getting so damned insolent these days. My principle is, tip them sixpence regardless of the distance, and if they argue, let them have it. Only yesterday I had one shouting at my back all down the street because I gave him sixpence. But we've got to stand up to them.'

My cousin Jessie is a tall girl, broad-shouldered, aged about twenty-five. But she looks eighteen. She has light brown hair which she wears falling loose around her face, which is round and young and sharp-chinned. Her wide, light blue eyes are virginal and fierce. She is altogether like the daughter of a Viking, particularly when battling with bus conductors, taxi men, and porters. She and my Aunt Emma carry on permanent guerrilla warfare with the lower orders; an entertainment I begrudge neither of them, because their lives are dreary in the extreme. Besides, I believe their antagonists enjoy it. I remember once, after a set-to between Cousin Jessie and a taxi driver, when she had marched smartly off, shoulders swinging, he chuckled appreciatively and said: 'That's a real old-fashioned type, that one. They don't make them like that these days.'

'Have you bought your dress?' I asked.

'I've got it on,' she said.

Cousin Jessie always wears the same outfit: a well-cut suit, a round-necked jersey, and a string of pearls. She looks very nice in it.

'Then we might as well go and get it over,' I said.

'Mummy is coming, too,' she said. She looked at me aggressively.

'Oh well,' I said.

'But I told her I would *not* have her with me while I was buying my things. I told her to come and pick me up here. I will *not* have her choosing my clothes for me.'

'Quite right,' I said.

My Aunt Emma was coming towards us from the tearoom at the corner, where she had been biding her time. She is a very large woman, and she wears navy blue and pearls and white gloves like a policeman on traffic duty. She has a big, heavy-jowled, sorrowful face; and her bulldog eyes are nearly always fixed in disappointment on her daughter.

'There!' she said as she saw Jessie's suit. 'You might just as well have had me with you.'

'What do you mean?' said Jessie quickly.

'I went in to Renée's this morning and told them you were coming, and I asked them to show you that suit. And you've bought it. You see, I do know your tastes as I know my own.'

Jessie lifted her sharp battling chin at her mother, who dropped her eyes in modest triumph and began poking at the pavement with the point of her umbrella.

'I think we'd better get started,' I said.

Aunt Emma and Cousin Jessie, sending off currents of angry electricity into the air all around them, fell in beside me, and we proceeded up the street.

'We can get a bus at the top,' I said.

'Yes, I think that would be better,' said Aunt Emma. 'I don't think I could face the insolence of another taxi driver today.'

'No,' said Jessie, 'I couldn't either.'

We went to the top of the bus, which was empty, and sat side by side along the two seats at the very front.

'I hope this man of yours is going to do Jessie justice,' said Aunt Emma.

'I hope so too,' I said. Aunt Emma believes that every writer lives in a whirl of photographers, press conferences, and publishers' parties. She thought I was the right person to choose a photographer. I wrote to say I wasn't. She wrote back to say it was the least I could do. 'It doesn't matter in the slightest anyway,' said Jessie, who always speaks in short, breathless, battling sentences, as from an unassuageably painful inner integrity that she doesn't expect anyone else to understand.

It seems that at the boarding house where Aunt Emma and Jessie live, there is an old inhabitant who has a brother who is a TV producer. Jessie had been acting in *Quiet Wedding* with the local Reps. Aunt Emma thought that if there was a nice photograph of Jessie, she could show it to the TV producer when he came to tea with his brother at the boarding house, which he was expected to do any weekend now; and if Jessie proved to be photogenic, the TV producer would whisk her off to London to be a TV star.

What Jessie thought of this campaign I did not know. I never did know what she thought of her mother's plans for her future. She might conform or she might not; but it was always with the same fierce and breathless integrity of indifference.

'If you're going to take that attitude, dear,' said Aunt Emma, 'I really don't think it's fair to the photographer.'

'Oh, Mummy!' said Jessie.

'There's the conductor,' said Aunt Emma, smiling bitterly. 'I'm not paying a penny more than I did last time. The fare from Knightsbridge to Little Duchess Street is threepence.'

'The fares have gone up,' I said.

'Not a penny more,' said Aunt Emma.

But it was not the conductor. It was two middle-aged people, who steadied each other at the top of the stairs and then sat down, not side by side, but one in front of the other. I thought this was odd, particularly as the woman leaned forward over the man's shoulder and said in a loud parrot voice: 'Yes, and if you turn my goldfish out of doors once more, I'll tell the landlady to turn *you* out. I've warned you before.'

The man, in appearance like a damp, grey, squashed felt hat, looked in front of him and nodded with the jogging of the bus.

She said, 'And there's fungus on my fish. You needn't think I don't know where it came from.'

Suddenly he remarked in a high insistent voice, 'There are all those little fishes in the depths of the sea, all those little fishes. We explode all these bombs at them, and we're not going to be forgiven for that, are we, we're not going to be forgiven for blowing up the poor little fishes.'

She said, in an amiable voice, 'I hadn't thought of that,' and she left her seat behind him and sat in the same seat with him.

I had known that the afternoon was bound to get out of control at some point but this conversation upset me. I was relieved when Aunt Emma restored normality by saying: '*There*. There never used to be people like *that*. It's the Labour Government.'

'Oh, Mummy,' said Jessie, 'I'm not in the mood for politics this afternoon.'

We had arrived at the place we wanted, and we got down off the bus. Aunt Emma gave the bus conductor ninepence for the three of us, which he took without comment. 'And they're inefficient as well,' she said.

It was drizzling and rather cold. We proceeded up the street, our heads together under Aunt Emma's umbrella.

Then I saw a newsboard with the item: Stalin Is Dying. I stopped and the umbrella went jerking up the pavement without me. The newspaperman was an old acquaintance. I said to him, 'What's this, another of your sales boosters?' He said: 'The old boy's had it, if you ask me. Well, the way he's lived – the way I look at it, he's had it coming to him. Must have the constitution of a bulldozer.' He folded up a paper and gave it to me. 'The way I look at it is that it doesn't do anyone any good to live that sort of life. Sedentary. Reading reports and sitting at meetings. That's why I like this job – there's plenty of fresh air.'

A dozen paces away Aunt Emma and Jessie were standing facing me, huddled together under the wet umbrella. 'What's the matter, dear?' shouted Aunt Emma. 'Can't you see, she's buying a newspaper,' said Jessie crossly.

The newspaperman said, 'It's going to make quite a change, with *him* gone. Not that I hold much with the goings-on out there. But they aren't used to democracy much, are they? What I mean is, if people aren't used to something, they don't miss it.'

I ran through the drizzle to the umbrella. 'Stalin's dying,' I said.

'How do you know?' said Aunt Emma suspiciously.

'It says so in the newspaper.'

'They said he was sick this morning, but I expect it's just propaganda. I won't believe it till I see it.'

'Oh don't be silly, Mummy. How can you *see* it?' said Jessie.

We went on up the street. Aunt Emma said: 'What do you think, would it have been better if Jessie had bought a nice pretty afternoon dress?'

'Oh, Mummy,' said Jessie, 'can't you see she's upset? It's the same for her as it would be for us if Churchill was dead.'

'Oh, my *dear*!' said Aunt Emma, shocked, stopping dead. An umbrella spoke scraped across Jessie's scalp, and she squeaked. 'Do put that umbrella down now. Can't you see it's stopped raining?' she said, irritably, rubbing her head.

Aunt Emma pushed and bundled at the umbrella until it collapsed, and Jessie took it and rolled it up. Aunt Emma, flushed and frowning, looked dubiously at me. 'Would you like a nice cup of tea?' she said.

'Jessie's going to be late,' I said. The photographer's door was just ahead.

'I do hope this man's going to get Jessie's expression,' said Aunt Emma. 'There's never been one yet that got her *look*.'

Jessie went crossly ahead of us up some rather plushy stairs in a hallway with mauve and gold striped wallpaper. At the top there was a burst of Stravinsky as Jessie masterfully opened a door and strode in. We followed her into what seemed to be a drawing room, all white and grey and gold. The *Rites of Spring* tinkled a baby chandelier overhead; and there was no point in speaking until our host, a charming young man in a black velvet jacket, switched off the machine, which he did with an apologetic smile.

'I do hope this is the right place,' said Aunt Emma. 'I have brought my daughter to be photographed.'

'Of course it's the right place,' said the young man. 'How delightful of you to come!' He took my Aunt Emma's white-gloved hands in his own and seemed to press her down on to a large sofa; a pressure to which she responded with a confused blush. Then he looked at me. I sat down quickly on another divan, a long way from Aunt Emma. He looked professionally at Jessie, smiling. She was standing on the carpet, hands linked behind her back, like an admiral on the job, frowning at him.

'You don't look at all relaxed,' he said to her gently. 'It's really no use at all, you know, unless you are really relaxed all over.'

'I'm perfectly relaxed,' said Jessie. 'It's my cousin here who isn't relaxed.'

I said, 'I don't see that it matters whether I'm relaxed or not, because it's not me who is going to be photographed.' A book fell off the divan beside me on the floor. It was *Prancing Nigger* by Ronald Firbank. Our host dived for it, anxiously.

'Do you read our Ron?' he asked.

'From time to time,' I said.

'Personally I never read anything else,' he said. 'As far as I am concerned he said the last word. When I've read him all through, I begin again at the beginning and read him through again. I don't see that there's any point in anyone ever writing another word after Firbank.'

This remark discouraged me, and I did not feel inclined to say anything.

'I think we could all do with a nice cup of tea,' he said. 'While I'm making it, would you like the gramophone on again?'

'I can't stand modern music,' said Jessie.

'We can't all have the same tastes,' he said. He was on his way to a door at the back, when it opened and another young man came in with a tea tray. He was as light and lithe as the first, with the same friendly ease of manner. He was wearing black jeans and a purple sweater, and his hair looked like two irregular glossy black wings on his head.

'Ah, bless you, dear!' said our host to him. Then to us: 'Let me introduce my friend and assistant, Jackie Smith. My name you know. Now if we all have a nice cup of tea, I feel that our vibrations might become just a *little* more harmonious.'

All this time Jessie was standing-at-ease on the carpet. He

handed her a cup of tea. She nodded towards me, saying, 'Give it to her.' He took it back and gave it to me. 'What's the matter, dear?' he asked. 'Aren't you feeling well?'

'I am perfectly well,' I said, reading the newspaper.

'Stalin is dying,' said Aunt Emma. 'Or so they would like us to believe.'

'Stalin?' said our host.

'That man in Russia,' said Aunt Emma.

'Oh, you mean old Uncle Joe. Bless him.'

Aunt Emma started. Jessie looked gruffly incredulous.

Jackie Smith came and sat down beside me and read the newspaper over my shoulder. 'Well, well,' he said. 'Well, well, well, well.' Then he giggled and said: 'Nine doctors. If there were fifty doctors I still wouldn't feel very safe, would you?'

'No, not really,' I said.

'Silly old nuisance,' said Jackie Smith. 'Should have bumped him off years ago. Obviously outlived his usefulness at the end of the war, wouldn't you think?'

'It seems rather hard to say,' I said.

Our host, a teacup in one hand, raised the other in a peremptory gesture, 'I don't like to hear that kind of thing,' he said. 'I really don't. God knows, if there's one thing I make a point of never knowing a thing about, it's politics, but during the war Uncle Joe and Roosevelt were absolutely my pin-up boys. But absolutely!'

Here Cousin Jessie, who had neither sat down nor taken a cup of tea, took a stride forward and said angrily: 'Look, do you think we could get this *damned* business over with?' Her virginal pink cheeks shone with emotion, and her eyes were brightly unhappy.

'But, my *dear*!' said our host, putting down his cup. 'But of course. If you feel like that, of course.'

He looked at his assistant, Jackie, who reluctantly laid down the newspaper and pulled the cords of a curtain, revealing an alcove full of cameras and equipment. Then they both thoughtfully examined Jessie. 'Perhaps it would help,' said our host, 'if you could give me an idea what you want it for? Publicity? Dust jackets? Or just for your lucky friends?'

'I don't know and I don't care,' said Cousin Jessie.

Aunt Emma stood up and said: 'I would like you to catch her expression. It's just a little *look* of hers . . .'

Jessie clenched her fists at her.

'Aunt Emma,' I said, 'don't you think it would be a good idea if you and I went out for a little?'

'But my *dear* . . .'

But our host had put his arm around her and was easing her to the door. 'There's a duck,' he was saying. 'You do want me to make a good job of it, don't you? And I never could really do my best, even with the most sympathetic lookers-on.'

Again Aunt Emma went limp, blushing. I took his place at her side and led her to the door. As we shut it, I heard Jackie Smith saying: 'Music, do you think?' And Jessie: 'I *loathe* music.' And Jackie again: 'We do rather find music helps, you know . . .'

The door shut and Aunt Emma and I stood at the landing window, looking into the street.

'Has that young man done *you*?' she asked.

'He was recommended to me,' I said.

Music started up from the room behind us. Aunt Emma's foot tapped on the floor. 'Gilbert and Sullivan,' she said. 'Well, she can't say she loathes that. But I suppose she would, just to be difficult.'

I lit a cigarette. *The Pirates of Penzance* abruptly stopped.

'Tell me, dear,' said Aunt Emma, suddenly roguish, 'about all the exciting things you are doing.'

Aunt Emma always says this; and always I try hard to think of portions of my life suitable for presentation to Aunt Emma. 'What have you been doing today, for instance?' I considered Bill; I considered Beatrice; I considered comrade Jean.

'I had lunch,' I said, 'with the daughter of a Bishop.'

'Did you, dear?' she said doubtfully.

Music again: Cole Porter. 'That doesn't sound right to me,' said Aunt Emma. 'It's modern, isn't it?' The music stopped. The door opened. Cousin Jessie stood there, shining with determination. 'It's no good,' she said. 'I'm sorry, Mummy, but I'm not in the mood.'

'But we won't be coming up to London again for another four months.'

Our host and his assistant appeared behind Cousin Jessie. Both were smiling rather bravely. 'Perhaps we had better all forget about it,' said Jackie Smith.

Our host said, 'Yes, we'll try again later, when everyone is really themselves.'

Jessie turned to the two young men and thrust out her hand at them. 'I'm very sorry,' she said, with her fierce virgin sincerity. 'I am really terribly sorry.'

Aunt Emma went forward, pushed aside Jessie, and shook their hands. 'I must thank you both,' she said, 'for the tea.'

Jackie Smith waved my newspaper over the three heads. 'You've forgotten this,' he said.

'Never mind, you can keep it,' I said.

'Oh, bless you, now I can read all the gory details.' The door shut on their friendly smiles.

'Well,' said Aunt Emma, 'I've never been more ashamed.'

'I don't care,' said Jessie fiercely. 'I really couldn't care less.'

We descended into the street. We shook each other's hands. We kissed each other's cheeks. We thanked each other. Aunt Emma and Cousin Jessie waved at a taxi. I got on a bus.

When I got home, the telephone was ringing. It was Beatrice. She said she had got my telegram, but she wanted to see me in any case. 'Did you know Stalin was dying?' I said.

'Yes, of course. Look, it's absolutely essential to discuss this business on the Copper Belt.'

'Why is it?'

'If we don't tell people the truth about it, who is going to?'

'Oh, well, I suppose so,' I said.

She said she would be over in an hour. I set out my typewriter and began to work. The telephone rang. It was comrade Jean. 'Have you heard the news?' she said. She was crying.

Comrade Jean had left her husband when he became a member of the Labour Party at the time of the Stalin–Hitler Pact, and ever since then had been living in bed-sitting rooms on bread, butter and tea, with a portrait of Stalin over her bed.

'Yes, I have,' I said.

'It's awful,' she said sobbing. 'Terrible. They've murdered him.'

'Who has? How do you know?' I said.

'He's been murdered by capitalist agents,' she said. 'It's perfectly obvious.'

'He was seventy-three,' I said.

'People don't die just like *that*,' she said.

'They do at seventy-three,' I said.

'We will have to pledge ourselves to be worthy of him,' she said.

'Yes,' I said, 'I suppose we will.'

WINE

A man and woman walked towards the boulevard from a little hotel in a side street.

The trees were still leafless, black, cold; but the fine twigs were swelling towards spring, so that looking upward it was with an expectation of the first glimmering greenness. Yet everything was calm, and the sky was a calm, classic blue.

The couple drifted slowly along. Effort, after days of laziness, seemed impossible; and almost at once they turned into a café and sank down, as if exhausted, in the glass-walled space that was thrust forward into the street.

The place was empty. People were seeking the midday meal in the restaurants. Not all: that morning crowds had been demonstrating, a procession had just passed, and its straggling end could still be seen. The sounds of violence, shouted slogans and singing, no longer absorbed the din of Paris traffic; but it was these sounds that had roused the couple from sleep.

A waiter leaned at the door, looking after the crowds, and he reluctantly took an order for coffee.

The man yawned; the woman caught the infection; and they laughed with an affectation of guilt and exchanged glances before their eyes, without regret, parted. When the coffee came, it remained untouched. Neither spoke. After some time the woman yawned again; and this time the man turned and looked at her critically, and she looked back. Desire asleep, they looked. This remained: that while everything which drove them slept, they accepted from each other a sad irony; they could look at each other without illusion, steady-eyed.

And then, inevitably, the sadness deepened in her till she consciously resisted it; and into him came the flicker of cruelty.

'Your nose needs powdering,' he said.

'You need a whipping boy.'

But always he refused to feel sad. She shrugged, and, leaving him to it, turned to look out. So did he. At the far end of the boulevard there was a faint agitation, like stirred ants, and she heard him mutter, 'Yes, and it still goes on . . .'

Mocking, she said, 'Nothing changes, everything always the same . . .'

But he had flushed. 'I remember,' he began, in a different voice. He stopped, and she did not press him, for he was gazing at the distant demonstrators with a bitterly nostalgic face.

Outside drifted the lovers, the married couples, the students, the old people. There the stark trees; there the blue, quiet sky. In a month the trees would be vivid green; the sun would pour down heat; the people would be brown, laughing, bare-limbed. No, no, she said to herself, at this vision of activity. Better the static sadness. And, all at once, unhappiness welled up in her, catching her throat, and she was back fifteen years in another country. She stood in blazing tropical moonlight, stretching her arms to a landscape that offered her nothing but silence and then she was running down a path where small stones glinted sharp underfoot, till at last she fell spent in a swathe of glistening grass. Fifteen years.

It was at this moment that the man turned abruptly and called the waiter and ordered wine.

'What,' she said humorously, 'already?'

'Why not?'

For the moment she loved him completely and maternally, till she suppressed the counterfeit and watched him wait, fidgeting, for the wine, pour it, and then set the two glasses before them beside the still-brimming coffee cups. But she was again remembering that night, envying the girl ecstatic with moonlight, who ran crazily through the trees in an unsharable desire for – but that was the point.

'What are you thinking of?' he asked, still a little cruel.

'Ohhh,' she protested humorously.

'That's the trouble, that's the trouble.' He lifted his glass, glanced at her, and set it down. 'Don't you want a drink?'

'Not yet.'

He left his glass untouched and began to smoke.

These moments demanded some kind of gesture – something

slight, even casual, but still an acknowledgement of the sep-
arateness of those two people in each of them; the one seen,
perhaps, as a soft-staring never-closing eye, observing, always
observing, with a tired compassion; the other, a shape of violence that struggled on in the cycle of desire and rest, creation
and achievement.

He gave it her. Again their eyes met in the grave irony,
before he turned away, flicking his fingers irritably against the
table; and she turned also, to note the black branches where the
sap was tingling.

'I remember,' he began; and again she said, in protest,
'Ohhh!'

He checked himself. 'Darling,' he said dryly, 'you're the only
woman I've ever loved.' They laughed.

'It must have been this street. Perhaps this café – only they
change so. When I went back yesterday to see the place where I
came every summer, it was a *pâtisserie*, and the woman had
forgotten me. There was a whole crowd of us – we used to go
around together – and I met a girl here, I think, for the first
time. There were recognized places for contacts; people
coming from Vienna or Prague, or wherever it was, knew the
places – it couldn't be this café, unless they've smartened it up.
We didn't have the money for all this leather and chromium.'

'Well, go on.'

'I keep remembering her, for some reason. Haven't thought
of her for years. She was about sixteen, I suppose. Very pretty
– no, you're quite wrong. We used to study together. She used
to bring her books to my room. I liked her, but I had my own
girl, only she was studying something else, I forget what.' He
paused again, and again his face was twisted with nostalgia, and
involuntarily she glanced over her shoulder down the street.
The procession had completely disappeared, not even the sound
of singing and shouting remained.

'I remember her because ...' And, after a preoccupied
silence: 'Perhaps it is always the fate of the virgin who comes
and offers herself, naked, to be refused.'

'What!' she exclaimed, startled. Also, anger stirred in her.
She noted it, and sighed. 'Go on.'

'I never made love to her. We studied together all that summer. Then, one weekend, we all went off in a bunch. None of us had any money, of course, and we used to stand on the pavements and beg lifts, and meet up again in some village. I was with my own girl, but that night we were helping the farmer get in his fruit, in payment for using his barn to sleep in, and I found this girl Marie was beside me. It was moonlight, a lovely night, and we were all singing and making love. I kissed her, but that was all. That night she came to me. I was sleeping up in the loft with another lad. He was asleep. I sent her back down to the others. They were all together down in the hay. I told her she was too young. But she was no younger than my own girl.' He stopped; and after all these years his face was rueful and puzzled. 'I don't know,' he said. 'I don't know why I sent her back.' Then he laughed. 'Not that it matters, I suppose.'

'Shameless hussy,' she said. The anger was strong now. 'You had kissed her, hadn't you?'

He shrugged. 'But we were all playing the fool. It was a glorious night – gathering apples, the farmer shouting and swearing at us because we were making love more than working, and singing and drinking wine. Besides, it was that time: the youth movement. We regarded faithfulness and jealousy and all that sort of thing as remnants of bourgeois morality.' He laughed again, rather painfully. 'I kissed her. There she was, beside me, and she knew my girl was with me that weekend.'

'You kissed her,' she said accusingly.

He fingered the stem of his wineglass, looking over at her and grinning. 'Yes, darling,' he almost crooned at her. 'I kissed her.'

She snapped over into anger. 'There's a girl all ready for love. You make use of her for working. Then you kiss her. You know quite well . . .'

'What do I know quite well?'

'It was a cruel thing to do.'

'I was a kid myself . . .'

'Doesn't matter.' She noted, with discomfort, that she was

almost crying. 'Working with her! Working with a girl of sixteen, all summer!'

'But we all studied very seriously. She was a doctor afterwards, in Vienna. She managed to get out when the Nazis came in, but . . .'

She said impatiently, 'Then you kissed her, on *that* night. Imagine her, waiting till the others were asleep, then she climbed up the ladder to the loft, terrified the other man might wake up, then she stood watching you sleep, and she slowly took off her dress and . . .'

'Oh, I wasn't asleep. I pretended to be. She came up dressed. Shorts and sweater – our girls didn't wear dresses and lipstick – more bourgeois morality. I watched her strip. The loft was full of moonlight. She put her hand over my mouth and came down beside me.' Again, his face was filled with rueful amazement. 'God knows, I can't understand it myself. She was a beautiful creature. I don't know why I remember it. It's been coming into my mind the last few days.' After a pause, slowly twirling the wineglass: 'I've been a failure in many things, but not with . . .' He quickly lifted her hand, kissed it, and said sincerely: 'I don't know why I remember it now, when . . .' Their eyes met, and they sighed.

She said slowly, her hand lying in his: 'And so you turned her away.'

He laughed. 'Next morning she wouldn't speak to me. She started a love affair with my best friend – the man who'd been beside me that night in the loft, as a matter of fact. She hated my guts, and I suppose she was right.'

'Think of her. Think of her at that moment. She picked up her clothes, hardly daring to look at you . . .'

'As a matter of fact, she was furious. She called me all the names she could think of; I had to keep telling her to shut up, she'd wake the whole crowd.'

'She climbed down the ladder and dressed again, in the dark. Then she went out of the barn, unable to go back to the others. She went into the orchard. It was still brilliant moonlight. Everything was silent and deserted, and she remembered how you'd all been singing and laughing and making love. She went to the tree where you'd kissed her. The moon was shining on the apples. She'll never forget it, never, never!'

He looked at her curiously. The tears were pouring down her face.

'It's terrible,' she said. 'Terrible. Nothing could ever make up to her for that. Nothing, as long as she lived. Just when everything was most perfect, all her life, she'd suddenly remember that night, standing alone, not a soul anywhere, miles of damned empty moonlight . . .'

He looked at her shrewdly. Then, with a sort of humorous, deprecating grimace, he bent over and kissed her and said: 'Darling, it's not my fault; it just isn't my fault.'

'No,' she said.

He put the wineglass into her hands; and she lifted it, looked at the small crimson globule of warming liquid, and drank with him.

'Goodness! You gave me a start, Mary . . .'

Mary Brooke was quietly knitting beside the stove. 'Thought I'd drop in,' she said.

Annie Blake pulled off her hat and flopped a net of bread and vegetables on the table; at the same time her eyes were anxiously inspecting her kitchen: there was an unwashed dish in the sink, a cloth over a chair. 'Everything's in such a mess,' she said irritably.

Mary Brooke, eyes fixed on her knitting, said, 'Eh, sit down. It's clean as can be.'

After a hesitation Annie flopped herself into the chair and shut her eyes. 'Those stairs . . .' she panted. Then: 'Like a cuppa tea, Mary?'

Mary quickly pushed her knitting away and said, 'You sit still. I'll do it.' She heaved up her large, tired body, filled a kettle from the tap, and set it on the flame. Then, following her friend's anxious glance, she hung the dish cloth where it belonged and shut the door. The kitchen was so clean and neat it could have gone on exhibition. She sat down, reached for her knitting, and knitted without looking at it, contemplating the wall across the room. 'He was carrying on like anything last night,' she observed.

Annie's drooping lids flew open, her light body straightened. 'Yes?' she murmured casually. Her face was tense.

'What can you expect with that type? She doesn't get the beds made before dinnertime. There's dirt everywhere. He was giving it to her proper. Dirty slut, he called her.'

'She won't do for him what I did, that's certain,' said Annie bitterly.

'Shouting and banging until nearly morning – we all heard it.' She counted purl, plain, purl, and added: 'Don't last long, do it? Six months he's been with her now?'

'He never lifted his hand to me, *that's* certain,' said Annie victoriously. 'Never. I've got my pride, if others haven't.'

'That's right, love. Two purl. One plain.'

'Nasty temper he's got. I'd be up summer and winter at four, cleaning those offices till ten, then cleaning for Mrs Lynd till dinnertime. Then if he got home and found his dinner not ready, he'd start to shout and carry on – well, I'd say, if you can't wait five minutes, get home and cook it yourself, I'd say. I bring in as much as you do, don't I? But he never lifted a finger. Bone lazy. Men are all the same.'

Mary gave her friend a swift, searching glance, then murmured, 'Eh, you can't tell *me* . . .'

'I'd have the kids and the cleaning and the cooking, and working all day – sometimes when he was unemployed I'd bring in all the money . . . and he wouldn't even put the kettle on for me. Women's work, he said.'

'Two purl, plain.' But Mary's kindly face seemed to suggest that she was waiting to say something else. 'We all know what it is,' she agreed at last, patiently.

Annie rose lightly, pulled the shrieking kettle off the flame, and reached for the teapot. Seen from the back, she looked twenty, slim and erect. When she turned with the steaming pot, she caught a glimpse of herself; she set down the pot and went to the mirror. She stood touching her face anxiously. 'Look at me!' She pushed a long, sagging curl into position, then shrugged. 'Well, who's to care what I look like anyway?'

She began setting out the cups. She had a thin face, sharpened by worry, and small sharp blue eyes. As she sat down, she nervously felt her hair. 'I must get the curlers on to my hair,' she muttered.

'Heard from the boys?'

Annie's hand fell and clenched itself on the table. 'Not a word from Charlie for months. They don't think . . . he'll turn up one fine day and expect his place laid, if I know my Charlie. Tommy's after a job in Manchester, Mrs Thomas said. But I had a nice letter from Dick . . .' Her face softened; her eyes were soft and reminiscent. 'He wrote about his father. Should he come down and speak to the old so and so for me, he said. I wrote back and said that was no way to speak of his father. He should respect him, I said, no matter what he's done. It's not his place to criticize his father, I said.'

'You're lucky in your boys, Annie.'

'They're good workers, no one can say they aren't. And they've never done anything they shouldn't. They don't take after their dad, *that's* certain.'

At this, Mary's eyes showed a certain tired irony. 'Eh, Annie – but we all do things we shouldn't.' This gaining no response from the bitter Annie, she added cautiously, 'I saw him this morning in the street.'

Annie's cup clattered down into the saucer. 'Was he alone?'

'No. But he took me aside – he said I could give you a message if I was passing this way – he might be dropping in this evening instead of tomorrow with your money, he said. Thursday *she* goes to her mother's – I suppose he thinks while the cat's away . . .'

Annie had risen, in a panic. She made herself sit down again and stirred her tea. The spoon tinkled in the cup with the quivering of her hand. 'He's regular with the money, anyway,' she said heavily. 'I didn't have to take him into court. He offered. And I suppose he needn't, now the boys are out keeping themselves.'

'He still feels for you, Annie . . .' Mary was leaning forward, speaking in a direct appeal. 'He does, really.'

'He never felt for anyone but himself,' snapped Annie. 'Never.'

Mary let a sigh escape her. 'Oh, well . . .' she murmured. 'Well, I'll be getting along to do the supper.' She stuffed her knitting into her carryall and said consolingly: 'You're lucky. No one to get after you if you feel like sitting a bit. No one to worry about but yourself . . .'

'Oh, don't think I'm wasting any tears over *him*. I'm taking it easy for the first time in my life. You slave your life out for your man and your kids. Then off they go, with not so much as a thank you. Now I can please myself.'

'I wouldn't mind being in your place,' said Mary loyally. At the door she remarked, apparently at random, 'Your floor's so clean you could eat off it.'

The moment Mary was gone, Annie rushed into her apron and began sweeping. She got down on her knees to polish the floor, and then took off her dress and washed herself at the sink. She combed her dragging wisps of pale hair and did each one up neatly with a pin till her face was surrounded by a ring of little sausages. She put back her dress and sat down at the table. Not a moment too soon. The door opened, and Rob Blake stood there.

He was a thin, rather stooping man, with an air of apology. He said politely, 'You busy, Annie?'

'Sit down,' she commanded sharply. He stooped loosely in the doorway for a moment, then came forward, minding his feet. Even so she winced as she saw the dusty marks on the gleaming linoleum. 'Take it easy,' he said with friendly sarcasm. 'You can put up with my dust once a week, can't you?'

She smiled stiffly, her blue eyes fastened anxiously on him, while he pulled out a chair and sat down. 'Well, Annie?'

To this conciliatory opening she did not respond. After a moment she remarked, 'I heard from Dick. He's thinking of getting married.'

'Getting married, now? That puts us on the shelf, don't it?'

'*You*'re not on any shelf that I can see,' she snapped.

'Now – Annie . . .' he deprecated, with an appealing smile. She showed no signs of softening. Seeing her implacable face, his smile faded, and he took an envelope from his pocket and pushed it over.

'Thanks,' she said, hardly glancing at it. Then that terrible bitterness came crowding up, and he heard the words: 'If you can spare it from *her*.'

He let that one pass; he looked steadily at his wife, as if seeking a way past that armour of anger. He watched her, passing the tip of his tongue nervously over his lips.

'Some women know how to keep themselves free from kids and responsibilities. They just do this and that, and take up with anyone they please. None of the dirty work for *them*.'

He gave a sigh, and was on the point of getting up, when she demanded, 'Like a cuppa tea?'

'I wouldn't mind.' He let himself sink back again.

While she worked at the stove, her back to him, he was looking around the kitchen; his face had a look of tired, disappointed irony. An ageing man, but with a dogged set to his shoulders. Trying to find the right words, he remarked, 'Not so much work for you now, Annie.'

But she did not answer. She returned with the two cups and put the sugar into his for him. This wifely gesture encouraged him. 'Annie,' he began, 'Annie – can't we talk this over . . .' He was stirring the tea clumsily, not looking at it, leaning forward. The cup knocked over. 'Oh, look what you've done,' she cried out. 'Just look at the mess.' She snatched up a cloth and wiped the table.

'It's only a drop of tea, Annie,' he protested at last, shrinking a little aside from her furious energy.

'Only a drop of tea – I can polish and clean half the day, and then in a minute the place is like a pig sty.'

His face darkened with remembered irritation.

'Yes, I've heard,' she went on accusingly, 'she lets the beds lie until dinner, and the place isn't cleaned from one week to the next.'

'At least she cares more for me than she does for a clean floor,' he shouted. Now they looked at each other with hatred.

At this delicate moment there came a shout: 'Rob. Rob!'

She laughed angrily. 'She's got you where she wants you – waits and spies on you and now she comes after you.'

'Rob! You there, Rob?' It was a loud, confident, female voice.

'She sounds just what she is, a proper . . .'

'Shut up,' he interrupted. He was breathing heavily. 'You keep that tongue of yours quiet, now.'

Her eyes were full of tears, but the blue shone through, bright and vengeful. ' "Rob, Rob" – and off you trot like a little dog.'

He got up from the table heavily, as a loud knock came at the door.

Annie's mouth quivered at the insult of it. And *his* first instinct was to stand by her – she could see that. He looked apologetically at her, then went to the door, opened it an inch, and said in a low, furious voice: 'Don't you do that now. Do you hear me!' He shut the door, leaned against it, facing Annie. 'Annie,' he said again, in an awkward appeal. 'Annie . . .'

But she sat at her table, hands folded in a trembling knot before her, her face tight and closed against him.

'Oh, all right!' he said at last despairingly, angry. 'You've always got to be in the right about everything, haven't you? That's all that matters to you – if you're in the right. Bloody plaster saint, you are.' He went out quickly.

She sat quite still, listening until it was quiet. Then she drew a deep breath and put her two fists to her cheeks, as if trying to keep them still. She was sitting thus when Mary Brooke came in. 'You let him go?' she said incredulously.

'And good riddance, too.'

Mary shrugged. Then she suggested bravely, 'You shouldn't be so hard on him, Annie – give him a chance.'

'I'd see him dead first,' said Annie through shaking lips. Then: 'I'm forty-five, and I might as well be on the dust heap.' And then, after a pause, in a remote, cold voice: 'We've been together twenty-five years. Three kids. And then he goes off with that . . . with that . . .'

'You're well rid of him, and that's a fact,' agreed Mary swiftly.

'Yes. I am, and I know it . . .' Annie was swaying from side to side in her chair. Her face was stony, but the tears were trickling steadily down, following a path worn from nose to chin. They rolled off and splashed on to her white collar.

'Annie,' implored her friend. 'Annie . . .'

Annie's face quivered, and Mary was across the room and had her in her arms. 'That's right, love, that's right, that's right, love,' she crooned.

'I don't know what gets into me,' wept Annie, her voice coming muffled from Mary's large shoulder. 'I can't keep my wicked tongue still. He's fed up and sick of that – cow, and I drive him away. I can't help it. I don't know what gets into me.'

'There now, love, there now, love.' The big, fat, comfortable woman was rocking the frail Annie like a baby. 'Take it easy, love. He'll be back, you'll see.'

'You think he will?' asked Annie, lifting her face up to see if her friend was lying to comfort her.

'Would you like me to go and see if I can fetch him back for you now?'

In spite of her longing, Annie hesitated. 'Do you think it'll be all right?' she said doubtfully.

'I'll go and slip in a word when *she's* not around.'

'Will you do that, Mary?'

Mary got up, patting at her crumpled dress. 'You wait here, love,' she said imploringly. She went to the door and said as she went out: 'Take it easy, now, Annie. Give him a chance.'

'I go running after him to ask him back?' Annie's pride spoke out of her wail.

'Do you want him back or don't you?' demanded Mary, patient to the last, although there was a hint of exasperation now. Annie did not say anything, so Mary went running out.

Annie sat still, watching the door tensely. But vague, rebellious, angry thoughts were running through her head: If I want to keep him, I can't ever say what I think, I can't ever say what's true – I'm nothing to him but a convenience, but if I say so he'll just up and off . . .

But that was not the whole truth; she remembered the affection in his face, and for a moment the bitterness died. Then she remembered her long hard life, the endless work, work, work – she remembered, all at once, as if she were feeling it now, her aching back when the children were small; she could see him lying on the bed reading the newspaper when she could hardly drag herself . . . It's all very well, she cried out to herself, it's not right, it just isn't right . . . A terrible feeling of injustice was gripping her; and it was just this feeling she must push down, keep under, if she wanted him. For she knew finally – and this was stronger than anything else – that without him there would be no meaning in her life at all.

THE OTHER WOMAN

Rose's mother was killed one morning crossing the street to do her shopping. Rose was fetched from work, and a young policeman, awkward with sympathy, asked questions and finally said: 'You ought to tell your Dad, miss, he ought to know.' It had struck him as strange that she had not suggested it, but behaved as if the responsibility for everything must of course be hers. He thought Rose was too composed to be natural. Her mouth was set and there was a strained look in her eyes. He insisted; Rose sent a message to her father; but when he came she put him straight into bed with a cup of tea. Mr Johnson was a plump, fair little man, with wisps of light hair lying over a rosy scalp, and blue, candid, trustful eyes. Then she came back to the kitchen and her manner told the policeman that she expected him to leave. From the door he said diffidently: 'Well, I'm sorry, miss, I'm really sorry. A terrible thing – you can't rightly blame the lorry-driver, and your mum – it wasn't her fault, either.' Rose turned her white, shaken face, her cold and glittering eyes towards him and said tartly: 'Being sorry doesn't mend broken bones.' That last phrase seemed to take her by surprise, for she winced, her face worked in a rush of tears, and then she clenched her jaw again. 'Them lorries,' she said heavily, 'them machines, they ought to be stopped, that's what I think.' This irrational remark encouraged the policeman: it was nearer to the tears, the emotion that he thought would be good for her. He remarked encouragingly: 'I daresay, miss, but we couldn't do without them, could we now?' Rose's face did not change. She said politely: 'Yes?' It was sceptical and dismissing; that monosyllable said finally: 'You keep your opinions, I'll keep mine.' It examined and dismissed the whole machine age. The young policeman, still lingering over his duty, suggested: 'Isn't there anybody to come and sit with you? You don't look too good, miss, and that's a fact.'

'There isn't anybody,' said Rose briefly, and added: 'I'm all right.' She sounded irritated, and so he left. She sat down at the table and was shocked at herself for what she had said. She thought: I ought to tell George . . . But she did not move. She stared vaguely around the kitchen, her mind dimly churning around several ideas. One was that her father had taken it hard, she would have her hands full with him. Another, that policemen, officials – they were all nosy parkers, knowing what was best for everybody. She found herself staring at a certain picture on the wall, and thinking: 'Now I can take that picture down. Now she's gone I can do what I like.' She felt a little guilty, but almost at once she briskly rose and took the picture down. It was of a battleship in a stormy sea, and she hated it. She put it away in a cupboard. Then the white empty square on the wall troubled her, and she replaced it by a calendar with yellow roses on it. Then she made herself a cup of tea and began cooking her father's supper, thinking: I'll wake him up and make him eat, do him good to have a bite of something hot.

At supper her father asked: 'Where's George?' Her face closed against him in irritation and she said: 'I don't know.' He was surprised and shocked, and he protested: 'But Rosie, you ought to tell him, it's only right.' Now, it was against this knowledge that she had been arming herself all day; but she knew that sooner or later she must tell George, and when she had finished the washing-up she took a sheet of writing-paper from the drawer of the dresser and sat down to write. She was as surprised as her father was: Why didn't she want to tell George? Her father said, with the characteristic gentle protest: 'But, Rosie, why don't you give him a ring at the factory? They'd give him the message.' Rose made as if she had not heard. She finished the letter, found some coppers in her bag for a stamp and went out to post it. Afterwards she found herself thinking of George's arrival with the reluctance that deserved the name of fear. She could not understand herself, and soon went to bed in order to lose herself in sleep. She dreamed of the lorry that had killed her mother; she dreamed, too, of an enormous black machine, relentlessly moving its great arms back and forth, back and forth, in a way that was menacing to Rose.

George found the letter when he returned from work the following evening. His first thought was: 'Why couldn't she have got killed next week, after we were married, instead of now?' He was shocked at the cruel and selfish idea. But he and Rose had been going together now for three years, and he could not help feeling that it was cruel of fate to cloud their wedding with this terrible, senseless death. He had not liked Rose's mother: he thought her a fussy and domineering woman; but to be killed like that, all of a sudden, in her vigorous fifties— He thought suddenly: 'Poor little Rosie, she'll be upset bad, and there's her Dad, he's just like a big baby; I'd better get to her quick.' He was putting the letter in his pocket when it struck him: 'Why did she write? Why didn't she telephone to the works?' He looked at the letter and saw that Mrs Johnson had been killed as long ago as yesterday morning. At first he was too astonished to be angry; then he was extraordinarily angry. 'What!' he muttered, 'why the hell – what's she doing?' He was a member of the family, wasn't he? – or as good as. And she wrote him stiff little letters, beginning *Dear George*, and ending, *Rose* – no love, not even a sincerely. But underneath the anger he was deeply dismayed. He was remembering that there had been a listlessness, an apathy about her recently that could almost be taken as indifference. For instance, when he took her to see the two rooms that would be their home, she had made all kinds of objections instead of being as delighted as he was. 'Look at all those stairs,' she had said, 'it's so high up,' and so on. You might almost think she wasn't keen on marrying him – but this idea was insupportable, and he abandoned it quickly. He remembered that at the beginning, three years ago, she had pleaded for them to marry at once; she didn't mind taking a chance, she had said; lots of people got married on less money than they had. But he was a cautious man and he talked her into waiting for some kind of security. That's where he made his mistake, he decided now; he should have taken her at her word and married her straight off, and then ... He hastened across London to comfort Rose; and all the time his thoughts of her were uneasy and aggrieved; and he felt as anxious as a lost child.

When he entered the kitchen it was with no clear idea of what to expect; but he was surprised to find her seated at her usual place at the table, her hands folded idly before her, pale, heavy-lidded, but quite composed. The kitchen was spotless and there was a smell of soapsuds and clean warmth. Evidently the place had just been given a good scrub.

Rose turned heavy eyes on him and said: 'It was good of you to come over, George.'

He had been going to give her a comforting kiss, but this took him by surprise. His feelings of outrage deepened. 'Hey,' he said, accusingly, 'what's all this, Rosie, why didn't you let me know?'

She looked upset, but said, evasively: 'It was all over so quick, and they took her away – there didn't seem no point in getting you disturbed too.'

George pulled out a chair and sat opposite her. He had thought that there was nothing new to learn about Rose, after three years. But now he was giving her troubled and apprehensive glances; she seemed a stranger. In appearance she was small and dark, rather too thin. She had a sharp, pale face, with an irregular prettiness about it. She usually wore a dark skirt and a white blouse. She would sit up at night to wash and iron the blouse so that it would always be fresh. This freshness, the neatness, was her strongest characteristic. 'You look as if you could be pulled through a hedge backwards and come out with every hair in order,' he used to tease her. To which she might reply: 'Don't make me laugh. How could I?' She would be quite serious; and at such moments he might sigh, humorously, admitting that she had no sense of humour. But really he liked her seriousness, her calm practicality: he relied on it. Now he said, rather helplessly: 'Don't take on, Rosie, everything's all right.'

'I'm not taking on,' she replied unnecessarily, looking quietly at him, or rather, through him, with an air of patient waiting. He was now more apprehensive than angry. 'How's your Dad?' he asked.

'I've put him to bed with a nice cup of tea.'

'How's he taking it?'

She seemed to shrug. 'Well, he's upset, but he's getting over it now.'

And now, for the life of him, he could think of nothing to say. The clock's ticking seemed very loud, and he shifted his feet noisily. After a long silence he said aggressively: 'This won't make any difference to us, it'll be all right next week, Rosie?'

He knew that it wasn't all right when, after a further pause, she turned her eyes towards him with a full, dark, vague stare: 'Oh, well, I don't know . . .'

'What do you mean?' he challenged quickly, leaning across at her, forcibly, so that she might be made to respond: 'What do you mean, Rosie, let us have it now.'

'Well – there's Dad,' she replied, with that maddening vagueness.

'You mean we shan't get married?' he shouted angrily. 'Three years, Rosie . . .' As her silence persisted: 'Your Dad can live with us. Or – he might be getting married again – or something.'

Suddenly she laughed, and he winced; her moments of rough humour always disconcerted him. At the same time they pained him because they seemed brutal. 'You mean to say,' she said, clumsily jeering, 'you mean you hope he gets married again, even if no one else'd ever think of it.' But her eyes were filled with tears. They were lonely and self-sufficing tears. He slowly fell back into his chair, letting his hands drop loosely. He simply could not understand it. He could not understand her. It flashed into his mind that she intended not to marry him at all, but this was too monstrous a thought, and he comforted himself: 'She'll be all right by tomorrow, it's the shock, that's all. She liked her ma, really, even though they scrapped like two cats.' He was just going to say: 'Well, if I can't do anything I'll be getting along; I'll come and see you tomorrow,' when she asked him carefully, as if it were an immense effort for her to force her attention on to him: 'Would you like a cuppa tea?'

'Rose!' he shouted miserably.

'What?' She sounded unhappy but stubborn; and she was unreachable, shut off from him behind a barrier of – what? He did not know. 'Oh, go to hell then,' he muttered, and got up and stamped out of the kitchen. At the door he gave her an appealing glance, but she was not looking at him. He slammed the door hard. Afterwards he thought guiltily: She's upset, and then I treat her bad.

But Rose did not think of him when he had gone. She remained where she was, for some time, looking vaguely at the calendar with the yellow roses. Then she got up, washed her hands, hung her apron on the hook behind the door, as usual, and went to bed. 'That's over,' she said to herself, meaning George. She began to cry. She knew she would not marry him – rather, *could* not marry him. She did not know why this was impossible or why she was crying: she could not understand her own behaviour. Up till so few hours before she had been going to marry George, live with him in the little flat: everything was settled. Yet, from the moment she had heard the shocked voices saying outside in the street: Mrs Johnson's dead, she's been killed – from that moment, or so it seemed now, it had become impossible to marry George. One day he had meant everything to her, he represented her future, and the next, he meant nothing. The knowledge was shocking to her; above all she prided herself on being a sensible person; the greatest praise she could offer was: 'You got sense,' or 'I like people to behave proper, no messing about.' And what she felt was not sensible, therefore, she could not think too closely about it. She cried for a long time, stifling her sobs so that her father could not hear them where he lay through the wall. Then she lay awake and stared at the square of light that showed chimney-pots and the dissolving yellowish clouds of a rainy London dawn, scolding herself scornfully: What's the good of crying? while she mopped up the tears that rose steadily under her lids and soaked down her cheeks to the already damp pillow.

Next morning when her father asked over breakfast cups: 'Rosie, what are you going to do about George?' she replied calmly, 'It's all right, he came last night and I told him.'

'You told him what?' He spoke cautiously. His round, fresh face looked troubled, the clear, rather childlike blue eyes were not altogether approving. His workmates knew him as a jaunty, humorous man with a warm, quick laugh and ingrained opinions about life and politics. In his home he was easy and uncritical. He had been married for twenty-five years to a woman who had outwardly let him do as he pleased while taking all the responsibility on herself. He knew this. He used to say of his wife: 'Once she's got an idea into her head you might as well whistle at a wall!' And now he was looking at his daughter as he had at the mother. He did not know what she had planned, but he knew nothing he said would make any difference.

'Everything's all right, Dad,' Rose said quietly.

I daresay, he thought; but what's it all about? He asked: 'You don't have to get ideas into your head about not getting married. I'm easy.' Without looking at him she filled his cup with the strong, brown, sweet tea he loved, and said again: 'It's all right.' He persisted: 'You don't want to make any mistakes now, Rosie, you're upset, and you want to give yourself time to have a good think about things.'

To this there was no reply at all. He sighed and took his newspaper to the fire. It was Sunday. Rose was cooking the dinner when George came in. Jem, the father, turned his back on the couple, having nodded at George, thus indicating that as far as he was concerned they were alone. He was thinking: George's a good bloke, she's a fool if she gives him up.

'Well, Rosie?' said George, challengingly, the misery of the sleepless night bursting out of him.

'Well what?' temporized Rose, wiping dishes. She kept her head lowered and her face was pale and set hard. Confronted thus, with George's unhappiness, her decision did not seem so secure. She wanted to cry. She could not afford to cry now, in front of him. She went to the window so that her back might be turned to him. It was a deep basement, and she looked up at the rubbish-can and railings showing dirty black against the damp, grey houses opposite. This had been her view of the world since she could remember. She heard George saying, uncertainly: 'You marry me on Wednesday, the way we fixed it, and your Dad'll be all right, he can stay here or live with us, just as you like.'

'I'm sorry,' said Rose after a pause.

'But why, Rosie, why?'

Silence. 'Don't know,' she muttered. She sounded obstinate but unhappy. Grasping this moment of weakness in her, he laid his hand on her shoulder and appealed: 'Rosie girl, you're upset, that's all it is.' But she tensed her shoulder against him and then, since his hand remained there, jerked herself away and said angrily: 'I'm sorry. It's no good. I keep telling you.'

'Three years,' he said slowly, looking at her in amazed anger. 'Three years! And now you throw me over.'

She did not reply at once. She could see the monstrousness of what she was doing and could not help herself. She had loved him then. Now he exasperated her. 'I'm not throwing you over,' she said defensively.

'So you're not!' he shouted in derision, his face clenched in pain and rage. 'What are you doing then?'

'I don't know,' she said helplessly.

He stared at her, suddenly swore under his breath and went to the door: 'I'm not coming back,' he said, 'you're just playing the fool with me, Rosie. You shouldn't 've treated me like this. No one'd stand for it, and I'm not going to.' There was no sound from Rose, and so he went out.

Jem slowly let down the paper and remarked: 'You want to think what you're doing, Rosie.'

She did not reply. The tears were pouring down her face, but she wiped them impatiently away and bent to the oven. Later that day Jem watched her secretly over the top of the paper. There was a towel-rail beside the dresser. She was unscrewing it and moving it to a different position. She rolled the dresser itself into the opposite corner and then shifted various ornaments on the mantelpiece. Jem remembered that over each of these things she had bickered with her mother: the women could not agree about where the dresser would stand best, or the height of the towel-rail. So now Rose was having her own way, thought Jem, amazed at the sight of his daughter's quiet but determined face. The moment her mother was dead she moved everything to suit herself ... Later she made tea and sat down opposite him, in her mother's chair. Women, thought Jem, half humorous, half shocked at the persistence of the thing. And she was throwing over a nice, decent chap just because of – what? At last he shrugged and accepted it; he knew she would have her way. Also, at the bottom of his heart, he was pleased. He would never have put any pressure on her to give up marriage, but he was glad that he did not have to move, that he could stay in his old ways without disturbance. She's still young, he comforted himself; there's plenty of time for her to marry.

A month later they heard George had married someone else. Rose had a pang of regret, but it was the kind of regret one feels for something inevitable, that could not have been otherwise. When they met in the street, she said, 'Hullo, George,' and he gave her a curt, stiff nod. She even felt a little hurt because he would not let bygones be; that he felt he had to store resentment. If she could greet him nicely, as a friend, then it was unkind of him to treat her coldly ... She glanced with covert interest at the girl who was his wife, and waited for a greeting; but the girl averted her face and stared coldly away. She knew about Rose; she knew she had got George on the rebound.

This was in 1938. The rumours and the fear of war were still more an undercurrent in people's minds than a part of their thinking. Vaguely, Rose and her father expected that everything would continue as they were. About four months after the mother's death, Jem said one day: 'Why don't you give up your work now. We can manage without what you earn, if we're careful.'

'Yes?' said Rose, in the sceptical way which already told him his pleading was wasted. 'You've got too much,' he persisted. 'Cleaning and cooking, and then out all day at work.'

'Men,' she said simply, with a good-natured but dismissing sniff.

'There's no sense in it,' he protested, knowing he was wasting his breath. His wife had insisted on working until Rose was sixteen and could take her place. 'Women should be independent,' she had said. And now Rose was saying: 'I like to be independent.'

Jem said: 'Women. They say all women want is a man to keep them, but you and your mother, you go on as if I'm trying to do you out of something when I say you mustn't work.'

'Women here and women there,' said Rose. 'I don't know about *women*. All I know is what I think.'

Jem was that old type of Labour man who has been brought up in the trade union movement. He went to meetings once or twice a week, and sometimes his friends came in for a cup of tea and an argument. For years he had been saying to his wife: 'If they paid you proper, it'd be different. You work ten hours a day, and it's all for the bosses.' Now he used the argument on Rose, and she said: 'Oh, politics, I'm not interested.' Her father said: 'You're as stubborn as a mule, like your mother.'

'Then I am,' said Rose, good-humouredly. She would have said she had not 'got on' with her mother; she had had to fight to become independent of that efficient and possessive woman. But in this she agreed with her: it had been instilled into her ever since she could remember, that women must look after themselves. Like her mother, she was indulgent about the trade union meetings, as if they were a childish amusement that men should be allowed: and she voted Labour to please him, as her mother had done. And every time her father pleaded with her to give up her job at the bakery she inexorably replied: 'Who knows what might happen? It's silly not to be careful.' And so she continued to get up early in order to clean the basement kitchen and the two little rooms over it that was their home; then she made the breakfast, and went out to shop. Then she went to the bakery, and at six o'clock came back to cook supper for her father. At weekends she had a grand clean-up of the whole place, and cooked puddings and cakes. They were in bed most nights by nine. They never went out. They listened to the radio while they ate, and they read the newspapers. It was a hard life, but Rose did not think of it as hard. If she had ever used words like happiness she would have said she was happy. Sometimes she thought wistfully, not of George, but of the baby his wife was going to have. Perhaps, after all, she had made a terrible mistake? Then she squashed the thought and comforted herself: There's plenty of time, there's no hurry, I couldn't leave Dad now.

When the war started she accepted it fatalistically, while her father was deeply upset. His vision of the future had been the old socialist one: everything would slowly get better and better; and one day the working man would get into power by the automatic persuasion of common sense, and then – but his picture of that time was not so clear. Vaguely he thought of a house with a little garden and a holiday by the sea once a year. The family had never been able to afford a proper holiday. But the war cut right across this vision.

'Well, what did you expect?' asked Rose satirically.

'What do you mean?' he demanded aggressively. 'If Labour'd been in, it wouldn't have happened.'

'Maybe, maybe not.'

'You're just like your mother,' he complained again. 'You haven't got any logic.'

'Well, you've been going to meetings for years and years, and you make resolutions, and you talk, but there's a war just the same.' She felt as if this ended the argument. She felt, though she could never have put it into words, that there was a deep basic insecurity, that life itself was an enemy to be placated and humoured, liable at any moment to confront her, or people like her, with death or destitution. The only sensible thing to do was to gather together every penny that came along and keep it safe. When her mother had been alive, she paid thirty shillings of the two pounds a week she earned towards the housekeeping. Now that thirty shillings went straight into the post office. When the newspapers and the wireless blared war and horror at her, she thought of that money, and it comforted her. It didn't amount to much, but if something happened ... What that *something* might be, she did not clearly know. But life was terrible, there was no justice – had not her own mother been killed by a silly lorry crossing the street she had crossed every day of her life for twenty-five years ... that just proved it. And now there was a war, and all sorts of people were going to be hurt, all for nothing – that proved it too, if it needed any proof. Life was frightening and dangerous – therefore, put money into the post office; hold on to your job, work, and – put money into the post office.

Her father sat over the wireless set, bought newspapers,

argued with his cronies, trying to make sense of the complicated, cynical movements of power politics, while the family pattern of life dissolved into the slogans and noise of war, and the streets filled with uniforms and rumours. 'It's all Hitler,' he would say aggressively to Rose.

'Maybe, maybe not.'

'Well, he started it, didn't he?'

'I'm not interested who started it. All I know is, ordinary people don't want war. And there's war all the time. They make me sick if you want to know – and you men make me sick, too. If you were young enough, you'd be off like the rest of them,' she said accusingly.

'But, Rosie,' he said, really shocked. 'Hitler's got to be stopped, hasn't he?'

'Hitler,' she said scornfully. 'Hitler and Churchill and Stalin and Roosevelt – they all make me sick, if you want to know. And that goes for your Attlee too.'

'Women haven't got any logic,' he said, in despair.

So they came not to discuss the war at all, they merely suffered it. Slowly, Rose came to use the same words and slogans as everyone else; and like everyone else, with the deep, sad knowledge that it was all talk, and what was really happening in the world was something vast and terrible, beyond her comprehension; and perhaps it was wonderful, too, if she only knew – but she could never hope to understand. Better get on with the job, live as best she could, try not to be afraid and – put money in the post office.

Soon she switched to a job in a munitions factory. She felt she ought to do something for the war, and also, she was paid much better than in the bakery. She did fire-watching, too. Often she was up till three or four and then woke at six to clean and cook. Her father continued as a bricklayer and did fire-watching three or four nights a week. They were both permanently tired and sad. The war went on, month after month, year after year, food was short, it was hard to keep warm, the searchlights wheeled over the dark wilderness of London, the bombs fell screaming, and the black-out was like a weight on their minds and spirits. They listened to the news, read the newspapers, with the same look of bewildered but patient courage; and it seemed as if the war was a long, black, noisome tunnel from which they would never emerge.

In the third year Jem fell off a ladder one cold, foggy morning and injured his back. 'It's all right, Rose,' he said. 'I can get back to work all right.'

'You're not working,' she said flatly. 'You're sixty-seven. That's enough now, you've been working since you was fourteen.'

'There won't be enough coming in every week.'

'Won't there?' she said triumphantly. 'You used to go on at me for working. Aren't you glad now? With your bit of pension and what I get, I can still put some away every week if I try. Funny thing,' she said reflectively, not without grim humour: 'It was two pounds a week when there was peace, and I was supposed to be grateful for it. Comes a war and they pay you like you was a queen. I'm getting seven pounds a week now, one way and another. So you take things easy, and if I find you getting back to work, with your back as it is, and your rheumatism, you'll catch it from me, I'm telling you.'

'It's not right for me to sit at home, with the war and all,' he said uneasily.

'Well, did you make the war? No! You have some sense now.'

Now things were not so hard for Rose because when Jem could get out of bed he cleaned the rooms for her and there was a cup of tea waiting when she came in at night. But there was an emptiness in her and she could not pretend to herself there was not. One day she saw George's wife in the street with a little girl of about four, and stopped her. The girl was hostile, but Rose said hurriedly: 'I wanted to know, how's George?' Rather unwillingly came the reply: 'He's all right, so far, he's in North Africa.' She held the child to her as she spoke, as if for comfort, and the tears came into Rose's eyes. The two women stood hesitating on the pavement, then Rose said appealingly: 'It must be hard for you.' 'Well, it'll be over some day – when they've stopped playing soldiers,' was the grim reply; and at this Rose smiled in sympathy and the women suddenly felt friendly towards each other. 'Come over some time if you like,' said George's wife, slowly; and Rose said quickly: 'I'd like to ever so much.'

So Rose got into the habit of going over once a week to the rooms that had originally been got ready for herself. She went because of the little girl, Jill. She was secretly asking herself now: Did I make a mistake then? Should I have married George?— But even as she asked the question she knew it was futile: she could have behaved in no other way; it was one of those irrational emotional things that seem so slight and meaningless, but are so powerful. And yet, time was passing, she was nearly thirty, and when she looked in the mirror she was afraid. She was very thin now, nothing but a white-faced shrimp of a girl, with lank, tired, stringy black hair. Her sombre dark eyes peered anxiously back at her over hollowed and bony cheeks. 'It's because I work so hard,' she comforted herself. 'No sleep, that's what it is, and the bad food, and those chemicals in the factory ... it'll be better after the war.' It was a question of endurance; somehow she had to get through the war, and then everything would be all right. Soon she looked forward all week to the Sunday night when she went over to George's wife, with a little present for Jill. When she lay awake at nights she thought not of George, nor of the men she met at the factory who might have become interested in her, but of children. 'What with the war and all the men getting killed,' she sometimes worried, 'perhaps it's too late. There won't be any men left by the time they've finished killing them all off.' But if her father could have managed for himself before, he could not now; he was really dependent on her. So she always pushed away her fears and longings with the thought: 'When the war's over we can eat and sleep again, and then I'll look better, and then perhaps ...'

Not long before the war ended Rose came home late one night, dragging her feet tiredly along the dark pavement, thinking that she had forgotten to buy anything for supper. She turned into her street, was troubled by a feeling that something was wrong, looked down towards the house where she lived, and stopped dead. There were heaps of smoking rubble showing

against the reddish glare of fire. At first she thought: 'I must
have come to the wrong street in the black-out.' Then she
understood and began to run towards her home, clutching her
handbag tightly, holding the scarf under her chin. At the edge
of the street was a deep crater. She nearly fell into it, but
righted herself and walked on stumblingly among bomb refuse
and tangling wires. Where her gate had been she stopped. A
group of people were standing there. 'Where's my father?' she
demanded angrily. 'Where is he?' A young man came forward
and said, 'Take it easy, miss.' He laid a hand on her shoulder.
'You live here? I think your Dad was an unlucky one.' The
words brought no conviction to her and she stared at him,
frowning. 'What have you done with him?' she asked, accusingly. 'They took him away, miss.' She stood passively, then
she heavily lifted her head and looked around her. In this part
of the street all the houses were gone. She pushed her way
through the people and stood looking down at the steps to the
basement door. The door was hanging loose from the frame,
but the glass of the window was whole. 'It's all right,' she said,
half-aloud. She took a key from her handbag and slowly descended the steps over a litter of bricks. 'Miss, miss,' called the
young man, 'you can't go down there.' She made no reply, but
fitted the key into the door and tried to turn it. It would not turn,
so she pushed the door, it swung in on its one remaining hinge,
and she went inside. The place looked as it always did, save
that the ornaments on the mantelpiece had been knocked to the
floor. It was half-lit from the light of burning houses over the
street. She was slowly picking up the ornaments and putting
them back when a hand was laid on her arm. 'Miss,' said a
compassionate voice, 'you can't stay down here.'

'Why shouldn't I?' she retorted, with a flash of stubbornness.

She looked upwards. There was a crack across the ceiling and
dust was still settling through the air. But a kettle was boiling
on the stove. 'It's all right,' she announced. 'Look, the gas is
still working. If the gas is all right then things isn't too bad,
that stands to reason, doesn't it now?'

'You've got the whole weight of the house lying on that ceiling,' said the man dubiously.

'The house has always stood over the ceiling hasn't it,' she said, with a tired humour that surprised him. He could not see what was funny, but she was grinning heavily at the joke. 'So nothing's changed,' she said, airily. But there was a look on her face that worried him, and she was trembling in a hard, locked way, as if her muscles were held rigid against the weakness of her flesh. Sudden spasmodic shudders ran through her, and then she shut her jaw hard to stop them. 'It's not safe,' he protested again, and she obediently gazed around her to see. The kettle and the pans stood as they had ever since she could remember; the cloth on the table was one her mother had embroidered, and through the cracked window she would see the black, solid shape of the dustcan, though beyond it there were no silhouettes of grey houses, only grey sky spurting red flame. 'I think it's all right,' she said, stolidly. And she did. She felt safe. This was her home. She lifted the kettle and began making tea. 'Have a cup?' she inquired, politely. He did not know what to do. She took her cup to the table, blew off the thick dust and began stirring in sugar. Her trembling made the spoon tinkle against the cup.

'I'll be back,' he announced suddenly, and went out, meaning to fetch someone who would know how to talk to her. But now there was no one outside. They had all gone over to the burning houses; and after a little indecision he thought: I'll come back later, she's all right for the moment. He helped with the others over at the houses until very late, and he was on his way home when he remembered: That kid, what's she doing? Almost, he went straight home. He had not had his clothes off for nights, he was black and grimy, but he made the effort and returned to the basement under the heap of rubble. There was a faint glow beneath the ruin and, peering low, he saw two candles on the table, while a small figure sat sewing beside them. Well I'll be ... he thought, and went in. She was darning socks. He went beside her and said: 'I've come to see if you're all right.' Rose worked on her sock and replied calmly: 'Yes, of course I'm all right, but thanks for dropping in.' Her eyes were enormous, with a wild look, and her mouth was trembling like that of an old woman. 'What are you doing?' he asked, at a loss. 'What do

you think?' she said tartly. Then she looked wonderingly at the
sock which was stretched across her palm and shuddered. 'Your
Dad's sock?' he said carefully; and she gave him an angry
glance and began to cry. That's better, he thought, and went
forward and made her lean against him while he said aloud:
'Take it easy, take it easy, miss.' But she did not cry for long.
Almost at once she pushed him away and said: 'Well, there's no
need to let the socks go to waste. They'll do for someone.'

'That's right, miss.' He stood hesitantly beside her and, after
a moment, she lifted her head and looked at him. For the first
time she saw him. He was a slight man, of middle height, who
seemed young because of the open, candid face, though his hair
was greying. His pleasant grey eyes rested compassionately on
her and his smile was warm. 'Perhaps you'd like them,' she
suggested. 'And there's his clothes, too – he didn't have anything very special, but he always looked after his things.' She
began to cry again, this time more quietly, with small, shudder-
ing sobs. He sat gently beside her, patting her hand as it lay on
the table, repeating, 'Take it easy, miss, take it easy, it's all
right.' The sound of his voice soothed her and soon she came to
an end, dried her eyes and said in a matter-of-fact voice:
'There, I'm just silly, what's the use of crying?' She got up,
adjusted the candles so that they would not gutter over the
cloth, and said: 'Well, we might as well have a cup of tea.' She
brought him one, and they sat drinking in silence. He was
watching her curiously; there was something about her that
tugged at his imagination. She was such an indomitable little
figure sitting there staring out of sad, tired eyes, under the ruins
of her home, like a kind of waif. She was not pretty, he decided,
looking at the small, thin face, at the tired locks of black hair
lying tidily beside it. He felt tender towards her; also he was
troubled by her. Like everyone who lived through the big cities
during the war, he knew a great deal about nervous strain;
about shock; he could not have put words around what he knew,
but he felt there was still something very wrong with Rose;
outwardly, however, she seemed sensible, and so he suggested:
'You'd better get yourself some sleep. It'll be morning soon.'

'I've got to be getting to work. I'm working an early shift.'

He said: 'If you feel like it,' thinking it might be better for her to work. And so he left her, and went back home to get some sleep.

That next evening he came by expecting to find her gone, and saw her sitting at the table, in the yellow glow from the candles, her hands, lying idly before her, staring at the wall. Everything was very tidy, and the dust had been removed. But the crack in the ceiling had perceptibly widened. 'Hasn't anyone been to see you?' he asked carefully. She replied evasively: 'Oh, some old nosy parkers came and said I mustn't stay.' 'What did you tell them?' She hesitated and then said: 'I said I wasn't staying here, I was with some friends.' He scratched his head, smiling ruefully: he could imagine the scene. 'Those old nosy parkers,' she went on resentfully, 'interfering, telling people what to do.'

'You know, miss, I think they were right, you ought to move out.'

'I'm staying here,' she announced defiantly, with un-mistakable fear. 'Nothing's getting me out. Not all the king's horses.'

'I don't expect they could spare the king's horses,' he said, trying to make her laugh; but she replied seriously, after considering it: 'Well, even if they could.' He smiled tenderly at her literal-mindedness, and suggested on an impulse: 'Come to the pictures with me, doesn't do any good to sit and mope.'

'I'd like to, but it's Sunday, see?'

'What's the matter with a Sunday?'

'Every Sunday I go and see a friend of mine who has a little girl . . .' she began to explain; and then she stopped, and went pale. She scrambled to her feet and said: 'Oh oh, I never thought . . .'

'What's wrong, what's up?'

'Perhaps that bomb got them too, they were along this street – oh dear, oh dear, I never came to think – I'm wicked, that's what I am . . .' She had taken up her bag and was frantically wrapping her scarf around her head.

'Here, miss, don't go rushing off – I can find out for you, perhaps I know – what was her name?'

She told him. He hesitated for a moment and then said: 'You're having bad luck, and that's a fact. She was killed the same time.'

'She?' asked Rose, quickly.

'The mother was killed, the kid's all right, it was playing in another room.'

Rose slowly sat down, thinking deeply, her hand still holding the scarf together at her chin. Then she said: 'I'll adopt her, that's what I'll do.'

He was surprised that she showed no sort of emotion at the death of the woman, her friend. 'Hasn't the kid got a dad?' he asked. 'He's in North Africa,' she said. 'Well, he'll come back after the war, he might not want you to adopt the kid.' But she was silent, and her face was hard with determination. 'Why this kid in particular?' he asked. 'You'll have kids of your own one day.'

She said evasively: 'She's a nice kid, you should see her.' He left it. He could see that there was something here too deep for him to grasp. Again he suggested: 'Come to the pictures and take your mind off things.' Obediently she rose and placed herself at his disposal, as it were. Walking along the streets she turned this way and that at a touch of his hand, but in spirit she was not with him. He knew that she sat through the film without seeing it. 'She's in a bad way,' he said helplessly to himself. 'It's time she snapped out of it.'

But Rose was thinking only of Jill. Her whole being was now concentrated on the thought of the little girl. Tomorrow she would find out where she was. Some nosy parkers would have got hold of her – that was certain; they were always bossing other people. She would take Jill away from them and look after her – they could stay in the basement until the house got rebuilt . . . Rose was awake all night, dreaming of Jill; and next day she did not go to work. She went in search of the child. She found her grandmother had taken her. She had never thought of the grandmother, and the discovery was such a shock that she came back to the basement not knowing how she walked or what she did. The fact that she could not have the child seemed more terrible than anything else; it was as if she had been deprived maliciously of something she had a right to; something had been taken away from her – that was how she felt.

Jimmie came that night. He was asking himself why he kept returning, what it would come to; and yet he could not keep away. The image of Rose, the silent, frightened little girl – which was how he saw her – stayed with him all day. When he entered the basement she was sitting as usual by the candles, staring before her. He saw with dismay that she had made no effort to clean the place, and that her hair was untidy. This last fact seemed worse than anything.

He sat beside her, as usual, and tried to think of some way to make her 'snap out of it'. At last he remarked: 'You ought to be making some plans to move, Rose.' At this, she irritably shrugged her shoulders. She wished he would stop pestering her with this sort of reminder. At the same time she was glad to have him there. She would have liked him to stay beside her silently; his warm friendliness wrapped her about like a blanket, but she could never relax into it because there was a part of her mind alert against him for fear of what he might say.

She was afraid, really, that he might talk of her father. Not once had she allowed herself to think of it – her father's death, as it must have been. She said to herself the words: My father's dead, just as she had once said to herself: My mother's dead. Never had she allowed those words to form into images of death. If they had been ordinary deaths, deaths one could understand, it would have been different. People dying of illness or age, in bed; and then the neighbours coming, and then the funeral – that was understandable, that would have been different. But not the senselessness of a black bomb falling out of the sky, dropped by a nice young man in an aeroplane, not the silly business of a lorry running someone over – no, she could not bear to think of it. Underneath the surface of living was a black gulf, full of senseless horror. All day, at the factory (where she helped to make other bombs) or in the basement at night, she made the usual movements, said the expected things, but never allowed herself to think of death. She said: My father's been killed, in a flat, ordinary voice, without letting pictures of death arise into her mind.

And now here was Jimmie, who had come into her life just when she needed his warmth and support most; and even this was two-faced, because it was the same Jimmie who made these remarks, forcing her to think . . . she would not think, she refused to respond. Jimmie noticed that whenever he made a remark connected in any way with the future, or even with the war, a blank, nervous look came on to her face and she turned away her eyes. He did not know what to do. For that evening he left it, and came back next day. This was the sixth day after the bomb, and he saw that the crack in the ceiling was bulging heavily downwards from the weight on top of it, and when a car passed, bits of plaster flaked down in a soft white rain. It was really dangerous. He had to do something. And still she sat there, her hands lying loosely in front of her, staring at the wall. He decided to be cruel. His heart was hammering with fright at what he was going to do; but he announced in a loud and cheerful voice: 'Rose, your father's dead, he's not going to come back.'

She turned her eyes vaguely towards him; it seemed as if she had not heard at all. But he had to go on now. 'Your Dad's had it,' he said brightly. 'He's copped it. He's dead as a doornail, and it's no use staying here.'

'How do you know?' she asked faintly. 'Sometimes there are mistakes. Sometimes people come back, don't they?'

This was much worse than he had thought. 'He won't come back. I saw him myself.'

'No,' she protested, sharply drawing breath.

'Oh, yes I did. He was lying on the pavement, smashed to smithereens.' He was waiting for her face to change. So far, it was obstinate, but her eyes were fixed on him like a scared rabbit's. 'Nothing, left,' he announced, jauntily, 'his legs were gone – nothing there at all, and he didn't have a head left either . . .'

And now Rose got to her feet with a sudden angry movement, and her eyes were small and black. 'You . . .' she began. Her lips shook. Jimmie remained seated. He was trying to look casual, even jaunty. He was forcing himself to smile. Underneath he was very frightened. Supposing this was the wrong thing? Supposing she went clean off her rocker ... supposing ... He passed his tongue quickly over his lips and glanced at her to see how she was. She was still staring at him. But now she seemed to hate him. He wanted to laugh from fright. But he stood up and, with an appearance of deliberate brutality, said: 'Yes, Rosie girl, that's how it is, your Dad's nothing but a bleeding corpse – that's good, bleeding!' And now, he thought, I've done it properly! 'You—' began Rose again, her face contracted with hatred. 'You—' And such a stream of foul language came from her mouth that it took him by surprise. He had expected her to cry, to break down. She shouted and raved at him, lifting her fists to batter at his chest. Gently holding her off he said silently to himself, giving himself courage: 'Ho, ho, Rosie my girl, what language, naughty, naughty!' Out loud he said, with uneasy jocularity: 'Hey, take it easy, it's not my fault now ...' He was surprised at her strength. The quiet, composed, neat little Rose was changed into a screaming hag, who scratched and kicked and clawed. 'Get out of here you—' and she picked up a candlestick and threw it at him. Holding his arm across his face, he retreated backwards to the door, gave it a kick with his heel, and went out. There he stood, waiting, with a half-rueful, half-worried smile on his face, listening. He was rubbing the scratches on his face with his handkerchief. At first there was silence, then loud sobbing. He straightened himself slowly. I might have hurt her bad, talking like that, he thought; perhaps she'll never get over it. But he felt reassured; instinctively he knew he had done the right thing. He listened to the persistent crying for a while, and then wondered: Yes, but what do I do now? Should I go back again now, or wait a little? And more persistent than these worries was another: And what then? If I go back now, I'll let myself in for something and no mistake. He slowly retreated from Rose's door, down the damaged street, to a pub at the corner, which had not been hit. Must have a drink and a bit of a think ... Inside the pub he leaned quietly by the counter, glass in hand, his grey eyes dark with worry. He heard someone say: 'Well handsome, and what's been biting you?' He looked up, smiling, and saw Pearl. He had known her for some time – nothing serious; they exchanged greetings and bits of talk over the counter when he dropped in. He liked Pearl, but now he wanted to be left alone. She lingered and said again: 'How's your wife?' He frowned quickly, and did not reply. She made a grimace as if to say: Well, if you don't want to be sociable I'm not going to force you! But she remained where she was, looking at him closely. He was thinking: I shouldn't have started it, I shouldn't have taken her on. No business of mine what happened to her ... And then, unconsciously straightening himself, with a a small, desperate smile that was also triumphant: 'You're in trouble again, my lad, you're in for it now!' Pearl remarked in an offhand way: 'You'd better get your face fixed up – been in a fight?' He lifted his hand to his face and it came away covered with blood. 'Yes,' he said, grinning, 'with a spitfire.' She laughed, and he laughed with her. The words presented Rose to him in a new way. Proper little spitfire, he said to himself, caressing his cheek. Who would have thought Rose had all that fire in her? Then he set down the glass, straightened his tie, wiped his cheek with his handkerchief, nodded to Pearl with his debonair smile, and went out. Now he did not hesitate. He went straight back to the basement.

Rose was washing clothes in the sink. Her face was swollen and damp with crying, but she had combed her hair. When she saw him she went red, trying to meet his eyes, but could not. He went straight over to her and put his arms around her. 'Here, Rosie, don't get worked up now.' 'I'm sorry,' she said, with prim nervousness, trying to smile. Her eyes appealed to him. 'I don't know what came over me, I don't really.'

'It's all right, I'm telling you.'

But now she was crying from shame. 'I never use them words. Never. I didn't know I knew them. I'm not like that. And now you'll think ...' He gathered her to him and felt her shoulders shaking. 'Now don't you waste any more time thinking about it. You were upset – well, I wanted you to be upset, I did it on purpose, don't you see, Rosie? You couldn't go on like that, pretending to yourself.' He kissed the part of her cheek that was not hidden in his shoulder. 'I'm sorry, I'm ever so sorry,' she wept, but she sounded much better.

He held her tight and made soothing noises. At the same time he had the feeling of a man sliding over the edge of a dangerous mountain. But he could not stop himself now. It was much too late. She said, in a small voice: 'You were quite right, I know you were. But it was just that I couldn't bear to think. I didn't have anybody but Dad. It's been him and me together for ever so long. I haven't got anybody at all . . .' The thought came into her mind and vanished: Only George's little girl. She belongs to me by rights.

Jimmie said indignantly: 'Your Dad – I'm not saying anything against him, but it wasn't right to keep you here looking after him. You should have got out and found yourself a nice husband and had kids.' He did not understand why, though only for a moment, her body hardened and rejected him. Then she relaxed and said submissively: 'You mustn't say anything against my Dad.'

'No,' he agreed, mildly, 'I won't.' She seemed to be waiting. 'I haven't got anything now,' she said, and lifted her face to him. 'You've got me,' he said at last, and he was grinning a little from sheer nervousness. Her face softened, her eyes searched his, and she still waited. There was a silence, while he struggled with common sense. It was far too long a silence, and she was already reproachful when he said: 'You come with me, Rosie, I'll look after you.'

And now she collapsed against him again and wept: 'You do love me, don't you, you do love me?' He held her and said: 'Yes, of course, I love you.' Well that was true enough. He did. He didn't know why, there wasn't any sense in it, she wasn't even pretty, but he loved her. Later she said: 'I'll get my things together and come to where you live.'

He temporized, with an anxious glance at the ominous ceiling: 'You stay here for a bit. I'll get things fixed first.'

'Why can't I come now?' She looked in a horrified, caged way around the basement as if she couldn't wait to get out of it – she who had clung so obstinately to its shelter.

'You just trust me now, Rosie. You pack your things, like a good girl. I'll come back and fetch you later.' She clutched his shoulders and looked into his face and pleaded: 'Don't leave me here long – that ceiling – it might fall.' It was as if she had only just noticed it. He comforted her, put her persuasively away from him, and repeated he would be back in half an hour. He left her sorting out her belongings in worried haste, her eyes fixed on the ceiling.

And now what was he going to do? He had no idea. Flats – they weren't hard to find, with so many people evacuated; yes, but here it was after eleven at night, and he couldn't even lay hands on the first week's rent. Besides, he had to give his wife some money tomorrow. He walked slowly through the damaged streets, in the thick dark, his hands in his pockets, thinking: Now you're in a fix, Jimmie boy, you're properly in a fix.

About an hour later his feet took him back. Rose was seated at the table, and on it were two cardboard boxes and a small suitcase – her clothes. Her hands were folded together in front of her.

'It's all right?' she inquired, already on her feet.

'Well, Rosie, it's like this—' he sat down and tried for the right words. 'I should've told you. I haven't got a place really.'

'You've got no place to sleep?' she inquired, incredulously. He avoided her eyes and muttered: 'Well, there's complications.' He caught a glimpse of her face and saw there – pity! It made him want to swear. Hell, this was a mess, and what was he to do? But the sorrowful warmth of her face touched him and, hardly knowing what he was doing, he let her put her arms around him, while he said: 'I was bombed out last week.'

'And you were looking after me, and you had no place yourself?' she accused him, tenderly. 'We'll be all right. We'll find a place in the morning.

'That's right, we'll have our own place and – can we get married soon?' she inquired shyly, going pink.

At this, he laid his face against hers, so that she could not look at him, and said: 'Let's get a place first, and we can fix everything afterwards.'

She was thinking. 'Haven't you got no money?' she inquired, diffidently at last. 'Yes, but not the cash. I'll have it later.' He was telling himself again: You're properly in the soup, Jimmie, in – the – soup!

'I've got two hundred pounds in the post office,' she offered, smiling with shy pride, as she fondled his hair. 'And there's the furniture from here – it's not hurt by the bomb a bit. We can furnish nicely.'

'I'll give you back the money later,' he said desperately.

'When you've got it. Besides, my money is yours now,' she said, smiling tenderly at him. '*Ours.*' She tasted the word delicately, inviting him to share her pleasure in it.

Jimmie was essentially a man who knew people, got around, had irons in the fire and strings to pull; and by next afternoon he had found a flat. Two rooms and a kitchen, a cupboard for the coal, hot and cold water, and a share of the bathroom downstairs. Cheap, too. It was the top of an old house, and he was pleased that one could see trees from Battersea Park over the tops of the buildings opposite. Rose'll like it, he thought. He was happy now. All last night he had lain on the floor beside her in the ruinous basement, under the bulging ceiling, consumed by dubious thoughts; now these had vanished, and he was optimistic. But when Rose came up the stairs with her packages she went straight to the window and seemed to shrink back. 'Don't you like it, Rosie?' 'Yes, I like it, but . . .' Soon she laughed and said, apologetically: 'I've always lived underneath – I mean, I'm not used to being so high up.' He kissed her and teased her and she laughed too. But several times he noticed that she looked unhappily down from the window and quickly came away, with a swift, uncertain glance around at the empty rooms. All her life she had lived underground, with buses and cars rumbling past above eye-level, the weight of the big old house heavy over her, like the promise of protection. Now she was high above streets and houses, and she felt unsafe. Don't be silly, she told herself. You'll get used to it. And she gave herself to the pleasure of arranging furniture, putting things away. She took a hundred pounds of her money out of the post office and bought – but what she bought was chiefly for him. A chest for his clothes: she teased him because he had so many; a small wireless set; and finally a desk for him to work on, for he had said he was studying for an engineering degree of some kind. He asked her why she bought nothing for herself, and she said, defensively, that she had plenty. She had arranged the new flat to look like her old home. The table stood the same way, the calendar with yellow roses hung on the wall, and she worked happily beside her stove, making the same movements she had used for years; for the cupboard, the drying-line and the drain-ing-board had been fixed exactly as they had been 'at home'. Unconsciously, she still used that phrase. 'Here,' he protested, 'isn't this home now?' She said seriously: 'Yes, but I can't get used to it.' 'Then you'd better get used to it,' he complained, and then kissed her to make amends for his resentment. When this had happened several times he let out: 'Anyway, the base-ment's fallen in, I passed today, and it's filled with bricks and stuff.' He had intended not to tell her. She shrank away from him and went quite white. 'Well, you knew it wasn't going to stay for long,' he said. She was badly shaken. She could not bear to think of her old home gone; she could imagine it, the great beams slanting into it, filled with dirty water – she imagined it and shut out the vision for ever. She was quiet and listless all that day, until he grew angry with her. He was quite often angry. He would protest when she bought things for him. 'Don't you like it?' she would inquire, looking puzzled. 'Yes, I like it fine, but . . .' And later she was hurt because he seemed reluctant to use the chest, or the desk.

There were other points where they did not understand each other. About four weeks after they moved in she said: 'You aren't much of a one for home, are you?' He said, in genuine astonishment: 'What do you mean? I'm stuck here like . . .' He stopped, and put a cigarette in his mouth to take the place of speech. From his point of view he had turned over a new leaf; he was a man who hated to be bound, to spend every evening the same way; and now he came to Rose most evenings straight from work, ate supper with her, paid her sincere compliments on her cooking, and then – well, there was every reason why he should come, he would be a fool not to! He was consumed by secret pride in her. Fancy Rose, a girl like her, living with her

old man all these years, like a girl shut into a convent, or not
much better — you'd think there was something wrong with a girl
who got to be thirty before having a man in her bed! But there
was nothing wrong with Rose. And at work he'd think of their
nights and laugh with deep satisfaction. She was all right, Rose
was. And then, slowly, a doubt began to eat into the pride. It
wasn't natural that she'd been alone all those years. Besides,
she was a good-looker. He laughed when he remembered that
he had thought her quite ugly at first. Now that she was happy,
and in a place of her own, and warmed through with love, she
was really pretty. Her face had softened, she had a delicate
colour in her thin cheeks, and her eyes were deep and wel-
coming. It was like coming home to a little cat, all purring and
pliable. And when he took her to the pictures he walked
proudly by her, conscious of the other men's glances at her. And
yet he was the first man who had had the sense to see what she
could be? — hmm, not likely, it didn't make sense.

He talked to Rose, and suddenly the little cat showed its
sharp and unpleasant claws. 'What is it you want to know?' she
demanded coldly, after several clumsy remarks from him.
'Well, Rosie — it's that bloke George, you said you were going
to marry him when you were a kid still?'

'What of it?' she said, giving him a cool glance.

'You were together for a long time?'

'Three years,' she said flatly.

'Three years!' he exclaimed. He had not thought of anything
so serious. 'Three years is a long time.'

She looked at him with a pleading reproach that he entirely
failed to understand. As far as she was concerned the delight
Jimmie had given her completely cancelled out anything she
had known before. George was less than a memory. When she
told herself that Jimmie was the first man she had loved, it was
true, because that was how she felt. The fact that he could now
question it, doubting himself, weakened the delight, made her
unsure not only of him but of herself. How could he destroy
their happiness like this! And into the reproach came contempt.
She looked at him with heavy, critical eyes; and Jimmie felt
quite wild with bewilderment and dismay — she could look at

him like that! – then that proved she had been lying when she said he was the first – if she had said so … 'But, Rosie,' he blustered, 'it stands to reason. Engaged three years, and you tell me …'

'I've never told you anything,' she pointed out, and got up from the table and began stacking the dishes ready for washing.

'Well, I've a right to know, haven't I?' he cried out, unhappily.

But this was very much a mistake. 'Right?' she inquired in a prim, disdainful voice. She was no longer Rose, she was something much older. She seemed to be hearing her mother speaking. 'Who's talking about rights?' She dropped the dishes neatly into the hot, soapy water and said: 'Men! I've never asked you what you did before me. And I'm not interested either, if you want to know. And what I did, if I did anything, doesn't interest you neither.' Here she turned on the tap so that the splashing sounds made another barrier. Her ears filled with the sound of water, she thought: Men, they always spoil everything. She had forgotten George, he didn't exist. And now Jimmie brought him to life and made her think of him. Now she was forced to wonder: Did I love him as much then? Was it the same as this? And if her happiness with George had been as great as now it was with Jimmie, then that very fact seemed to diminish love itself and make it pathetic and uncertain. It was as if Jimmie were doing it on purpose to upset her. That, at any rate, was how she felt.

But across the din of the running water Jimmie shouted: 'So I'm not interested, is that it?'

'No, you'd better not be interested,' she announced, and looked stonily before her, while her hands worked among the hot, slippery plates. 'So that's how it is?' he shouted again, furiously.

To which she did not reply. He remained leaning at the table, calling Rose names under his breath, but at the same time conscious of bewilderment. He felt that all his possessive masculinity was being outraged and flouted; there was, however, no doubt that she felt as badly treated as he did. As she did not relent he went to her and put his arms around her. It was necessary for him to destroy this aloof and wounded-looking female and restore the loving, cosy woman. He began to tease: 'Spitfire, little cat, that's what you are.' He pulled her hair and held her arms to her sides so that she could not dry the plates. She remained unresponsive. Then he saw that the tears were running down her immobile and stubborn cheeks, and in a flush of triumph picked her up and carried her over to the bed. It was all quite easy, after all.

But maybe not so easy, because late that night, in a studiously indifferent voice, Rose inquired from the darkness at his side: 'When are we going to get married?' He stiffened. He had forgotten – or almost – about this. Hell, wasn't she satisfied? Didn't he spend all his evenings here? He might just as well be married, seeing what she expected of him. 'Don't you trust me, Rosie?' he inquired at last. 'Yes, I trust you,' she said, rather doubtfully, and waited. 'There's reasons why I can't marry you just now.' She remained silent, but her silence was like a question hanging in the dark between them. He did not reply, but turned and kissed her. 'I love you, Rosie, you know that, don't you?' Yes, she knew that; but about a week later he left her one morning saying: 'I can't come tonight, Rosie. I've got to put in some work on this exam.' He saw her glance at the desk she had bought him and which he had never used. 'I'll be along tomorrow as usual,' he said quickly, wanting to escape from the troubled, searching eyes.

She asked suddenly: 'Your wife getting anxious about you?'

He caught his breath and stared at her: 'Who told you?' She laughed derisively. 'Well, who told you?'

'No one told me,' she said, with contempt.

'Then I must have been talking in my sleep,' he muttered, anxiously.

She laughed loudly: ' "Someone told me." "Talking in your sleep" – you must think I'm stupid.' And with a familiar, maddening gesture, she turned away and picked up a dishcloth.

'Leave the dishes alone, they're clean, anyway,' he shouted.

'Don't shout at me like that.'

'Rose,' he appealed after a moment, 'I was going to tell you, I just couldn't tell you – I tried to, often.'

'Yes?' she said, laconically. That *yes* of hers always exasperated him. It was like a statement of rock-bottom disbelief, a basic indifference to himself and the world of men. It was as if she said: There's only one person I can rely on – myself.

'Rosie, she won't divorce me, she won't give me my freedom.' These dramatic words were supplied straight to his tongue by the memory of a film he had seen the week before. He felt ashamed of himself. But her face had changed. 'You should have told me,' she said; and once again he was disconcerted because of the pity in her voice. She had instinctively turned to him with a protective movement. Her arms went around him and he let his head sink on her shoulder with that old feeling that he was being swept away, that he had no control over the things he did and said. Hell, he thought, even while he warmed to her tenderness: to hell with it. I never meant to get me and Rosie into this fix. In the meantime she held him comfortingly, bending her face to his hair, but there was a rigidity in her pose that told him she was still waiting. At last she said: 'I want to have kids. I'm not getting any younger.' He tightened his arms around her waist while he thought: I never thought of that. For he had two children of his own. Then he thought: She's right. She should have kids. Remember how she got worked up over that other kid in the blitz? Women need to have kids. He thought of her with his child, and pride stirred in him. He realized he would be pleased if she got pregnant, and felt even more at sea. Rose said: 'Ask her again, Jimmie. Make her divorce you. I know women get spiteful and that about divorces, but if you talk to her nice—' He miserably promised that he would. 'You'll ask her tonight?' she insisted. 'Well . . .' the fact was, that he had not intended to go home tonight. He wanted to have an evening to himself – go to the pub, see some of his pals, even work for an hour or so. 'Weren't you going home tonight?' she asked, incredulously, seeing his face. 'No, I meant it, I want to do some work. I've got to get this exam, Rosie. I know I can take it if I work a little. And then I'm qualified. Just now I'm not one thing and I'm not the other.' She accepted this with a sigh, then pleaded: 'Go home tomorrow then and ask her.'

'But tomorrow I want to come and see you, Rosie, don't you

want me?' She sighed again, not knowing that she did, and smiled: 'You're nothing but a baby, Jimmie.' He began coaxing: 'Come on, be nice, Rosie, give me a kiss.' He felt it was urgently necessary for him to have her warm and relaxed and loving again before he could leave her with a quiet mind. And so she was – but not entirely. There was a thoughtful line across her forehead and her mouth was grave and sad. Oh, to hell with it, he thought, as he went off. To hell with them all.

The next evening he went to Rose anxiously. He had drunk himself gay and debonair in the pub, he had flirted a little with Pearl, talked sarcastically about women and marriage, and finally gone home to sleep. He had breakfast with his family, avoided his wife's sardonic eye, and went off to work with a bad hangover. At the factory, as always, he became absorbed in what he was doing. It was a small factory which made precision instruments. He was highly skilled, but in status an ordinary workman. He knew, had known for a long time, that with a little effort he could easily take an examination which would lift him into the middle classes as far as money was concerned. It was the money he cared about, not the social aspect of it. For years his wife had been nagging at him to better himself, and he had answered impatiently because, for her, what mattered was to outdo their neighbours. This he despised. But she was right for the wrong reasons. It was a question of devoting a year of evenings to study. What was a year of one's life? Nothing. And he had always found examinations easy. That day, at the factory, he had decided to tell Rose that she would not see as much of him in future. He swore angrily to himself that she must understand a man had a duty to himself. He was only forty, after all . . . And yet, even while he spoke firmly to himself and to the imaginary Rose, he saw a mental picture of the desk she had bought him that stood unused in the living room of the flat. 'Well, who's stopping you from working?' she would inquire, puzzled. Genuinely puzzled, too. But he could not work in that flat, he knew that; although in the two months before he had met Rose he was working quite steadily in his evenings. That day he was cursing the fate that had linked him with Rose; and by evening he was hurrying to her as if some terrible thing might happen if he were not there by supper-time. He was expecting her to be cold and distant, but she fell into his arms as if he had been away for weeks. 'I missed you,' she said, clinging to him. 'I was so lonely without you.'

'It was only one night,' he said, jauntily, already reassured.

'You were gone two nights last week,' she said, mournfully. At once he felt irritated. 'I didn't know you counted them up,' he said, trying to smile. She seemed ashamed that she had said it. 'I just get lonely,' she said, kissing him guiltily. 'After all . . .'

'After all what?' His voice was aggressive.

'It's different for you,' she defended herself. 'You've got — other things.' Here she evaded his look. 'But I go to work, and then I come home and wait for you. There's nothing but you to look forward to.' She spoke hastily, as if afraid to annoy him, and then she put her arms around his neck and kissed him coaxingly and said: 'I've cooked you something you like — can you smell it?' And she was the warm and affectionate woman he wanted her to be. Later he said: 'Listen, Rosie girl, I've got to tell you something. That exam — I must start working for it.' She said, gaily, at once: 'But I told you already, you can work here at the desk and I'll sew while you work, and it'll be lovely.' The idea seemed to delight her, but his heart chilled at it. It seemed to him quite insulting to their romantic love that she should not mind his working, that she should suggest prosaic sewing — just like a wife. He spent the next few evenings with her, newly in love, absorbed in her. And he felt hurt when she suggested hurriedly — for she was afraid of a rebuff — 'If you want to work tonight, I don't mind, Jimmie.' He said laughing: 'Oh, to hell with work, you're the only work I want.' She was flattered, but the thoughtful line was marked deep across her forehead. About a fortnight after his wife was first mentioned she delicately inquired: 'Have you asked her about the divorce?'

He turned away, saying evasively, 'She wouldn't listen just now.' He was not looking at her, but he could feel her heavy, questioning look on him. His irritation was so strong that he had to make an effort to control it. Also he was guilty, and that guilt he could understand even less than the irritation. He all at once became very gay, so that his mood infected her, and they were giggling and laughing like two children. 'You're just conventional, that's what you are,' he said, pulling her hair. 'Conventional?' she tasted the big word doubtfully. 'Women always want to get married. What do you want to get married for? Aren't we happy? Don't we love each other? Getting married would just spoil it.' But theoretical statements like this always confused Rose. She would consider each of them separately, with a troubled face, rather respectful of the intellectual minds that had formulated them. And while she considered them, the current of her emotions ran steadily and deep, unconnected with words. From the gulf of love in which she was sunk she murmured, fondly: 'Oh, you – you just talk and talk.' 'Men are polygamous,' he said gaily, 'it's a fact, scientists say so.' 'What are women then?' she asked, keeping her end up. 'They aren't polygamous.' She considered this seriously, as was her way, and said doubtfully: 'Yes?' 'Hell,' he expostulated, half seriously, half laughing, 'you're telling me you're polygamous?' But Rose moved uneasily, with a laugh, away from him. To connect a word like polygamous, reeking as it did of the 'nosy parkers' who were, she felt, her chief enemy in life, with herself, was too much to ask of her. Silence. 'You're thinking of George,' he suddenly shouted, jealously. 'I wasn't doing any such thing,' she said, indignantly. Her genuine indignation upset him. He always hated it when she was serious. As far as he was concerned, he had just been teasing her – he thought.

Once she said: 'Why do you always look cross when I say what I think about something?' Now that surprised him – didn't she always say what she thought? 'I don't get cross, Rosie, but why do you take everything so serious?' To this she remained silent, in the darkness. He could see the small, thoughtful face turned away from him, lit by the bleak light from the window. The thoughtfulness seemed to him like a reproach. He liked her childish and responsive. 'Don't I make you happy, Rose?' He sounded miserable. 'Happy?' she said, testing the word. Then she unexpectedly laughed and said: 'You talk so funny sometimes you make me laugh.' 'I don't see what's funny, you've no sense of humour, that's what's wrong with you.' But instead of responding to his teasing voice, she thought it over and said seriously: 'Well I laugh at things, don't I? I must be laughing at something then. My Dad used to say I hadn't any sense of humour. I used to say to him: "How do you know what I laugh at isn't as funny as what you laugh at?" ' He said, wryly, after a moment, 'When you laugh, it's like you're not laughing at all, it's something nasty.' 'I don't know what you mean.' 'I ask you if you're happy and you laugh – what's funny about being happy?' Now he was really resentful. Again she meditated about it, instead of responding – as he had hoped – with a laugh or some reassurance that he made her perfectly happy. 'Well, it stands to reason,' she concluded, 'people who talk about happy or unhappy, and then the long words – and the things you say, women are like this, and men are like that, and polygamous and all the rest – well . . .' 'Well?' he demanded. 'Well, it just seems funny to me,' she said lamely. For she could have found no words at all for what she felt, that deep knowledge of the dangerousness and the sadness of life. Bombs fell on old men, lorries killed people, and the war went on and on, and the nights when he did not come to her she would sit by herself, crying for hours, not knowing why she was crying, looking down from the high window at the darkened, ravaged streets – a city dark with the shadow of war.

In the early days of their love Jimmie had loved best the hours of tender, aimless, frivolous talk. But now she was, it seemed, always grave. And she questioned him endlessly about his life, about his childhood. 'Why do you want to know?' he would inquire, unwilling to answer. And then she was hurt. 'If you love someone, you want to know about them, it stands to reason.' So he would give simple replies to her questions, the facts, not the spirit, which she wanted. 'Was your Mum good to you?' she would ask, anxiously. 'Did she cook nice?' She wanted him to talk about the things he had felt; but he would reply, shortly: 'Yes,' or 'Not bad.'

'Why don't you want to tell me?' she would ask, puzzled.

He repeated that he didn't mind telling her; but all the same he hated it. It seemed to him that no sooner had one of those long, companionable silences fallen, in which he could drift off into a pleasant dream, than the questions began. 'Why didn't you join up in the war?' she asked once. 'They wouldn't have me, that's why.' 'You're lucky,' she said, fiercely. 'Lucky nothing, I tried over and over. I wanted to join.'

And then, to her obstinate silence, he said: 'You're queer. You've got all sorts of ideas. You talk like a pacifist; it's not right when there's a war on.'

'Pacifist!' she cried, angrily. 'Why do you use all these silly words? I'm not anything.'

'You ought to be careful, Rosie, if you go saying things like that where people can hear you, they'll think you're against the war, you'll get into trouble.'

'Well, I am against the war, I never said I wasn't.'

'But Rosie—'

'Oh, shut up. You make me sick. You all make me sick. Everybody just talks and talks, and those fat old so-and-so's talking away in Parliament, they just talk so they can't hear themselves think. Nobody knows anything and they pretend they do. Leave me alone, I don't want to listen.' He was silent. To this Rose he had nothing to say. She was a stranger to him. Also, he was shocked: he was a talker who liked picking up phrases from books and newspapers and using them in a verbal game. But she, who could not use words, who was so deeply inarticulate, had her own ideas and stuck to them. Because he used words so glibly she tried to become a citizen of his country – out of love for him and because she felt herself lacking. She would sit by the window with the newspapers and read earnestly, line by line, having first overcome her instinctive shrinking from the language of violence and hatred that filled them. But the war news, the slogans, just made her exhausted and anxious. She turned to the more personal. 'War takes toll of marriage,' she would read. 'War disrupts homes.' Then she dropped the paper and sat looking before her, her brow puzzled. That headline was about her, Rose. And again, she would read the divorces; some judge would pronounce: 'This unscrupulous woman broke up a happy marriage and . . .' Again the paper dropped while Rose frowned and thought. That meant herself. She was one of those bad women. She was The Other Woman. She might even be that ugly thing, A Co-

Respondent ... But she didn't feel like that. It didn't make sense. So she stopped reading the newspapers, she simply gave up trying to understand.

She felt she was not on an intellectual level with Jimmie, so instinctively she fell back on her feminine weapons – much to his relief. She was all at once very gay, and he fell easily into the mood. Neither of them mentioned his wife for a time. It was their happiest time. After love, lying in the dark, they talked aimlessly, watching the sky change through moods of cloud and rain and tinted light, watching the searchlights. They took no notice of raids or danger. The war was nearly over, and they spoke as if it had already ended. 'If we was killed now, I shouldn't mind,' she said, seriously, one night when the bombs were bad. He said: 'We're not going to get killed, they can't kill us.' It sounded a simple statement of fact: their love and happiness was proof enough against anything. But she said again, earnestly: 'Even if we was killed, it wouldn't matter. I don't see how anything afterwards could be as good as this now.'

'Ah, Rosie, don't be so serious always.'

It was not long before they quarrelled again – because she was so serious. She was asking questions again about his past. She was trying to find out why the army wouldn't have him. He would never tell her. And then he said, impatiently, one night: 'Well, if you must know, I've got ulcers ... ah, for God's sake, Rosie, don't fuss, I can't stand being fussed.' For she had given a little cry and was holding him tight. 'Why didn't you tell me? I haven't been cooking the proper things for you.'

'Rose, for crying out aloud, don't go on.'

'But if you've got ulcers you must be fed right, it stands to reason.' And next evening when she served him some milk pudding, saying anxiously: 'This won't hurt your stomach,' he flared up and said, 'I told you, Rosie, I won't have you coddling me.' Her face was loving and stubborn and she said: 'But you've got no sense ...'

'For the last time, I'm not going to put up with it.'

She turned away, her mouth trembling, and he went to her and said desperately: 'Now don't you take on, Rosie, you mean it nicely, but I don't like it, that's why I didn't tell you before.

Get it?' She responded to him, listlessly, and he found himself thinking, angrily: 'I've got two wives, not one . . .' They were both dismayed and unhappy because their happiness was so precarious it could vanish overnight just because of a little thing like ulcers and milk pudding.

A few days later he ate in heavy silence through the supper she had provided, and then sarcasm broke out of him: 'Well, Rosie, you've decided to humour me, that's what it is.' The meal had consisted of steamed fish, baked bread and very weak tea, which he hated. She looked uncomfortable, but said obstinately: 'I went to a friend of mine who's a chemist at the corner, and he told me what it was right for you to eat.' Involuntarily he got up, his face dark with fury. He hesitated, then he went out, slamming the door.

He stood moodily in the pub, drinking. Pearl came across and said: 'What's eating you tonight?' Her tone was light, but her eyes were sympathetic. The sympathy irritated him. He ground out: 'Women!' slammed down his glass and turned to go. 'Doesn't cost you anything to be polite,' she said tartly, and he replied: 'Doesn't cost you anything to leave me alone.' Outside he hesitated a moment, feeling guilty. Pearl had been a friend for so long, and she had a soft spot for him – also, she knew about his wife, and about Rose, and made no comment, seemed not to condemn. She was a nice girl, Pearl was – he went back and said, hastily: 'Sorry, Pearl, didn't mean it.' Without waiting for a reply he left again, and this time set off for home.

The woman he called his wife looked up from her sewing and asked briefly: 'What do you want now?'

'Nothing.' He sat down, picked up a paper and pretended to read, conscious of her glances. They were not hostile. They had gone a long way beyond that, and the fact that she seemed scarcely interested in him was a relief after Rose's persistent, warm curiosity – like loving white fingers strangling him, he thought involuntarily. 'Want something to eat?' she inquired at last.

'What have you got?' he inquired cautiously, thinking of the tasteless steamed fish and baked bread he had just been offered.

'Help yourself,' she returned, and he went to the cupboard on the landing, filled a plate with bread and mustard pickles and cheese, and came back to the room where she was. She glanced at his plate, but made no comment. After a while he asked sarcastically: 'Aren't you going to tell me I shouldn't eat pickles?'

'Couldn't care less,' she returned equably. 'If you want to kill yourself, it's your funeral.' At this he laughed loudly, and she joined him. Later, she asked: 'Staying here the night?'

'If you don't mind.' At this she gave a snort of derisive laughter, got up and said: 'Well, I'm off to bed. You can't have the sofa because the kids have got a friend and he's got it. You'll have to put a blanket and a cushion on the floor.'

'Thanks,' he said, indifferently. 'How are the kids?' he inquired, as an afterthought.

'Fine – if you're interested.'

'I asked, didn't I?' he replied, without heat. All this conversation had been conducted quietly, indifferently, and the undercurrent was almost amiable. An outsider would have said they hardly knew each other. When she had gone he took a blanket from a drawer, wrapped it round his legs, and settled himself in a chair. He had meant to think about himself and Rose, but instead he dropped off at once. He left the house early, before anyone was awake. All day at the factory he thought: About Rose, what must I do about Rose? After work he went instinctively to the pub. Pearl stood quietly behind the counter, showing him by her manner that she was not holding last night's bad humour against him. He meant to have one drink and go, but he had three. He liked Pearl's cheerful humour. She told him that her young man was playing about with another girl, and added, as if it hardly concerned her: 'There's plenty of fish in the sea after all.'

'That's right,' he said, non-committally.

'Well, we all have our troubles,' she said, with a half-humorous sigh.

'Yes – for what they're worth.' At this he felt a pang of guilt because he had been thinking of Rose. Pearl was giving him a keen look. Then she said: 'I didn't say he hadn't been worth it.

But now that other girl's getting all the benefit . . .' Here she laughed grimly.

He liked this cheerful philosophy, and could not prevent himself saying: 'He's got no sense, turning you up.' He looked with appreciation at her crown of bright yellow curls, at her shapely body. Her eyes brightened, and he said good night quickly, and left. He mustn't get mixed up with Pearl now, he was thinking.

It was after eight. Usually he was with Rose by seven. He lagged down the street, thinking of what he would say to her, and entered the flat with a blank mind. For some reason he was very tired. Rose had eaten by herself, cleared the table, and now sat beside it, frowning over a newspaper. 'What are you reading?' he asked, for something to break the ice. Looking over her shoulder he saw that she had marked a column headed: 'Surplus Women Present Problem to Churches'. He was surprised.

'That's what I am, a surplus woman,' she said, and gave that sudden, unexpected laugh.

'What's funny?' he asked, uncomfortably.

'I've a right to laugh if I want,' she retorted. 'Better than crying, anyhow.'

'Oh, Rose,' he said, helplessly, 'oh, Rose stop it now . . .' She burst into tears and clung to him. But this was not the end, and he knew it. Later that night she said: 'I want to tell you something . . .' and he thought: Now I'm for it – whatever it is.

'You were home last night, weren't you?'

'Yes,' he said, alertly.

A pause, and then she asked: 'What did she say?'

'About what?' It was a fact that he did not immediately understand her. '*Jimmie,*' she said incredulously, under her breath and he said: 'Rosie, it's no good, I told you that before.'

She did not immediately reply, but when she did her voice was very bitter: 'Well, I see how it is now.'

'You don't see at all,' he said sarcastically.

'Well, then, tell me?' He was silent. Her silence was like a persistent question. Again he felt as if the warm, soft fingers were wrapping around him. He felt suffocated. 'There's nothing to explain, I just can't help it.' A pause, and then she said in the flat, laconic way he hated: 'Yes?' That was all. For the time being, at least. A week later she said, calmly: 'I went to see Jill's Granny today.'

His heart faltered and he thought: Now what? 'Well?' he inquired.

'George was killed last month. In Italy.'

He felt triumph, then he said guiltily: 'I'm sorry.' She waved this away and said: 'I told her Granny that I want to adopt Jill.'

'But Rose . . .' Then he saw her face and quailed.

'I want kids,' she said fiercely. He dropped his gaze.

'Her Granny won't want to give her up.'

'I'm not so sure. At first she said no, then she thought it over a bit. She's getting old now – eighty next year. She thinks perhaps Jill'd be better with me.'

'You want to have the kid *here*?' he asked, incredulously.

'Why shouldn't I?'

'You're working all day.' She was silent, he looked at her – and slowly coloured.

'Listen a minute,' she began, persuasively – not unpleasantly at all, though every word wounded Jimmie. 'I furnished this place. It was my furniture and my money. And I've got a hundred still in the post office in case of accidents – I'll need it; now the war's over we won't be earning so much money, if I know anything. So far, I've not been . . .' But here her instinctive delicacy overcame her, and she could not go on. She wanted to say that she paid for the food, paid for everything. Lately, even the rent. One week he had said, apologetically, that he hadn't the cash, and that if she could do it this once – but now it was a regular thing.

'You want me to give you the money so you can stay here with the kid?' he inquired, cautiously. She was blushing with embarrassment. 'No, no,' she said, quickly. 'Listen. If you can just pay the rent – that would be enough. I could get a part-time job, just the mornings. Jill goes to school now, and I'd manage somehow.'

He digested this silently. He was thinking, incredulously:

She wants to have a kid here, a kid's always in the way — that means she can't love me any more. He said, slowly: 'Well, Rosie, if that's what you want, then go ahead.'

Her face cleared into vivid happiness and she came running to him in the old way and kissed him and said: 'Oh, Jimmie; oh, Jimmie . . .' He held her and thought, bitterly, that all this joy was not because of him, all she cared about was the kid — women! But at the back of his mind were two other thoughts: First, that he did not know how he would find the money to pay the rent unless he passed that examination soon, and the other was that the authorities would never let Rose have Jill.

Next evening Rose was despondent. 'Did you see the officials?' he asked at last.

'Yes.' She would not look at him. She was staring helpless down from the window.

'Wasn't it any good?'

'They said I must prove myself a fit and proper person. So I said that I was. I told them I'd known Jill since she was born. I said I knew her mother and father.'

'That's true enough,' he could not help interjecting, jealously. She gave him a cold look and said: 'Don't start that now. I told them her Granny was too old, and I could easily look after Jill.'

'Well then?'

She was silent, then, wringing her hands unconsciously, she cried out: 'They wasn't nice, they wasn't nice to me at all. There were two of them, a woman and a man. They said: How could I support Jill? I said I could get money. They said I must show them papers and things . . .' She was silently crying now, but she did not come to him. She stayed at the window, her back turned, shutting him out of her sorrow. 'They asked me, how could a working girl look after a child, and I said I'd do it easy, and they said, did I have a husband . . .' Here she leaned her head against the wall and sobbed bitterly. After a time he said: 'Well, Rosie, it looks as if I'm no good for you. Perhaps you'd better give me up and get yourself a proper husband.' At this she jerked her head up, looked incredulously at him and cried: 'Jimmie! How could I give you up . . .' He went to her, thinking, in relief: 'She loves me better after all.' He meant: better than the child.

It seemed that Rose had accepted her defeat. For some days she talked sorrowfully about 'those nosy parkers' at the Council. She was even humorous, though in the way that made him uneasy. 'I'll go to them,' she said, smiling grimly, 'I'll go and I'll say: I can't help being a surplus woman. Don't blame me, blame the war, it's not my fault that they keep killing all the men off in their silly wars . . .'

And then his jealousy grew unbearable and he said: 'You love Jill better than me.' She laughed in amazement, and said, 'Don't be a baby, Jimmie.' 'Well, you must. Look how you go on and on about that kid. It's all you think about.'

'There isn't no sense in you being jealous of Jill.'

'Jealous,' he said, roughly. 'Who says I'm jealous?'

'Well, if you're not, what are you then?'

'Oh, go to hell, go to hell,' he muttered to himself, as he put his arms around her. Aloud he said: 'Come on, Rosie girl, come on, stop being like this, be like you used to be, can't you?'

'I'm not any different,' she said patiently, submitting to his caresses with a sigh.

'So you're not any different,' he said, exasperatedly. Then, controlling himself with difficulty he coaxed: 'Rosie, Rosie, don't you love me a little . . .'

For the truth was he was becoming obsessed with the difference in Rose. He thought of her continuously as she had been. It was like dreaming of another woman, she was so changed now. At work, busy with some job that needed all his attention, he would start as if stung, and mutter: 'Rose – oh, to hell with her!' He was remembering, with anguish, how she had run across the room to welcome him, how responsive she had been, how affectionate. He thought of her patient kindliness now, and wanted to swear. After work he would go straight to the flat, reaching it even before she did. The lights would be out, the rooms cold, like a reminder of how Rose had changed. She would come in, tired, laden with string-bags, to find him seated at the table staring at her, his eyes black with jealousy. 'This place is as cold as a street-corner,' he would say, angrily. She looked at him, sighed, then said, reasonably: 'But Jimmie, look, here's where I keep the sixpences for the gas – why don't you light the fire?' Then he would go to her, holding down her arms as he kissed her, and she would say: 'Just leave me a minute, Jimmie. I must get the potatoes on or there'll be no supper.'

'Can't the potatoes wait a minute?'

'Let me get my arms free, Jimmie.' He held them, so she would carefully reach them out from under the pressure of his grip, and put the string-bags on the table. Then she would turn to kiss him. He noticed that she would be glancing worriedly at the curtains, which had not been drawn, or at the rubbish-pail, which had not been emptied. 'You can't even kiss me until you've done all the housework,' he cried, sullenly. 'All right then, you tip me the wink when you've got a moment to spare and you don't mind being kissed.'

To this she replied, listlessly but patiently: 'Jimmie, I come straight home from work and there's nothing ready, and before you didn't come so early.'

'So now you're complaining because I come straight here. Before, you complained because I dropped in for a drink somewhere first.'

'I never complained.'

'You sulked, even if you didn't complain.'

'Well, Jimmie,' she said, after a sorrowful pause, as she peeled the potatoes. 'If I went to drink with a boy-friend you wouldn't like it either.'

'That means Pearl, I suppose. Anyway, it's quite different.'

'Why is it different?' she asked, reasonably. 'I don't like to go to pubs by myself, but if I did I don't see why not, I don't see why men should do one thing and women another.'

These sudden lapses into feminism always baffled him. They seemed so inconsistent with her character. He left that point and said: 'You're jealous of Pearl, that's what it is.'

He wanted her, of course, to laugh, or even quarrel a little, so the thing could be healed by kisses, but she considered it, thoughtfully, and said: 'You can't help being jealous if you love someone.'

'Pearl!' he snorted. 'I've known her for years. Besides, who told you?'

'You always think that nobody ever notices things,' she said, sadly. 'You're always so surprised.'

'Well, how did you know?'

'People always tell you things.'

'And you believe *people*.'

A pause. Then: 'Oh, Jimmie, I don't want to quarrel all the time, there isn't any sense in it.' This sad helplessness satisfied him, and he was able to take her warmly in his arms. 'I don't mean to quarrel either,' he murmured.

But they quarrelled continuously. Every conversation was bound to end, it seemed, either in Pearl or in George. Or their tenderness would lapse into tired silence, and he would see her staring quietly away from him, thinking. 'What are you getting so serious about now, Rosie?' 'I was thinking about Jill. Her Granny's too old. Jill's shut up in that kitchen all day – just think, those old nosy parkers say I'm not a fit and proper person for Jill, but at least I'd take her for walks on Sunday . . .'

'You want Jill because of George,' he would grind out, gripping her so tight she had to ease her arms free. 'Oh, stop it, Jimmie, stop it.'

'Well, it's true.'

'If you want to think it, I can't stop you.' Then the silence of complete estrangement.

After some weeks of this he went back to the pub one evening. 'Hullo, stranger,' said Pearl. Her eyes shone welcomingly over at him.

'I've been busy, one way or another,' he said.

'I bet,' she said, satirically, challenging him with her look.

He could not resist it. 'Women,' he said, 'women.' And he took a long drain from his glass.

'Don't you talk that way to me,' she said, with a short laugh. 'My boy-friend's just got himself married. Didn't so much as send me an invite to the wedding.'

'He doesn't know what's good for him.'

Her wide, blue eyes swung around and rested obliquely on him before she lowered them to the glasses she was rinsing. 'Perhaps there are others who don't neither.'

He hesitated and said: 'Maybe, maybe not.' Caution held him back. Yet they had been flirting cheerfully for so long, out of sheer good-nature. The new hesitation was dangerous in itself, and gave depth to their casual exchanges. He thought to himself: Careful, Jimmie, boy, you're off again if you're not careful. He decided he should go to another pub. Yet he came back, every evening, for he looked forward to the moment when he stood in the doorway, and then she saw him, and her eyes warmed to him as she said lightly: 'Hullo, handsome, what trouble have you been getting yourself into today?' He got into the way of staying for an hour or more, instead of the usual half hour. He leaned quietly against the counter, his coat collar turned up round his face, while his grey eyes rested appreciatively on Pearl. Sometimes she grew self-conscious and said: 'Your eyes need a rest,' and he replied, coolly: 'If you don't want people to look at you, better buy yourself another jumper.' He would think, with a sense of disloyalty: Why doesn't Rosie buy herself one like that? But Rose always wore her plain, dark skirts and her neat blouses, pinned at the throat with a brooch.

Afterwards he climbed the stairs to the flat thinking, anxiously: Perhaps today she'll be like she used to be? He would expectantly open the door, thinking: Perhaps she'll smile when she sees me and come running over . . .

But she would be at the stove, or seated at the table waiting, and she gave him that tired, patient smile before beginning to dish up the supper. His disappointment dragged down his spirits, but he forced himself to say: 'Sorry, I'm late, Rosie.' He braced himself for a reproach, but it never came, though her eyes searched him anxiously, then lowered as if afraid he might see a reproach in them.

'That's all right,' she replied, carefully, setting the dishes down and pulling out the chair for him.

Always, he could not help looking to see if she was still 'fussing' about the food. But she was taking trouble to hide the precautions she took to feed him sensibly. Sometimes he would probe sarcastically: 'I suppose your friend the chemist said that peas were good for ulcers – how about a bit of fried onions, Rosie?'

'I'll make you some tomorrow,' she would reply. And she averted her eyes, as if she were wincing, when he pulled the pickle bottle towards him and heaped mustard pickle over his fish. 'You only live once,' he remarked, jocularly.

'That's right.' And then, in a prepared voice: 'It's your stomach, after all.'

'That's what I always said.' To himself he said: Might be my bloody wife. For his wife had come to say at last: 'It's your stomach, if you want to die ten years too soon . . .'

If he had attacks of terrible pain in the night, after a plateful of fried onions, or chips thick with tomato sauce, he would lie rigid beside her, concealing it, just as he had with his wife. Women fussing! Fussing women!

He asked himself continually why he did not break it off. A dozen times he had said to himself: That's enough now, it's no good, she doesn't love me, anyway. Yet by evening he was back at the pub, flirting tentatively with Pearl, until the time came when he could delay no longer. And back he went, as if dragged, to Rose. He could not understand it. He was behaving badly – and he could not help himself; he should be studying for his exam – and he couldn't bring himself to study; it would be so easy to make Rose happy – and he couldn't take the decisive step; he should decide not to return to Pearl in the evenings, and he could not keep away. What was it all about? Why did people just go on doing things, as if they were dragged along against their will, even against what they enjoyed?

One Saturday evening Rose said: 'Tomorrow I won't be here.'

He clutched at her hand and demanded: 'Why not? Where are you going?'

'I'm going to take Jill out all day and then have supper with her Granny.'

Breathing quickly, his lips set hard, he brought out: 'No time for me any more, eh?'

'Oh, Jimmie, have some sense.'

Next morning he lay in bed and watched her dress to go out. She was smiling, her face soft with pleasure. She kissed him consolingly before she left, and said: 'It's only on Sundays, Jimmie.'

So it's going to be every Sunday, he thought, miserably.

In the evening he went to the pub. It was Pearl's evening off. He had thought of asking her along to the pictures, but he didn't know where she lived. He went to his home. The children were in bed and his wife had gone to see a neighbour. He felt as if everyone had let him down. At last he went back to the flat and waited for Rose. When she came he sat quietly, an angry little smile on his face, while she chatted animatedly about Jill. In bed he turned his back on her and lay gazing at the greyish light at the window. It couldn't go on, he thought; what was the point of it? Yet he was back next evening as usual.

Next Sunday she asked him to go with her to see Jill.

'What the hell!' he exclaimed, indignantly.

She was hurt. 'Why not, Jimmie? She's so sweet. She's such a good girl. She's got long golden ringlets.'

'I suppose George had long yellow ringlets, too,' he said, sardonically.

She looked at him blankly, shrugged, and said no more. When she had gone he went to Pearl's house – for he had asked for the address – and took her to the pictures. They were careful and polite with each other. She watched him secretly: his face was tight with worry; he was thinking of Rose with that damned brat – she was happy with Jill, when she couldn't even raise a smile for him! When he said good night, Pearl drawled out: 'Do you even know what the film was called?'

He laughed uncomfortably and said: 'Sorry, Pearl, got things on my mind.'

'Thanks for the information.' But she was not antagonistic; she sounded sympathetic. He was grateful for her understanding. He hastily kissed her cheek and said: 'You're a nice kid, Pearl.' She flushed and quickly put her arms around his neck and kissed him again. Afterwards he thought uneasily: If I just lifted my little finger I could have her.

At home Rose was cautious with him and did not mention

Jill until he did. She was afraid of him. He saw it, and it made him half-wild with frustration. Anyone'd think that he was cruel to her! 'For crying out aloud, Rose,' he pleaded, 'what's the matter with you, why can't you be nice to me?'

To which she sighed and asked in a dry, tired voice: 'I suppose Pearl is nice to you.'

'Hell, Rosie, I have to do something when you're away.'

'I asked you to come with me, didn't I?'

They were on the verge of some crisis, and both knew it, and for several days they were treating each other almost like strangers, for fear of an explosion. They hardly dare let their eyes meet.

On the following Saturday evening Rose inquired: 'Made a date with Pearl for tomorrow?'

He was going to deny it, but she went on implacably: 'Things can't go on like this, Jimmie.' He was silent, and then she asked suddenly: 'Jimmie, did you ever really ask your wife to divorce you?'

He exploded: 'Hell, Rosie, are you going back to that now?'

'I suppose you are thinking it's not my affair and I'm interfering,' she said, and laughed with that unexpected, grim humour of hers.

Rose went off to Jill in the morning without another word to him. As for him, he went to Pearl. The girl was gentle with him: 'If you don't feel like the pictures, you don't have to take me,' she said, sympathetically. So they went to a café and he said, abruptly: 'You know, Pearl, it's no good getting to like me, women think I'm poison when they get to know better.' He was grinning savagely and his hands were clenched. She reached out, took one of them and said: 'It's for me to say what I want, isn't it?'

'Don't say I didn't warn you,' he said at random, putting his arm around her, feeling that he had, by this remark, absolved himself of all responsibility for Pearl. He was thinking of Rose. She'd be back home by now. Well, it'd do her good not to find him there. She just took him for granted, and it was a fact. But after a restless five minutes he said: 'I better be getting along.' When he left her, Pearl said: 'I love you, Jimmie, don't forget that. I'd do anything for you, anything . . .' She ran into the house, and he saw she was crying. She loves me, at any rate, he thought, thinking angrily of Rose. Slowly he climbed the long, dark stairs. He was very tired again. I must get some sleep, he mused, dimly, this can't go on, it wears a man out, I'll go straight to bed and sleep.

But he opened the door on bright light; she was already in, seated at the table. She was still in her best clothes: a neat grey suit, white blouse, brooch; and her hair looked as if she had just combed it. Her face was what held him: she looked tight-lipped, determined, even triumphant. What's up? he thought.

'Don't go to bed straight away,' she said – for he was throwing off his shoes and coat. 'There's something we've got to do.'

'It'd better be pretty important,' he said. 'I'm dead on my feet.'

'For once you'd better stay on your feet.' This brutal note was new and astonishing from Rose.

'What's going on?'

'You'll see in a minute.'

He almost ignored her and went to bed; but at last he compromised by pushing the pillows against the wall and leaning on them. 'Wake me up when the mystery's ripe,' he said, and dropped off at once.

Rose remained at the table in a stiff attitude, watching the door and listening. The day before she had made a decision. Or rather, a decision had been made for her. It had come into her head: Why not write and ask? She'll know . . . At first the idea had shocked her. It was a terrible thing to do, contrary to what she felt to be the right way to behave. And yet from the moment it entered her head, the idea gathered strength until she could think of nothing else. At last she sat down and wrote:

Dear Mrs Pearson, I am writing to you on a matter which is personal to us both, and I hope it gives no offence, because I am not writing in that spirit. I am Rose Johnson, and your husband has been courting me for two years since before the war stopped. He says you live separate and you won't divorce him. I want things to be straight and proper now, and I've been thinking perhaps if we have a little talk, things will be straight. If this meets with your approval, Jimmie will be home tomorrow night, ten or so, and we could all three have a talk. Believing me, I mean no trouble or offence.

This letter she had carried herself to the house and dropped through the letter-slot. Afterwards, she could not go away. She walked guiltily up the street, and then down, her eyes fixed on the windows. That was where *she* lived. Her heart was so heavy with jealous love it was as if her very feet were weighted. That was where Jimmie had lived with *her*. That was where his children lived. She hoped to get a glimpse of them, and looked searchingly at some children playing in the street, trying to find his eyes, his features in their faces. There was a little boy she thought might be his son and she found herself smiling at the child, her eyes filled with tears. Then, finally, she walked past the house and thought: If only it'd come to an end, I can't bear it no longer, I can't bear it . . .

There were footsteps, Rose half-rose to open the door, but they went past. Later, when she had given up hope, there were steps again, and they stopped at the door. Now the moment had come. Rose was faint with anxiety and could hardly cross the floor. She thought: I mustn't wake Jimmie, he's so tired. She opened the door with an instinctive gesture of warning towards the sleeping man. Mrs Pearson glanced at him, smiled in a tight-lipped fashion, and came in, making her heels click loudly. Rose had created for herself many pictures of this envied woman, Jimmie's wife. She had imagined her, for some reason, fair, frail, pretty – rather like Pearl, whom she had seen in the street once. But she was not like that at all. She was a big, square woman, heavy on her feet. Her face was square and good-humoured, her brown eyes calm and direct. Her dark, greying hair was tightly waved, too close around her head for the big features. 'Well,' she said in a normal voice, with a good-humoured nod at Rose, 'the prisoner's sleeping before the execution.'

'Oh, no,' breathed Rose, in dismay: 'It's not like that at all.'

Mrs Pearson looked curiously at her, shrugged, and laid her bag on the table. 'Thanks for the letter,' she said. 'It's about time you found out.'

'Found out what?' asked Rose quickly.

Jimmie stirred, looked blankly over at the women and then scrambled quickly to his feet. 'What the hell?' he asked, involuntarily. And then, very angry: 'What are you poking your nose in for?'

'She asked me to come,' said his wife, quietly. She sat down. 'Come and sit down, Jimmie, and let's talk it over.'

He looked quite baffled. Then he, too, shrugged, lit a cigarette and came to the table. 'OK, get it over,' he said jauntily. He glanced incredulously at Rose. She could do this to him, he thought, hurt to the very bone – and she says she loves me . . . He was set hard against Rose, hard against his wife . . . Well, let them do as they liked.

'Now listen, Jimmie,' said his wife, reasonably, as to a child, 'it seems you've been telling this poor child a lot of lies.' He sat tight and said nothing. She waited, then went on, looking at Rose: 'This is the truth. We've been married ten years. We've got two kids. We were happy at first – well, nothing unusual in that. Then he got fed up. Nothing unusual in that either. In any case, he's not a man who can settle to anything. I used to be unhappy, and then I got used to it. I thought: Well, we can't change our natures. Jimmie doesn't mean any harm, he just drifts into everything. Then the war started, and you know how things were. I was working night-shifts, and he too, and there was a girl at his factory, and they got together.' She paused, looking at Jimmie like a presiding judge, but he said nothing. He smoked, looking down at the table with a small angry smile. 'I got fed up and said we'd better separate. Then he came running back and said it wouldn't happen again, he didn't really want a divorce.' Jimmie stirred, opened his mouth to say something, then shut it again. 'You were going to say?' inquired his wife, pleasantly. 'Nothing. Go on, enjoy yourself.'

'Isn't it true?'

He shrugged, she waited and then went on: 'So everything was all right for a month or so. And then he started up with the girl again . . .'

'Pearl?' Rose suddenly asked.

He snorted derisively: 'Pearl, that's all she can think of.'

'Who's Pearl?' asked Mrs Pearson, alertly. 'She's a new one on me.'

'Never mind,' said Rose. 'Go on.'

'But this time I'd had enough. I said either me or her.' Addressing Rose, excluding Jimmie, she said: 'If there's one thing he can't do, it's make up his mind to anything.'

'Yes,' agreed Rose, involuntarily. Then she flushed and looked guiltily at Jimmie.

'Go on, enjoy yourselves,' he said, sarcastically.

'*We* haven't been enjoying ourselves, *you* have.'

'That's what you think.'

'Oh, have it your own way. You always do. But now I'm talking to Rose. When I said either her or me, he got into a proper state. The root of the matter was, he wanted both of us. Men are naturally bigamists, he said.'

'Yes,' said Rose again, quickly.

'Oh, for crying out aloud, can't you two ever take a joke. It was a joke. What did you think? I wanted to be married to two women at once? One's enough.'

'You have been married to two women at once,' said his wife, tartly. 'Whether you liked it or not. Or as good as.' The two women were looking at each other, smiling grimly. Jimmie glanced at them, got up and went to the window. 'Let me know when you've finished,' he said.

Rose made an impulsive movement towards him. 'Oh sit down, the trouble with you is you're too soft with him. I was too.'

From the window Jimmie said: 'Soft as concrete.' To Rose he made a gesture indicating his wife: 'Just take a good look at her and see how soft she is.' Rose looked, flushed, and said: 'Jimmie, I didn't mean anything nasty for you.'

'You didn't?' That was contemptuous.

'Well,' said Mrs Pearson, loudly, interrupting this exchange: 'At last I got the pip and divorced him.'

Rose drew in her breath. Her eyes were frantic. 'You're *divorced*?' She stared at Jimmie, waiting for him to deny it, but he kept his back turned. 'Jimmie, it isn't true, is it?'

Mrs Pearson said, with rough kindliness, 'Now don't get upset, Rose. It's time you knew what's what. We got divorced three years ago. I got the kids, and he's supposed to pay me two pounds a week for them. But if the other girl thought he was going to marry her she made a mistake. He was courting me for three years and then I had to put my foot down. He said he couldn't live without me, but at the registry he looked like a man being executed.'

Jimmie said, in cold fury: 'If you want to know the truth, she wouldn't marry me, she married someone else.'

'I daresay. She learned some sense, I expect. You never told her you were married, and she got shocked into her senses when she found out.'

'Go on,' said Rose, 'I want to hear the end of it.'

'There wasn't any end, that's the point. After the divorce Jimmie was popping in and out as if he belonged in the house. "Here," I used to say, "I thought we were divorced." But if he was short of a place to sleep, or he wanted somewhere to read, or his ulcers was bad, he'd drop in for a meal or the use of the sofa. And he still does,' she concluded.

Rose was crying now. 'Why did you lie to me, Jimmie,' she implored, gazing at his impervious back. 'Why? You didn't have to lie to *me*.'

He said miserably: 'What was the use, Rosie? I have to pay two pounds a week to her. I couldn't do that and give you a proper home too.'

Rose gave a helpless sort of gesture and sat silently, while the tears ran steadily down. Mrs Pearson watched her, not unkindly. 'What's the use of crying?' she inquired. 'He's no good to you. And you say he's got another woman already! Who's this Pearl?'

Rose said: 'He takes her to the pictures and she wants to marry him.'

'How the hell do you know?' he asked, turning around and facing them at last.

Rose glanced pleadingly at him and said softly: 'But Jimmie, everybody knows.'

'I suppose you've been down talking to Pearl,' he said, contemptuously. 'Women!'

'Of course I didn't.' She was shocked. 'I wouldn't do no such thing. But everyone knows about it.'

'Who's everyone this time?'

'Well, there's my friend at the shop at the corner, who keeps my bit extra for me when there's biscuits or something going. He told me Pearl was crazy for you, and he said people said you were going to marry her.'

'Jesus,' he said simply, sitting on the bed. 'Women.'

'Just like him,' commented Mrs Pearson dryly. 'He always thinks he's the invisible man. He can just carry on in broad daylight and no one'll notice what he's doing. He's always surprised when they do. He was going out with that other girl for months, and the whole factory knew it, but when I mentioned it he thought I'd had a private detective on to him.'

'Well,' said Rose, helplessly, at last. 'I don't know, I really don't.'

She said again, with that rough warmth: 'Now don't you mind too much, Rosie. You're well out of it, believe me.'

Rose's lips trembled again. Mrs Pearson got up, sat by her and patted her shoulders. 'There now,' she said, as Rose collapsed. 'Now don't take on. There, there,' she soothed, while over Rose's head she gave her husband a deadly look. Jimmie was sitting on the edge of the bed, smoking, looking badly shaken. What he was thinking was: That Rose could do this to me – how could she do it to me?

'I haven't got nothing,' wailed Rose. 'I haven't got anything or anybody anywhere.'

Mrs Pearson went on patting. Her face was thoughtful. She made soothing noises, and then she asked suddenly, out of the blue: 'Listen, Rose, how'd you like to come and live with me?'

Rose stopped crying from the shock, lifted her face and said: 'What did you say?'

'I expect you're surprised.' Mrs Pearson looked surprised at herself. 'I just thought of it – I'm starting a cake shop next month. I saved a bit during the war. I was looking for someone to help me with it. You could live in my place if you like. It's only got three rooms and a kitchen, but we'd manage.'

'The house isn't yours?'

Mrs Pearson laughed: 'I suppose my lord told you he owned the whole house? Not on your life. I've got the basement.'

'The basement,' said Rose, intently.

'Well, it's warm and dry and in one piece, more than can be said for most basements.'

'It's safer, too,' said Rose, slowly.

'Safer?'

'If there's bombing or something.'

'I suppose so,' said Mrs Pearson, rather puzzled at this. Rose was gazing eagerly into her face. 'You've got the kids,' said Rose, slowly.

'They're no trouble, really. They're at school.'

'I didn't mean that – could I have a kid – no, listen, I'd be wanting to adopt a kid if I came to you. If I lived with you I'd be a fit and proper person and those nosy parkers would let me have her.'

'You want to adopt a kid?' said Mrs Pearson, rather put out. She glanced at Jimmie, who said: 'You say things about me – but look at her. She was engaged to a man, and he was killed and all she thinks about is his kid.'

'Jimmie . . .' began Rose, in protest. But Mrs Pearson asked: 'Hasn't the kid got a mother?'

'The blitz,' said Rose, simply.

After a pause Mrs Pearson said thoughtfully: 'I suppose there's no reason why not.'

Rose's face was illuminated. 'Mrs Pearson,' she prayed, 'Mrs Pearson – if I could have Jill, if only I could have Jill . . .'

Mrs Pearson said dryly: 'I can't see me cluttering myself up with kids if I didn't have to. You wouldn't catch me marrying and getting kids if I had my chance over again, but it takes all sorts to make a world.'

'Then it'd be all right?'

Mrs Pearson hesitated: 'Yes, why not?'

Jimmie gave a short laugh. 'Women,' he said. 'Women.'

'You can talk,' said his wife.

Rose looked shyly at him. 'What are you going to do now?' she asked.

'A fat lot you care,' he said, bitterly.

'He's going to marry Pearl, I don't think,' commented his wife.

Rose said slowly: 'You ought to marry Pearl, you know, Jimmie. You did really ought to marry her. It's not right. You shouldn't make her unhappy, like me.'

Jimmie stood before them, hands in pockets, trying to look nonchalant. He was slowly nodding his head as if his worst suspicions were being confirmed. 'So now you've decided to marry me off,' he said, savagely.

'Well, Jimmie,' said Rose, 'she loves you, everyone knows that, and you've been taking her out and giving her ideas – and – and – you could have this flat now, I don't want it. You better have it, anyway, you can't get flats now the war's finished. And you and Pearl could live here.' She sounded as if she were pleading for herself.

'For crying out aloud,' said Jimmie, astonished, gazing at her.

Mrs Pearson was looking shrewdly at him. 'You know, Jimmie, it's not a bad idea, Rose is quite right.'

'What-a-at? You too?'

'It's about time you stopped messing around. You messed around with Rose here, and I told you time and time again, you should either marry her or not, I said.'

'You *knew* about me?' said Rose, dazedly.

'Well, no harm in that,' said Mrs Pearson, impatiently. 'Be your age, Rose. Of course, I knew. When he came home I used to say to him: You do right by that poor girl. You can't expect her to go hanging about, missing her chances, just to give you an easy life and somewhere to play nicely at nights.'

'I told Rose,' he said, abruptly. 'I told her often enough I wasn't good enough for her, I said.'

'I bet you did,' said his wife, shortly.

'Didn't I, Rose?' he asked her.

Rose was silent. Then she shrugged. 'I just don't understand,' she said at last. And then, after a pause: 'I suppose you're just made that way.' And then, after a longer pause: 'But you ought to marry Pearl now.'

'Just to please you, I suppose!' He turned challengingly to his wife: 'And you, too, I suppose. You want to see me safely tied up to someone, don't you?'

'No one's going to marry me, stuck with two kids,' said his wife. 'I don't see why you shouldn't be tied too, if we're going to look at it that way.'

'And you can't see why I shouldn't marry Pearl when I've got to pay you two pounds a week?'

Mrs Pearson said on an impulse: 'If you marry Pearl, I'll let you off the two pounds. I'm going to make a good thing out of my cake shop, I expect, and I won't need your bit.'

'And if I don't marry her, then I must go on paying you the two pounds?'

'Fair enough,' she said, calmly.

'Blackmail,' he said, bitterly. 'Blackmail, that's what it is.'

'Call it what you like.' She got up and lifted her handbag from the table. 'Well, Rose,' she said. 'All this has been sudden, spur of the moment sort of thing. Perhaps you'd like to think about it. I'm not one for rushing into things myself, in the usual way. I wouldn't like you to come and then be sorry after.'

Rose had unconsciously risen and was standing by her. 'I'll come with you now, if it's all right. I'll get my things tomorrow. I wouldn't want to stay here tonight.' She glanced at Jimmie, then averted her face.

'She's afraid of staying here with me,' said Jimmie with bitter triumph.

'Quite right. I know you.' She mimicked his voice: *'Don't go back on me, Rose, don't you trust me?'*

Rose winced and muttered: 'Don't do that.'

'Oh, I know him, I know him. And you'd have to put chains on him and drag him to the registry. It's not that he doesn't want to marry you. I expect he does, when all's said. But it just kills him to make up his mind.'

'Staying with me, Rosie?' asked Jimmie, suddenly – the gambler playing his last card. He watched her with bright eyes, waiting, almost sure of his power to make her stay.

Rose looked unhappily from him to Mrs Pearson.

Mrs Pearson watched her with a half-smile; that smile seemed to say: I'm not implicated, settle it for yourself, it makes no difference to me. But aloud she said: 'You're a fool if you stay, Rosie.'

'Let her decide,' said Jimmie, quietly. He was thinking: If she cares anything she'll stay with me, she'll stand by me. Rose gazed pitifully at him and wavered. It flashed across her mind: He's just trying to prove something to his wife, he doesn't really want me at all. But she could not take her eyes away. There he sat, upright but easy, his hair ruffled lightly on his forehead, his handsome grey eyes watching her. She thought, wildly: Why does he just sit there waiting? If he loved me he'd come across and put his arms around me and ask me nicely to stay with him, and I would – if he'd only do that . . .

But he remained quiet, challenging her to move; and slowly the tension shifted and Rose drooped away from him with a sigh. She turned to Mrs Pearson. He couldn't really love her or he wouldn't have just sat there – that's what she felt.

'I'll come with you,' she said, heavily.

'That's a sensible girl, Rose.'

Rose followed the older woman with dragging feet.

'You won't regret it,' said Mrs Pearson. 'Men – they're more trouble than they're worth, when all is said. Women have to look after themselves these days, because if they don't, no one will.'

'I suppose so,' said Rose, reluctantly. She stood hesitating at the door, looking hopefully at Jimmie. Even now – she thought – even now, if he said one word she'd run back to him and stay with him.

But he remained motionless, with that bitter little smile about his mouth.

'Come on, Rose,' said Mrs Pearson. 'Come, if you're coming. We'll miss the Underground.'

And Rose followed her. She was thinking, dully: 'I'll have Jill, that's something. And by the time she grows up perhaps there won't be wars and bombs and things, and people won't act silly any more.'

THE EYE OF GOD IN PARADISE

O— in the Bavarian Alps is a charming little village. It is no more charming, however, than ten thousand others; although it is known to an astonishing number of people, some of whom have actually been there, while others have savoured its attractions in imagination only. Pleasure resorts are like film stars and royalty who – or so one hopes – must be embarrassed by the figures they cut in the fantasies of people who have never met them. The history of O— is fascinating; for this is true of every village. Its location has every advantage, not least that of being so near to the frontier that when finally located on the map it seems to the exuberant holiday-making fancy that one might toss a stone from it into Austria. This is, of course, not the case, since a high wall of mountains forms a natural barrier to any such adventure, besides making it essential that all supplies for O— and the ten or a dozen villages in the valley above it must come from Germany. This wall of mountains is in fact the reason why O— is German, and has always been German; although its inhabitants, or so it would seem from the songs and stories they offer the summer and winter visitors on every possible occasion, take comfort from the belief that Austria is at least their spiritual home. And so those holiday-makers who travel there in the hope of finding the attractions of two countries combined are not so far wrong. And there are those who go there because of the name, which is a homely, simple, gentle name, with none of the associations of, let us say, Berchtesgaden, a place in which one may also take one's ease, if one feels so inclined. O— has never been famous; never has the spotlight of history touched it. It has not been one of those places that no one ever heard of until woken into painful memory, like Seoul, or Bikini, or, for that matter, this same Berchtesgaden, although that is quite close enough for discomfort.

Two holiday-makers who had chosen O— out of the several hundred winter resorts that clamoured for their patronage were standing in one of the upper streets on the evening of their arrival there. The charming little wooden houses weighted with snow, the delightful little streets so narrow and yet so dignified as to make the great glittering cars seem pretentious and out of place, the older inhabitants in their long dark woollen skirts and heavy clogs, even a sleigh drawn by ribboned horses and full of holiday-makers – all this was attractive, and undeniably what they had come for; particularly as slopes suitable for skiing stretched away on every side. Yet there was no denying that something weighed on them; they were uneasy. And what this thing was does not need to be guessed at, since they had not ceased to express it, and very volubly, since their arrival.

This was a pleasure resort; it existed solely for its visitors. In winter, heavy with snow, and ringing with the shouts of swooping skiers; in summer, garlanded with flowers and filled with the sounds of cowbells – it was all the same: summer and winter dress were nothing but masks concealing the fact that this village had no existence apart from its flux of visitors, which it fed and supplied by means of the single rickety little train that came up from the lowlands of Bavaria, and which in turn it drained of money spent freely on wooden shoes, carved and painted wooden bottles, ironwork, embroidered aprons, ski trousers and sweaters, and those slender curved skis themselves that enabled a thousand earth-plodders to wing over the slopes all through the snow months.

The fact is that for real pleasure a pleasure resort should have no one in it but its legitimate inhabitants, oneself, and perhaps one's friends. Everyone knows it, everyone feels it; and this is the insoluble contradiction of tourism; and perhaps the whole edifice will collapse at that moment when there is not one little town, not one village in the whole of Europe that has not been, as the term is, exploited. No longer will it be possible to drive one's car away into the mountains in search of that un-spoiled village, that Old-World inn by the stream; for when one arrives most certainly a professional host will hasten out, offering professional hospitality. What then? Will everyone stay at home?

But what of poor, war-denuded Europe whose inhabitants continue to live, a little sullenly perhaps, under the summer and winter eyes of their visitors, eyes that presumably are searching for some quality, some good, that they do not possess themselves, since otherwise why have they travelled so far from themselves in order to examine the lives of other people?

These were the sort of reflections – which, it must be confessed, could scarcely be more banal – that were being exchanged by our two travellers.

There they stood, outside a little wayside booth, or open shop, that sold, not carved bottles or leather aprons, but real vegetables and butter and cheese. These goods were being bought by a group of American wives who were stationed here with their husbands as part of the army of occupation. Or rather, their husbands were part of the machinery which saw to it that American soldiers stationed all over the American zone of occupation could have pleasant holidays in the more attractive parts of Europe.

Between small, green-painted houses, the snow was pitted and rutted in the narrow street, glazed with the newly frozen heat of tramping feet. In places it was stained yellow and mounded with dark horse droppings, and there was a strong smell of urine mingling with the fresh tang of winter cabbage, giving rise to further reflections about the superiority of automobiles over horses – and even, perhaps, of wide streets over narrow ones, for at every moment the two travellers had to step down off the small pavement into the strong-smelling snow to allow happy groups of skiers to pass by; had to stand back again to make room for the cars that were trying to force a passage up to the big hotels where the American soldiers were holidaying with their wives or girls.

There were so many of the great powerful cars, rocking fast and dangerously up over the slippery snow, that it was hard to preserve the illusion of an unspoiled mountain village. And so the two lifted their eyes to the surrounding forests and peaks. The sun had slipped behind the mountains, but had left their snowfields tinted pink and gold, sentinelled by pine groves which, now that the light had gone from them, loomed black and rather sinister, inevitably suggesting wolves, witches, and other creatures from a vanished time – a suggestion, however, tinged with bathos, since it was obvious that wolves or witches would have got short shrift from the mighty creators of those powerful machines. The tinted glitter of the smooth slopes and the black stillness of the woods did their best to set the village in a timelessness not disturbed by the gear and machinery of the travelling cages that lifted clear over intervening valleys to the ledge of a mountain where there was yet another hotel and the amenities of civilization. And perhaps it was a relief, despite all the intrusions of the machinery of domesticity and comfort, to rest one's eyes on those forests, those mountains, whose savagery seemed so innocent. The year was 1951; and, while the inhabitants of the village seemed almost feverishly concerned to present a scene of carefree charm, despite all their efforts the fact which must immediately strike everyone was that most of the people in the streets wore the uniform of the war which was six years past, and that the language most often overheard was American. But it was not possible to stand there, continually being edged this way and that on and off the pavement, with one's eyes fixed determinedly on natural beauty, particularly as the light was going fast and now the houses, shops, and hotels were taking their nocturnal shape and spilling the white pallor of electricity from every door and window, promising warmth, promising certain pleasure. The mountains had massed themselves, black against a luminous sky. Life had left them and was concentrating down in the village. Everywhere came groups of skiers hastening home for the night, and everywhere among them those men and women who proclaimed themselves immediately and at first glance as American. Why? Our two stood there, looking into first one face and then the next, trying to define what it was that set them apart. A good-looking lot, these new policemen of Europe. And well-fed, well-dressed ... They were distinguished above all, perhaps, by their assurance! Or was this noisy cheerfulness nothing more than the expression of an inner guilt because the task of policing and preserving order earned such attractive holidays? In which case, it was rather to their credit than not.

But when the four army wives had finished their bargaining at the vegetable and dairy stall and went up the steep street, walking heavily because of their crammed baskets, they so dominated the scene in their well-cut trousers and their bright jackets that the women selling produce and the locals who had been waiting patiently for the four to conclude their shopping seemed almost unimportant, almost like willing extras in a crowd-scene from a film called perhaps *Love in the Alps*, or *They Met in the Snow*.

And six years had been enough to still in the hearts of these Germans – for Germans they were, although Austria was no more than a giant's stone-throw away – all the bitterness of defeat? They were quite happy to provide a homely and picturesque background for whatever nationalities might choose to visit them, even if most were American and many British – as our two conscientiously added, trying not to dissociate themselves from their responsibilities, even though they felt very strongly that the representatives of *their* country were much too naturally modest and tactful to appropriate a scene simply by the fact that they were in it.

It was hard to believe; and the knowledge of the secret angers, or at the very best, an ironical patience, that must be burning in the breasts of their hosts, the good people of the village of O—, deepened an uneasiness which was almost (and this was certainly irrational) a guilt which should surely have no place in the emotions of a well-deserved holiday.

Guilt about what? It was absurd.

Yet, from the moment they had arrived on the frontier – the word still came naturally to them both – and had seen the signs in German; had heard the language spoken all around them; had passed through towns whose names were associated with the savage hate and terror of headlines a decade old – from that moment had begun in both the complicated uneasiness of which they were so ashamed. Neither had admitted it to the other; both were regretting they had come. Why – they were both thinking – why submit ourselves when we are on holiday and won't be able to afford another one for goodness knows how long, to something that must be unpleasant? Why not say simply and be done with it that, for us, Germany is poisoned? We never want to set foot in it again or hear the language spoken or see a sign in German. We simply do not want to think about it; and if we are unjust and lacking in humanity and reason and good sense then – why not? One cannot be expected to be reasonable about everything.

Yet here they were.

The man remarked, after a long silence: 'Last time I was here there was nothing of *that*.'

Down the other side of the street, pressed close to the wall to avoid a big car that was going by, came a group of five girls in local peasant costume. All day these girls had been serving behind the counters, or in the restaurants, wearing clothes such as girls anywhere in Europe might wear. Now their individual faces had dwindled behind great white starched headdresses. Their bodies were nothing more than supports for the long-sleeved, long-skirted, extinguishing black dresses. The whole costume had something reminiscent of the prim fantasy of the habits of certain orders of nuns. They were plodding resignedly enough – since after all they were being well paid for doing this – down over the snow towards one of the big hotels where they would regale the tourists with folk songs before slipping home to change into their own clothes in time to spend an hour or so with their young men.

'Well, never mind, I suppose one does like to see it?' The woman slipped her arm through his.

'Oh, I suppose so, why not?'

They began to walk down the street, leaning on each other because of the slipperiness of the rutted snow.

It hung in the balance whether one or other of them might have said something like: Suppose we all stopped coming? Suppose there were no tourists at all; perhaps they would simply cease to exist? Like actors who devote so much of themselves to acting they have no emotions over for their own lives but continue to exist in whatever part they are playing . . .

But neither of them spoke. They turned into the main street of the village, where there were several large hotels and restaurants.

Very easily one of them might have remarked to the other, with a kind of grumbling good humour: It's all very well, all these things we're saying about tourists, but we are tourists ourselves.

Come, come, the other would have replied. Clearly we are tourists on a much higher level than most!

Then they would have both laughed.

But at the same moment they stopped dead, looking at some queer hopping figure that was coming along the pavement over the badly lighted snow. For a moment it was impossible to make out what this great black jumping object could be that was coming fast towards them along the ground. Then they saw it was a man whose legs had been amputated and who was hopping over the snow like a frog, his body swinging and jerking between his heavy arms like the body of some kind of insect.

The two saw the eyes of this man stare up at them as he went hopping past.

At the station that day, when they arrived, two men hacked and amputated by war almost out of humanity, one without arms, his legs cut off at the knee, one whose face was a great scarred eyeless hollow, were begging from the alighting holiday-makers.

'For God's sake,' said the man suddenly, as if this were nothing but a continuation of what they had been saying, 'for God's sake, let's get out of here.'

'Oh, *yes*,' she agreed instantly. They looked at each other, smiling, acknowledging in that smile all that they had not said that day.

'Let's go back. Let's find somewhere in France.'

'We shouldn't have come.'

They watched the cripple lever himself up over a deep door-step, dragging his body up behind his arms, using the stump of his body as a support while he reached up with long arms to ring the bell.

'What about the money?' she asked.

'We'll go home when it runs out.'

'Good, we'll go back tomorrow.'

Instantly they felt gay; they were leaving tomorrow.

They walked along the street, looking at the menus outside the hotels. He said, 'Let's go in here. It's expensive, but it's the last night.'

It was a big, brown, solid-looking hotel called the Lion's Head; and on the old-fashioned gilded signboard was a great golden lion snarling down at them.

Inside was a foyer, lined with dark, shining wood; there were dark, straight-backed wooden settles around the walls and heavy arrangements of flowers in massive brass tubs. Glass doors opened into the restaurant proper. This was a long room lined with the same gleaming dark wood, and in each corner stood even larger brass tubs crammed with flowers. The table-cloths were heavy white damask; a profusion of cutlery and glass gleamed and glittered. It was a scene of solid middle-class comfort. A waiter showed them to an empty table at one side. The menu was placed between them. They exchanged a grimace, for the place was far too expensive for them, particularly as now they were committed to spending so much of their money on fares away and out of Germany into France – a country where they would feel no compulsion at all to make disparaging and ironical remarks about tourists or tourism.

They ordered their dinner and, while they waited, sat examining the other diners. The Americans were not here. Their hotels were the big, new, modern ones at the top of the village. The clientele here was solidly German. Again the two British tourists were conscious of a secret, half-ashamed unease. They looked from one face to another, thinking: Six years ago, what were you doing? And you – and you? We were mortal enemies then; now we sit in the same room, eating together. You were the defeated.

This last was addressed as a reminder to themselves, for no people could have looked less defeated than these. A more solid, sound, well-dressed, comfortable crowd could not be imagined; and they were eating with the easy satisfaction of those who cannot imagine ever being short of a meal. Yet six years ago . . .

The waiter brought two plates of soup, very big plates, monogrammed with the sign of the Lion's Head, so full that they asked him to take them away and divide one portion between the two of them. For they had observed that a single portion (served on large metal dishes) of any dish here was enough for two English stomachs. Not that they were not more than willing to do as well as these people around them – the defeated whose capacity seemed truly incredible. But one day in this country of hearty eaters had not enlarged their stomachs to German capacity; and now that they were leaving not later than tomorrow, it was too late.

They consumed their half-portions of very strong meat soup, full of vegetables; and pointed out to each other that, even so, their plates held twice as much as they would in England; and continued to dart curious, half-guilty glances at their fellow diners.

Six years ago these people were living amid ruins, in cellars, behind any scrap of masonry that remained standing. They were half-starved, and their clothes were rags. An entire generation of young men were dead. Six years. A remarkable nation, surely.

The jugged hare came and was eaten with appreciation.

They had ordered pastries with cream; but alas, before they could eat them, they had to restore themselves with strong cups of coffee.

Back in France, they told themselves and each other, they would find themselves at home, at table as well as spiritually. By this time tomorrow, they would be in France. And now, with the last meal over and the bill to pay, came the moment of general reckoning, soon over, and in fact accomplished hastily on the back of an envelope.

To take a train, third-class, back to the nearest suitable spot in the French Alps would use up half of their available currency; and it would be a choice of staying out their full three weeks and eating one meal a day – and that a very slender meal – or staying a week and then going home.

They did not look at each other as they reached this final depressing conclusion. They were thinking, of course, that they were mad to leave at all. If to come to Germany was the result of some sort of spiritual quixotry, a symptom of moral philanthropy suitable only for liberal idealists whom – they were convinced – they both despised, then to leave again was simply weak-minded. In fact, their present low-spiritedness was probably due to being over-tired, for they had spent two successive nights sitting upon hard wooden train seats, sleeping fitfully on each other's shoulders.

They would have to stay. And now that they reached this conclusion, depression settled on them both; and they looked at the rich Germans who surrounded them with a gloomy hatred which, in their better moments, they would have utterly repudiated.

Just then the waiter came forward, followed by an energetically striding young man apparently fresh from a day's skiing, for his face was flaming scarlet under untidy shags of sandy hair. They did not want him at their table, but the restaurant was now quite full. The waiter left their bill on the tablecloth; and they occupied themselves in finding the right change, under the interested inspection of the young sportsman, who, it seemed, was longing to advise them about money and tips. Resenting his interest, they set themselves to be patient. But the waiter did not return for some time, so busy was he at the surrounding tables; and they watched a party of new arrivals who were settling down at a nearby table that had been reserved for them. There came first a handsome woman in her early middle age, unfastening a shaggy, strong-looking fur coat of the kind worn for winter sports or bad weather outdoors. She flung this open on her chair, making a kind of nest, in which she placed herself, wrapping it closely around her legs. She was wearing a black wool dress, full-skirted and embroidered in bright colours, a dress which flirted with the idea of peasant naïvety. Having arranged herself, she raised her face to greet the rest of her family with a smile that seemed to mock and chide them for taking so long to follow after her. It was a handsome face: she was a fine-looking woman, with her fair curling hair, and a skin bronzed deep with the sun and oil of many weeks of winter sport. Next came a young lad, obviously her son, a very tall, good-looking, attractive youth, who began teasing her because of her hurry to begin eating. He flashed his white strong teeth at her, and his young blue eyes, until she playfully took his arm and shook him. He protested. Then both, with looks of mock concern because this was a public place, desisted, lowered their voices, and sat laughing while the daughter, a delightfully pretty girl of fifteen or so, and the father, a heavy, good-humoured gentleman, took the two empty chairs. The family party was complete. The waiter was attentive for their order, which was for four tall glasses of beer, which they insisted on having that moment, before they could order or even think of food. The waiter hurried off to fetch the beer, while they settled down to study the menus. And one could be sure that there would be no half-portions for this family, either for financial reasons or because they suffered from limitations of appetite.

Watching this family, it came home to the couple from Britain that what they were resenting was very likely their sheer capacity for physical enjoyment. Since, like all British people of their type, they spent a great deal of emotional energy on complaining about the inability of their countrymen to experience joy and well-being, they told themselves that what they felt was both churlish and inconsistent. The woman said to the man in a conciliating, apologetic, almost resigned voice, 'They really are extraordinarily good-looking.'

To this he responded with a small ironical grimace; and he returned his attention to the family.

Mother, father, and son were laughing over some joke, while the girl turned a very long tapering glass of beer between thumb and forefinger of a thin, tanned hand so that the frost beads glittered and spun. She was staring out of the family group, momentarily lost to it, a fair, dreaming tendril of a girl with an irregular wedge of a little face. Her eyes wandered over the people at the tables, encountered those of our couple, and lingered in open, bland curiosity. It was a gaze of frank unselfconsciousness, almost innocence; the gaze of a protected

child who knew she might commit no folly on her own individual account, since the family stood between her and the
results of folly. Yet, just then, she chose to be out of the family
group; or at least, she gazed out of it as one looks through an
open door. Her pale, pretty eyes absorbed what she wanted of
the British couple, and, at their leisure, moved on to the other
diners; and all the time her fingers moved slowly up and down
the slim cold walls of her beer glass. The woman, finding in
this girl a poetic quality totally lacking from the stolid burghers
who filled this room, indicated her to the man by saying: 'She's
charming.' Again he grimaced, as if to say: Every young girl is
poetic. And: She'll be her mother in ten years.

Which was true. Already the family had become aware of the
infidelity of this, their youngest member; already the handsome
mother was leaning over her daughter, rallying her for her
dreamy inattention, claiming her by little half-caressing, peremptory exclamations. The solid, kindly father laid his brown
and capable hand on the girl's white-wool-covered forearm
and bent towards her with solicitude, as if she were sick. The
boy put a large forkful of meat into his mouth and ate it rumi-
nantly, watching his sister with an irreverent grin. Then he said
in a low tone some word that was clearly an old trumpet for
disagreement between them, for she swung her chin towards
him petulantly with a half-reproachful and half-resentful epi-
thet. The brother went on grinning, protective but derisive; the
father and mother smiled tenderly at each other because of the
brother-and-sister sparring.

No, clearly, this young girl had no chance of escaping from
the warm prison of her family; and in a few years she would be
a capable, handsome, sensual woman, married to some manu-
facturer carefully chosen for her by her father. That is, she
would be unless another war or economic cataclysm intervened
and plunged all her people into the edge-of-disaster hunger-
bitten condition from which they had just emerged. Though
they did not look as if they had . . .

Returned full circle to the point of their complicated and
irrational dislike, the man and woman raised ironical eyes at
each other, and the man said briefly: 'Blond beasts.'

These two were of another family of mankind from most of the people in the restaurant.

The man was Scotch, small-built, nervous, energetic, with close-springing black hair, white freckled skin, quick, deep blue eyes. He tended to be sarcastic about the English, among whom, of course, he had spent most of his life. He was busy, hard-working, essentially pragmatic, practical, and humane. Yet above and beyond all these admirably useful qualities was something else, expressed in his characteristic little grimace of ironical bitterness, as if he were saying: Well, yes, and then?

As for her, she was small, dark, and watchful, Jewish in appearance and arguably by inheritance, since there had been a Jewish great-grandmother who had escaped from pogrom-loving Poland in the last century and married an Englishman. More potent than the great-grandmother was the fact that her fiancé, a medical student and a refugee from Austria, had been killed in the early days of the war flying over this same country in which they now sat and took their holiday. Mary Parrish was one of those people who had become conscious of their claims to being Jewish only when Hitler drew their attention to the possibility they might have some.

She now sat and contemplated the handsome German family and thought: Ten years ago ... She was seeing them as executioners.

As for the man, who had taken his name, Hamish, from a string of possible names, some of them English, because of another kind of national pride, he had served in his capacity as a doctor on one of the commissions that, after the war, had tried to rescue the debris of humanity the war had left all over Europe.

It was no accident that he had served on this commission. Early in 1939 he had married a German girl, or rather, a Jewish girl, studying in Britain. In July of that year she had made a brave and foolhardy attempt to rescue some of her family who had so far escaped the concentration camps, and had never been heard of since. She had simply vanished. For all Hamish knew, she was still alive somewhere. She might very well be in this village of O—. Ever since yesterday morning when they entered

Germany, Mary had been watching Hamish's anxious, angry, impatient eyes moving, preoccupied, from the face of one woman to another: old women, young women; women on buses, trains, platforms; women glimpsed at the end of a street; a woman at a window. And she could feel him thinking: Well, and if I did see her, I wouldn't recognize her.

And his eyes would move back to hers; she smiled; and he gave his small, bitter, ironical grimace.

They were both doctors, both hard-working and conscientious, both very tired because, after all, while living in Britain has many compensations, it is hard work, this business of maintaining a decent level of life with enough leisure for the pursuits that make life worth-while, or at least to cultivated people, which they both were, and determined to remain. They were above all, perhaps, tired people.

They were tired and they needed to rest. This was their holiday. And here they sat, knowing full well that they were pouring away energies into utterly useless, irrelevant and, above all, unfair emotions.

The word 'unfair' was one they both used without irony.

She said, 'I think one week in France would be better than three here. Let's go. I really do think we should.'

He said, 'Let's go into one of the smaller villages higher up the valley. They are probably just ordinary mountain villages, not tarted-up like this place.'

'We'll go tomorrow,' she agreed with relief.

Here they both became alert to the fact that the young man who had sat down at their table was watching them, at the same time as he heartily chewed a large mouthful of food, and looked for an inlet into their conversation. He was an unpleasant person. Tall, with an uncoordinated, bony look, his blue eyes met the possibilities of their reaction to him with a steady glare of watchful suspicion out of an ugly face whose skin had a peculiar harsh red texture. The eyes of our couple had been, unknown to them, returning again and again to this remarkable scarlet face, and at the back of their minds they had been thinking professionally: A fool to overheat himself in this strong reflected light up here.

Now, at the same moment, the two doctors realized that the surface of his face was a skin-graft; that the whole highly-coloured, shiny, patchy surface, while an extraordinarily skilful reconstruction of a face, was nothing but a mask, and what the face had been before must be guessed at. They saw, too, that he was not a young man, but, like themselves, in early middle age. Instantly pity fought with their instinctive dislike of him; and they reminded themselves that the aggressive glare of the blue eyes was the expression of the pitiful necessity of a wounded creature to defend itself.

He said in stiff but good English, or rather, American: 'I must beg your pardon for interrupting your conversation, and beg leave to introduce myself – Dr Schröder. I wish to place myself at your service. I know this valley well, and can recommend hotels in the other villages.'

He was looking at Hamish, as he had from the time he began speaking; though he gave a small, minimal bow when Mary Parrish introduced herself and instantly returned his attention to the man.

Both the British couple felt discomfort; but it was hard to say whether this was because of the man's claim on their pity; because of their professional interest in him, which they must disguise; or because of the impolite insistence of his manner.

'That is very kind of you,' said Hamish; and Mary murmured that it was very kind. They wondered whether he had heard Hamish's 'blond beasts'. They wondered what other indiscretions they might have committed.

'As it happens,' said Dr Schröder, 'I have a very good buddy who runs a guest house at the top of the valley. I was up there this morning, and she has a dandy room to let.'

Once again they indicated that it was very kind of him.

'If it is not too early for you, I shall be taking the 9.30 autobus up the valley tomorrow for a day's skiing, and I shall be happy to assist you.'

And now it was necessary to take a stand one way or the other. Mary and Hamish glanced at each other inquiringly; and immediately Dr Schröder said, with a perceptible increase of tension in his manner, 'As you know, at this time in the season, it is hard to find accommodation.' He paused, seemed to assure himself of their status by a swift inspection of their clothes and general style, and added: 'Unless you can afford one of the big hotels – but they are not of the cheapest.'

'Actually,' said Mary, trying to make of what he must have heard her say before a simple question of caprice: 'Actually we were wondering whether we might not go back to France? We are both very fond of France.'

But Dr Schröder was not prepared to take this from them. 'If it is a question of skiing, then the weather report announced today that the snow is not as good in the French Alps as it is with us. And, of course, France is much more expensive.'

They agreed that this was so; and he continued to say that if they took the empty room at his buddy's guest house it would cost them much less than it would at a German pension, let alone a French pension. He examined their clothes again and remarked, 'Of course, it must be hard for you to have such unfortunate restrictions with your travel allowance. Yes, it must be annoying. For people of a good salary and position it must be annoying.'

For both these two the restrictions of the travel allowance merely confirmed a fact; they could not have afforded more than the allowance in any case. They realized that Dr Schröder was quite unable to decide whether they were rich and eccentric English people who notoriously prefer old clothes to new clothes, or whether they were rich people deliberately trying to appear poor, or whether they were poor. In the first two cases they would perhaps be eager to do some trade in currency with him? Was that what he wanted?

It seemed it was; for he immediately said that he would be very happy to lend them a modest sum of dough, in return for which he would be glad if they would do the same for him when he visited London, which he intended to do very soon. He fastened the steady glare of his eyes on their faces, or rather, on Hamish's face, and said: 'Of course, I am prepared to offer every guarantee.' And he proceeded to do so. He was a doctor attached to a certain hospital in the town of S—, and his salary was regular. If they wished to make independent inquiries they were welcome to do so.

And now Hamish intervened to make it clear that they could not afford to spend on this vacation one penny more than the travel allowance. For a long moment Dr Schröder did not believe him. Then he examined their clothes again and openly nodded.

Now, perhaps, the man would go away?

Not at all. He proceeded to deliver a harangue on the subject of his admiration for Britain. His love for the entire British nation, their customs, their good taste, their sportsmanship, their love of fair play, their history, and their art were the ruling passions of his life. He went on like this for some minutes, while the British couple wondered if they ought to confess that their trade was the same as his. But, if they did, presumably it would let them in for even closer intimacy. And by a hundred of the minute signs which suffice for communication between people who know each other well, they had said that they disliked this man intensely and wished only that he would go away.

But now Dr Schröder inquired outright what profession his new friend Mr Anderson pursued; and when he heard that they were both doctors, and attached to hospitals whose names he knew, his expression changed. But subtly. It was not surprise, but rather the look of a prosecutor who has been cross-examining witnesses and at last got what he wants.

And the British couple were beginning to understand what it was Dr Schröder wanted of them. He was talking with a stiff, brooding passion of resentment about his position and prospects as a doctor in Germany. For professional people, he said, Germany was an unkind country. For the business people – yes. For the artisans – yes. The workers were all millionaires these days, yes sir! Better far to be a plumber or an electrician than a doctor. The ruling dream of his life was to make his way to Britain, and there become an honoured – and, be it understood – a well-paid member of his profession.

Here Doctors Anderson and Parrish pointed out that foreign

doctors were not permitted to practise in Britain. They might lecture; they might study; but they might not practise. Not unless, added Dr Parrish, possibly reacting to the fact that not once had this man done more than offer her the barest minimum of politeness until he had recognized that she, as well as Hamish, was a doctor and therefore possibly of use to him – not unless they were refugees, and even then they must take the British examinations.

Dr Schröder did not react to the word 'refugee'.

He returned to a close cross-examination about their salaries and prospects, dealing first with Mary's, and then, in more detail, with Hamish. At last, in response to their warning that for him to become a doctor in Britain would be much more difficult than he seemed to think, he replied that in this world everything was a question of pulling strings. In short, he intended they should pull strings for him. It was the most fortunate occurrence of his life that he had happened to meet them that evening, the happiest and the best-timed . . .

At this, the eyes of the British couple met on a certain suspicion. Ten minutes later in the talk it emerged that he knew the lady who ran the house where they had taken a room, and therefore he probably had heard from her that she had a British doctor as a lodger. Very likely he had arranged with the waiter to be put at their table. For he must know the people of the village well: he had been coming for his winter holidays to O— since he was a small child – Dr Schröder held out his hand below table level to show how small. Yes, all those years of winters O— had known Dr Schröder, save for the years of war, when he was away serving his country.

There was a small stir in the restaurant. The family were rising, gathering their wraps, and departing. The lady first, her shaggy brown coat slung over her handsome shoulders, her rosy lower lip caught by her white teeth as she searched for belongings she might have forgotten. Then she extended her smile, so white against the clear brown skin, and waited for her son to take her by the shoulder and propel her, while she laughed protesting, to the door. There, when it opened, she shivered playfully, although it was only the door to the vestibule. Behind her came the pretty, rather languid girl; then the stout authoritative father, shepherding his family away and out to the snow-cold air. The family vanished, leaving their table a mess of empty glasses, plates, broken bread, cheeses, fruit, wine. The waiter cleared the table with a look as if he found it a privilege.

The British couple also rose and said to Dr Schröder that they would think over his suggestion and perhaps let him know in the morning. His thin-skinned shiny face tilted up at them, and levelled into an affronted mask as he stood up and said, 'But I understood all arrangements were made.'

And how had they got themselves into this position, where they could not exercise simple freedom of choice without upsetting this extremely dislikeable person? But they knew how. It was because he was a wounded man, a cripple; because they knew that his fixed aggression was part of his laudable determination not to let that shockingly raw face drive him into self-pity and isolation. They were doctors, and they were reacting above all to the personality of a cripple. When they said that they were tired and intended to go to bed early, and he replied instantly, insulted, that he would be happy to accompany them to a certain very pleasant place of entertainment, they knew that they could bring themselves to do no more than say they could not afford it.

They knew he would immediately offer to be their host. He did, and they politely refused as they would refuse an ordinary acquaintance, and were answered by the man who could tolerate no refusal, because if he once accepted a refusal, he would be admitting to himself that his face put him outside simple human intercourse.

Dr Schröder, who had spent all the winter holidays of his life in this valley, naturally knew the proprietor of the hotel where he proposed to take them; and he guaranteed them a pleasant and relaxing evening while he fixed on them a glare of suspicious hate.

They walked together under the snow-weighted eaves of the houses, over snow rutted by the hundred enormous American cars which had rocked over it that day, to the end of the street where there was a hotel whose exterior they had already inspected earlier that day and rejected on the grounds that anything inside it must necessarily be too expensive for them. Immediately outside, on the seared snow, sat the man without legs they had seen earlier. Or rather he stood, his head level with their hips, looking as if he were buried to hip-level in the snow, holding out a cloth cap to them. His eyes had the same bold, watchful glare as those of Dr Schröder.

Dr Schröder said, 'It's a disgrace that these people should be allowed to behave like this. It makes a bad impression on our visitors.' And he led the British couple past the cripple with a look of angry irritation.

Inside was a long room sheltered by glass on two sides from the snow which could be seen spinning down through the areas of yellow light conquered from the black mass of the darkness by the room and its warmth and its noise and its people. It was extraordinarily pleasant to enter this big room, so busy with pleasure, and to see the snow made visible only during its passage through the beams from the big windows, as if the wildness of the mountain valley had been admitted just so far as would give the delight of contrast to the guests who could see savagery as a backdrop of pretty, spinning white flakes.

There was a small band, consisting of piano, clarinet and drum, playing the kind of jazz that makes a pleasant throb, like a blood-beat, behind conversation.

The family had moved themselves from the table in the restaurant to a table here and sat as before in a close group. The British couple found an empty table near them, which Dr Schröder approved; and when the waiter came knew they had been right – the drinks were very expensive and this was not a place where one might lightly sip one drink for a whole evening while richer people drank seriously. One was expected to drink; people were drinking, although a small beer cost nearly ten shillings. They saw, too, that Dr Schröder's boast that he had special privileges here because he was a friend of the proprietor was untrue. His passport here, as everywhere else, was his raw, shiny face. When the proprietor glanced towards him during his hospitable passage among the tables, he did so with a nod and a smile, but it was a smile that had the over-kindness of controlled hostility. And his eyes lingered briefly on the British couple who, after this inspection, were forced to feel that everyone else in this place was German. The Americans were in their own rich hotels; the impoverished British in the cheap guest houses; this place was for wealthy Germans. And the British couple wondered at the insistence of Dr Schröder in bringing them here. Was it possible that he really believed he had a special place in the heart of the proprietor? Yes, it was; he kept smiling and nodding after the turned back of the fat host, as if to say: You see, he knows me; then smiling at them, proud of his achievement. For which he was prepared to pay heavily in actual money. He counted out the price of the drinks with the waiter with a painful care for the small change of currency that they understood very well. What recompense could they possibly give this man; what was he wanting so badly? Was it really only that he wanted to live and work in Britain?

Again Dr Schröder began to talk, and again of his admiration for their country, leaning across the table, looking into their faces, as if this was a message of incalculable importance to them both.

He was interrupted by the clarinet player who stood up, took a note from the regular ground-throb of the music, and began to develop a theme of his own from it. Couples went on to a small area of shiny floor not occupied by tables, and which was invaded at every moment by the hurrying waiters with their trays of drinks. They were dancing, these people, for the pleasure not of movement, but of contact. A dozen or a score of men and women, seemingly held upright by the pressure of the seated guests around them, idled together, loosely linked, smiling, sceptical, good-natured with the practice of pleasure.

Immediately the dancing was broken up because the group of folk singers had come in at the big glass entrance door, in their demure conventual dress, and now stood by the band waiting.

The woman at the next table gave a large cheerful shrug and said, 'This is the fifth time. This is my fifth home-evening.' People turned to smile at the words *heimat-abend*, indulgent with the handsome woman and her look of spoiled enjoyment. Already one of the folk singers was moving among the tables to collect their fee, which was high; and already the rich papa was thrusting towards the girl a heap of money, disdaining the change with a shake of his head – change, however, which she did not seem in any urgency to give him. When she reached the table where our couple sat with Dr Schröder, Hamish paid, and not with good grace. After all, the prices were high enough here without having to pay more for folk songs which one did not necessarily want to listen to at all.

When the girl had made her rounds and collected her money, she rejoined the group, which formed itself together near the band and sang, one after another, songs of the valley, in which yodelling figured often and loudly, earning loud applause.

It was clear that Dr Schröder, who listened to the group with a look of almost yearning nostalgia, did not feel its intrusion as an irritant at all. Folk songs, his expression said, were something he could listen to all night. He clapped often and glanced at his guests, urging them to share his sentimental enjoyment.

At last the group left; the clarinet summoned the dancers to the tiny floor; and Dr Schröder resumed his hymn of love for Britain. Tragic, he said, having stated and restated the theme of praise – tragic that these two countries had ever had to fight at all. Tragic that natural friends should have been divided by the machinations of interested and sinister groups. The British couple's eyes met ironically over the unspoken phrase, international Jewry, and even with the consciousness of being pedantic, if not unfair. But Dr Schröder did not believe in the unstated. He said that international Jewry had divided the two natural masters of Europe, Germany and Britain; and it was his passionate belief that in the future these two countries should work together for the good of Europe and thus, obviously, of the whole world. Dr Schröder had had good friends, friends who were almost brothers, killed on the front; where British and German troops had been manoeuvred into hostility; and he grieved over them even now as one does for sacrificed victims.

Dr Schröder paused, fixed them with the glare of his eyes, and said: 'I wish to tell you that I, too, was wounded; perhaps you have not noticed. I was wounded on the Russian front. My life was despaired of. But I was saved by the skill of our doctors. My entire face is a witness to the magnificent skill of our German doctors.'

The British couple hastened to express their surprise and congratulations. Oddly enough, they felt a lessened obligation towards compassion because of Dr Schröder's grotesque and touching belief that his face was nearly normal enough to be unnoticed. He said that the surface of his face had burned off when a tank beside him had exploded into pieces, showering him with oil. He had fought for three years with the glorious armies of his country all over the Ukraine. He spoke like a survivor from the Grande Armée to fellow admirers of 'The Other', inviting and expecting interested congratulation. 'Those Russians,' he said, 'are savages. Barbarians. No one would believe the atrocities they committed. Unless you had seen it with your own eyes you would not believe the brutality the Russians are capable of.'

The British couple, now depressed into silence, and even past the point where they could allow their eyes to meet in ironical support of each other, sat watching the languidly revolving dancers.

Dr Schröder said insistently, 'Do you know that those Russians would shoot at our soldiers as they walked through the streets of a village? An ordinary Russian peasant, if he got the chance, would slaughter one of our soldiers? And even the women – I can tell you cases of Russian women murdering our soldiers after pretending to be buddies with them.'

Mary and Hamish kept their peace and wondered how Dr Schröder had described to himself the mass executions, the hangings, the atrocities of the German army in Russia. They did not wonder for long, for he said, 'We were forced to defend ourselves. Yes, I can tell you that we had to defend ourselves against the savagery of those people. The Russians are monsters.'

Mary Parrish roused herself to say, 'Not such monsters,

perhaps, as the Jews?' And she tried to catch and hold the fanatic eyes of their host with her own. He said, 'Ah, yes, we had many enemies.' His eyes, moving fast from Hamish's face to Mary's, paused and wavered. It occurred to him perhaps that they were not entirely in accordance with him. For a second his ugly, blistered mouth twisted in what might have been doubt. He said politely, 'Of course, our Führer went too far in his zeal against our enemies. But he understood the needs of our country.'

'It is the fate of great men,' said Hamish, in the quick sarcastic voice that was the nearest he ever got to expressed anger, 'to be misunderstood by the small-minded.'

Dr Schröder was now unmistakably in doubt. He was silent, examining their faces with his eyes, into which all the expression of his scarred face was concentrated, while they suffered the inner diminishment and confusion that happens when the assumptions on which one bases one's life are attacked. They were thinking dubiously that this was the voice of madness. They were thinking that they knew no one in Britain who would describe it as anything else. They were thinking that they were both essentially, self-consciously, of that element in their nation dedicated to not being insular, to not falling into the errors of complacency; and they were, at this moment, feeling something of the despair that people like them had felt ten, fifteen years ago, watching the tides of madness rise while the reasonable and the decent averted their eyes. At the same time they were feeling an extraordinary but undeniable reluctance to face the fact that Dr Schröder might represent any more than himself. No, they were assuring themselves, this unfortunate man is simply a cripple, scarred mentally as well as physically, a bit of salvage from the last war.

At this moment the music again stopped, and there was an irregular clapping all over the room; clearly there was to be a turn that the people there knew and expected.

Standing beside the piano was a small, smiling man who nodded greetings to the guests. He was dark, quick-eyed, with an agreeable face that the British couple instinctively described as 'civilized'. He nodded to the pianist, who began to improvise an accompaniment to his act; he was half-singing, half-talking the verse of a song or ballad about a certain general whose name the British couple did not recognize. The accompaniment was a steady, military-sounding thump-thump against which the right hand wove fragments of 'Deutschland Uber Alles' and the 'Horst Wessel Song'. The refrain was: 'And now he sits in Bonn.'

The next verse was about an admiral, also now sitting in Bonn.

The British couple understood that the song consisted of the histories of a dozen loyal German militarists who had been over-zealous in their devotion to their Führer; had been sentenced by the Allied courts of justice to various terms of imprisonment, or to death; 'and now they sat in Bonn'.

All that was fair enough. It sounded like a satire on Allied policy in Germany which – so both these conscientious people knew and deplored – tended to be over-generous to the ex-murderers of the Nazi regime. What could be more heartening than to find their own view expressed there, in this comfortable resort of the German rich? And what more surprising?

They looked at Dr Schröder and saw his eyes gleaming with pleasure. They looked back at the urbane, ironical little singer, who was performing with the assurance of one who knows himself to be perfectly at one with his audience, and understood that this was the type of ballad adroitly evolved to meet the needs of an occupied people forced to express themselves under the noses of a conqueror. True that the American army was not here, in this room, this evening; but even if they had been, what possible exception could they have taken to the words of this song?

It was a long ballad, and when it was ended there was very little applause. Singer and audience exchanged with each other smiles of discreet understanding, and the little man bowed this way and that. He then straightened himself, looked at the British couple, and bowed to them. It was as if the room caught its breath. Only when they looked at Dr Schröder's face, which showed all the malicious delight of a child who had thumbed his nose behind teacher's back, did they understand what a demonstration of angry defiance that bow had been. And they understood, with a sinking of the heart, the depths of furious revengeful humiliation which made such a very slight gesture so extremely satisfying to these rich burgesses, who merely glanced discreetly, smiling slightly, at these conquerors in their midst – conquerors who were so much shabbier than they were, so much more worn and tired – and turned away, exchanging glances of satisfaction, to their batteries of gleaming glasses filled with wine and with beer.

And now Mary and Hamish felt that this demonstration, which presumably Dr Schröder had shared in, perhaps even invited, released them from any obligation to him; and they looked at him with open dislike, indicating that they wished to leave.

Besides, the waiter stood beside them, showing an open insolence that was being observed and admired by the handsome matron and her husband and her son; the girl was, as usual, dreaming some dream of her own and not looking at anyone in particular. The waiter bent over them, put his hands on their still half-filled glasses, and asked what they would have.

Hamish and Mary promptly drank what remained of their beer and rose. Dr Schröder rose with them. His whole knobbly, ugly body showed agitation and concern. Surely they weren't going? Surely, when the evening was just beginning, and very soon they would have the privilege of hearing again the talented singer who had just retired, but only for a short interval. Did they realize that he was a famous artist from M—, a man who nightly sang to crammed audiences, who was engaged by the management of this hotel, alas, only for two short weeks of the winter season?

This was either the most accomplished insolence or another manifestation of Dr Schröder's craziness. For a moment the British couple wondered if they had made a mistake and had misunderstood the singer's meaning. But one glance around the faces of the people at the near tables was enough: each face expressed a discreetly hidden smile of satisfaction at the rout of the enemy – routed by the singer, and by the waiter, their willing servant who was nevertheless at this moment exchanging democratic grins of pleasure with the handsome matron.

Dr Schröder was mad, and that was all there was to it. He both delighted in the little demonstration of hostility and, in some involved way of his own, wanted them to delight in it – probably out of brotherly love for him. And now he was quite genuinely agitated and hurt because they were going.

The British couple went out, past the smiling band, past the conscious waiter, while Dr Schröder followed. They went down the iced steps of the hotel and stopped by the legless man who was still rooted in the snow like a plant, where Hamish gave him all the change he had, which amounted to the price of another round of drinks had they stayed in the big warm room.

Dr Schröder watched this and said at once, with indignant reproach, 'You should not do this. It is not expected. Such people should be locked away.' All his suspicion had returned; they must, obviously, be rich, and they had been lying to him.

Mary and Hamish went without speaking down the snow-soft street, through a faint fall of white snow; and Dr Schröder came striding behind them, breathing heavily. When they reached the door of the little house where they had a room, he ran around them and stood facing them, saying hurriedly, 'And so I shall see you tomorrow at the autobus, nine-thirty.'

'We will get in touch with you,' said Hamish politely, which, since they did not know his address, and had not asked for it, was as good as dismissing him.

Dr Schröder leaned towards them, examining their faces with his gleaming, suspicious eyes. He said, 'I will attend you in the morning,' and left them.

They let themselves in and ascended the shallow wooden stairs to their room in silence. The room was low and comfortable, gleaming with well-polished wood. There were an old-fashioned rose-patterned jug and basin on the washstand and an enormous bed laden with thick eiderdowns. A great, shining, blue-tiled stove filled half a wall. Their landlady had left a note pinned to one of the fat pillows, demanding politely that they should leave, in their turn, a note for her outside their door, saying at what hour they wished to receive their breakfast tray. She was the widow of the pastor. She now lived by letting this

room to the summer and winter visitors. She knew this couple
were not married because she had had, by regulation, to take
down particulars from their passports. She had said nothing of
any disapproval she might have felt. The gods of the tourist
trade must not be offended by any personal prejudice she might
hold; and she must have prejudices, surely, as the widow of a
man of God, even against a couple so obviously respectable as
this one?

Mary said, 'I wish she'd turn us out in a fit of moral indignation. I wish someone would have a fit of moral indignation
about something, instead of everything simmering and fes-
tering in the background.'

To which he replied, with the calm of a practical man, 'We
will get up extremely early and leave this valley before our
friend Dr Fascist can see us. I don't think I could bear to
exchange even one more word with him.' He wrote a short note
to the widow of the pastor, demanding breakfast for seven
o'clock; left it outside the door; and, thus well organized, invited Mary to come to bed and stop worrying.

They got into bed and lay side by side. This was not a night
when their arms could hold any comfort for each other. This
was a night when they were not a couple, they were two people.
Their dead were in the room with them – if Lise, his wife,
could be called dead. For how were they to know? War above
all breeds a knowledge of the fantastic, and neither of them
heard one of the extraordinary and impossible stories of escape,
coincidence and survival without thinking: Perhaps Lise is
alive somewhere after all. And the possible aliveness of
Hamish's dead wife had kept alive the image of the very young
medical student who, being a medical student, had no right to
risk himself in the air at all; but who had in fact taken wing out
of his furious misery and anger because of the Nazis and had
crashed in flames a year later. These two, the pretty and vivacious Lise and the gallant and crusading airman, stood by the
enormous, eiderdown-weighted bed and said softly: You must
include us, you must include us.

And so it was a long time before Mary and Hamish slept.

Both awoke again in the night, aware of the snow-sheen on

the windowpanes, listening to the soft noises of the big porcelain stove which sounded as if there were a contented animal breathing beside them in the room. Now they thought that they were leaving this valley because, out of some weakness of character apparently inherent in both of them, they had put themselves in a position where, if they took a room higher up the valley, it would have to be a room chosen for them by Dr Schröder, since they could not bring themselves to be finally rude to him because of that scarred face of his.

No, they preferred to conclude that Dr Schröder summed up in his personality and being everything they hated in this country, Germany, the great catalyst and mirror of Europe: summed it up and presented it to them direct and unambiguously, in such a way that they must reject or accept it.

Yet how could they do either? For to meet Dr Schröder at all made it inevitable that these two serious and conscience-driven people must lie awake and think: One nation is not very different from another ... (For if one did not take one's stand on this proposition where did one end?) And therefore it followed that they must think: What in Britain corresponds to Dr Schröder? What unpleasant forces are this moment simmering in the sewers of our national soul that might explode suddenly into shapes like Dr Schröder? Well then? And what deplorable depths of complacency there must be in us both that we should feel so superior to Dr Schröder – that we should wish only that he might be pushed out of sight somewhere, like a corpse in a house full of living people; or masked like a bad smell; or exorcized like an evil spirit?

Were they or were they not on holiday? They were; and therefore exempt by definition from lying awake and thinking about the last war; lying awake and worrying about the possible next war; lying awake and wondering what perverse masochism had brought them here at all.

At the dead and silent hour of four, when not a light glimmered anywhere in the village, they were both awake, lying side by side in the great feather-padded bed, discussing Dr Schröder in depth. They analysed him politically, psychologically, and medically – particularly medically – and at such length that when the maid came in with their early breakfast they were extremely reluctant to wake up. But they forced themselves to wake, to eat and to dress, and then went downstairs where their landlady was drinking coffee in her kitchen. They put their problem to her. Yesterday they had agreed to stay with her for a week. Today they wanted to leave. Since it was the height of the season presumably she would let her room today? If not, of course they would be delighted to pay what they were morally bound to do.

Frau Stohr dismissed the subject of payment as irrelevant. At this time of the year her bell rang a dozen times a day with inquiries for rooms by people who had arrived at the station and hoped, usually over-optimistically, to find empty rooms in the village. Frau Stohr was upset that her two guests wished to leave. They were not comfortable? They were badly served?

They hastened to assure her that the place was everything they wanted. At the moment they felt it was. Frau Stohr was the most pleasant sight in an early morning after a night of conscience-searching. She was a thin and elderly lady, her white hair drawn back into a tight knot which was stuck through with stiff utilitarian pins almost the size of knitting needles. Her face was severe, but tranquil and kindly. She wore a long, full, black woollen skirt, presumably a practical descendant of the great woollen skirts of the local peasant costume. She wore a long-sleeved striped woollen blouse fastened high at the throat with a gold brooch.

They found it very hard to say that they wanted to leave the valley the day after arriving in it. The rectitude of this admirable old lady made it difficult. So they said they had decided to take a room farther up the valley where the snow slopes organized for skiing would be closer to the villages. For, above all, they did not want to hurt Frau Stohr's national feelings; they intended to slip quietly down to the station and take the first train away from the place, away and out of Germany into France.

Frau Stohr instantly agreed. She had always thought it more suitable for the serious skiers to find homes farther up the valley. But there were people who came to the winter sports not for the sport, but for the atmosphere of the sport. As for herself she never tired of seeing the young people at their tricks on the snow. Of course, when she had been a girl, it was not a question of tricks at all; skis were simply a means of getting from one place to another quickly ... but now, of course, all that had changed, and someone like herself who had been almost born on skis, like all the children of the valley, would find it embarrassing to stand on skis again with nothing to show in the way of jumps and turns. Of course, at her age she seldom left the house, and so she did not have to expose her deficiencies. But her two guests, being serious skiers, must be feeling frustrated, knowing that all the long runs, and the big ski lifts were at the head of the valley. Luckily she knew of a lady in the last village of the valley who had a free room and would be just the person to look after them.

Here she mentioned the name of the lady recommended by Dr Schröder the night before, and it was extraordinary how this name, yesterday associated with every kind of unpleasantness, became attractive and reassuring, simply because it came from the lips of Frau Stohr.

Mary and Hamish exchanged looks and came to a decision without speaking. In the sober light of early morning, all the very sound arguments against leaving the valley returned to them. And after all, Dr Schröder was staying in O— itself, and not in the village thirty miles up the valley. At worst he might come and visit them.

Frau Stohr offered to telephone Frau Länge, who was a good woman and an unfortunate one. Her husband had been killed in the last war. Here Frau Stohr smiled at them with the gentle tolerance of the civilized who take it for granted that war between nations need not destroy their common humanity and understanding. Yes, yes, as long as men were so stupid there would be wars and, afterwards, widows like poor Frau Länge, who had lost not only her husband but her two sons, and now lived alone with her daughter, taking in lodgers.

Frau Stohr and the British couple, united on the decent common ground of the international humanitarian conscience, smiled at each other, thinking compassionately of Frau

Länge. Then Frau Stohr went to the telephone and engaged the room on behalf of her two guests, for whom she was prepared to vouch personally. Then they settled the bill, thanked each other, and separated – Mary and Hamish with their cases in their hands and their skis over their shoulders towards the bus stop, and Frau Stohr to her knitting and her cup of coffee in her big heated kitchen.

It was a clear morning, the sun sparkling pinkly over the slopes of snow where the pine trees stood up, stiff and dark. The first bus of the day was just leaving, and they found places in it. They sat behind two small pigtailed blonde girls who saw nobody else in the bus, but held each other's hands and sang one folk song after another in small, clear voices. Everyone in the bus turned to smile with affectionate indulgence at them. The bus climbed slowly up and up, along the side of the snow-filled valleys; and as the skiing villages came into sight, one after another, the bus stopped, shedding some passengers and taking on others, but always full; up and up while the two small girls sang, holding hands, looking earnestly into each other's faces, so as to be sure they were keeping time, and never once repeating a song.

The British couple thought it unlikely that they could find, in their own country, two small girls who could sing, without repeating themselves, for two solid hours of a bus journey, even if their British stiff-lippedness would allow them to open their mouths in public in the first place. These two singing children comforted Mary and Hamish quite remarkably. This was the real Germany – rather old-fashioned, a bit sentimental, warm, simple, kindly. Dr Schröder and what he stood for was an unlucky and not very important phenomenon. Everything they had felt yesterday was the result of being overtired. Now they examined the pleasant villages through which they passed with anticipation, hoping that the one they were committed to would be equally as full of modest wooden chalets and apparently inexpensive restaurants.

It was. At the very head of the valley where the mountain barrier beyond which lay Innsbruck rose tall and impregnable, there was a small village, as charming as all the others. Here,

somewhere, was the house of Frau Länge. They made inquiries at a hotel and were directed. A path ran off from the
village uphill among the pine woods to a small house about a
mile away. The isolation of this house appealed naturally to the
instincts of the British couple, who trudged towards it over
cushions of glittering snow, feeling grateful to Frau Stohr. The
path was narrow, and they had constantly to stand aside while
skiers in bright clothes whizzed past them, laughing and
waving. The proficiency of the sun-bronzed gods and goddesses
of the snowfields discouraged Mary and Hamish, and perhaps
half the attraction of that isolated house was that they could
make their tame flights over the snow in comparative privacy.

The house was square, small, wooden; built on a low mound
of snow in a space surrounded by pine woods. Frau Länge was
waiting for them at her front door, smiling. For some reason
they had imagined her in the image of Frau Stohr; but she was
a good twenty years younger, a robust, straw-headed, red-
cheeked woman wearing a tight scarlet sweater and a tight
bright blue skirt. Behind her was a girl, obviously her daughter,
a healthy, brown, flaxen-haired girl. Both women occupied
themselves with a frank and intensive examination of their new
guests for the space of time it took them to cross the snow to the
house. The room they were given was at the front of the house,
looking away from the village up into a side valley. It was a
room like the one they had occupied for the one night at Frau
Stohr's; low, large, gleaming with waxed wood, and warmed by
an enormous tiled stove. Frau Länge took their passports to
write down their particulars, and when she returned them it
was with a change of manner which made Mary Parrish and
Hamish Anderson know they had been accepted into a freemasonry with their hostess. She said, while her frankly vulgar
blue eyes continued a minute examination of them and their
belongings, that her dear aunt, Frau Stohr, who was not really
her aunt, just a second cousin, called Aunt out of respect for her
age and position as widow of the pastor, had spoken for them;
that she had every confidence in any person recommended from
that quarter. And she had heard, too, from dear Dr Schröder,
who was an old friend, a friend of many years, ah – what a

brave man. Did they notice his face? Yes, truly? Did they know that for two years he had lain in hospital while a new face was moulded for him and covered with skin taken from his thighs? Poor man. Yes, it was the barbarity of those Russians that was responsible for Dr Schröder's face. Here she gave an exaggerated sigh and a shrug and left them.

They reminded themselves that they had hardly slept for three nights of their precious holiday, and this doubtless accounted for their present lack of enthusiasm for the idea of putting on skis. They went to sleep and slept the day through; that evening they were served a heavy meal in the living room by Frau Länge herself, who stood chatting to them until they asked her to sit down. Which she did, and proceeded to cross-examine them about the affairs of the British royal family. It was impossible to exaggerate the degree of enthusiasm aroused in Frau Länge by the royal family. She followed every move made by any member of it through a dozen illustrated papers. She knew what they all ate, how they liked things cooked, and how served. She knew the type of corset favoured by the Queen, the names of the doctors attending her, the methods of upbringing planned for the royal children, the favourite colours of the two royal Elizabeths and the royal Margaret.

The British couple, who were by temperament republicans and who would have described themselves as such had the word not, at that time, been rather *vieux jeu*, acquired an impressive amount of information about 'their' royal family, and felt inadequate, for they were unable to answer any of her questions.

To escape from Frau Länge they went back to their room. They discovered that this house was not at all as isolated as it had seemed during the day when the pine trees had concealed from them buildings farther up the little side valley. Lights sparkled in the trees, and it seemed that there were at least two large hotels less than half a mile away. Music streamed towards them across the dark snow.

In the morning they found there were two American hotels; that is, hotels specifically for the recreation of American troops. Frau Länge used the word American with a mixture of admiration and hatred. And she took it for granted that they, who were after all partners with the Americans (and the Russians of course) in this business of policing the defeated country, should share this emotion with her. It was because they shared with her, Frau Länge, the quality of not being rich.

'Ah,' she said, with a false and hearty shrug of her shoulders, a false humility in her voice, 'it is a terrible thing, the way they come here and behave as if they owned our country.' And she stood at the window, while the British couple ate their breakfast, watching the American soldiers and their wives and their girl friends swooping past down the slopes; and on her face was a bitter envy, an admiring spite, as if she were thinking. Yes? Then wait and see!

Later that day they saw the daughter standing displayed on her doorstep in well-cut ski trousers and sweater, like a girl in a poster, looking at the American soldiers. And they heard her call out, every time a single man went past: 'Yank-ee. Yank-ee.' The soldier would look up and wave, and she waved back shouting: 'I love you, Buddy.' At last one came over; and the two went off on skis, down to the village.

Frau Länge, who had seen them watching, said, 'Ach, these young girls, I was one myself.' She waited until they smiled their tolerant complicity – and waited in such a way they felt they could do no less, seeing that their passports proved they had no right to different standards; and said, 'Yes, when one is young one is foolish. I remember how I fell in love with every man I saw. Ach, yes, it was so. I was living in Munich when I was a girl. Yes, youth has no discrimination. I was in love with our Führer, yes, it is true. And before that in love with a Communist leader who lived in our street. And now I tell my Lili it is lucky that she falls in love with the American army, because she is in love with democracy.' Frau Länge giggled and sighed.

At all the heavy meals she served them – sausage and *sauerkraut* and potatoes; *sauerkraut*, potatoes, and beef stew – she stood by them, talking, or sat modestly at the other end of the polished wood table, one plump forearm resting before her, one hand stroking and arranging her bright yellow hair, and talked and talked. She told them the history of her life while they ate.

Her mother died of hunger in the First World War. Her father was a carpenter. Her elder brother was a political; he was a Social Democrat, and so she had been a Social Democrat, too. And then he had been a Communist and so she voted for the Communists, God forgive her. And then there came the Führer and her brother told her he was a good man, and so she became a Nazi. Of course, she was very young and foolish in those days. She told them, giggling, how she had stood in those vast crowds while the Führer spoke, shrieking with enthusiasm. 'For my brother was in the uniform, yes, and he was so good-looking, you would never believe it!'

The British couple remembered listening on the radio to the sound of those fanatic crowds roaring and yelling approval to the dedicated, hysterical, drum-beating voice; they watched Frau Länge and imagined her a young girl, sweating and scarlet-faced, yelling with the thousands, arm in arm with her girl friend, who was of course in love with the uniformed brother. Then, afterwards cooling her sore throat with beer in a café, she would perhaps have giggled with the girl friend at the memory of her intoxication. Or perhaps she had not giggled. At any rate, she had married and come here to the mountains and had three children.

And now her man was dead, killed on the front near Stalingrad. And one son had been killed in North Africa, and another at Avranches. And when her Lili leaned out of the window giggling and waving at a passing American soldier she giggled and said, with a glance at the British couple, 'Lucky for us we aren't in the Russian zone, because if so Lili would have loved a Russki.' And Lili giggled and leaned farther out of the window and waved and called, 'Buddy, I love you.'

Frau Länge, conscious perhaps that the continued politeness of her British guests need not necessarily mean agreement, would sometimes straighten her shoulders into prim self-righteousness, look in front of her with lowered and self-conscious eyelids, and say with a murmuring shocked rectitude: 'Yes, Lili, say what you like, but we are lucky this time to have English people as guests. They are people like ourselves who have suffered from this terrible war. And they will go back home and tell their friends what we suffer because our country is divided. For it is clear they are shocked. They did not know of the humiliations we have to undergo.'

At this Mary Parrish and Hamish Anderson would say nothing at all, but politely passed each other the salt or the dumplings and shortly afterwards excused themselves and went to their room. They were sleeping a good deal, for, after all, they were people kept permanently short of sleep. And they ate heartily if not well. They skied a little and lay often in the sun, acquiring a layer of brown that they would lose within a week of returning to London. They were feeling rested. They were in a lethargy of physical contentment. They listened to Frau Länge, accepted her scolding because of their total ignorance of the manners and habits of the royal families of Europe, watched the daughter go off with this US soldier or that; and when Dr Schröder arrived one afternoon to take coffee with Frau Länge, they were happy to join the party. Frau Länge had explained to them that it was the dream of Dr Schröder's life to reach the United States. Unfortunately, every attempt he had made to do this had failed. It was, perhaps, easy for them to arrange a visa for Dr Schröder from London? No? It was difficult there, too? Ach, if she were a young woman she too would to go the United States; that was the country of the future, was it not? She did not blame Dr Schröder that he wished so much to go there. And if she were in a position to assist him, they must believe her that she would, for friends should always help each other.

They had decided that it was Frau Länge's plan to marry Lili to the doctor. But it seemed Lili did not share this idea, for although she knew he was coming, she did not appear that evening. And perhaps Frau Länge was not altogether sorry, for while the word flirtation could hardly be used of a relationship like this one, it was extremely amiable. Frau Länge sighed a great deal, her silly blue eyes fastened on the terrible shining mask of her friend's face, saying, 'Ach, mein Gott, mein Gott, mein Gott!' while Dr Schröder accepted the tribute like a film star bored with flattery, making polite gestures of repudiation with one hand, using the other to eat with.

He stayed the night, ostensibly on the old sofa in the kitchen.

In the morning he woke Mary and Hamish at seven to say that unfortunately he was leaving the valley because he was due to take up his duties at the hospital, that he was delighted to have been of service to them, that he hoped they would arrange their return journey so as to pass through the city where his hospital was, and asked for their assurances that they would.

The departure of Dr Schröder brought it home to them that their own holiday would end in a week and that they were bored, or on the point of becoming bored. They had much better rouse themselves, leave the snow mountains, and go down to one of the cities below, take a cheap room, and make an effort to meet some ordinary people. By this they meant neither the rich industrialists who frequented this valley, nor people like Frau Stohr, who were manifestly something left over from an older and more peaceful time; nor like Frau Länge and her daughter Lili; nor like Dr Schröder. Saying goodbye to Frau Länge was almost painless, for, as she said instantly, a day never passed without at least one person knocking on her door and asking for a room because, as everyone in the village knew, she gave good value for money. This was true; Frau Länge was a natural landlady; she had given them far more than had been contracted for in the way of odd cups of coffee and above all in hours of fraternal conversation. But at last she accepted their plea that they wanted to spend a week in their professional guise, seeing hospitals and making contact with their fellow-doctors. 'In that case,' she said at once, 'it is lucky that you know Dr Schröder, for there could be no better person to show you everything that you need to see.' They said that they would look up Dr Schröder the moment they arrived, if they should happen to pass through his town, and with this the goodbyes were made.

They made the journey by bus down the long winding valley to the mother village, O—, caught the little rickety train, spent another uncomfortable night sitting up side by side on the hard wooden benches, and at last reached the city of Z—, where they found a small room in a cheap hotel. And now they were pledged to contact ordinary people and widen their view of present-day Germany. They took short walks through the streets of the city surrounded by ordinary people, looked into their faces, as tourists do, made up stories about them, and got into brief conversations from which they made large generalizations. And, like every earnest tourist, they indulged in fantasies of how they would stop some pleasant-faced person in the street and say: We are ordinary people, completely representative of the people of our country. You are obviously an ordinary person, representative of yours. Please divulge and unfold yourself to us, and we will do the same.

Whereupon this pleasant-faced person would let out an exclamation of delight, strike his forehead with his fist and say: But my friends! There is nothing I would like better. With which he would take them to his house, flat, or room; and a deathless friendship would begin, strong enough to outlast any international misunderstandings, accidents, incidents, wars, or other phenomena totally undesired by the ordinary people on both sides.

They did not contact Dr Schröder, since they had taken good care not to choose the town he was working in. But from time to time they thought how pleasant it would have been if Dr Schröder had not been such an utterly disgusting person; if he had been a hard-working, devoted, idealistic doctor like themselves, who could initiate them into the medical life of Germany, or at least, of one city, without politics entering their intercourse at all.

Thinking wistfully along these lines led them into a course of action foreign to their naturally diffident selves. It so happened that about a year before, Dr Anderson had got a letter from a certain Dr Kroll who was attached to a hospital just outside the city of Z— congratulating him on a paper he had published recently and enclosing a paper of his own which dealt with a closely related line of research. Hamish remembered reading Dr Kroll's paper and diagnosing it as typical of the work put out by elderly and established doctors who are no longer capable of ploughing original furrows in the field of medicine but, because they do not wish to seem as if they have lost all interest in original research, from time to time put out a small and harmless paper which amounts to an urbane comment on the work of other people. In short, Dr Anderson had despised the paper sent to him by his colleague in Germany and had done no more than write him a brief letter of thanks. Now he remembered the incident and told Mary Parrish about it, and both wondered if they might telephone Dr Kroll and introduce themselves. When they decided that they should, it was with a definite feeling that they were confessing a defeat. Now they were going to be professional people, nothing more. The 'ordinary people' had totally eluded them. Conversations with three workmen (on buses), two housewives (in cafés), a businessman (on a train), two waitresses and two maids (at the hotel) had left them dissatisfied. None of these people had come out with the final, pithy, conclusive statement about modern Germany that they so badly needed. In fact none of them had said more than what their counterparts in Britain would have done. The nearest to a political comment any of them had made was the complaint by one of the maids that she did not earn enough money and would very likely go to England where, she understood, wages were much higher.

No, contact with that real, sound, old-fashioned, healthy Germany, as symbolized by the two little girls singing on the bus, had failed them. But certainly it must be there. Something which was a combination of the rather weary irony of the refugees both had known, the bitter affirmation of the songs of Bertolt Brecht, the fighting passion of a Dimitrov (though of course Dimitrov was not a German); the innocence of the little girls, the crashing chords of Beethoven's Fifth. These qualities were fused in their minds into the image of a tired, sceptical, sardonic, but tough, personage, a sort of civilized philosopher prepared at any moment to pick up a rifle and fight for the good and the right and the true. But they had not met anyone remotely like this. As for the two weeks up in the valley, they had simply wiped them out. After all, was it likely that a valley given up wholly to the pursuit of pleasure, and all the year round at that, could be representative of anything but itself?

They would simply accept the fact that they had failed, and

ring up Dr Kroll, and spend the remaining days of their holiday acquiring information about medicine. They rang up Dr Kroll who, rather to their surprise, remembered the interesting correspondence he had had with Dr Anderson and invited them to spend the next morning with him. He sounded not at all like the busy head of a hospital, but more like a host. Having made this arrangement, Doctors Parrish and Anderson were on the point of going out to find some cheap restaurant – for their reserve of money was now very small indeed – when Dr Schröder was announced to them. He had travelled that afternoon all the way from S— especially to greet them, having heard from his buddy Frau Länge that they were here. In other words, he must have telephoned or wired Frau Länge, who knew their address since she was forwarding letters for them; his need for them was so great that he had also travelled all the way from S—, an expensive business, as he did not hesitate to point out.

The British couple, once again faced with the scarred face and bitter eyes of Dr Schröder, once again felt a mixture of loathing and compassion and limply made excuses because they had chosen to stop in this town and not in S—. They said they could not possibly afford to spend the evening, as he wanted to do, in one of the expensive restaurants; refused to go as his guests since he had already spent so much money on coming to meet them; and compromised on an agreement to drink beer with him. This they did in various beer cellars where the cohorts of the Führer used to gather in the old days. Dr Schröder told them this in a way that could be taken either as if he were pointing out a tourist attraction, or as if he were offering them the opportunity to mourn a lost glory with him. His manner towards them now fluctuated between hostility and a self-abasing politeness. They, for their part, maintained their own politeness, drank their beer, occasionally caught each other's eye, and suffered through an evening which, had it not been for Dr Schröder, might have been a very pleasant one. From time to time he brought the conversation around to the possibilities of his working in Britain; and they repeated their warnings, until at last, although he had not mentioned the United States, they explained that getting visas to live in that

part of the world would be no easier in Britain than it was here.
Dr Schröder was not at all discomposed when they showed
that they were aware of his real objective. Not at all; he behaved as if he had told them from the start that the United
States was his ideal country. Just as if he had never sung songs
of praise to Britain, he now disparaged Britain as part of
Europe, which was dead and finished, a parasite on the healthy
body of America. Quite obviously all people of foresight would
make their way to America – he assumed that they, too, had
seen this obvious truth, and had possibly already made their
plans? Of course he did not blame anyone for looking after
himself first, that was a rule of nature; but friends should help
each other. And who knew but that once they were all in America Dr Schröder might be in a position to help Doctors
Anderson and Parrish? The wheel of chance might very well
bring such a thing to pass. Yes, it was always advisable in this
world to plan well ahead. As for himself, he was not ashamed to
admit that it was his first principle; that was why he was sitting
this evening in the city of Z—, at their service. That was why he
had arranged a day's leave from his own hospital – not the
easiest thing to do, this, since he had just returned from a fortnight's holiday – in order to be their guide around the hospitals
of Z—.

Mary and Hamish, after a long stunned silence, said that his
kindness to them was overwhelming. But unfortunately they
had arranged to spend tomorrow with Dr Kroll of such-and-
such a hospital.

The eyes of Dr Schröder showed a sudden violent animation. The shiny stretched mask of his face deepened its scarlet and, after a wild angry flickering of blue light at the name
Kroll, the eyes settled into a steady, almost anguished glare of
inquiry.

It appeared that at last they had hit upon, quite by chance,
the way to silence Dr Schröder.

'Dr Kroll,' he said, with the sigh of a man who, after long
searching, finds the key. 'Dr Kroll. I see. Yes.'

At last he had placed them. It seemed that Dr Kroll's status
was so high, and therefore, presumably, their status also, that

he could not possibly aspire to any equality with them. Perfectly understandable that they did not need to emigrate to America, being the close friends of Dr Kroll. His manner became bitter, brooding, and respectful, and at the most suggested that they might have said, nearly three weeks ago on that first evening in O—, that they were intimates of Dr Kroll, thereby saving him all this anguish and trouble and expense.

Dr Kroll, it emerged, was a man loaded with honours and prestige, at the very height of his profession. Of course, it was unfortunate that such a man should be afflicted in the way he was . . .

And how was Dr Kroll afflicted?

Why, didn't they know? Surely, they must! Dr Kroll was for six months in every year a voluntary patient in his own hospital – yes, that was something to admire, was it not? – that a man of such brilliance should, at a certain point in every year, hand over his keys to his subordinates and submit to seeing a door locked upon himself, just as, for the other six months, he locked doors on other people. It was very sad, yes. But of course they must know all this quite well, since they had the privilege of Dr Kroll's friendship.

Mary and Hamish did not like to admit that they had not known it was a mental hospital that Dr Kroll administered. If they did, they would lose the advantage of their immunity from Dr Schröder who had, obviously, already relinquished them entirely to a higher sphere. Meanwhile, since his evening was already wasted, and there was time to fill in, he was prepared to talk.

By the time the evening had drawn to a close in a beer cellar where one drank surrounded by great wooden barrels from which the beer was drawn off direct into giant-sized mugs – the apotheosis of all beer cellars – they had formed an image of Dr Kroll as a very old, Lear-like man, proud and bitter in the dignified acceptance of his affliction; and although neither of them had any direct interest in the problems of the mentally sick, since Mary Parrish specialized in small children and Hamish Anderson in geriatrics, they were sympathetically looking forward to meeting this courageous old man.

The evening ended without any unpleasantness because of

the invisible presence of Dr Kroll. Dr Schröder returned them to the door of their hotel, shook their hands, and wished them a happy conclusion to their holiday. The violent disharmony of his personality had been swallowed entirely by the self-abasing humility into which he had retreated, with which he was consoling himself. He said that he would look them up when he came to London, but it was merely conventional. He wished them a pleasant reunion with Dr Kroll and strode off through the black, cold, blowing night towards the railway station, springing on his long lean legs like a black-mantled grass-hopper – a hooded, bitter, energetic shape whirled about by flurries of fine white snow that glittered in the streetlights like blown salt or sand.

Next morning it was still snowing. The British couple left their hotel early to find the right bus stop, which was at the other end of the city in a poor suburb. The snow fell listlessly from a low grey sky, and fine shreds of dingy snow lay sparse on the dark earth. The bombs of the recent war had laid the streets here flat for miles around. The streets were etched in broken outlines, and the newly laid railway lines ran clean and shining through them. The station had been bombed, and there was a wooden shed doing temporary duty until another could be built. A dark-wrapped, dogged crowd stood bunched around the bus stop. Nearby a mass of workmen were busy on a new building that rose fine and clean and white out of the miles of damaged houses. They looked like black and energetic insects at work against the stark white of the walls. The British couple stood hunching their cold shoulders and shifting their cold feet with the German crowd, and watched the builders. They thought that it was the bombs of their country which had created this havoc; thought of the havoc created in their country by the bombs of the people they now stood shoulder to shoulder with, and sank back slowly into a mood of listless depression. The bus was a long time coming. It seemed to grow colder. From time to time people drifted past to the station shed or added themselves to the end of the bus queues, or a woman went past with a shopping basket. Behind the ruined buildings rose the shapes and outlines of the city that had been destroyed and the outlines of the city that would be rebuilt. It was as if they stood solid among the ruins and ghosts of dead cities and cities not yet born. And Hamish's eyes were at work again on the faces of the people about them, fixed on the face of an old shawled woman who was passing; and it seemed as if the crowd, like the streets, became transparent and fluid, for beside them, behind them, among them stood the dead. The dead of two wars peopled the ruined square and jostled the living, a silent snowbound multitude.

The silence locked the air. There was a low, deep thudding that seemed to come from under the earth. It was from a machine at work on the building site. The machine, low in the dirty snow, lifted black grappling arms like a wrestler or like someone in prayer; and the sound of its labouring travelled like a sensation of movement through the cold earth, as if the soil were hoarsely breathing. And the workmen swarmed and worked around the machine and over the steep sides of the new building. They were like children playing with bricks. Half an hour before a giant of a man in black jackboots had strode past their block building and carelessly kicked it down. Now the children were building it again, under the legs of a striding race of great black-booted giants. At any moment another pair of trampling black legs might come straddling over the building and down it would go, down into ruin, to the accompaniment of crashing thunder and bolts of lightning. All over the soil of patient Europe, soil soaked again and again by blood, soil broken again and again by angry metal, the small figures were at work, building their bright new houses among the shells and the ruins of war; and in their eyes was the shadow from the great marching jackbooted feet, and beside each of them, beside every one of them, their dead, the invisible, swarming, memoried dead.

The crowd continued to wait. The machine kept up its hoarse breathing. From time to time a shabby bus came up, a few people climbed in, the bus went off, and more people came dark-clothed through the thinly falling snow to join the crowd, which was very similar to a British crowd in its stolid disciplined quality of patience.

At last a bus with the number they had been told to look for drew up, and they got into it with a few other people. The bus was half empty. Almost at once it left the city behind. Dr Kroll's hospital, like so many of the similar hospitals in Britain, was built well outside the city boundaries so that the lives of healthy people might not be disturbed by thoughts of those who had to retreat behind the shelter of high walls. The way was straight on a good narrow road, recently rebuilt, over flat black plains streaked and spotted with snow. The quiet, windless air was full of fine particles of snow that fell so slowly it seemed that the sky was falling, as if the slow weight of the snow dragged the grey covering over the black flat plains down to the earth. They travelled forward in a world without colour.

Dr Kroll's hospital made itself visible a long way off over the plain. It consisted of a dozen or more dark, straight buildings set at regular angles to each other, like the arrangement of the sheds in the concentration camps of the war. Indeed, at a distance, the resemblance to the mechanical order of a concentration camp was very great; but as the bus drew nearer the buildings grew and spread into their real size and surrounded themselves with a regular pattern of lawns and shrubs.

The bus set them down outside a heavy iron gate; and at the entrance of the main building, which was high and square, they were welcomed by a doctor whose enthusiasm was expressly delegated from Dr Kroll, who was impatiently waiting for them upstairs. They went up several staircases and along many corridors, and thought that whatever bleak impression this place might give from the outside, great care had been given to banishing bleakness from within. The walls were all covered by bright pictures, which there was no time to examine now, as they hurried after their busy guide; flowers stood on high pedestals at every turning of the corridor, and the walls and ceiling and woodwork were painted in clean white and blue. They were thinking sympathetically of the storm-driven Lear whom they were so soon to meet, as they passed through these human and pleasant corridors; they were even thinking that perhaps it was an advantage to have as director of a mental hospital a man who knew what it was like to spend time inside it as a victim. But their guide remarked, 'This is, of course, the administrative block and the doctors' quarters. Dr Kroll will be happy to show you the hospital itself later.'

With this he shook them by the hand, nodded a goodbye and went, leaving them outside the half-open door of what looked like a middle-class living room.

A hearty voice called out that they must come in; and they went into a suite of two rooms, half-divided by sheets of sliding glass, brightly lighted, pleasantly furnished, and with nothing in it reminiscent of an office but a single small desk in the farther of the two rooms. Behind the desk sat a handsome man of late middle age who was rising to greet them. It occurred to them, much too late, that this must be Dr Kroll; and so their greetings, because they were shocked, were much less enthusiastic than his. His greetings were in any case much more like a host's than a colleague's. He was apparently delighted to see them and pressed them to sit down while he ordered them some coffee. This he did by going to the house telephone on the desk in the room beyond the pane of glass; and the two looked at each other, exchanging surprise, and then, finally, pleasure.

Dr Kroll was, to begin with, extremely distinguished, and they remembered something Dr Schröder had said the night before, to the effect that he came from an old and respected family; that he was, in short, an aristocrat. They had to accept the word when looking at Dr Kroll himself, even though they could not conceivably take it from Dr Schröder. Dr Kroll was rather tall and managed to combine heaviness and leanness in a remarkable way, for while he was a man of whom one instinctively wondered how much he must weigh when he stood on a scale, he was not fat, or even plump. But he was heavy; and his face, which had strong and prominent bones, carried a weight of large-pored flesh. Yet one would have said, because of the prominent dome of pale forehead and because of the large, commanding nose, and because of the deep dark lively eyes, that it was a lean face. And his movements were not those of a heavy man; he had quick impatient gestures and his large, handsome hands were in constant movement. He returned, smiling, from giving orders about the coffee, sat down in an easy chair opposite the two British doctors, and proceeded to entertain them in the most urbane and pleasant way in the world.

He spoke admirable English, he knew a good deal about Britain, and he now discussed the present state of affairs in Britain with assurance.

His admiration for Britain was immense. And this time the British couple were flattered. This was something very different from hearing praise from that appalling Dr Schröder. Until the coffee came, and while they were drinking it, and for half an hour afterwards, they discussed Britain and its institutions. The British couple listened to a view of Britain that they disagreed with profoundly, but without irritation, since it was natural that a man like this should hold conservative ideas. Dr Kroll believed that a limited monarchy was the best guarantee against disorder and was, in fact, the reason for the well-known British tolerance, which was a quality he admired more than any other. Speaking as a German, and therefore peculiarly equipped to discuss the dangers of anarchy, he would say that the best thing the Allied Armies could have done would have been to impose upon Germany a royal family, created, if necessary, from the shreds and fragments of the unfortunately dwindling royal families of Europe. Further, he believed that this should have been done at the end of the First World War, at the Treaty of Versailles. When Britain, usually so perspicacious in matters of this kind, had left Germany without a royal safeguard, they had made the worst mistake of their history. For a royal family would have imposed good conduct and respect for institutions and made an upstart like Hitler impossible.

At this point the eyes of the British pair met again, though briefly. There was no doubt that to hear Hitler described as an upstart revived some of the sensations they felt when listening to Dr Schröder or Frau Länge. A few seconds later they heard him being referred to as a mongrel upstart, an unease definitely set in, beneath the well-being induced by the good coffee and their liking for their host.

Dr Kroll developed his theme for some time, darting his lively and intelligent glances at them, offering them more coffee, offering them cigarettes, and demanded from them an account of how the Health Service worked in Britain. He took it for granted that neither would approve of a scheme which gave people something for nothing, and he commiserated with them for their subjection to state tyranny. They ventured to point out to him certain advantages they felt it had; and at last he nodded and admitted that a country as stable and well-ordered as their own might very well be able to afford extravagant experiments that would wreck other countries – his own, for instance. But he did feel disturbed when he saw their country, which he regarded as the bulwark of decency against socialism in Europe, giving in to the mob.

Here they suggested that they did not want to take up more of his time than was necessary; he must be very busy. For surely the director of such a large hospital could not possibly afford to devote so much time to every foreign doctor who wished to see over it? Or could it be his devotion to Britain that made him so ready to devote his time to them?

At any rate, he seemed disappointed at being reminded of what they had come for. He even sighed and sat silent a little, so that Dr Anderson, out of politeness, mentioned the paper he had received from him so that they might, if Dr Kroll wished it, discuss the subject of their research. But Dr Kroll merely sighed again, and said that these days he had very little time for original work; such was the penalty one must pay for accepting the burdens of administration. He rose, all his animation gone, and invited them to step into the other room beyond the glass panel where he would collect his keys. So the three of them went into the inner drawing room, which was an office because of the desk and the telephone; and there Mary Parrish's attention was drawn to a picture on the wall above the desk. At a distance of six or eight feet it was a gay fresh picture of a cornfield painted from root-vision, or field-mouse view. The sheaves of corn rose startlingly up, bright and strong, mingled with cornflowers and red poppies, as if one were crouching in the very centre of a field. But as one walked towards the picture it vanished, it became a confusion of bright paint. It was finger-painted. The surface of the canvas was as rough as a ploughed field. Mary Parrish walked up to it, into the bright paint, took a few steps back, and back again; and, behold, the picture re-created itself, the cornfield strong and innocent, with something of the sensual innocence of Renoir's pictures. She was so absorbed, that she started when Dr Kroll dropped a heavy hand on her shoulder and demanded, Was she fond of painting? Instantly both she and Hamish assured him that they were enthusiastically fond of pictures.

Dr Kroll dropped back on the surface of his very neat desk – so neat one could not help wondering how much it was used – the very large black bunch of keys he had removed from it; and he stood in front of the cornfield picture, his hands on Mary's shoulder.

'This,' he said, 'is what I am really interested in. Yes, yes; this, you must agree, is more interesting than medicine.'

They agreed, since they had just understood that this was the artist in person. Dr Kroll proceeded to take out from a large cupboard set into the wall a thick stack of pictures, all finger-painted, all with the rough staring surface of thick paint, all of which created themselves at ten paces into highly organized and original pictures.

Soon both rooms were full of pictures that leaned against chairs, tables, walls and along the sliding glass panels. Dr Kroll, his fine hands knotted together in anxiety because of their possible reception of his work, followed them around as they gazed at one picture after another. It became evident that the pictures separated themselves into two categories. There were those, like the cornfield, done in bright clear colours, very fresh and lyrical. Then there were those which, close up, showed grim rutted surfaces of dirty black, grey, white, a sullen green and – recurring again and again – a characteristic sullen shade of red – a dark, lightless, rusty red like old blood. These pictures were all extraordinary and macabre, of graveyards and skulls and corpses, of war scenes and bombed buildings and screaming women and houses on fire with people falling from burning windows like ants into flames. It was quite extra-

ordinary how, in the space of a few seconds, these two conventional and pretty rooms had been transformed by these
pictures into an exhibition of ghoulishness, particularly as the
scenes of the pictures were continually vanishing altogether
into areas of thick paint that had been smeared, rubbed, piled,
worked all over the canvas an inch or so thick by the handsome
fingers of Dr Kroll. Standing at six feet from one picture, the
proper distance to view the work of Dr Kroll, the picture they
had been examining five moments before, and which they had
now moved away from, lost its meaning and disintegrated into
a surface of jumbled and crusted colour. They were continually
stepping forward or stepping back from chaos into moments of
brief, clear, startling illumination. And they could not help
wondering if Dr Kroll was gifted with a peculiar vision of his
own, a vision perhaps of his fingertips, which enabled him to
see his work as he stood up against it, rubbing and plastering
the thick paint on to the canvas; they even imagined him as a
monster with arms six feet long, standing back from his canvas
as he worked on it like a clambering spider. The quality of
these pictures was such that, as they examined them, they could
not help picturing the artist as a monster, a maniac, or kind of
gifted insect. Yet, turning to look at Dr Kroll, there he stood, a
handsome man who was the very essence of everything that was
conservative, correct, and urbane.

Mary, at least, was feeling a little giddy. She sought out the
battling blue eyes of her partner, Hamish, and understood that
he felt the same. For this was an exact repetition of their en-
counter with Dr Schröder with his scarred face that demanded compassion. In saying what they thought of his work to
Dr Kroll, they must remember that they were speaking to a
man who gallantly and bravely volunteered to hand the keys of
sanity over to a subordinate and retired into madness for six
months of the year, when, presumably, he painted these horrible pictures, whose very surfaces looked like the oozing,
shredding substance of decomposing flesh.

Meanwhile, there he stood beside them, searching their faces
anxiously.

They said, in response to his appeal, that this was obviously a real and strong talent. They said that his work was striking and original. They said they were deeply impressed.

He stood silent, not quite smiling, but with a quizzical look behind the fine eyes. He was judging them. He knew what they were feeling and was condemning them, in the same way as the initiated make allowances for the innocent.

Dr Anderson remarked that it must be admitted that the pictures were rather strong? Not to everybody's taste, perhaps? Perhaps rather savage?

Dr Kroll, smiling urbanely, replied that life tended sometimes to be savage. Yes, that was his experience. He deepened his smile and indicated the cornfield on the wall behind his desk and said that he could see Dr Anderson preferred pictures like that one?

Dr Anderson took his stand, and very stubbornly, on the fact that he preferred that picture to any of the others he had seen.

Mary Parrish moved to stand beside Dr Anderson and joined him in asserting that to her mind this picture was entirely superior to all the others; she preferred the few bright pictures, all of which seemed to her to be loaded with a quality of sheer joy, a sensuous joy, to the others which seemed to her – if he didn't mind her saying so – simply horrible.

Dr Kroll turned his ironical, dark gaze from one face to the other and remarked: 'So.' And again, accepting their bad taste: 'So.'

He remarked, 'I am subject to fits of depression. When I am depressed, naturally enough, I paint these pictures.' He indicated the lightless pictures of his madness. 'And when I am happy again, and when I have time – for, as I have said, I am extremely busy – I paint pictures such as these . . .' His gesture towards the cornfield was impatient, almost contemptuous. It was clear that he had hung the joyous cornfield on the wall of his reception room because he expected all his guests or visiting colleagues to have the bad taste to prefer it.

'So,' he said again, smiling dryly.

At which, Mary Parrish – since he was conveying a feeling of total isolation – said quickly, 'But we are very interested. We would love to see some more, if you have time.'

It seemed that he needed very much to hear her say this. For the ironical condemnation left his face and was succeeded by the pathetic anxiety of the amateur artist to be loved for his work. He said that he had had two exhibitions of his paintings, that he had been misunderstood by the critics, who had praised the paintings he did not care for, so that he would never again expose himself publicly to the stupidity of critics. He was dependent for sympathy on the understanding minority, some of them chance visitors to his hospital; some of them even – if they did not mind his saying so – inmates of it. He would, for two such delightful guests as his visitors from England, be happy to show more of his work.

With this he invited them to step into a passage behind his office. Its walls were covered from floor to ceiling with pictures. Also the walls of the passage beyond it.

It was terrifying to think of the energy this man must have when he was 'depressed'. Corridor after corridor opened up, the walls all covered with canvases loaded with thick, crusted paint. Some of the corridors were narrow, and it was impossible to stand far enough back for the pictures to compose themselves. But it seemed that Dr Kroll was able to see what his hands had done even when he was close against the canvas. He would lean into a big area of thick, dry paint from which emerged fragmentarily a jerky branch that looked like a bombed tree, or a bit of cracked bone, or a tormented mouth, and say: 'I call this picture "Love".' Or Victory, or Death; for he liked this kind of title. 'See? See that house there? See how I've put the church?' And the two guests gazed blankly at the smears of paint and wondered if perhaps this canvas represented the apotheosis of his madness and had no form in it at all. But if they stepped back against the opposite wall as far as they could, and leaned their heads back to gain an extra inch of distance, they could see that there was a house or a church. The house was also a skull; and the dead grey walls of the church oozed rusty blood, or spilled a gout of blood over the sills of its windows, or its door ejected blood like a person's mouth coughing blood.

Depression again weighed on the pair who, following after the dignified back of Dr Kroll as he led them into yet another picture-filled corridor, instinctively reached for each other's hands, reached for the warm contact of healthy flesh.

Soon their host led them back into the office, where he offered them more coffee. They refused politely but asked to see his hospital. Dr Kroll carelessly agreed. It was not, his manner suggested, that he did not take his hospital seriously, but that he would much rather, now he had been given the privilege of a visit from these rarely sympathetic people, share with them his much higher interests: his love for their country, his art. But he would nevertheless escort them around the hospital.

Again he took up the great bundle of black keys and went before them down the corridor they had first entered by. Now they saw that the pictures they had noticed then were all by him; these were the pictures he despised and hung for public view. But as they passed through a back door into a courtyard he paused, held up his keys, smiling, and indicated a small picture by the door. The picture was of the keys. From a scramble of whitey-grey paint came out, very black and hard and shining, a great jangling bunch of keys that also looked like bells, and, from certain angles, like staring eyes. Dr Kroll shared a smile with them as if to say: An interesting subject?

The three doctors went across a courtyard into the first block, which consisted of two parallel very long wards, each filled with small, tidy, white beds that had a chair and a locker beside them. On the beds sat, or leaned, or lay, the patients. Apart from the fact that they tended to be listless and staring, there was nothing to distinguish this ward from the ward of any public hospital. Dr Kroll exchanged brisk greetings with certain of his patients; discouraged an old man who grasped his arm as he passed and said that he had a momentous piece of news to tell him which he had heard that moment over his private wireless station, and which affected the whole course of history; and passed on smiling through this building into the next. There was nothing new here. This block, like the last, had achieved the ultimate in reducing several hundred human beings into complete identity with each other. Dr Kroll said, almost impatiently, that if you had seen one of these wards you had seen them all, and took off at a tangent across a courtyard to another of these regular blocklike buildings which was full of women. It occurred to the British pair that the two buildings on the other side of the court had men in them only; and they asked Dr Kroll if he kept the men in the line of buildings on one side of the court, and the women on the other – for there was a high wire fence down the court, with a door in it that he opened and locked behind him. 'Why, that is so,' said Dr Kroll indifferently.

'Do the men and the women meet – in the evenings, perhaps?'

'Meet? No.'

'Not at social evenings? At dances perhaps? At some meals during the week?'

Here Dr Kroll turned and gave his guests a tolerant smile. 'My friends,' he said, 'sex is a force destructive enough even when kept locked up. Do you suggest that we should mix the sexes in a place like this, where it is hard enough to keep people quiet and unexcited?'

Dr Anderson remarked that in progressive mental hospitals in Britain it was a policy to allow men and women to mix together as much as was possible. For what crime were these poor people being punished, he inquired hotly, that they were treated as if they had taken perpetual vows of celibacy?

Dr Parrish noted that the word 'progressive' fell very flat in this atmosphere. Such was the power of Dr Kroll's conservative personality that it sounded almost eccentric.

'So?' commented Dr Kroll. 'So the administrators of your English hospitals are prepared to give themselves so much unnecessary trouble?'

'Do the men and women never meet?' insisted Dr Parrish.

Dr Kroll said tolerantly that at night they behaved like naughty schoolchildren and passed each other notes through the wire.

The British couple fell back on their invincible politeness and felt their depression inside them like a fog. It was still snowing lightly through the heavy grey air.

Having seen three buildings all full of women of all ages,

lying and sitting about in the listlessness of complete idleness, they agreed with Dr Kroll it was enough; they were prepared to end their tour of inspection. He said that they must return with him for another cup of coffee, but first he had to make a short visit, and perhaps they would be kind enough to accompany him. He led the way to another building set rather apart from the others, whose main door he opened with an enormous key from his bunch of keys. As soon as they were inside it became evident that this was the children's building. Dr Kroll was striding down the main passage, calling aloud for some attendant who appeared to take instructions.

Meanwhile, Mary Parrish, doctor who specialized in small children, finding herself at the open door of a ward looked in, and invited Dr Anderson to do the same. It was a very large room, very clean, very fresh, with barred windows. It was full of cots and small beds. In the centre of the room a five-year-old child stood upright against the bars of a cot. His arms were confined by a straitjacket, and because he could not prevent himself from falling, he was tied upright against the bars with a cord. He was glaring around the room, glaring and grinding his teeth. Never had Mary seen such a desperate, wild, suffering little creature as this one. Immediately opposite the child sat a very large towheaded woman, dressed in heavy striped grey material, like a prison dress, knitting as comfortably as if she were in her kitchen.

Mary was speechless with horror at the sight. She could feel Hamish stiff and angry beside her.

Dr Kroll came back down the passage, saw them, and said amiably: 'You are interested? So? Of course, Dr Parrish, you said children are your field. Come in, come in.' He led the way into the room, and the fat woman stood up respectfully as he entered. He glanced at the straitjacketed child and moved past it to the opposite wall, where there was a line of small beds, placed head to foot. He pulled back the coverings one after another, showing a dozen children aged between a year and six years – armless children, limbless children, children with enormous mis-shapen heads, children with tiny heads and monstrous bodies. He pulled the coverings off, one after another, replacing them as soon as Mary Parrish and Hamish Anderson had seen what he was showing them, and remarked: 'Modern drugs are a terrible thing. Now these horrors are kept alive. Before, they died of pneumonia.'

Hamish said, 'The theory is, I believe, that medical science advances so fast that we should keep even the most apparently hopeless people alive in case we find something that can save them?'

Dr Kroll gave them the ironical smile they had seen before, and said, 'Yes, yes, yes. That is the theory. But for my part . . .'

Mary Parrish was watching the imprisoned little boy, who glared from a flushed wild face, straining his small limbs inside the thick stuff of the straitjacket. She said, 'In Britain strait-jackets are hardly ever used. Certainly not for children.'

'So?' commented Dr Kroll. 'So? But sometimes it is for the patient's own good.'

He advanced towards the boy and stood before the bars of the cot, looking at him. The child glared back like a wild animal into the eyes of the big doctor. 'This one bites if you go too near him,' commented Dr Kroll; and with a nod of his head invited them to follow him out.

'Yes, yes,' he remarked, unlocking the big door and locking it behind them, 'there are things we cannot say in public, but we may agree in private that there are many people in this hospital who would be no worse for a quick and painless death.'

Again he asked that they should excuse him, and he strode off to have a word with another doctor who was crossing the court in his white coat, with another big bunch of black keys in his hand.

Hamish said, 'This man told us that he has directed this hospital for thirty years.'

'Yes, I believe he did.'

'So he was here under Hitler.'

'The mongrel upstart, yes.'

'And he would not have kept his job unless he had agreed to sterilize Jews, serious mental defectives, and communists. Did you remember?'

'No, I'd forgotten.'

'So had I.'

They were silent a moment, thinking of how much they had liked, how much they still liked, Dr Kroll.

'Any Jew or mental defective or communist unlucky enough to fall into Dr Kroll's hands would have been forcibly sterilized. And the very ill would have been killed outright.'

'Not necessarily,' she objected feebly. 'After all, perhaps he refused. Perhaps he was strong enough to refuse.'

'Perhaps.'

'After all, even under the worst governments there are always people in high places who use their influence to protect weak people.'

'Perhaps.'

'And he might have been one.'

'We should keep an open mind?' he inquired, quick and sarcastic. They stood very close together under the cold snow in a corner of the grey courtyard. Twenty paces away, beyond walls and locked doors, a small boy, naked save for a straitjacket and tied to bars like an animal, was grinding his teeth and glaring at the fat knitting wardress.

Mary Parrish said miserably, 'We don't know, after all. We shouldn't condemn anyone without knowing. For all we know he might have saved the lives of hundreds of people.'

At this point Dr Kroll came back, swinging his keys.

Hamish inquired blandly, 'It would interest us very much to know if Hitler's regime made any difference to you professionally?'

Dr Kroll considered this question as he strolled along beside them. 'Life was easy for no one during that time,' he said.

'But as regards medical policy?'

Dr Kroll gave this question his serious thought, and said, 'No, they did not interfere very much. Of course, on certain questions, the gentlemen of the Nazi regime had sensible ideas.'

'Such as? For instance?'

'Oh, questions of hygiene? Yes, one could call them questions of social hygiene.' He had led them to the door of the main building, and now he said: 'You will, I hope, join me in a cup of coffee before you leave? Unless I can persuade you to stay and have a meal with us?'

'I think we should catch our bus back to town,' said Hamish, speaking firmly for both of them. Dr Kroll consulted his watch. 'Your bus will not be passing for another twenty minutes.' They accompanied him back through the picture-hung corridors to his office.

'And I would like so much to give you a memento of your visit,' he said, smiling at them both. 'Yes, I would like that. No, wait for one minute, I want to show you something.'

He went to the wall cupboard and took out a flat object wrapped in a piece of red silk. He unwrapped the silk and brought forth another picture. He set this picture against the side of the desk and invited them to stand back and look at it. They did so, already prepared to admire it, for it was a product of one of the times when he was not depressed. It was a very large picture, done in clear blues and greens, the picture of a forest – an imaginary forest with clear streams running through it, a forest where impossibly brilliant birds flew, and full of plants and trees created in Dr Kroll's mind. It was beautiful, full of joy and tranquillity and light. But in the centre of the sky glared a large black eye. It was an eye remote from the rest of the picture; and obviously what had happened was that Dr Kroll had painted his fantasy forest, and then afterwards, looking at it during some fit of misery, had painted in that black, condemnatory, judging eye.

Mary Parrish stared back at the eye and said, 'It's lovely; it's a picture of paradise.' She felt uncomfortable at using the word paradise in the presence of Hamish, who by temperament was critical of words like these.

But Dr Kroll smiled with pleasure, and laid his heavy hand on her shoulder, and said: 'You understand. Yes, you understand. That picture is called *The Eye of God in Paradise*. You like it?'

'Very much,' she said, afraid that he was about to present that picture to her. For how could they possibly transport such a big picture all the way back to Britain and what would she do with it when she got there? For it would be dishonest to paint out the black, wrathful eye: one respected, naturally, an artist's conception even if one disagreed with it. And she could not endure to live with that eye, no matter how much she liked the rest of the picture.

But it seemed that Dr Kroll had no intention of parting with the picture itself, which he wrapped up again in its red silk and hid in the cupboard. He took from a drawer a photograph of the picture and offered it to her, saying, 'If you really like my picture – and I can see that you do, for you have a real feeling, a real understanding – then kindly take this as a souvenir of a happy occasion.'

She thanked him, and both she and Hamish looked with polite gratitude at the photograph. Of course it gave no idea at all of the original. The subtle blues and greens had gone, were not hinted at; and even the softly-waving grasses, trees, plants, foliage, were obliterated. Nothing remained but a reproduction of crude crusts of paint, smeared thick by the fingers of Dr Kroll, from which emerged the hint of a branch, the suggestion of a flower. Nothing remained except the black, glaring eye, the eye of a wrathful and punishing God. It was the photograph of a roughly-scrawled eye, as a child might have drawn it – as, so Mary could not help thinking, that unfortunate straitjacketed little boy might have drawn the eye of God, or of Dr Kroll, had he been allowed to get his arms free and use them.

The thought of that little boy hurt her; it was still hurting Hamish who stood politely beside her. She knew that the moment they could leave this place and get on to the open road where the bus passed would be the happiest of her life.

They thanked Dr Kroll profoundly for his kindness, insisted they were afraid they might miss their bus, said goodbye, and promised letters and an exchange of medical papers of interest to them all – promised, in short, eternal friendship.

Then they left the big building and Dr Kroll and emerged into the cold February air. Soon the bus came and picked them up, and they travelled back over the flat black plain to the city terminus.

The terminus was exactly as it had been four or five hours before. Under the low grey sky lay the black chilled earth, the ruins of streets, the already softening shapes of bomb craters, the big new shining white building covered with the energetic shapes of workers. The bus queue still waited patiently, huddled into dark, thick clothes, while a thin bitter snow drifted down, down, hardly moving, as if the sky itself were slowly falling.

Mary Parrish took out the photograph and held it in her chilly gloved hand.

The black angry eye glared up at them.

'Tear it up,' he said.

'No,' she said.

'Why not? What's the use of keeping the beastly thing?'

'It wouldn't be fair,' she said seriously, returning it to her handbag.

'Oh, *fair*,' he said bitterly, with an impatient shrug.

They moved off side by side to the bus stop where they would catch a bus back to their hotel. Their feet crunched sharply on the hard earth. The stillness, save for the small shouts of the men at work on the half-finished building, save for the breathing noise of the machine, was absolute. And this queue of people waited like the other across the square, waited eternally, huddled up, silent, patient, under the snow; listening to the silence, under which seemed to throb from the depths of the earth the memory of the sound of marching feet, of heavy, black-booted, marching feet.

ONE OFF THE SHORT LIST

When he had first seen Barbara Coles, some years before, he only noticed her because someone said: 'That's Johnson's new girl.' He certainly had not used of her the private erotic formula: *Yes, that one*. He even wondered what Johnson saw in her. 'She won't last long,' he remembered thinking, as he watched Johnson, a handsome man, but rather flushed with drink, flirting with some unknown girl while Barbara stood by a wall looking on. He thought she had a sullen expression.

She was a pale girl, not slim, for her frame was generous, but her figure could pass as good. Her straight yellow hair was parted on one side in a way that struck him as gauche. He did not notice what she wore. But her eyes were all right, he remembered: large, and solidly green, square-looking because of some trick of the flesh at their corners. Emerald-like eyes in the face of a schoolgirl, or young schoolmistress who was watching her lover flirt and would later sulk about it.

Her name sometimes cropped up in the papers. She was a stage decorator, a designer, something on those lines.

Then a Sunday newspaper had a competition for stage design and she won it. Barbara Coles was one of the 'names' in the theatre, and her photograph was seen about. It was always serious. He remembered having thought her sullen.

One night he saw her across the room at a party. She was talking with a well-known actor. Her yellow hair was still done on one side, but now it looked sophisticated. She wore an emerald ring on her right hand that seemed deliberately to invite comparison with her eyes. He walked over and said: 'We have met before, Graham Spence.' He noted, with discomfort, that he sounded abrupt. 'I'm sorry, I don't remember, but how do you do?' she said, smiling. And continued her conversation.

He hung around a bit, but soon she went off with a group of people she was inviting to her home for a drink. She did not invite Graham. There was about her an assurance, a carelessness, that he recognized as the signature of success. It was then, watching her laugh as she went off with her friends, that he used the formula: 'Yes, *that one.*' And he went home to his wife with enjoyable expectation, as if his date with Barbara Coles were already arranged.

His marriage was twenty years old. At first it had been stormy, painful, tragic – full of partings, betrayals and sweet reconciliations. It had taken him at least a decade to realize that there was nothing remarkable about this marriage that he had lived through with such surprise of the mind and the senses. On the contrary, the marriages of most of the people he knew, whether they were first, second or third attempts, were just the same. His had run true to form even to the serious love affair with the young girl for whose sake he had *almost* divorced his wife – yet at the last moment had changed his mind, letting the girl down so that he must have her for always (not unpleasurably) on his conscience. It was with humiliation that he had understood that this drama was not at all the unique thing he had imagined. It was nothing more than the experience of everyone in his circle. And presumably in everybody else's circle too?

Anyway, round about the tenth year of his marriage he had seen a good many things clearly, a certain kind of emotional adventure went from his life, and the marriage itself changed.

His wife had married a poor youth with a great future as a writer. Sacrifices had been made, chiefly by her, for that future. He was neither unaware of them, nor ungrateful; in fact he felt permanently guilty about it. He at last published a decently successful book, then a second which now, thank God, no one remembered. He had drifted into radio, television, book reviewing.

He understood he was not going to make it; that he had become – not a hack, no one could call him that – but a member of that army of people who live by their wits on the fringes of the arts. The moment of realization was when he was in a pub one lunchtime near the BBC where he often dropped in to meet others like himself: he understood that was why he went there –

they *were* like him. Just as that melodramatic marriage had turned out to be like everyone else's – except that it had been shared with one woman instead of with two or three – so it had turned out that his unique talent, his struggles as a writer had led him here, to this pub and the half dozen pubs like it, where all the men in sight had the same history. They all had their novel, their play, their book of poems, a moment of fame, to their credit. Yet here they were, running television programmes about which they were cynical (to each other or to their wives) or writing reviews about other people's books. Yes, that's what he had become, an impresario of other people's talent. These two moments of clarity, about his marriage and about his talent, had roughly coincided; and (perhaps not by chance) had coincided with his wife's decision to leave him for a man younger than himself who had a future, she said, as a playwright. Well, he had talked her out of it. For her part she had to understand he was not going to be the T. S. Eliot or Graham Greene of our time – but after all, how many were? She must finally understand this, for he could no longer bear her awful bitterness. For his part he must stop coming home drunk at five in the morning, and starting a new romantic affair every six months which he took so seriously that he made her miserable because of her implied deficiencies. In short he was to be a good husband. (He had always been a dutiful father.) And she a good wife. And so it was: the marriage became stable, as they say.

The formula: *Yes, that one* no longer implied a necessarily sexual relationship. In its more mature form, it was far from being something he was ashamed of. On the contrary, it expressed a humorous respect for what he was, for his real talents and flair, which had turned out to be not artistic after all, but to do with emotional life, hard-earned experience. It expressed an ironical dignity, a proving to himself not only: I can be honest about myself, but also: I have earned the best in *that* field whenever I want it.

He watched the field for the women who were well known in the arts, or in politics; looked out for photographs, listened for bits of gossip. He made a point of going to see them act, or dance, or orate. He built up a not unshrewd picture of them. He would either quietly pull strings to meet her or – more often, for there was a gambler's pleasure in waiting – bide his time until he met her in the natural course of events, which was bound to happen sooner or later. He would be seen out with her a few times in public, which was in order, since his work meant he had to entertain well-known people, male and female. His wife always knew, he told her. He might have a brief affair with this woman, but more often than not it was the appearance of an affair. Not that he didn't get pleasure from other people envying him – he would make a point, for instance, of taking this woman into the pubs where his male colleagues went. It was that his real pleasure came when he saw her surprise at how well she was understood by him. He enjoyed the atmosphere he was able to set up between an intelligent woman and himself: a humorous complicity which had in it much that was unspoken, and which almost made sex irrelevant.

On to the list of women with whom he planned to have this relationship went Barbara Coles. There was no hurry. Next week, next month, next year, they would meet at a party. The world of well-known people in London is a small one. Big and little fishes, they drift around, nose each other, flirt their fins, wriggle off again. When he bumped into Barbara Coles, it would be time to decide whether or not to sleep with her.

Meanwhile he listened. But he didn't discover much. She had a husband and children, but the husband seemed to be in the background. The children were charming and well brought up, like everyone else's children. She had affairs, they said; but while several men he met sounded familiar with her, it was hard to determine whether they had slept with her, because none directly boasted of her. She was spoken of in terms of her friends, her work, her house, a party she had given, a job she had found someone. She was liked, she was respected, and Graham Spence's self-esteem was flattered because he had chosen her. He looked forward to saying in just the same tone: 'Barbara Coles asked me what I thought about the set and I told her quite frankly . . .'

Then by chance he met a young man who did boast about Barbara Coles; he claimed to have had the great love affair with her, and recently at that; and he spoke of it as something generally known. Graham realized how much he had already become involved with her in his imagination because of how perturbed he was now, on account of the character of this youth, Jack Kennaway. He had recently become successful as a magazine editor – one of those young men who, not as rare as one might suppose in the big cities, are successful from sheer impertinence, effrontery. Without much talent or taste, yet he had the charm of his effrontery. 'Yes, I'm going to succeed, because I've decided to; yes, I may be stupid, but not so stupid that I don't know my deficiencies. Yes, I'm going to be successful because you people with integrity, etc., etc., simply don't believe in the possibility of people like me. You are too cowardly to stop me. Yes, I've taken your measure and I'm going to succeed because I've got the courage, not only to be unscrupulous, but to be quite frank about it. And besides, you admire me, you must, or otherwise you'd stop me . . .' Well, that was young Jack Kennaway, and he shocked Graham. He was a tall, languishing young man, handsome in a dark melting way, and, it was quite clear, he was either asexual or homosexual. And this youth boasted of the favours of Barbara Coles; boasted, indeed, of her love. Either she was a raving neurotic with a taste for neurotics; or Jack Kennaway was a most accomplished liar; or she slept with anyone. Graham was intrigued. He took Jack Kennaway out to dinner in order to hear him talk about Barbara Coles. There was no doubt the two were pretty close – all those dinners, theatres, weekends in the country – Graham Spence felt he had put his finger on the secret pulse of Barbara Coles; and it was intolerable that he must wait to meet her; he decided to arrange it.

It became unnecessary. She was in the news again, with a run of luck. She had done a successful historical play, and immediately afterwards a modern play, and then a hit musical. In all three, the sets were remarked on. Graham saw some interviews in newspapers and on television. These all centred around the theme of her being able to deal easily with so many different styles of theatre; but the real point was, of course, that she was a woman, which naturally added piquancy to the thing. And

now Graham Spence was asked to do a half-hour radio interview with her. He planned the questions he would ask her with
care, drawing on what people had said of her, but above all on
his instinct and experience with women. The interview was to
be at nine-thirty at night; he was to pick her up at six from the
theatre where she was currently at work, so that there would be
time, as the letter from the BBC had put it, 'for you and Miss
Coles to get to know each other'.

At six he was at the stage door, but a message from Miss
Coles said she was not quite ready, could he wait a little. He
hung about, then went to the pub opposite for a quick one, but
still no Miss Coles. So he made his way backstage, directed by
voices, hammering, laughter. It was badly lit, and the group of
people at work did not see him. The director, James Poynter,
had his arm around Barbara's shoulders. He was newly well-
known, a carelessly good-looking young man reputed to be intelligent. Barbara Coles wore a dark blue overall, and her flat
hair fell over her face so that she kept pushing it back with the
hand that had the emerald on it. These two stood close, side by
side. Three young men, stagehands, were on the other side of a
trestle which had sketches and drawings on it. They were
studying some sketches. Barbara said, in a voice warm with
energy: 'Well, so I thought if we did *this* – do you see, James?
What do you think, Steven?' 'Well, love,' said the young man
she called Steven, 'I see your idea, but I wonder if . . .' 'I think
you're right, Babs,' said the director. 'Look,' said Barbara,
holding one of the sketches towards Steven, 'look, let me show
you.' They all leaned forward, the five of them, absorbed in the
business.

Suddenly Graham couldn't stand it. He understood he was
shaken to his depths. He went off stage, and stood with his back
against a wall in the dingy passage that led to the dressing
rooms. His eyes were filled with tears. He was seeing what a
long way he had come from the crude, uncompromising, admirable young egomaniac he had been when he was twenty. That
group of people there – working, joking, arguing, yes, that's
what he hadn't known for years. What bound them was the
democracy of respect for each other's work, a confidence in

H

themselves and in each other. They looked like people banded together against a world which they – no, not despised, but which they measured, understood, would fight to the death, out of respect for what *they* stood for, for what *it* stood for. It was a long time since he felt part of that balance. And he understood that he had seen Barbara Coles when she was most herself, at ease with a group of people she worked with. It was then, with the tears drying on his eyelids, which felt old and ironic, that he decided he would sleep with Barbara Coles. It was a necessity for him. He went back through the door on to the stage, burning with this single determination.

The five were still together. Barbara had a length of blue gleaming stuff which she was draping over the shoulder of Steven, the stagehand. He was showing it off, and the others watched. 'What do you think, James?' she asked the director. 'We've got that sort of dirty green, and I thought . . .' 'Well,' said James, not sure at all, 'well, Babs, well . . .'

Now Graham went forward so that he stood beside Barbara, and said: 'I'm Graham Spence, we've met before.' For the second time she smiled socially and said: 'Oh I'm sorry, I don't remember.' Graham nodded at James, whom he had known, or at least had met off and on, for years. But it was obvious James didn't remember him either.

'From the BBC,' said Graham to Barbara, again sounding abrupt, against his will. 'Oh I'm sorry, I'm so sorry, I forgot all about it. I've got to be interviewed,' she said to the group. 'Mr Spence is a journalist.' Graham allowed himself a small smile ironical of the word journalist, but she was not looking at him. She was going on with her work. 'We should decide tonight,' she said. 'Steven's right.' 'Yes, I am right,' said the stagehand. 'She's right, James, we need that blue with that sludge-green everywhere.' 'James,' said Barbara, 'James, what's wrong with it? You haven't said.' She moved forward to James, passing Graham. Remembering him again, she became contrite. 'I'm sorry,' she said, 'we can none of us agree. Well, look' – she turned to Graham – 'you advise us, we've got so involved with it that . . .' At which James laughed, and so did the stagehands. 'No, Babs,' said James, 'of course Mr Spence can't advise. He's just this moment come in. We've got to decide. Well, I'll give you till tomorrow morning. Time to go home, it must be six by now.'

'It's nearly seven,' said Graham, taking command.

'It isn't!' said Barbara, dramatic. 'My God, how terrible, how appalling, how could I have done such a thing . . .' She was laughing at herself. 'Well, you'll have to forgive me, Mr Spence, because you haven't got any alternative.'

They began laughing again: this was clearly a group joke. And now Graham took his chance. He said firmly, as if he were her director, in fact copying James Poynter's manner with her: 'No, Miss Coles, I won't forgive you, I've been kicking my heels for nearly an hour.' She grimaced, then laughed and accepted it. James said: 'There, Babs, that's how you ought to be treated. We spoil you.' He kissed her on the cheek, she kissed him on both his, the stagehands moved off. 'Have a good evening, Babs,' said James, going, and nodding to Graham. Who stood concealing his pleasure with difficulty. He knew, because he had had the courage to be firm, indeed, peremptory, with Barbara, that he had saved himself hours of manoeuvring. Several drinks, a dinner – perhaps two or three evenings of drinks and dinners – had been saved because he was now on this footing with Barbara Coles, a man who could say: 'No, I won't forgive you, you've kept me waiting.'

She said: 'I've just got to . . .' and went ahead of him. In the passage she hung her overall on a peg. She was thinking, it seemed, of something else, but seeing him watching her, she smiled at him, companionably: he realized with triumph it was the sort of smile she would offer one of the stagehands, or even James. She said again: 'Just one second . . .' and went to the stage-door office. She and the stage doorman conferred. There was some problem. Graham said, taking another chance: 'What's the trouble, can I help?' – as if he could help, as if he expected to be able to. 'Well . . .' she said, frowning. Then, to the man: 'No, it'll be all right. Good night.' She came to Graham. 'We've got ourselves into a bit of a fuss because half the set's in Liverpool and half's here and – but it will sort itself out.' She stood, at ease, chatting to him, one colleague to another. All this was admirable, he felt; but there would be a bad moment when they emerged from the special atmosphere of the theatre into the street. He took another decision, grasped her arm firmly, and said: 'We're going to have a drink before we do anything at all, it's a terrible evening out.' Her arm felt resistant, but remained within his. It was raining outside, luckily. He directed her, authoritative: 'No, not that pub, there's a nicer one around the corner.' 'Oh, but I like this pub,' said Barbara, 'we always use it.'

'Of course you do,' he said to himself. But in that pub there would be the stagehands, and probably James, and he'd lose contact with her. He'd become a *journalist* again. He took her firmly out of danger around two corners, into a pub he picked at random. A quick look around – no, they weren't there. At least, if there were people from the theatre, she showed no sign. She asked for a beer. He ordered her a double Scotch, which she accepted. Then, having won a dozen preliminary rounds already, he took time to think. Something was bothering him – what? Yes, it was what he had observed backstage, Barbara and James Poynter. Was she having an affair with him? Because if so, it would all be much more difficult. He made himself see the two of them together, and thought with a jealousy surprisingly strong: *Yes, that's it.* Meantime he sat looking at her, seeing himself look at her, *a man gazing in calm appreciation at a woman*: waiting for her to feel it and respond. She was examining the pub. Her white woollen suit was belted, and had a not unprovocative suggestion of being a uniform. Her flat yellow hair, hastily pushed back after work, was untidy. Her clear white skin, without any colour, made her look tired. Not very exciting, at the moment, thought Graham but maintaining his appreciative pose for when she would turn and see it. He knew what she would see: he was relying not only on the 'warm kindly' beam of his gaze, for this was merely a reinforcement of the impression he knew he made. He had black hair, a little greyed. His clothes were loose and bulky – masculine. His eyes were humorous and appreciative. He was not, never had been, concerned to lessen the impression of being settled, dependable: the husband and father. On the contrary, he knew women found it reassuring.

When she at last turned she said, almost apologetic: 'Would you mind if we sat down? I've been lugging great things around all day.' She had spotted two empty chairs in a corner. So had he, but rejected them, because there were other people at the table. 'But my dear, of course!' They took the chairs, and then Barbara said: 'If you'll excuse me a moment.' She had remembered she needed make-up. He watched her go off, annoyed with himself. She was tired; and he could have understood, protected, sheltered. He realized that in the other pub, with the people she had worked with all day, she would not have thought: 'I must make myself up, I must be on show.' That was for outsiders. She had not, until now, considered Graham an outsider, because of his taking his chance to seem one of the working group in the theatre; but now he had thrown this opportunity away. She returned armoured. Her hair was sleek, no longer defenceless. And she had made up her eyes. Her eyebrows were untouched, pale gold streaks above the brilliant green eyes whose lashes were blackened. Rather good, he thought, the contrast. Yes, but the moment had gone when he could say: Do you know you had a smudge on your cheek? Or – my dear girl! – pushing her hair back with the edge of a brotherly hand. In fact, unless he was careful, he'd be back at starting point.

He remarked: 'That emerald is very cunning' – smiling into her eyes.

She smiled politely, and said: 'It's not cunning, it's an accident, it was my grandmother's.' She flirted her hand lightly by her face, though, smiling. But that was something she had done before, to a compliment she had had before, and often. It was all social, she had become social entirely. She remarked: 'Didn't you say it was half-past nine we had to record?'

'My dear Barbara, we've got two hours. We'll have another drink or two, then I'll ask you a couple of questions, then we'll drop down to the studio and get it over, and then we'll have a comfortable supper.'

'I'd rather eat now, if you don't mind. I had no lunch, and I'm really hungry.'

'But my dear, of course.' He was angry. Just as he had been surprised by his real jealousy over James, so now he was thrown off balance by his anger: he had been counting on the long quiet dinner afterwards to establish intimacy. 'Finish your drink and I'll take you to Nott's.' Nott's was expensive. He glanced at her assessingly as he mentioned it. She said: 'I wonder if you know Butler's? It's good and it's rather close.' Butler's was good, and it was cheap, and he gave her a good mark for liking it. But Nott's it was going to be. 'My dear, we'll get into a taxi and be at Nott's in a moment, don't worry.'

She obediently got to her feet: the way she did it made him understand how badly he had slipped. She was saying to herself: Very well, he's like that, then all right, I'll do what he wants and get it over with . . .

Swallowing his own drink he followed her, and took her arm in the pub doorway. It was polite within his. Outside it drizzled. No taxi. He was having bad luck now. They walked in silence to the end of the street. There Barbara glanced into a side street where a sign said: BUTLER'S. Not to remind him of it, on the contrary, she concealed the glance. And here she was, entirely at his disposal, they might never have shared the comradely moment in the theatre.

They walked half a mile to Nott's. No taxis. She made conversation: this was, he saw, to cover any embarrassment he might feel because of a half-mile walk through rain when she was tired. She was talking about some theory to do with the theatre, with designs for theatre building. He heard himself saying, and repeatedly: Yes, yes, yes. He thought about Nott's. There he took the headwaiter aside, gave him a pound, and instructions. They were put in a corner. Large Scotches appeared. The menus were spread. 'And now, my dear,' he said, 'I apologize for dragging you here, but I hope you'll think it's worth it.'

'Oh, it's charming, I've always liked it. It's just that . . .' She stopped herself saying: it's such a long way. She smiled at him, raising her glass, and said: 'It's one of my very favourite places, and I'm glad you dragged me here.' Her voice was flat with tiredness. All this was appalling; he knew it; and he sat thinking how to retrieve his position. Meanwhile she fingered the menu. The headwaiter took the order, but Graham made a gesture which said: Wait a moment. He wanted the Scotch to take effect before she ate. But she saw his silent order; and, without annoyance or reproach, leaned forward to say, sounding patient: 'Graham, please, I've got to eat, you don't want me drunk when you interview me, do you?'

'They are bringing it as fast as they can,' he said, making it sound as if she were greedy. He looked neither at the headwaiter nor at Barbara. He noted in himself, as he slipped farther and farther away from contact with her, a cold determination growing in him; one apart from, apparently, any conscious act of will, that come what may, if it took all night, he'd be in her bed before morning. And now, seeing the small pale face, with the enormous green eyes, it was for the first time that he imagined her in his arms. Although he had said: *Yes, that one,* weeks ago, it was only now that he imagined her as a sensual experience. Now he did, so strongly that he could only glance at her, and then away towards the waiters who were bringing food.

'Thank the Lord,' said Barbara, and all at once her voice was gay and intimate. 'Thank heavens. Thank every power that is . . .' She was making fun of her own exaggeration; and, as he saw, because she wanted to put him at his ease after his boorishness over delaying the food. (She hadn't been taken in, he saw, humiliated, disliking her.) 'Thank all the gods of Nott's,' she went on, 'because if I hadn't eaten inside five minutes I'd have died, I tell you.' With which she picked up her knife and fork and began on her steak. He poured wine, smiling with her, thinking that *this* moment of closeness he would not throw away. He watched her frank hunger as she ate, and thought: Sensual – it's strange I hadn't wondered whether she would be or not.

'Now,' she said, sitting back, having taken the edge off her hunger: 'Let's get to work.'

He said: 'I've thought it over very carefully – how to present you. The first thing seems to me, we must get away from that old chestnut: Miss Coles, how extraordinary for a woman to be so versatile in her work . . . I hope you agree?' This was his trump card. He had noted, when he had seen her on television, her polite smile when this note was struck. (The smile he had seen so often tonight.) This smile said: All right, if you *have* to be stupid, what can I do?'

Now she laughed and said: 'What a relief. I was afraid you were going to do the same thing.'

'Good, now you eat and I'll talk.'

In his carefully prepared monologue he spoke of the different styles of theatre she had shown herself mistress of, but not directly: he was flattering her on the breadth of her experience; the complexity of her character, as shown in her work. She ate, steadily, her face showing nothing. At last she asked: 'And how did you plan to introduce this?'

He had meant to spring that on her as a surprise, something like: Miss Coles, a surprisingly young woman for what she has accomplished (she was thirty? thirty-two?) and a very attractive one . . . 'Perhaps I can give you an idea of what she's like if I say she could be taken for the film star Marie Carletta . . .' The Carletta was a strong earthy blonde, known to be intellectual. He now saw he could not possibly say this: he could imagine her cool look if he did. She said: 'Do you mind if we get away from all that – my manifold talents, et cetera . . .' He felt himself stiffen with annoyance; particularly because this was not an accusation, he saw she did not think him worth one. She had assessed him: This is the kind of man who uses this kind of flattery and therefore . . . It made him angrier that she did not even trouble to say: Why did you do exactly what you promised you wouldn't? She was being invincibly polite, trying to conceal her patience with his stupidity.

'After all,' she was saying, 'it is a stage designer's job to design what comes up. Would anyone take, let's say Johnnie Cranmore' (another stage designer) 'on to the air or television and say: How very versatile you are because you did that musical about Java last month and a modern play about Irish labourers this?'

He battened down his anger. 'My dear Barbara, I'm sorry. I didn't realize that what I said would sound just like the mixture as before. So what shall we talk about?'

'What I was saying as we walked to the restaurant: can we get away from the personal stuff?'

Now he almost panicked. Then, thank God, he laughed from nervousness, for she laughed and said: 'You didn't hear one word I said.'

'No, I didn't. I was frightened you were going to be furious because I made you walk so far when you were tired.'

They laughed together, back to where they had been in the theatre. He leaned over, took her hand, kissed it. He said: 'Tell me again.' He thought: Damn, now she's going to be earnest and intellectual.

But he understood he had been stupid. He had forgotten himself at twenty – or, for that matter, at thirty; forgotten one could live inside an idea, a set of ideas, with enthusiasm. For in talking about her ideas (also the ideas of the people she worked with) for a new theatre, a new style of theatre, she was as she had been with her colleagues over the sketches or the blue material. She was easy, informal, almost chattering. This was how, he remembered, one talked about ideas that were a breath of life. The ideas, he thought, were intelligent enough; and he would agree with them, with her, if he believed it mattered a damn one way or another, if any of these enthusiasms mattered a damn. But at least he now had the key, he knew what to do. At the end of no more than half an hour, they were again two professionals, talking about ideas they shared, for he remembered caring about all this himself once. *When? How many years ago was it that he had been able to care?*

At last he said: 'My dear Barbara, do you realize the impossible position you're putting me in? Margaret Ruyen who runs this programme is determined to do you personally, the poor woman hasn't got a serious thought in her head.'

Barbara frowned. He put his hand on hers, teasing her for the frown: 'No, wait, trust me, we'll circumvent her.' She smiled. In fact Margaret Ruyen had left it all to him, had said nothing about Miss Coles.

'They aren't very bright – the brass,' he said. 'Well, never mind: we'll work out what we want, do it, and it'll be a *fait accompli*.'

'Thank you, what a relief. How lucky I was to be given you to interview me.' She was relaxed now, because of the whisky, the food, the wine, above all because of this new complicity against Margaret Ruyen. It would all be easy. They worked out five or six questions, over coffee, and took a taxi through rain to the studios. He noted that the cold necessity to have her, to make her, to beat her down, had left him. He was even seeing himself, as the evening ended, kissing her on the cheek and going home to his wife. This comradeship was extraordinarily pleasant. It was balm to the wound he had not known he carried until that evening, when he had had to accept the justice of the word *journalist*. He felt he could talk for ever about the state of the theatre, its finances, the stupidity of the government, the philistinism of . . .

At the studios he was careful to make a joke so that they walked in on the laugh. He was careful that the interview began at once, without conversation with Margaret Ruyen; and that from the moment the green light went on, his voice lost its easy familiarity. He made sure that not one personal note was struck during the interview. Afterwards, Margaret Ruyen, who was pleased, came forward to say so; but he took her aside to say that Miss Coles was tired and needed to be taken home at once: for he knew this must look to Barbara as if he were squaring a producer who had been expecting a different interview. He led Barbara off, her hand held tight in his against his side. 'Well,' he said, 'we've done it, and I don't think she knows what hit her.'

'Thank you,' she said, 'it really was pleasant to talk about something sensible for once.'

He kissed her lightly on the mouth. She returned it, smiling. By now he felt sure that the mood need not slip again, he could hold it.

'There are two things we can do,' he said. 'You can come to my club and have a drink. Or I can drive you home and you can give me a drink. I have to go past you.'

'Where do you live?'

'Wimbledon.' He lived, in fact, at Highgate; but she lived in Fulham. He was taking another chance, but by the time she found out, they would be in a position to laugh over his ruse.

'Good,' she said. 'You can drop me home then. I have to get up early.' He made no comment. In the taxi he took her hand; it was heavy in his, and he asked: 'Does James slave-drive you?'

'I didn't realize you knew him – no, he doesn't.'

'Well I don't know him intimately. What's he like to work with?'

'Wonderful,' she said at once. 'There's no one I enjoy working with more.'

Jealousy spurted in him. He could not help himself: 'Are you having an affair with him?'

She looked: what's it to do with you? but said: 'No, I'm not.'

'He's very attractive,' he said, with a chuckle of worldly complicity. She said nothing, and he insisted: 'If I were a woman I'd have an affair with James.'

It seemed she might very well say nothing. But she remarked: 'He's married.'

His spirits rose in a swoop. It was the first stupid remark she had made. It was a remark of such staggering stupidity that . . . he let out a humouring snort of laughter, put his arm around her, kissed her, said: 'My dear little Babs.'

She said: 'Why Babs?'

'Is that the prerogative of James? And of the stagehands?' he could not prevent himself adding.

'I'm only called that at work.' She was stiff inside his arm.

'My dear Barbara, then . . .' He waited for her to enlighten and explain, but she said nothing. Soon she moved out of his arm, on the pretext of lighting a cigarette. He lit it for her. He noted that his determination to lay her, and at all costs, had come back. They were outside her house. He said quickly: 'And now, Barbara, you can make me a cup of coffee and give me a brandy.' She hesitated; but he was out of the taxi, paying, opening the door for her. The house had no lights on, he noted.

He said: 'We'll be very quiet so as not to wake the children.'

She turned her head slowly to look at him. She said, flat, replying to his real question: 'My husband is away. As for the children, they are visiting friends tonight.' She now went ahead of him to the door of the house. It was a small house, in a terrace of small and not very pretty houses. Inside a little, bright intimate hall, she said: 'I'll go and make some coffee. Then, my friend, you must go home because I'm very tired.'

The *my friend* struck him deep, because he had become vulnerable during their comradeship. He said, gabbling: 'You're annoyed with me – oh, please don't, I'm sorry.'

She smiled, from a cool distance. He saw, in the small light from the ceiling, her extraordinary eyes. 'Green' eyes are hazel, are brown with green flecks, are even blue. Eyes are chequered, flawed, changing. Hers were solid green, but really, he had never seen anything like them before. They were like very deep water. They were like – well, emeralds; or the absolute clarity of green in the depths of a tree in summer. And now, as she smiled almost perpendicularly up at him, he saw a darkness come over them. Darkness swallowed the clear green. She said: 'I'm not in the least annoyed.' It was as if she had yawned with boredom. 'And now I'll get the things . . . in there.' She nodded at a white door and left him. He went into a long, very tidy white room, that had a narrow bed in one corner, a table covered with drawings, sketches, pencils. Tacked to the walls with drawing pins were swatches of coloured stuffs. Two small chairs stood near a low round table: an area of comfort in the working room. He was thinking: I wouldn't like it if my wife had a room like this. I wonder what Barbara's husband . . .? He had not thought of her till now in relation to her husband, or to her children. Hard to imagine her with a frying pan in her hand, or for that matter, cosy in the double bed.

A noise outside: he hastily arranged himself, leaning with one arm on the mantelpiece. She came in with a small tray that had cups, glasses, brandy, coffeepot. She looked abstracted. Graham was on the whole flattered by this: it probably meant she was at ease in his presence. He realized he was a little tight and rather tired. Of course, she was tired too, that was why she was vague. He remembered that earlier that evening he had lost a chance by not using her tiredness. Well now, if he were intelligent . . . She was about to pour coffee. He firmly took the coffeepot out of her hand, and nodded at a chair. Smiling, she obeyed him: 'That's better,' he said. He poured coffee, poured brandy, and pulled the table towards her. She watched him. Then he took her hand, kissed it, patted it, laid it down gently. Yes, he thought, I did that well.

Now, a problem. He wanted to be closer to her, but she was fitted into a damned silly little chair that had arms. If he were to sit by her on the floor . . .? But no, for him, the big bulky reassuring man, there could be no casual gestures, no informal postures. Suppose I scoop her out of the chair on to the bed? He drank his coffee as he plotted. Yes, he'd carry her to the bed, but not yet.

'Graham,' she said, setting down her cup. She was, he saw with annoyance, looking tolerant. 'Graham, in about half an hour I want to be in bed and asleep.'

As she said this, she offered him a smile of amusement at this situation – man and woman manoeuvring, the great comic situation. And with part of himself he could have shared it. Almost, he smiled with her, laughed. (Not till days later he exclaimed to himself: Lord, what a mistake I made, not to share the joke with her then: that was where I went seriously wrong.) But he could not smile. His face was frozen, with a stiff pride. Not because she had been watching him plot; the amusement she now offered him took the sting out of that; but because of his revived determination that he was going to have his own way, he was going to have her. He was not going home. But he felt that he held a bunch of keys, and did not know which one to choose.

He lifted the second small chair opposite to Barbara, moving aside the coffee table for this purpose. He sat in this chair, leaned forward, took her two hands, and said: 'My dear, don't make me go home yet, don't, I beg you.' The trouble was, nothing had happened all evening that could be felt to lead up to these words and his tone – simple, dignified, human being pleading with human being for surcease. He saw himself leaning forward, his big hands swallowing her small ones; he saw his face, warm with the appeal. And he realized he had meant the words he used. They were nothing more than what he felt. He wanted to stay with her because she wanted him to, because he was her colleague, a fellow worker in the arts. He needed this desperately. But she was examining him, curious rather than surprised, and from a critical distance. He heard himself saying: 'If James were here, I wonder what you'd do?' His voice was aggrieved; he saw the sudden dark descend over her eyes, and she said: 'Graham, would you like some more coffee before you go?'

He said: 'I've been wanting to meet you for years. I know a good many people who know you.'

She leaned forward, poured herself a little more brandy, sat back, holding the glass between her two palms on her chest. An odd gesture: Graham felt that this vessel she was cherishing between her hands was herself. A patient, long-suffering gesture. He thought of various men who had mentioned her. He thought of Jack Kennaway, wavered, panicked, said: 'For instance, Jack Kennaway.'

And now, at the name, an emotion lit her eyes – what was it? He went on, deliberately testing this emotion, adding to it: 'I had dinner with him last week – oh, quite by chance! – and he was talking about you.'

'Was he?'

He remembered he had thought her sullen, all those years ago. Now she seemed defensive, and she frowned. He said: 'In fact he spent most of the evening talking about you.'

She said in short, breathless sentences, which he realized were due to anger: 'I can very well imagine what he says. But surely you can't think I enjoy being reminded that ...' She broke off, resenting him, he saw, because he forced her down on to a level she despised. But it was not his level either: it was all her fault, all hers! He couldn't remember not being in control of a situation with a woman for years. Again he felt like a man teetering on a tightrope. He said, trying to make good use of

Jack Kennaway, even at this late hour: 'Of course, he's a charming boy, but not a man at all.'

She looked at him, silent, guarding her brandy glass against her breasts.

'Unless appearances are totally deceptive, of course.' He could not resist probing, even though he knew it was fatal.

She said nothing.

'Do you know you are supposed to have had the great affair with Jack Kennaway?' he exclaimed, making this an amused expostulation against the fools who could believe it.

'So I am told.' She set down her glass. 'And now,' she said, standing up, dismissing him. He lost his head, took a step forward, grabbed her in his arms, and groaned: 'Barbara!'

She turned her face this way and that under his kisses. He snatched a diagnostic look at her expression – it was still patient. He placed his lips against her neck, groaned 'Barbara' again, and waited. She would have to do something. Fight free, respond, something. She did nothing at all. At last she said: 'For the Lord's sake, Graham!' She sounded amused: he was again being offered amusement. But if he shared it with her, it would be the end of this chance to have her. He clamped his mouth over hers, silencing her. She did not fight him off so much as blow him off. Her mouth treated his attacking mouth as a woman blows and laughs in water, puffing off waves or spray with a laugh, turning aside her head. It was a gesture half annoyance, half humour. He continued to kiss her while she moved her head and face about under the kisses as if they were small attacking waves.

And so began what, when he looked back on it afterwards, was the most embarrassing experience of his life. Even at the time he hated her for his ineptitude. For he held her there for what must have been nearly half an hour. She was much shorter than he, he had to bend, and his neck ached. He held her rigid, his thighs on either side of hers, her arms clamped to her side in a bear's hug. She was unable to move, except for her head. When his mouth ground hers open and his tongue moved and writhed inside it, she still remained passive. And he could not

stop himself. While with his intelligence he watched this ridiculous scene, he was determined to go on, because sooner or
later her body must soften in wanting his. And he could not
stop because he could not face the horror of the moment when
he set her free and she looked at him. And he hated her more,
every moment. Catching glimpses of her great green eyes, open
and dismal beneath his, he knew he had never disliked anything
more than those 'jewelled' eyes. They were repulsive to him. It
occurred to him at last that even if by now she wanted him, he
wouldn't know it, because she was not able to move at all. He
cautiously loosened his hold so that she had an inch or so
leeway. She remained quite passive. As if, he thought derisively, she had read or been told that the way to incite men
maddened by lust was to fight them. He found he was thinking:
Stupid cow, so you imagine I find you attractive, do you?
You've got the conceit to think that!

The sheer, raving insanity of this thought hit him, opened his
arms, his thighs, and lifted his tongue out of her mouth. She
stepped back, wiping her mouth with the back of her hand, and
stood dazed with incredulity. The embarrassment that lay in
wait for him nearly engulfed him, but he let anger postpone it.
She said positively apologetic, even, at this moment, humorous: 'You're crazy, Graham. What's the matter, are you drunk?
You don't seem drunk. You don't even find me attractive.'

The blood of hatred went to his head and he gripped her
again. Now she had got her face firmly twisted away so that he
could not reach her mouth, and she repeated steadily as he
kissed the parts of her cheeks and neck that were available to
him: 'Graham, let me go, do let me go, Graham.' She went on
saying this; he went on squeezing, grinding, kissing and licking.
It might go on all night: it was a sheer contest of wills, nothing
else. He thought: It's only a really masculine woman who
wouldn't have given in by now out of sheer decency of the flesh!
One thing he knew, however: that she would be in that bed, in
his arms, and very soon. He let her go, but said: 'I'm going to
sleep with you tonight, you know that, don't you?'

She leaned with hand on the mantelpiece to steady herself.
Her face was colourless, since he had licked all the make-up off.

She seemed quite different: small and defenceless with her large mouth pale now, her smudged green eyes fringed with gold. And now, for the first time, he felt what it might have been supposed (certainly by her) he felt hours ago. Seeing the small damp flesh of her face, he felt kinship, intimacy with her, he felt intimacy of the flesh, the affection and good humour of sensuality. He felt she was flesh of his flesh, his sister in the flesh. He felt desire for her, instead of the will to have her; and because of this, was ashamed of the farce he had been playing. Now he desired simply to take her into bed in the affection of his senses.

She said: 'What on earth am I supposed to do? Telephone for the police, or what?' He was hurt that she still addressed the man who had ground her into sulky apathy; she was not addressing *him* at all.

She said: 'Or scream for the neighbours, is that what you want?'

The gold-fringed eyes were almost black, because of the depth of the shadow of boredom over them. She was bored and weary to the point of falling to the floor, he could see that.

He said: 'I'm going to sleep with you.'

'But how can you possibly want to?' – a reasonable, a civilized demand addressed to a man who (he could see) she believed would respond to it. She said: 'You know I don't want to, and I know you don't really give a damn one way or the other.'

He was stung back into being the boor because she had not the intelligence to see that the boor no longer existed; because she could not see that this was a man who wanted her in a way which she must respond to.

There she stood, supporting herself with one hand, looking small and white and exhausted, and utterly incredulous. She was going to turn and walk off out of simple incredulity, he could see that. 'Do you think I don't mean it?' he demanded, grinding this out between his teeth. She made a movement – she was on the point of going away. His hand shot out on its own volition and grasped her wrist. She frowned. His other hand grasped her other wrist. His body hove up against hers to start the pressure of a new embrace. Before it could, she said: 'Oh Lord, no, I'm not going through all that again. Right, then.'

'What do you mean – right, then?' he demanded.

She said: 'You're going to sleep with me. OK. Anything rather than go through that again. Shall we get it over with?'

He grinned, saying in silence: 'No darling, oh no you don't, I don't care what words you use, I'm going to have you now and that's all there is to it.'

She shrugged. The contempt, the weariness of it, had no effect on him, because he was now again hating her so much that wanting her was like needing to kill something or someone.

She took her clothes off, as if she were going to bed by herself: her jacket, skirt, petticoat. She stood in white bra and panties, a rather solid girl, brown-skinned still from the summer. He felt a flash of affection for the brown girl with her loose yellow hair as she stood naked. She got into bed and lay there, while the green eyes looked at him in civilized appeal: Are you really going through with this? Do you have to? Yes, his eyes said back: I do have to. She shifted her gaze aside, to the wall, saying silently: Well, if you want to take me without any desire at all on my part, then go ahead, if you're not ashamed. He was not ashamed, because he was maintaining the flame of hate for her which he knew quite well was all that stood between him and shame. He took off his clothes, and got into bed beside her. As he did so, knowing he was putting himself in the position of raping a woman who was making it elaborately clear he bored her, his flesh subsided completely, sad, and full of reproach because a few moments ago it was reaching out for his sister whom he could have made happy. He lay on his side by her, secretly at work on himself, while he supported himself across her body on his elbow, using the free hand to manipulate her breasts. He saw that she gritted her teeth against his touch. At least she could not know that after all this fuss he was not potent.

In order to incite himself, he clasped her again. She felt his smallness, writhed free of him, sat up and said: 'Lie down.'

While she had been lying there, she had been thinking: The only way to get this over with is to make him big again, otherwise I've got to put up with him all night. His hatred of her was giving him a clairvoyance: he knew very well what went on through her mind. She had switched on, with the determination to *get it all over with*, a sensual good humour, a patience. He lay down. She squatted beside him, the light from the ceiling blooming on her brown shoulders, her flat hair falling over her face. But she would not look at his face. Like a bored, skilled wife, she was; or like a prostitute. She administered to him, she was setting herself to please him. Yes, he thought, she's sensual, or she could be. Meanwhile she was succeeding in defeating the reluctance of his flesh, which was the tender token of a possible desire for her, by using a cold skill that was the result of her contempt for him. Just as he decided: Right, it's enough, now I shall have her properly, she made him come. It was not a trick, to hurry or cheat him, what defeated him was her transparent thought: Yes, that's what he's worth.

Then, having succeeded, and waited for a moment or two, she stood up, naked, the fringes of gold at her loins and in her armpits speaking to him a language quite different from that of her green, bored eyes. She looked at him and thought, showing it plainly: What sort of man is it who . . .? He watched the slight movement of her shoulders: a just-checked shrug. She went out of the room: then the sound of running water. Soon she came back in a white dressing gown, carrying a yellow towel. She handed him the towel, looking away in politeness as he used it. 'Are you going home now?' she inquired hopefully, at this point.

'No, I'm not.' He believed that now he would have to start fighting her again, but she lay down beside him, not touching him (he could feel the distaste of her flesh for his) and he thought: Very well, my dear, but there's a lot of the night left yet. He said aloud: 'I'm going to have you properly tonight.' She said nothing, lay silent, yawned. Then she remarked consolingly, and he could have laughed outright from sheer surprise: 'Those were hardly conducive circumstances for making love.' She was *consoling* him. He hated her for it. A proper little slut: I forced her into bed, she doesn't want me, but she still has to make me feel good, like a prostitute. But even while he hated her, he responded in kind, from the habit of sexual generosity. 'It's because of my admiration for you, because ... after all, I was holding in my arms one of the thousand women.'

A pause. 'The thousand?' she inquired, carefully.

'The thousand especial women.'

'In Britain or in the world? You choose them for their brains, their beauty – what?'

'Whatever it is that makes them outstanding,' he said, offering her a compliment.

'Well,' she remarked at last, inciting him to be amused again: 'I hope that at least there's a short list you can say I am on, for politeness' sake.'

He did not reply for he understood he was sleepy. He was still telling himself that he must stay awake when he was slowly waking and it was morning. It was about eight. Barbara was not there. He thought: My God! What on earth shall I tell my wife? Where was Barbara? He remembered the ridiculous scenes of last night and nearly succumbed to shame. Then he thought, reviving anger: If she didn't sleep beside me here I'll never forgive her ... He sat up, quietly, determined to go through the house until he found her and, having found her, to possess her, when the door opened and she came in. She was fully dressed in a green suit, her hair done, her eyes made up. She carried a tray of coffee, which she set down beside the bed. He was conscious of his big loose hairy body, half uncovered. He said to himself that he was not going to lie in bed, naked, while she was dressed. He said: 'Have you got a gown of some kind?' She handed him, without speaking, a towel, and said: 'The bathroom's second on the left.' She went out. He followed, the towel around him. Everything in this house was gay, intimate – not at all like her efficient working room. He wanted to find out where she had slept, and opened the first door. It was the kitchen, and she was in it, putting a brown earthenware dish into the oven. 'The next door,' said Barbara. He went hastily past the second door, and opened (he hoped quietly) the third.

It was a cupboard full of linen. 'This door,' said Barbara, behind him.

'So all right then, where did you sleep?'

'What's it to do with you? Upstairs, in my own bed. Now, if you have everything, I'll say goodbye, I want to get to the theatre.'

'I'll take you,' he said at once.

He saw again the movement of her eyes, the dark swallowing the light in deadly boredom. 'I'll take you,' he insisted.

'I'd prefer to go by myself,' she remarked. Then she smiled: 'However, you'll take me. Then you'll make a point of coming right in, so that James and everyone can see – that's what you want to take me for, isn't it?'

He hated her, finally, and quite simply, for her intelligence; that not once had he got away with anything, that she had been watching, since they had met yesterday, every movement of his campaign for her. However, some fate or inner urge over which he had no control made him say sentimentally: 'My dear, you must see that I'd like at least to take you to your work.'

'Not at all, have it on me,' she said, giving him the lie direct. She went past him to the room he had slept in. 'I shall be leaving in ten minutes,' she said.

He took a shower fast. When he returned, the workroom was already tidied, the bed made, all signs of the night gone. Also, there were no signs of the coffee she brought in for him. He did not like to ask for it, for fear of an outright refusal. Besides, she was ready, her coat on, her handbag under her arm. He went, without a word, to the front door, and she came after him, silent.

He could see that every fibre of her body signalled a simple message: Oh God, for the moment when can I be rid of this boor! She was nothing but a slut, he thought.

A taxi came. In it she sat as far away from him as she could. He thought of what he should say to his wife.

Outside the theatre she remarked: 'You could drop me here, if you liked.' It was not a plea, she was too proud for that. 'I'll take you in,' he said, and saw her thinking: Very well, I'll go through with it to shame him. He was determined to take her in and hand her over to her colleagues, he was afraid she would give him the slip. But far from playing it down, she seemed determined to play it his way. At the stage door, she said to the doorman: 'This is Mr Spence, Tom – do you remember, Mr Spence from last night?' 'Good morning, Babs,' said the man, examining Graham, politely, as he had been ordered to do.

Barbara went to the door to the stage, opened it, held it open for him. He went in first, then held it open for her. Together they walked into the cavernous, littered, badly lit place and she called out: 'James, James!' A man's voice called out from the front of the house: 'Here, Babs, why are you so late?'

The auditorium opened before them, darkish, silent, save for an early-morning busyness of charwomen. A vacuum cleaner roared, smally, somewhere close. A couple of stagehands stood looking up at a drop which had a design of blue and green spirals. James stood with his back to the auditorium, smoking. 'You're late, Babs,' he said again. He saw Graham behind her, and nodded. Barbara and James kissed. Barbara said, giving allowance to every syllable. 'You remember Mr Spence from last night?' James nodded: How do you do? Barbara stood beside him, and they looked together up at the blue-and-green backdrop. Then Barbara looked again at Graham, asking silently: All right now, isn't that enough? He could see her eyes, sullen with boredom.

He said, 'Bye, Babs. Bye, James. I'll ring you, Babs.' No response, she ignored him. He walked off slowly, listening for what might be said. For instance: 'Babs, for God's sake, what are you doing with him?' Or she might say: 'Are you wondering about Graham Spence? Let me explain.'

Graham passed the stagehands who, he could have sworn, didn't recognize him. Then at last he heard James's voice to Barbara: 'It's no good, Babs, I know you're enamoured of that particular shade of blue, but do have another look at it, there's a good girl . . .' Graham left the stage, went past the office where the stage doorman sat reading a newspaper. He looked up, nodded, went back to his paper. Graham went to find a taxi, thinking: I'd better think up something convincing, then I'll telephone my wife.

Luckily he had an excuse not to be at home that day, for this evening he had to interview a young man (for television) about his new novel.

A WOMAN ON A ROOF

It was during the week of hot sun, that June.

Three men were at work on the roof, where the leads got so hot they had the idea of throwing water on to cool them. But the water steamed, then sizzled; and they made jokes about getting an egg from some woman in the flats under them, to poach it for their dinner. By two it was not possible to touch the guttering they were replacing, and they speculated about what workmen did in regularly hot countries. Perhaps they should borrow kitchen gloves with the egg? They were all a bit dizzy, not used to the heat; and they shed their coats and stood side by side squeezing themselves into a foot-wide patch of shade against a chimney, careful to keep their feet in the thick socks and boots out of the sun. There was a fine view across several acres of roofs. Not far off a man sat in a deck chair reading the newspapers. Then they saw her, between chimneys, about fifty yards away. She lay face down on a brown blanket. They could see the top part of her: black hair, a flushed solid back, arms spread out.

'She's stark naked,' said Stanley, sounding annoyed.

Harry, the oldest, a man of about forty-five, said: 'Looks like it.'

Young Tom, seventeen, said nothing, but he was excited and grinning.

Stanley said: 'Someone'll report her if she doesn't watch out.'

'She thinks no one can see,' said Tom, craning his head all ways to see more.

At this point the woman, still lying prone, brought her two hands up behind her shoulders with the ends of a scarf in them, tied it behind her back, and sat up. She wore a red scarf tied around her breasts and brief red bikini pants. This being the first day of the sun she was white, flushing red. She sat smoking, and did not look up when Stanley let out a wolf whistle. Harry said: 'Small things amuse small minds,' leading the way back to their part of the roof, but it was scorching. Harry said: 'Wait, I'm going to rig up some shade,' and disappeared down the skylight into the building. Now that he'd gone, Stanley and Tom went to the farthest point they could to peer at the woman. She had moved, and all they could see were two pink legs stretched on the blanket. They whistled and shouted but the legs did not move. Harry came back with a blanket and shouted: 'Come on, then.' He sounded irritated with them. They clambered back to him and he said to Stanley: 'What about your missus?' Stanley was newly married, about three months. Stanley said, jeering: 'What about my missus?' – preserving his independence. Tom said nothing, but his mind was full of the nearly naked woman. Harry slung the blanket, which he had borrowed from a friendly woman downstairs, from the stem of a television aerial to a row of chimney pots. This shade fell across the piece of gutter they had to replace. But the shade kept moving, they had to adjust the blanket, and not much progress was made. At last some of the heat left the roof, and they worked fast, making up for lost time. First Stanley, then Tom, made a trip to the end of the roof to see the woman. 'She's on her back,' Stanley said, adding a jest which made Tom snicker, and the older man smile tolerantly. Tom's report was that she hadn't moved, but it was a lie. He wanted to keep what he had seen to himself: he had caught her in the act of rolling down the little red pants over her hips, till they were no more than a small triangle. She was on her back, fully visible, glistening with oil.

Next morning, as soon as they came up, they went to look. She was already there, face down, arms spread out, naked except for the little red pants. She had turned brown in the night. Yesterday she was a scarlet and white woman, today she was a brown woman. Stanley let out a whistle. She lifted her head, startled, as if she'd been asleep, and looked straight over at them. The sun was in her eyes, she blinked and stared, then she dropped her head again. At this gesture of indifference, they all three, Stanley, Tom and old Harry, let out whistles and yells. Harry was doing it in parody of the younger men, making fun of them, but he was also angry. They were all angry because of her utter indifference to the three men watching her.

'Bitch,' said Stanley.

'She should ask us over,' said Tom, snickering.

Harry recovered himself and reminded Stanley: 'If she's married, her old man wouldn't like that.'

'Christ,' said Stanley virtuously, 'if my wife lay about like that, for everyone to see, I'd soon stop her.'

Harry said, smiling: 'How do you know, perhaps she's sunning herself at this very moment?'

'Not a chance, not on our roof.' The safety of his wife put Stanley into a good humour, and they went to work. But today it was hotter than yesterday; and several times one or the other suggested they should tell Matthew, the foreman, and ask to leave the roof until the heat wave was over. But they didn't. There was work to be done in the basement of the big block of flats, but up there they felt free, on a different level from ordinary humanity shut in the streets or the buildings. A lot more people came out on to the roofs that day, for an hour at midday. Some married couples sat side by side in deck chairs, the women's legs stockingless and scarlet, the men in vests with reddening shoulders.

The woman stayed on her blanket, turning herself over and over. She ignored them, no matter what they did. When Harry went off to fetch more screws, Stanley said: 'Come on.' Her roof belonged to a different system of roofs, separated from theirs at one point by about twenty feet. It meant a scrambling climb from one level to another, edging along parapets, clinging to chimneys, while their big boots slipped and slithered, but at last they stood on a small square projecting roof looking straight down at her, close. She sat smoking, reading a book. Tom thought she looked like a poster, or a magazine cover, with the blue sky behind her and her legs stretched out. Behind her a great crane at work on a new building in Oxford Street swung its black arm across the roofs in a great arc. Tom imagined himself at work on the crane, adjusting the arm to swing over and pick her up and swing her back across the sky to drop near him.

They whistled. She looked up at them, cool and remote, and went on reading. Again, they were furious. Or rather, Stanley was. His sun-heated face was screwed into rage as he whistled again and again, trying to make her look up. Young Tom stopped whistling. He stood beside Stanley, excited, grinning; but he felt as if he were saying to the woman: 'Don't associate me with *him*,' for his grin was apologetic. Last night he had thought of the unknown woman before he slept, and she had been tender with him. This tenderness he was remembering as he shifted his feet by the jeering, whistling Stanley, and watched the indifferent, healthy brown woman a few feet off, with the gap that plunged to the street between them. Tom thought it was romantic, it was like being high on two hilltops. But there was a shout from Harry, and they clambered back. Stanley's face was hard, really angry. The boy kept looking at him and wondered why he hated the woman so much, for by now he loved her.

They played their little games with the blanket, trying to trap shade to work under; but again it was not until nearly four that they could work seriously, and they were exhausted, all three of them. They were grumbling about the weather, by now. Stanley was in a thoroughly bad humour. When they made their routine trip to see the woman before they packed up for the day, she was apparently asleep, face down, her back all naked save for the scarlet triangle on her buttocks. 'I've got a good mind to report her to the police,' said Stanley, and Harry said: 'What's eating you? What harm's she doing?'

'I tell you, if she was my wife!'

'But she isn't, is she?' Tom knew that Harry, like himself, was uneasy at Stanley's reaction. He was normally a sharp young man, quick at his work, making a lot of jokes, good company.

'Perhaps it will be cooler tomorrow,' said Harry.

But it wasn't, it was hotter, if anything, and the weather forecast said the good weather would last. As soon as they were on the roof, Harry went over to see if the woman was there, and Tom knew it was to prevent Stanley going, to put off his bad humour. Harry had grown-up children, a boy the same age as Tom, and the youth trusted and looked up to him.

Harry came back and said: 'She's not there.'

'I bet her old man has put his foot down,' said Stanley, and Harry and Tom caught each other's eyes and smiled behind the young married man's back.

Harry suggested they should get permission to work in the basement, and they did, that day. But before packing up Stanley said: 'Let's have a breath of fresh air.' Again Harry and Tom smiled at each other as they followed Stanley up to the roof, Tom in the devout conviction that he was there to protect the woman from Stanley. It was about five-thirty, and a calm, full sunlight lay over the roofs. The great crane still swung its black arm from Oxford Street to above their heads. She was not there. Then there was a flutter of white from behind a parapet, and she stood up, in a belted, white dressing gown. She had been there all day, probably, but on a different patch of roof, to hide from them. Stanley did not whistle, he said nothing, but watched the woman bend to collect papers, books, cigarettes, then fold the blanket over her arm. Tom was thinking: If they weren't here, I'd go over and say . . . what? But he knew from his nightly dreams of her that she was kind and friendly. Perhaps she would ask him down to her flat? Perhaps . . . He stood watching her disappear down the skylight. As she went, Stanley let out a shrill derisive yell; she started, and it seemed as if she nearly fell. She clutched to save herself, they could hear things falling. She looked straight at them, angry. Harry said, facetiously: 'Better be careful on those slippery ladders, love.' Tom knew he said it to save her from Stanley, but she could not know it. She vanished, frowning. Tom was full of secret delight, because he knew her anger was for the others, not for him.

'Roll on some rain,' said Stanley, bitter, looking at the blue evening sky.

Next day was cloudless, and they decided to finish the work in the basement. They felt excluded, shut in the grey cement basement fitting pipes, from the holiday atmosphere of London in a heat wave. At lunchtime they came up for some air, but while the married couples, and the men in shirt-sleeves or vests, were there, she was not there, either on her usual patch of roof or where she had been yesterday. They all, even Harry, clambered about, between chimney pots, over parapets, the hot leads stinging their fingers. There was not a sign of her. They took off their shirts and vests and exposed their chests, feeling their feet sweaty and hot. They did not mention the woman. But Tom felt alone again. Last night she had asked him into her flat; it was big and had fitted white carpets and a bed with a padded white leather head top. She wore a black filmy négligé and her kindness to Tom thickened his throat as he remembered it. He felt she had betrayed him by not being there.

And again after work they climbed up, but still there was nothing to be seen of her. Stanley kept repeating that if it was as hot as this tomorrow he wasn't going to work and that's all there was to it. But they were all there next day. By ten the temperature was in the middle seventies, and it was eighty long before noon. Harry went to the foreman to say it was impossible to work on the leads in that heat; but the foreman said there was nothing else he could put them on, and they'd have to. At midday they stood, silent, watching the skylight on her roof open, and then she slowly emerged in her white gown, holding a bundle of blanket. She looked at them, gravely, then went to the part of the roof where she was hidden from them. Tom was pleased. He felt she was more his when the other men couldn't see her. They had taken off their shirts and vests, but now they put them back again, for they felt the sun bruising their flesh. 'She must have the hide of a rhino,' said Stanley, tugging at guttering and swearing. They stopped work, and sat in the shade, moving around behind chimney stacks. A woman came to water a yellow window box just opposite them. She was middle-aged, wearing a flowered summer dress. Stanley said to her: 'We need a drink more than them.' She smiled and said: 'Better drop down to the pub quick, it'll be closing in a minute.' They exchanged pleasantries, and she left them with a smile and a wave.

'Not like Lady Godiva,' said Stanley. 'She can give us a bit of a chat and a smile.'

'You didn't whistle at *her*,' said Tom, reproving.

'Listen to him,' said Stanley, 'you didn't whistle, then?'

But the boy felt as if he hadn't whistled, as if only Harry and Stanley had. He was making plans, when it was time to knock off work, to get left behind and somehow make his way over to the woman. The weather report said the hot spell was due to break, so he had to move quickly. But there was no chance of being left. The other two decided to knock off work at four, because they were exhausted. As they went down, Tom quickly climbed a parapet and hoisted himself higher by pulling his weight up a chimney. He caught a glimpse of her lying on her back, her knees up, eyes closed, a brown woman lolling in the sun. He slipped and clattered down, as Stanley looked for information: 'She's gone down,' he said. He felt as if he had protected her from Stanley, and that she must be grateful to him. He could feel the bond between the woman and himself.

Next day, they stood around on the landing below the roof, reluctant to climb up into the heat. The woman who had lent Harry the blanket came out and offered them a cup of tea. They accepted gratefully, and sat around Mrs Pritchett's kitchen an hour or so, chatting. She was married to an airline pilot. A smart blonde, of about thirty, she had an eye for the handsome sharp-faced Stanley; and the two teased each other while Harry sat in a corner, watching, indulgent, though his expression reminded Stanley that he was married. And young Tom felt envious of Stanley's ease in badinage; felt, too, that Stanley's getting off with Mrs Pritchett left his romance with the woman on the roof safe and intact.

'I thought they said the heat wave'd break,' said Stanley, sullen, as the time approached when they really would have to climb up into the sunlight.

'You don't like it, then?' asked Mrs Pritchett.

'All right for some,' said Stanley. 'Nothing to do but lie about as if it was a beach up there. Do you ever go up?'

'Went up once,' said Mrs Pritchett. 'But it's a dirty place up there, and it's too hot.'

'Quite right too,' said Stanley.

Then they went up, leaving the cool neat little flat and the friendly Mrs Pritchett.

As soon as they were up they saw her. The three men looked at her, resentful at her ease in this punishing sun. Then Harry said, because of the expression on Stanley's face: 'Come on, we've got to pretend to work, at least.'

They had to wrench another length of guttering that ran beside a parapet out of its bed, so that they could replace it. Stanley took it in his two hands, tugged, swore, stood up. 'Fuck it,' he said, and sat down under a chimney. He lit a cigarette. 'Fuck them,' he said. 'What do they think we are, lizards? I've got blisters all over my hands.' Then he jumped up and climbed over the roofs and stood with his back to them. He put his fingers either side of his mouth and let out a shrill whistle. Tom and Harry squatted, not looking at each other, watching him. They could just see the woman's head, the beginnings of her brown shoulders. Stanley whistled again. Then he began stamping with his feet, and whistled and yelled and screamed at the woman, his face getting scarlet. He seemed quite mad, as he stamped and whistled, while the woman did not move, she did not move a muscle.

'Barmy,' said Tom.

'Yes,' said Harry, disapproving.

Suddenly the older man came to a decision. It was, Tom knew, to save some sort of scandal or real trouble over the woman. Harry stood up and began packing tools into a length of oily cloth. 'Stanley,' he said, commanding. At first Stanley took no notice, but Harry said: 'Stanley, we're packing it in, I'll tell Matthew.'

Stanley came back, cheeks mottled, eyes glaring.

'Can't go on like this,' said Harry. 'It'll break in a day or so. I'm going to tell Matthew we've got sunstroke, and if he doesn't like it, it's too bad.' Even Harry sounded aggrieved, Tom noted. The small, competent man, the family man with his grey hair, who was never at a loss, sounded really off balance. 'Come on,' he said, angry. He fitted himself into the open square in the roof, and went down, watching his feet on the ladder. Then

Stanley went, with not a glance at the woman. Then Tom who, his throat beating with excitement, silently promised her in a backward glance: Wait for me, wait, I'm coming.

On the pavement Stanley said: 'I'm going home.' He looked white now, so perhaps he really did have sunstroke. Harry went off to find the foreman who was at work on the plumbing of some flats down the street. Tom slipped back, not into the building they had been working on, but the building on whose roof the woman lay. He went straight up, no one stopping him. The skylight stood open, with an iron ladder leading up. He emerged on to the roof a couple of yards from her. She sat up, pushing back her black hair with both hands. The scarf across her breasts bound them tight, and brown flesh bulged around it. Her legs were brown and smooth. She stared at him in silence. The boy stood grinning, foolish, claiming the tenderness he expected from her.

'What do you want?' she asked.

'I ... I came to ... make your acquaintance,' he stammered, grinning, pleading with her.

They looked at each other, the slight, scarlet-faced excited boy, and the serious, nearly naked woman. Then, without a word, she lay down on her brown blanket, ignoring him.

'You like the sun, do you?' he inquired of her glistening back.

Not a word. He felt panic, thinking of how she had held him in her arms, stroked his hair, brought him where he sat, lordly, in her bed, a glass of some exhilarating liquor he had never tasted in life. He felt that if he knelt down, stroked her shoulders, her hair, she would turn and clasp him in her arms.

He said: 'The sun's all right for you, isn't it?'

She raised her head, set her chin on two small fists. 'Go away,' she said. He did not move. 'Listen,' she said, in a slow reasonable voice, where anger was kept in check, though with difficulty; looking at him, her face weary with anger: 'If you get a kick out of seeing women in bikinis, why don't you take a sixpenny bus ride to the Lido? You'd see dozens of them, without all this mountaineering.'

She hadn't understood him. He felt her unfairness pale him. He stammered: 'But I like you, I've been watching you and ...'

'Thanks,' she said, and dropped her face again, turned away from him.

She lay there. He stood there. She said nothing. She had simply shut him out. He stood, saying nothing at all, for some minutes. He thought: She'll have to say something if I stay. But the minutes went past, with no sign of them in her, except in the tension of her back, her thighs, her arms – the tension of waiting for him to go.

He looked up at the sky, where the sun seemed to spin in heat; and over the roofs where he and his mates had been earlier. He could see the heat quavering where they had worked. 'And they expect us to work in these conditions!' he thought, filled with righteous indignation. The woman hadn't moved. A bit of hot wind blew her black hair softly, it shone, and was iridescent. He remembered how he had stroked it last night.

Resentment of her at last moved him off and away down the ladder, through the building, into the street. He got drunk then, in hatred of her.

Next day when he woke the sky was grey. He looked at the wet grey and thought, vicious: 'Well, that's fixed you, hasn't it now? That's fixed you good and proper.'

The three men were at work early on the cool leads, surrounded by damp drizzling roofs where no one came to sun themselves, black roofs, slimy with rain. Because it was cool now, they would finish the job that day, if they hurried.

HOW I FINALLY LOST MY HEART

It would be easy to say that I picked up a knife, slit open my side, took my heart out, and threw it away; but unfortunately it wasn't as easy as that. Not that I, like everyone else, had not often wanted to do it. No, it happened differently, and not as I expected.

It was just after I had had a lunch and a tea with two different men. My lunch partner I had lived with for (more or less) four and seven-twelfths years. When he left me for new pastures, I spent two years, or was it three, half dead, and my heart was a stone, impossible to carry about, considering all the other things weighing on one. Then I slowly, and with difficulty, got free, because my heart cherished a thousand adhesions to my first love – though from another point of view he could be legitimately described as either my second *real* love (my father being the first) or my third (my brother intervening).

As the folk song has it:

> I have loved but three men in my life,
> My father, my brother, and the man that
> took my life.

But if one were going to look at the thing from outside, without insight, he could be seen as (perhaps, I forget) the thirteenth, but to do that means disregarding the inner emotional truth. For we all know that those affairs or entanglements one has between *serious* loves, though they may number dozens and stretch over years, *don't really count.*

This way of looking at things creates a number of unhappy people, for it is well known that what doesn't really count for me might very well count for you. But there is no way of getting over this difficulty, for a *serious* love is the most important business in life, or nearly so. At any rate, most of us are engaged in looking for it. Even when we are in fact being very serious indeed with one person we still have an eighth of an eye cocked in case some stranger unexpectedly encountered might turn out to be even more serious. We are all entirely in agreement that we are in the right to taste, test, sip and sample a thousand people on our way to the *real* one. It is not too much to say that in our circles tasting and sampling is probably the second most important activity, the first being earning money. Or to put it another way, 'If you are serious about this thing, you go on laying everybody that offers until something clicks and you're all set to go.'

I have digressed from an earlier point: that I regarded this man I had lunch with (we will call him A) as my first love; and still do despite the Freudians, who insist on seeing my father as A and possibly my brother as B, making my (real) first love C. And despite, also, those who might ask: What about your two husbands and all those affairs?

What about them? I did not *really* love them, the way I loved A.

I had lunch with him. Then, quite by chance, I had tea with B. When I say B, here, I mean my *second* serious love, not my brother, or the little boys I was in love with between the ages of five and fifteen, if we are going to take fifteen (arbitrarily) as the point of no return . . . which last phrase is in itself a pretty brave defiance of the secular arbiters.

In between A and B (my count) there were a good many affairs, or samples, but they didn't score. B and I *clicked*, we went off like a bomb, though not quite as simply as A and I had clicked, because my heart was bruised, sullen, and suspicious because of A's throwing me over. Also there were all those ligaments and adhesions binding me to A still to be loosened, one by one. However, for a time B and I got on like a house on fire, and then we came to grief. My heart was again a ton weight in my side.

> If this were a stone in my side, a stone,
> I could pluck it out and be free . . .

Having lunch with A, then tea with B, two men who between them had consumed a decade of my precious years (I am not counting the test or trial affairs in between) and, it is fair to say, had balanced all the delight (plenty and intense) with misery (oh Lord, Lord) – moving from one to the other, in the course of an afternoon, conversing amiably about this and that, with meanwhile my heart giving no more than slight reminiscent tugs, the fish of memory at the end of a long slack line . . .

To sum up, it was salutary.

Particularly as that evening I was expecting to meet C, or someone who might very well turn out to be C – though I don't want to give too much emphasis to C, the truth is I can hardly remember what he looked like, but one can't be expected to remember the unimportant ones one has sipped or tasted in between. But after all, he might have turned out to be C, we might have *clicked*, and I was in that state of mind (in which we all so often are) of thinking: He might turn out to be the one. (I use a women's magazine phrase deliberately here, instead of saying, as I might: *Perhaps it will be serious.*)

So there I was (I want to get the details and atmosphere right) standing at a window looking into a street (Great Portland Street, as a matter of fact) and thinking that while I would not dream of regretting my affairs, or experiences, with A and B (it is better to have loved and lost than never to have loved at all), my anticipation of the heart because of spending an evening with a possible C had a certain unreality, because there was no doubt that both A and B had caused me unbelievable pain. Why, therefore, was I looking forward to C? I should rather be running away as fast as I could.

It suddenly occurred to me that I was looking at the whole phenomenon quite inaccurately. My (or perhaps I am permitted to say our?) way of looking at it is that one must search for an A, or a B, or a C or a D with a certain combination of desirable or sympathetic qualities so that one may click, or spontaneously combust: or to put it differently, one needs a person who, like a saucer of water, allows one to float off on him/her, like a transfer. But this wasn't so at all. Actually one carries with one a sort of burning spear stuck in one's side, that one waits for someone else to pull out; it is something painful, like a sore or a wound, that one cannot wait to share with someone else.

I saw myself quite plainly in a moment of truth: I was standing at a window (on the third floor) with A and B (to mention only the mountain peaks of my emotional experience) behind me, a rather attractive woman, if I may say so, with a mellowness that I would be the first to admit is the sad harbinger of age, but is attractive by definition, because it is a testament to the amount of sampling and sipping (I nearly wrote simpling and sapping) I have done in my time . . . there I stood, brushed, dressed, red-lipped, kohl-eyed, all waiting for an evening with a possible C. And at another window overlooking (I think I am right in saying) Margaret Street, stood C, brushed, washed, shaved, smiling: an attractive man (I think), and *he* was thinking: Perhaps she will turn out to be D (or A or 3 or ? or %, or whatever symbol he used). We stood, separated by space, certainly, in identical conditions of pleasant uncertainty and anticipation, and we both held our hearts in our hands, all pink and palpitating and ready for pleasure and pain, and we were about to throw these hearts in each other's face like snowballs, or cricket balls (How's that?) or, more accurately, like great bleeding wounds: 'Take my wound.' Because the last thing one ever thinks at such moments is that he (or she) will say: Take *my* wound, please remove the spear from *my* side. No, not at all, one simply expects to get rid of one's own.

I decided I must go to the telephone and say C! – You know that joke about the joke-makers who don't trouble to tell each other jokes, but simply say Joke 1, or Joke 2, and everyone roars with laughter, or snickers, or giggles appropriately . . . Actually one could reverse the game by guessing whether it was Joke C(b) or Joke A(d) according to what sort of laughter a person made to match the silent thought . . . Well, C (I imagined myself saying), the analogy is for our instruction: Let's take the whole thing as read or said. Let's not lick each other's sores; let's keep our hearts to ourselves. Because just consider it, C, how utterly absurd – here we stand at our re-spective windows with our palpitating hearts in our hands . . .

At this moment, dear reader, I was forced simply to put down the telephone with an apology. For I felt the fingers of my left hand push outwards around something rather large, light, and slippery – hard to describe this sensation, really. My hand is not large, and my heart was in a state of inflation after having had lunch with A, tea with B, and then looking forward to C . . . Anyway, my fingers were stretching out rather desper-ately to encompass an unknown, largish, lightish object, and I said: Excuse me a minute, to C, looked down, and there was my heart, in my hand.

I had to end the conversation there.

For one thing, to find that one has achieved something so often longed for, so easily, is upsetting. It's not as if I had been trying. To get something one wants simply by accident – no, there's no pleasure in it, no feeling of achievement. So to find myself heart-whole, or, more accurately, heart-less, or at any rate, rid of the damned thing, and at such an awkward moment, in the middle of an imaginary telephone call with a man who might possibly turn out to be C, well, it was irritating rather than not.

For another thing, a heart raw and bleeding and fresh from one's side, is not the prettiest sight. I'm not going into that at all. I was appalled, and indeed embarrassed that *that* was what had been loving and beating away all those years, because if I'd had any idea at all – well, enough of that.

My problem was how to get rid of it.

Simple, you'll say, drop it into the waste bucket.

Well, let me tell you, that's what I tried to do. I took a good look at this object, nearly died with embarrassment, and walked over to the rubbish can, where I tried to let it roll off my fingers. It wouldn't. It was stuck. There was my heart, a large red pulsing bleeding repulsive object, stuck to my fingers. What was I going to do? I sat down, lit a cigarette (with one hand, holding the matchbox between my knees), held my hand with the heart stuck on it over the side of the chair so that it could drip into a bucket, and considered.

If this were a stone in my hand, a stone,
I could throw it over a tree . . .

When I had finished the cigarette, I carefully unwrapped some tin foil, of the kind used to wrap food in when cooking, and I fitted a sort of cover around my heart. This was absolutely and urgently necessary. First, it was smarting badly. After all, it had spent some forty years protected by flesh and ribs and the air was too much for it. Secondly, I couldn't have any Tom, Dick and Harry walking in and looking at it. Thirdly, I could not look at it for too long myself, it filled me with shame. The tin foil was effective, and indeed rather striking. It is quite pliable and now it seemed as if there were a stylized heart balanced on my palm, like a globe, in glittering, silvery substance. I almost felt I needed a sceptre in the other hand to balance it . . . But the thing was, there is no other word for it, in bad taste. I then wrapped a scarf around hand and tin-foiled heart, and felt safer. Now it was a question of pretending to have hurt my hand until I could think of a way of getting rid of my heart altogether, short of amputating my hand.

Meanwhile I telephoned (really, not in imagination) C, who now would never be C. I could feel my heart, which was stuck so close to my fingers that I could feel every beat or tremor, give a gulp of resigned grief at the idea of this beautiful experience now never to be. I told him some idiotic lie about having flu. Well, he was all stiff and indignant, but concealing it urbanely, as I would have done, making a joke but allowing a tiny barb of sarcasm to rankle in the last well-chosen phrase. Then I sat down again to think out my whole situation.

There I sat.

What was I going to do?

There I sat.

I am going to have to skip about four days here, vital enough in all conscience, because I simply cannot go heartbeat by heartbeat through my memories. A pity, since I suppose this is what this story is about; but in brief: I drew the curtains, I took the telephone off the hook, I turned on the lights, I took the scarf off the glittering shape, then the tin foil, then I examined the heart. There were two-fifths of a century's experience to work through, and before I had even got through the first night, I was in a state hard to describe . . .

Or if I could pull the nerves from my skin
A quick red net to drag through a sea for fish . . .

By the end of the fourth day I was worn out. By no act of will, or intention, or desire, could I move that heart by a fraction – on the contrary, it was not only stuck to my fingers, like a sucked boiled sweet, but was actually growing to the flesh of my fingers and my palm.

I wrapped it up again in tin foil and scarf, and turned out the lights and pulled up the blinds and opened the curtains. It was about ten in the morning, an ordinary London day, neither hot nor cold nor clear nor clouded nor wet nor fine. And while the street is interesting, it is not exactly beautiful, so I wasn't looking at it so much as waiting for something to catch my attention while thinking of something else.

Suddenly I heard a tap-tap-tapping that got louder, sharp and clear, and I knew before I saw her that this was the sound of high heels on a pavement though it might just as well have been a hammer against stone. She walked fast opposite my window and her heels hit the pavement so hard that all the noises of the street seemed absorbed into that single tap-tap-clang-clang. As she reached the corner at Great Portland Street two London pigeons swooped diagonally from the sky very fast, as if they were bullets aimed to kill her; and then as they saw her they swooped up and off at an angle. Meanwhile she had turned the corner. All this has taken time to write down, but the thing happening took a couple of seconds: the woman's body hitting the pavement bang-bang through her heels then sharply turning the corner in a right angle; and the pigeons making another acute angle across hers and intersecting it in a fast sweep of displaced air. Nothing to all that, of course, nothing – she had gone off down the street, her heels tip-tapping, and the pigeons landed on my windowsill and began cooing. All gone, all vanished, the marvellous exact co-ordination of sound and movement, but it had happened, it had made me happy and exhilarated, I had no problems in this world, and I realized that the heart stuck to my fingers was quite loose. I couldn't get it off altogether, though I was tugging at it under the scarf and the tin foil, but almost.

I understood that sitting and analysing each movement of my pulse or beat of my heart through forty years was a mistake. I was on the wrong track altogether: this was the way to attach my red, bitter, delighted heart to my flesh for ever and ever . . .

> Ha! So you think I'm done! You think . . .
> Watch, I'll roll my heart in a mesh of rage
> And bounce it like a handball off
> Walls, faces, railings, umbrellas and pigeons' backs . . .

No, all that was no good at all, it just made things worse. What I must do is to take myself by surprise, as it were, the way I was taken by surprise over the woman and the pigeons and the sharp sounds of heels and silk wings.

I put on my coat, held my lumpy scarfed arm across my chest, so that if anyone said: What have you done with your hand? I could say: I've banged my finger in the door. Then I walked down into the street.

It wasn't easy to go among so many people, when I was worried that they were thinking: What has that woman done to her hand? because that made it hard to forget myself. And all the time it tingled and throbbed against my fingers, reminding me.

Now I was out I didn't know what to do. Should I go and have lunch with someone? Or wander in the park? Or buy myself a dress? I decided to go to the Round Pond, and walk around it by myself. I was tired after four days and nights without sleep. I went down into the Underground at Oxford Circus. Midday. Crowds of people. I felt self-conscious, but of course need not have worried. I swear you could walk naked down the street in London and no one would even turn round.

So I went down the escalator and looked at the faces coming up past me on the other side, as I always do; and wondered, as I

always do, how strange it is that those people and I should meet
by chance in such a way, and how odd that we would never see
each other again, or, if we did, we wouldn't know it. And I went
on to the crowded platform and looked at the faces as I always
do, and got into the train, which was very full, and found a seat.
It wasn't as bad as at rush hour, but all the seats were filled. I
leaned back and closed my eyes, deciding to sleep a little, being
so tired. I was just beginning to doze off, when I heard a
woman's voice muttering, or rather, declaiming:

> 'A gold cigarette case, well, that's a nice thing,
>   isn't it, I must say, a gold case, yes . . .'

There was something about this voice which made me open my
eyes: on the other side of the compartment, about eight persons
away, sat a youngish woman, wearing a cheap green cloth coat,
gloveless hands, flat brown shoes, and lisle stockings. She must
be rather poor – a woman dressed like this is a rare sight, these
days. But it was her posture that struck me. She was sitting half
twisted in her seat, so that her head was turned over her left
shoulder, and she was looking straight at the stomach of an
elderly man next to her. But it was clear she was not seeing it:
her young staring eyes were sightless, she was looking inwards.

She was so clearly alone, in the crowded compartment, that
it was not as embarrassing as it might have been. I looked
around, and people were smiling, or exchanging glances, or
winking, or ignoring her, according to their natures, but she was
oblivious of us all.

She suddenly aroused herself, turned so that she sat straight
in her seat, and directed her voice and her gaze to the opposite
seat:

> 'Well so that's what you think, you think that, you
>   think that do you, well, you think I'm just going
>   to wait at home for you, but you gave her a gold
>   case and . . .'

And with a clockwork movement of her whole thin person,

she turned her narrow pale-haired head sideways over her left shoulder, and resumed her stiff empty stare at the man's stomach. He was grinning uncomfortably. I leaned forward to look along the line of people in the row of seats I sat in, and the man opposite her, a young man, had exactly the same look of discomfort which he was determined to keep amused. So we all looked at her, the young, thin, pale woman in her private drama of misery, who was so completely unconscious of us that she spoke and thought out loud. And again, without particular warning or reason, in between stops, so it wasn't that she was disturbed from her dream by the train stopping at Bond Street, and then jumping forward again, she twisted her body frontways, and addressed the seat opposite her (the young man had got off, and a smart grey-curled matron had got in):

'Well I know about it now, don't I, and if you come in all smiling and pleased well then I know, don't I, you don't have to tell me, I know, and I've said to her, I've said, I know he gave you a gold cigarette case . . .'

At which point, with the same clockwork impulse, she stopped, or was checked, or simply ran out, and turned herself half around to stare at the stomach – the same stomach, for the middle-aged man was still there. But we stopped at Marble Arch and he got out, giving the compartment, rather than the people in it, a tolerant half-smile which said: I am sure I can trust you to realize that this unfortunate woman is stark staring mad . . .

His seat remained empty. No people got in at Marble Arch, and the two people standing waiting for seats did not want to sit by her to receive her stare.

We all sat, looking gently in front of us, pretending to ourselves and to each other that we didn't know the poor woman was mad and that in fact we ought to be doing something about it. I even wondered what I should say: Madam, you're mad – shall I escort you to your home? Or: Poor thing, don't go on like that, it doesn't do any good, you know – just leave him, that'll bring him to his senses . . .

And behold, after the interval that was regulated by her inner mechanism had elapsed, she turned back and said to the smart matron who received this statement of accusation with perfect self-command:

> 'Yes, I know! Oh yes! And what about my
> shoes, what about them, a golden cigarette
> case is what she got, the filthy bitch,
> a golden case . . .'

Stop. Twist. Stare. At the empty seat by her.

Extraordinary. Because it was a frozen misery, how shall I put it? A passionless passion – we were seeing unhappiness embodied, we were looking at the essence of some private tragedy – rather, Tragedy. There was no emotion in it. She was like an actress doing Accusation, or Betrayed Love, or Infidelity, when she has only just learned her lines and is not bothering to do more than get them right.

And whether she sat in her half-twisted position, her unblinking eyes staring at the greenish, furry, ugly covering of the train seat, or sat straight, directing her accusation to the smart woman opposite, there was a frightening immobility about her – yes, that was why she frightened us. For it was clear that she might very well (if the inner machine ran down) stay silent, for ever, in either twisted or straight position, or at any point between them – yes, we could all imagine her, frozen perpetually in some arbitrary pose. It was as if we watched the shell of some woman going through certain predetermined motions.

For *she* was simply not there. *What* was there, who she was, it was impossible to tell, though it was easy to imagine her thin, gentle little face breaking into a smile in total forgetfulness of what she was enacting now. She did not know she was in a train between Marble Arch and Queensway, nor that she was publicly accusing her husband or lover, nor that we were looking at her.

And we, looking at her, felt an embarrassment and shame that was not on her account at all . . .

Suddenly I felt, under the scarf and the tin foil, a lightening of my fingers, as my heart rolled loose.

I hastily took it off my palm, in case it decided to adhere there again, and I removed the scarf, leaving balanced on my knees a perfect stylized heart, like a silver heart on a Valentine card, though of course it was three-dimensional. This heart was not so much harmless, no that isn't the word, as artistic, but in very bad taste, as I said. I could see that the people in the train, now looking at me and the heart, and not at the poor mad-woman, were pleased with it.

I got up, took the four or so paces to where she was, and laid the tin-foiled heart down on the seat so that it received her stare.

For a moment she did not react, then with a groan or a mutter of relieved and entirely theatrical grief, she leaned for-ward, picked up the glittering heart, and clutched it in her arms, hugging it and rocking it back and forth, even laying her cheek against it, while staring over its top at her husband as if to say: Look what I've got, I don't care about you and your cigarette case, I've got a silver heart.

I got up, since we were at Notting Hill Gate, and, followed by the pleased congratulatory nods and smiles of the people left behind, I went out on to the platform, up the escalators, into the street, and along to the park.

No heart. No heart at all. What bliss. What freedom . . .

Hear that sound? That's laughter, yes.
That's me laughing, yes, that's me.

A MAN AND TWO WOMEN

Stella's friends the Bradfords had taken a cheap cottage in Essex for the summer, and she was going down to visit them. She wanted to see them, but there was no doubt there was something of a letdown (and for them too) in the English cottage. Last summer Stella had been wandering with her husband around Italy; had seen the English couple at a café table, and found them sympathetic. They all liked each other, and the four went about for some weeks, sharing meals, hotels, trips. Back in London the friendship had not, as might have been expected, fallen off. Then Stella's husband departed abroad, as he often did, and Stella saw Jack and Dorothy by herself. There were a great many people she might have seen, but it was the Bradfords she saw most often, two or three times a week, at their flat or hers. They were at ease with each other. Why were they? Well, for one thing they were all artists – in different ways. Stella designed wallpapers and materials; she had a name for it.

The Bradfords were real artists. He painted, she drew. They had lived mostly out of England in cheap places around the Mediterranean. Both from the North of England, they had met at art school, married at twenty, had taken flight from England, then returned to it, needing it, then off again: and so on, for years, in the rhythm of so many of their kind, needing, hating, loving England. There had been seasons of real poverty, while they lived on *pasta* or bread or rice, and wine and fruit and sunshine, in Majorca, southern Spain, Italy, North Africa.

A French critic had seen Jack's work, and suddenly he was successful. His show in Paris, then one in London, made money; and now he charged in the hundreds where a year or so ago he charged ten or twenty guineas. This had deepened his contempt for the values of the markets. For a while Stella thought that this was the bond between the Bradfords and herself. They were so very much, as she was, of the new generation of artists (and poets and playwrights and novelists) who had one thing in common, a cool derision about the racket. They were so very unlike (they felt) the older generation with their Societies and their Lunches and their salons and their cliques: their atmosphere of connivance with the snobberies of success. Stella, too, had been successful by a fluke. Not that she did not consider herself talented; it was that others as talented were unfêted, and unbought. When she was with the Bradfords and other fellow spirits, they would talk about the racket, using each other as yardsticks or fellow consciences about how much to give in, what to give, how to use without being used, how to enjoy without becoming dependent on enjoyment.

Of course Dorothy Bradford was not able to talk in quite the same way, since she had not yet been 'discovered'; she had not 'broken through'. A few people with discrimination bought her unusual delicate drawings, which had a strength that was hard to understand unless one knew Dorothy herself. But she was not at all, as Jack was, a great success. There was a strain here, in the marriage, nothing much; it was kept in check by their scorn for their arbitrary rewards of 'the racket'. But it was there, nevertheless.

Stella's husband had said: 'Well, I can understand that, it's like me and you – you're creative, whatever that may mean, I'm just a bloody TV journalist.' There was no bitterness in this. He was a good journalist, and besides he sometimes got the chance to make a good small film. All the same, there was that between him and Stella, just as there was between Jack and his wife.

After a time Stella saw something else in her kinship with the couple. It was that the Bradfords had a close bond, bred of having spent so many years together in foreign places, dependent on each other because of their poverty. It had been a real love marriage, one could see it by looking at them. It was now. And Stella's marriage was a real marriage. She understood she enjoyed being with the Bradfords because the two couples were equal in this. Both marriages were those of strong,

passionate, talented individuals; they shared a battling quality
that strengthened them, not weakened them.

The reason why it had taken Stella so long to understand this
was that the Bradfords had made her think about her own marriage, which she was beginning to take for granted, sometimes
even found exhausting. She had understood, through them, how
lucky she was in her husband; how lucky they all were. No
marital miseries; nothing of (what they saw so often in friends)
one partner in a marriage victim to the other, resenting the
other; no claiming of outsiders as sympathizers or allies in an
unequal battle.

There had been a plan for these four people to go off again to
Italy or Spain, but then Stella's husband departed, and Dorothy got pregnant. So there was the cottage in Essex instead, a
bad second choice, but better, they all felt, to deal with a new
baby on home ground, at least for the first year. Stella, telephoned by Jack (on Dorothy's particular insistence, he said),
offered and received commiserations on its being only Essex
and not Majorca or Italy. She also received sympathy because
her husband had been expected back this weekend, but had
wired to say he wouldn't be back for another month, probably –
there was trouble in Venezuela. Stella wasn't really forlorn; she
didn't mind living alone, since she was always supported by
knowing her man would be back. Besides, if she herself were
offered the chance of a month's 'trouble' in Venezuela, she
wouldn't hesitate, so it wasn't fair ... fairness characterized
their relationship. All the same, it was nice that she could drop
down (or up) to the Bradfords, people with whom she could
always be herself, neither more nor less.

She left London at midday by train, armed with food unob-
tainable in Essex: salamis, cheeses, spices, wine. The sun shone,
but it wasn't particularly warm. She hoped there would be
heating in the cottage, July or not.

The train was empty. The little station seemed stranded in a
green nowhere. She got out, cumbered by bags full of food. A
porter and a stationmaster examined, then came to succour her.
She was a tallish, fair woman, rather ample; her soft hair,
drawn back, escaped in tendrils, and she had great helpless-

looking blue eyes. She wore a dress made in one of the materials she had designed. Enormous green leaves laid hands all over her body, and fluttered about her knees. She stood smiling, accustomed to men running to wait on her, enjoying them enjoying her. She walked with them to the barrier where Jack waited, appreciating the scene. He was a smallish man, compact, dark. He wore a blue-green summer shirt, and smoked a pipe and smiled, watching. The two men delivered her into the hands of the third, and departed, whistling, to their duties.

Jack and Stella kissed, then pressed their cheeks together.

'Food,' he said, 'food', relieving her of the parcels.

'What's it like here, shopping?'

'Vegetables all right, I suppose.'

Jack was still Northern in this: he seemed brusque, to strangers; he wasn't shy, he simply hadn't been brought up to enjoy words. Now he put his arm briefly around Stella's waist, and said: 'Marvellous, Stell, marvellous.' They walked on, pleased with each other. Stella had with Jack, her husband had with Dorothy, these moments, when they said to each other wordlessly: If I were not married to my husband, if you were not married to your wife, how delightful it would be to be married to you. These moments were not the least of the pleasures of this four-sided friendship.

'Are you liking it down here?'

'It's what we bargained for.'

There was more than his usual shortness in this, and she glanced at him to find him frowning. They were walking to the car, parked under a tree.

'How's the baby?'

'Little bleeder never sleeps, he's wearing us out, but he's fine.'

The baby was six weeks old. Having the baby was a definite achievement: getting it safely conceived and born had taken a couple of years. Dorothy, like most independent women, had had divided thoughts about a baby. Besides, she was over thirty and complained she was set in her ways. All this – the difficulties, Dorothy's hesitations – had added up to an atmosphere which Dorothy herself described as 'like wondering if some damned horse is going to take the fence'. Dorothy would talk, while she was pregnant, in a soft staccato voice: 'Perhaps I don't really want a baby at all? Perhaps I'm not fitted to be a mother? Perhaps . . . and if so . . . and how . . .?'

She said: 'Until recently Jack and I were always with people who took it for granted that getting pregnant was a disaster, and now suddenly all the people we know have young children and baby-sitters and . . . perhaps . . . if . . .'

Jack said: 'You'll feel better when it's born.'

Once Stella had heard him say, after one of Dorothy's long troubled dialogues with herself: 'Now that's enough, that's enough, Dorothy.' He had silenced her, taking the responsibility.

They reached the car, got in. It was a second-hand job recently bought. 'They' (being the press, the enemy generally) 'wait for us' (being artists or writers who have made money) 'to buy flashy cars.' They had discussed it, decided that *not* to buy an expensive car if they felt like it would be allowing themselves to be bullied; but bought a second-hand one after all. Jack wasn't going to give *them* so much satisfaction, apparently.

'Actually we could have walked,' he said, as they shot down a narrow lane, 'but with these groceries, it's just as well.'

'If the baby's giving you a tough time, there can't be much time for cooking.' Dorothy was a wonderful cook. But now again there was something in the air as he said: 'Food's definitely not too good just now. You can cook supper, Stell, we could do with a good feed.'

Now Dorothy hated anyone in her kitchen, except, for certain specified jobs, her husband; and this was surprising.

'The truth is, Dorothy's worn out,' he went on, and now Stella understood he was warning her.

'Well, it is tiring,' said Stella soothingly.

'You were like that?'

Like *that* was saying a good deal more than just worn out, or tired, and Stella understood that Jack was really uneasy. She said, plaintively humorous: 'You two always expect me to remember things that happened a hundred years ago. Let me think . . .'

She had been married when she was eighteen, got pregnant at once. Her husband had left her. Soon she had married Philip, who also had a small child from a former marriage. These two children, her daughter, seventeen, his son, twenty, had grown up together.

She remembered herself at nineteen, alone, with a small baby. 'Well, I was alone,' she said. 'That makes a difference. I remember I was exhausted. Yes, I was definitely irritable and unreasonable.'

'Yes,' said Jack, with a brief reluctant look at her.

'All right, don't worry,' she said, replying aloud as she often did to things that Jack had not said aloud.

'Good,' he said.

Stella thought of how she had seen Dorothy, in the hospital room, with the new baby. She had sat up in bed, in a pretty bed jacket, the baby beside her in a basket. He was restless. Jack stood between basket and bed, one large hand on his son's stomach. 'Now, you just shut up, little bleeder,' he had said, as he grumbled. Then he had picked him up, as if he'd been doing it always, held him against his shoulder, and, as Dorothy held her arms out, had put the baby into them. 'Want your mother, then? Don't blame you.'

That scene, the ease of it, the way the two parents were together, had, for Stella, made nonsense of all the months of Dorothy's self-questioning. As for Dorothy, she had said, parodying the expected words but meaning them: 'He's the most beautiful baby ever born. I can't imagine why I didn't have him before.'

'There's the cottage,' said Jack. Ahead of them was a small labourer's cottage, among full green trees, surrounded by green grass. It was painted white, had four sparkling windows. Next to it a long shed or structure that turned out to be a greenhouse.

'The man grew tomatoes,' said Jack. 'Fine studio now.'

The car came to rest under another tree.

'Can I just drop in to the studio?'

'Help yourself.' Stella walked into the long, glass-roofed

shed. In London Jack and Dorothy shared a studio. They had
shared huts, sheds, any suitable building, all around the Mediterranean. They always worked side by side. Dorothy's end was
tidy, exquisite, Jack's lumbered with great canvases, and he
worked in a clutter. Now Stella looked to see if this friendly
arrangement continued, but as Jack came in behind her he
said: 'Dorothy's not set herself up yet. I miss her, I can tell
you.'

The greenhouse was still partly one: trestles with plants
stood along the ends. It was lush and warm.

'As hot as hell when the sun's really going, it makes up. And
Dorothy brings Paul in sometimes, so he can get used to a
decent climate young.'

Dorothy came in, at the far end, without the baby. She had
recovered her figure. She was a small dark woman, with neat,
delicate limbs. Her face was white, with scarlet rather irregular lips, and black glossy brows, a little crooked. So while she
was not pretty, she was lively and dramatic-looking. She and
Stella had their moments together, when they got pleasure from
contrasting their differences, one woman so big and soft and
blonde, the other so dark and vivacious.

Dorothy came forward through shafts of sunlight, stopped,
and said: 'Stella, I'm glad you've come.' Then forward again,
to a few steps off, where she stood looking at them. 'You two
look good together,' she said, frowning. There was something
heavy and over-emphasized about both statements, and Stella
said: 'I was wondering what Jack had been up to.'

'Very good, I think,' said Dorothy, coming to look at the new
canvas on the easel. It was of sunlit rocks, brown and smooth
with blue sky, blue water, and people swimming in spangles of
light. When Jack was in the South, he painted pictures that his
wife described as 'dirt and grime and misery' – which was how
they both described their joint childhood background. When he
was in England he painted scenes like these.

'Like it? It's good, isn't it?' said Dorothy.

'Very much,' said Stella. She always took pleasure from the
contrast between Jack's outward self – the small, self-contained
little man who could have vanished in a moment into a crowd

of factory workers in, perhaps, Manchester, and the sensuous bright pictures like these.

'And you?' asked Stella.

'Having a baby's killed everything creative in me – quite different from being pregnant,' said Dorothy, but not complaining of it. She had worked like a demon while she was pregnant.

'Have a heart,' said Jack; 'he's only just got himself born.'

'Well, I don't care,' said Dorothy. 'That's the funny thing, I *don't* care.' She said this flat, indifferent. She seemed to be looking at them both again from a small troubled distance. 'You two look good together,' she said, and again there was the small jar.

'Well, how about some tea?' said Jack, and Dorothy said at once: 'I made it when I heard the car. I thought better inside, it's not really hot in the sun.' She led the way out of the green-house, her white linen dress dissolving in lozenges of yellow light from the glass panes above, so that Stella was reminded of the white limbs of Jack's swimmers disintegrating under sun-light in his new picture. The work of these two people was always reminding one of each other, or each other's work, and in all kinds of ways: they were so much married, so close.

The time it took to cross the space of rough grass to the door of the little house was enough to show Dorothy was right: it was really chilly in the sun. Inside two electric heaters made up for it. There had been two little rooms downstairs, but they had been knocked into one fine low-ceilinged room, stone-floored, whitewashed. A tea table, covered with a purple checked cloth, stood waiting near a window where flowering bushes and trees showed through clean panes. Charming. They adjusted the heaters and arranged themselves so they could admire the English countryside through glass. Stella looked for the baby; Dorothy said: 'In the pram at the back.' Then she asked: 'Did yours cry a lot?'

Stella laughed and said again: 'I'll try to remember.'

'We expect you to guide and direct, with all your experience,' said Jack.

'As far as I can remember, she was a little demon for about

three months, for no reason I could see, then suddenly she became civilized.'

'Roll on the three months,' said Jack.

'Six weeks to go,' said Dorothy, handling teacups in a
languid indifferent manner Stella found new in her.

'Finding it tough going?'

'I've never felt better in my life,' said Dorothy at once, as if
being accused.

'You look fine.'

She looked a bit tired, nothing much; Stella couldn't see
what reason there was for Jack to warn her. Unless he meant
the languor, a look of self-absorption? Her vivacity, a friendly
aggressiveness that was the expression of her lively intelligence,
was dimmed. She sat leaning back in a deep airchair, letting
Jack manage things, smiling vaguely.

'I'll bring him in in a minute,' she remarked, listening to the
silence from the sunlit garden at the back.

'Leave him,' said Jack. 'He's quiet seldom enough. Relax,
woman, and have a cigarette.'

He lit a cigarette for her, and she took it in the same vague
way, and sat breathing out smoke, her eyes half closed.

'Have you heard from Philip?' she asked, not from politeness, but with sudden insistence.

'Of course she has, she got a wire,' said Jack.

'I want to know how she feels,' said Dorothy. 'How do you
feel, Stell?' She was listening for the baby all the time.

'Feel about what?'

'About his not coming back.'

'But he is coming back, it's only a month,' said Stella, and
heard, with surprise, that her voice sounded edgy.

'You see?' said Dorothy to Jack, meaning the words, not the
edge on them.

At this evidence that she and Philip had been discussed,
Stella felt, first, pleasure: because it was pleasurable to be
understood by two such good friends; then she felt discomfort,
remembering Jack's warning.

'See what?' she asked Dorothy, smiling.

'That's enough now,' said Jack to his wife in a flash of stubborn anger, which continued the conversation that had taken place.

Dorothy took direction from her husband, and kept quiet a moment, then seemed impelled to continue: 'I've been thinking it must be nice, having your husband go off, then come back. Do you realize Jack and I haven't been separated since we married? That's over ten years. Don't you think there's something awful in two grown people stuck together all the time like Siamese twins?' This ended in a wail of genuine appeal to Stella.

'No, I think it's marvellous.'

'But you don't mind being alone so much?'

'It's not *so* much, it's two or three months in a year. Well of course I mind. But I enjoy being alone, really. But I'd enjoy it too if we were together all the time. I envy you two.' Stella was surprised to find her eyes wet with self-pity because she had to be without her husband another month.

'And what does he think?' demanded Dorothy. 'What does Philip think?'

Stella said: 'Well, I think he likes getting away from time to time – yes. He likes intimacy, he enjoys it, but it doesn't come as easily to him as it does to me.' She had never said this before because she had never thought about it. She was annoyed with herself that she had had to wait for Dorothy to prompt her. Yet she knew that getting annoyed was what she must not do, with the state Dorothy was in, whatever it was. She glanced at Jack for guidance, but he was determinedly busy on his pipe.

'Well, I'm like Philip,' announced Dorothy. 'Yes, I'd love it if Jack went off sometimes. I think I'm being stifled being shut up with Jack day and night, year in year out.'

'Thanks,' said Jack, short but good-humoured.

'No, but I mean it. There's something humiliating about two adult people never for one second out of each other's sight.'

'Well,' said Jack, 'when Paul's a bit bigger, you buzz off for a month or so and you'll appreciate me when you get back.'

'It's not that I don't appreciate you, it's not that at all,' said Dorothy, insistent, almost strident, apparently fevered with restlessness. Her languor had quite gone, and her limbs jerked and moved. And now the baby, as if he had been prompted by his father's mentioning him, let out a cry. Jack got up, forestalling his wife, saying: 'I'll get him.'

Dorothy sat, listening for her husband's movements with the baby, until he came back, which he did, supporting the infant sprawled against his shoulder with a competent hand. He sat down, let his son slide on to his chest, and said: 'There now, you shut up and leave us in peace a bit longer.' The baby was looking up into his face with the astonished expression of the newly born, and Dorothy sat smiling at both of them. Stella understood that her restlessness, her repeated curtailed movements, meant that she longed – more, needed – to have the child in her arms, have its body against hers. And Jack seemed to feel this, because Stella could have sworn it was not a conscious decision that made him rise and slide the infant into his wife's arms. Her flesh, her needs, had spoken direct to him without words, and he had risen at once to give her what she wanted. This silent instinctive conversation between husband and wife made Stella miss her own husband violently, and with resentment against fate that kept them apart so often. She ached for Philip.

Meanwhile Dorothy, now the baby was sprawled softly against her chest, the small feet in her hand, seemed to have lapsed into good humour. And Stella, watching, remembered something she really had forgotten: the close, fierce physical tie between herself and her daughter when she had been a tiny baby. She saw this bond in the way Dorothy stroked the small head that trembled on its neck as the baby looked up into his mother's face. Why, she remembered it was like being in love, having a new baby. All kinds of forgotten or unused instincts woke in Stella. She lit a cigarette, took herself in hand; set herself to enjoy the other woman's love affair with her baby instead of envying her.

The sun, dropping into the trees, struck the windowpanes; and there was a dazzle and a flashing of yellow and white light into the room, particularly over Dorothy in her white dress and the baby. Again Stella was reminded of Jack's picture of the white-limbed swimmers in sun-dissolving water. Dorothy shielded the baby's eyes with her hand and remarked dreamily: 'This is better than any man, isn't it, Stell? Isn't it better than any man?'

'Well – no,' said Stella laughing. 'No, not for long.'

'If you say so, you should know . . . but I can't imagine ever . . . tell me, Stell, does your Philip have affairs when he's away?'

'For God's sake!' said Jack, angry. But he checked himself.

'Yes, I am sure he does.'

'Do you mind?' asked Dorothy, loving the baby's feet with her enclosing palm.

And now Stella was forced to remember, to think about having minded, minding, coming to terms, and the ways in which she now did not mind.

'I don't think about it,' she said.

'Well, I don't think I'd mind,' said Dorothy.

'Thanks for letting me know,' said Jack, short despite himself. Then he made himself laugh.

'And you, do you have affairs while Philip's away?'

'Sometimes. Not really.'

'Do you know, Jack was unfaithful to me this week,' remarked Dorothy, smiling at the baby.

'That's *enough*,' said Jack, really angry.

'No, it isn't enough, it isn't. Because what's awful is, I don't care.'

'Well why should you care, in the circumstances?' Jack turned to Stella. 'There's a silly bitch Lady Edith lives across that field. She got all excited, real live artists living down her lane. Well Dorothy was lucky, she had an excuse in the baby, but I had to go to her silly party. Booze flowing in rivers, and the most incredible people – you know. If you read about them in a novel you'd never believe . . . but I can't remember much after about twelve.'

'Do you know what happened?' said Dorothy. 'I was feeding the baby, it was terribly early. Jack sat straight up in bed and said: "Jesus, Dorothy, I've just remembered, I screwed that silly bitch Lady Edith on her brocade sofa." '

Stella laughed. Jack let out a snort of laughter. Dorothy

laughed, an unscrupulous chuckle of appreciation. Then she said seriously: 'But that's the point, Stella – the thing is, I don't care a tuppenny damn.'

'But why should you?' asked Stella.

'But it's the first time he ever has, and surely I should have minded?'

'Don't you be too sure of that,' said Jack, energetically puffing his pipe. 'Don't be too sure.' But it was only for form's sake, and Dorothy knew it, and said: 'Surely I should have cared, Stell?'

'No. You'd have cared if you and Jack weren't so marvellous together. Just as I'd care if Philip and I weren't . . .' Tears came running down her face. She let them. These were her good friends; and besides, instinct told her tears weren't a bad thing, with Dorothy in this mood. She said sniffing: 'When Philip gets home, we always have a flaming bloody row in the first day or two, about something unimportant, but what it's really about, and we know it, is that I'm jealous of any affair he's had and vice versa. Then we go to bed and make up.' She wept, bitterly, thinking of this happiness, postponed for a month, to be succeeded by the delightful battle of their day to day living.

'Oh Stella,' said Jack. 'Stell . . .' He got up, fished out a handkerchief, dabbed her eyes for her. 'There, love, he'll be back soon.'

'Yes, I know. It's just that you two are so good together and whenever I'm with you I miss Philip.'

'Well, I suppose we're good together?' said Dorothy, sounding surprised. Jack, bending over Stella with his back to his wife, made a warning grimace, then stood up and turned, commanding the situation. 'It's nearly six. You'd better feed Paul. Stella's going to cook supper.'

'Is she? How nice,' said Dorothy. 'There's everything in the kitchen, Stella. How lovely to be looked after.'

'I'll show you our mansion,' said Jack.

Upstairs were two small white rooms. One was the bedroom, with their things and the baby's in it. The other was an overflow room, jammed with stuff. Jack picked up a large

leather folder off the spare bed and said: 'Look at these, Stell.'
He stood at the window, back to her, his thumb at work in his
pipe bowl, looking into the garden. Stella sat on the bed,
opened the folder and at once exclaimed: 'When did she do
these?'

'The last three months she was pregnant. Never seen anything like it, she just turned them out one after the other.'

There were a couple of hundred pencil drawings, all of two
bodies in every kind of balance, tension relationship. The two
bodies were Jack's and Dorothy's, mostly unclothed, but not all.
The drawings startled, not only because they marked a real
jump forward in Dorothy's achievement, but because of their
bold sensuousness. They were a kind of chant, or exaltation
about their marriage. The instinctive closeness, the harmony
of Jack and Dorothy, visible in every movement they made
towards or away from each other, visible even when they
were not together, was celebrated here with a frank, calm
triumph.

'Some of them are pretty strong,' said Jack, the Northern
working-class boy reviving in him for a moment's puritanism.

But Stella laughed, because the prudishness masked pride:
some of the drawings were indecent.

In the last few of the series the woman's body was swollen in
pregnancy. They showed her trust in her husband, whose body,
commanding hers, stood or lay in positions of strength and
confidence.

In the very last Dorothy stood turned away from her husband, her two hands supporting her big belly, and Jack's hands
were protective on her shoulders.

'They are marvellous,' said Stella.

'They are, aren't they.'

Stella looked, laughing, and with love, towards Jack; for she
saw that his showing her the drawings was not only pride in his
wife's talent; but that he was using this way of telling Stella not
to take Dorothy's mood too seriously. And to cheer himself up.
She said, impulsively: 'Well that's all right then, isn't it?'

'What? Oh yes, I see what you mean, yes, I think it's all
right.'

'Do you know what?' said Stella, lowering her voice. 'I think Dorothy's guilty because she feels unfaithful to you.'

'*What?*'

'No, I mean, with the baby, and that's what it's all about.'

He turned to face her, troubled, then slowly smiling. There was the same rich unscrupulous quality of appreciation in that smile as there had been in Dorothy's laugh over her husband and Lady Edith. 'You think so?' They laughed together, irrepressibly and loudly.

'What's the joke?' shouted Dorothy.

'I'm laughing because your drawings are so good,' shouted Stella.

'Yes, they are, aren't they?' But Dorothy's voice changed to flat incredulity: 'The trouble is, I can't imagine how I ever did them, I can't imagine ever being able to do it again.'

'Downstairs,' said Jack to Stella, and they went down to find Dorothy nursing the baby. He nursed with his whole being, all of him in movement. He was wrestling with the breast, thumping Dorothy's plump pretty breast with his fists. Jack stood looking down at the two of them, grinning. Dorothy reminded Stella of a cat, half closing her yellow eyes to stare over her kittens at work on her side, while she stretched out a paw where claws sheathed and unsheathed themselves, making a small rip-rip-rip on the carpet she lay on.

'You're a savage creature,' said Stella, laughing.

Dorothy raised her small vivid face and smiled. 'Yes, I am,' she said, and looked at the two of them calm, and from a distance, over the head of her energetic baby.

Stella cooked supper in a stone kitchen, with a heater brought by Jack to make it tolerable. She used the good food she had brought with her, taking trouble. It took some time, then the three ate slowly over a big wooden table. The baby was not asleep. He grumbled for some minutes on a cushion on the floor, then his father held him briefly, before passing him over, as he had done earlier, in response to his mother's need to have him close.

'I'm supposed to let him cry,' remarked Dorothy. 'But why

should he? If he were an Arab or an African baby he'd be plastered to my back.'

'And very nice too,' said Jack. 'I think they come out too soon into the light of day, they should just stay inside for about eighteen months, much better all round.'

'Have a heart,' said Dorothy and Stella together, and they all laughed; but Dorothy added, quite serious: 'Yes, I've been thinking so too.'

This good nature lasted through the long meal. The light went cool and thin outside; and inside they let the summer dusk deepen, without lamps.

'I've got to go quite soon,' said Stella, with regret.

'Oh, no, you've got to stay!' said Dorothy, strident. It was sudden, the return of the woman who made Jack and Dorothy tense themselves to take strain.

'We all thought Philip was coming. The children will be back tomorrow night, they've been on holiday.'

'Then stay till tomorrow, I *want* you,' said Dorothy, petulant.

'But I can't,' said Stella.

'I never thought I'd want another woman around, cooking in my kitchen, looking after me, but I do,' said Dorothy, apparently about to cry.

'Well, love, you'll have to put up with me,' said Jack.

'Would you mind, Stell?'

'Mind *what*?' asked Stella, cautious.

'Do you find Jack attractive?'

'Very.'

'Well I know you do. Jack, do you find Stella attractive?'

'Try me,' said Jack, grinning; but at the same time signalling warnings to Stella.

'Well, then!' said Dorothy.

'A *ménage à trois*?' asked Stella laughing. 'And how about my Philip? Where does he fit in?'

'Well, if it comes to that, I wouldn't mind Philip myself,' said Dorothy, knitting her sharp black brows and frowning.

'I don't blame you,' said Stella, thinking of her handsome husband.

'Just for a month, till he comes back,' said Dorothy. 'I tell you what, we'll abandon this silly cottage, we must have been mad to stick ourselves away in England in the first place. The three of us'll just pack up and go off to Spain or Italy with the baby.'

'And what else?' inquired Jack, good-natured at all costs, using his pipe as a safety valve.

'Yes, I've decided I approve of polygamy,' announced Dorothy. She had opened her dress and the baby was nursing again, quietly this time, relaxed against her. She stroked his head, softly, softly, while her voice rose and insisted at the other two people: 'I never understood it before, but I do now. I'll be the senior wife, and you two can look after me.'

'Any other plans?' inquired Jack, angry now. 'You just drop in from time to time to watch Stella and me have a go, is that it? Or are you going to tell us when we can go off and do it, give us your gracious permission?'

'Oh I don't care what you do, that's the point,' said Dorothy, sighing, sounding forlorn, however.

Jack and Stella, careful not to look at each other, sat waiting.

'I read something in the newspaper yesterday, it struck me,' said Dorothy, conversational. 'A man and two women living together – here, in England. They are both his wives, they consider themselves his wives. The senior wife has a baby, and the younger wife sleeps with him – well, that's what it looked like, reading between the lines.'

'You'd better stop reading between lines,' said Jack. 'It's not doing you any good.'

'No, I'd like it,' insisted Dorothy. 'I think our marriages are silly. Africans and people like that, they know better, they've got some sense.'

'I can just see you if I did make love to Stella,' said Jack.

'Yes!' said Stella, with a short laugh which, against her will, was resentful.

'But I wouldn't mind,' said Dorothy, and burst into tears.

'Now, Dorothy, that's enough,' said Jack. He got up, took the baby, whose sucking was mechanical now, and said: 'Now listen, you're going right upstairs and you're going to sleep.

This little stinker's full as a tick, he'll be asleep for hours, that's my bet.'

'I don't feel sleepy,' said Dorothy, sobbing.

'I'll give you a sleeping pill, then.'

Then started a search for sleeping pills. None to be found.

'That's just like us,' wailed Dorothy, 'we don't even have a sleeping pill in the place ... Stella, I wish you'd stay, I really do. Why can't you?'

'Stella's going in just a minute, I'm taking her to the station,' said Jack. He poured some Scotch into a glass, handed it to his wife and said: 'Now drink that, love, and let's have an end of it. I'm getting fed-up.' He sounded fed-up.

Dorothy obediently drank the Scotch, got unsteadily from her chair and went slowly upstairs. 'Don't let him cry,' she demanded, as she disappeared.

'Oh you silly bitch,' he shouted after her. 'When have I let him cry? Here, you hold on a minute,' he said to Stella, handing her the baby. He ran upstairs.

Stella held the baby. This was almost for the first time, since she sensed how much another woman's holding her child made Dorothy's fierce new possessiveness uneasy. She looked down at the small, sleepy, red face and said softly: 'Well, you're causing a lot of trouble, aren't you?'

Jack shouted from upstairs: 'Come up a minute, Stell.' She went up, with the baby. Dorothy was tucked up in bed, drowsy from the Scotch, the bedside light turned away from her. She looked at the baby, but Jack took it from Stella.

'Jack says I'm a silly bitch,' said Dorothy, apologetic, to Stella.

'Well, never mind, you'll feel different soon.'

'I suppose so, if you say so. All right. I *am* going to sleep,' said Dorothy, in a stubborn, sad little voice. She turned over, away from them. In the last flare of her hysteria she said: 'Why don't you two walk to the station together? It's a lovely night.'

'We're going to,' said Jack, 'don't worry.'

She let out a weak giggle, but did not turn. Jack carefully deposited the now sleeping baby in the bed, about a foot from Dorothy. Who suddenly wriggled over until her small, defiant white back was in contact with the blanketed bundle that was her son.

Jack raised his eyebrows at Stella: but Stella was looking at mother and baby, the nerves of her memory filling her with sweet warmth. What right had this woman, who was in possession of such delight, to torment her husband, to torment her friend, as she had been doing – what right had she to rely on their decency as she did?

Surprised by these thoughts, she walked away downstairs, and stood at the door into the garden, her eyes shut, holding herself rigid against tears.

She felt a warmth on her bare arm – Jack's hand. She opened her eyes to see him bending towards her, concerned.

'It'd serve Dorothy right if I did drag you off into the bushes . . .'

'Wouldn't have to drag me,' he said; and while the words had the measure of facetiousness the situation demanded, she felt his seriousness envelop them both in danger.

The warmth of his hand slid across her back, and she turned towards him under its pressure. They stood together, cheeks touching, scents of skin and hair mixing with the smells of warmed grass and leaves.

She thought: What is going to happen now will blow Dorothy and Jack and that baby sky-high; it's the end of my marriage; I'm going to blow everything to bits. There was almost uncontrollable pleasure in it.

She saw Dorothy, Jack, the baby, her husband, the two half-grown children, all dispersed, all spinning downwards through the sky like bits of debris after an explosion.

Jack's mouth was moving along her cheek towards her mouth, dissolving her whole self in delight. She saw, against closed lids, the bundled baby upstairs, and pulled back from the situation, exclaiming energetically: 'Damn Dorothy, damn her, damn her, I'd like to kill her . . .'

And he, exploding into reaction, said in a low furious rage: 'Damn you both! I'd like to wring both your bloody necks . . .'

Their faces were at a foot's distance from each other, their eyes staring hostility. She thought that if she had not had the vision of the helpless baby they would now be in each other's arms — generating tenderness and desire like a couple of dynamos, she said to herself, trembling with dry anger.

'I'm going to miss my train if I don't go,' she said.

'I'll get your coat,' he said, and went in, leaving her defenceless against the emptiness of the garden.

When he came out, he slid the coat around her without touching her, and said: 'Come on, I'll take you by car.' He walked away in front of her to the car, and she followed meekly over rough lawn. It really was a lovely night.

A ROOM

When I first came into this flat of four small boxlike rooms, the bedroom was painted pale pink, except for the fireplace wall, which had a fanciful pink and blue paper. The woodwork was a dark purple, almost black. This paint is sold by a big decorating shop in the West End and is called Bilberry.

Two girls had the flat before me. Very little money, obviously, because the carpeting was going into holes and the walls were decorated with travel posters. The woman upstairs told me they often had parties that lasted all night. 'But I liked to hear them, I enjoy the sounds of life.' She was reproachful. I don't have parties often enough for her. The girls left no forwarding address, following the tradition for this flat. Over the years it has often happened that the bell rings and people ask for 'Angus Ferguson – I thought he lived here?' And the Maitlands? And Mrs Dowland? And the young Caitsbys? All these people, and probably many others, have lived in this flat, and departed leaving nothing behind. I know nothing about them, nor does anyone else in the building, though some of them have lived here for years.

I found the pink too assertive, and after several mistakes settled on white walls, leaving the plum-colour, or Bilberry, woodwork. First I had grey curtains, then blue ones. My bed is under the window. There is a desk, which I had meant to write on, but it is always too cluttered with papers. So I write in the living room or on the kitchen table. But I spend a lot of time in the bedroom. Bed is the best place for reading, thinking, or doing nothing. It is my room; it is where I feel I live, though the shape is bad and there are things about it that can never be anything but ugly. For instance, the fireplace was of iron – a bulging, knobbed, ornamented black. The girls had left it as it was, using a small gas heater in the opening. Its heavy ugliness kept drawing my eyes towards it; and I painted a panel from the ceiling downwards in the dark plum colour, so that the fireplace and the small thick shelf over it would be absorbed. On either side of the panel, since I could not have the whole wall in plum, which at night looks black, were left two panels of the absurd wallpaper, which has bright people like birds in pink and blue cages. The fireplace seemed less obtrusive, but my fire is a gas fire, a square solid shape of bronze, brought from an earlier flat where it did not look too bad. But it does not fit here at all. So the whole wall doesn't work, it fails to come off.

Another wall, the one beside my bed, is also deformed. Over the bed swells a grainy irregular lump two or more feet across. Someone – Angus Ferguson? The Maitlands? Mrs Dowland? – attempted to replace falling plaster and made a hash of it. No professional plasterer could have got away with such a pro-tuberance.

On the whole, this wall gives me pleasure: it reminds me of the irregular whitewashed walls of another house I lived in once. Probably I chose to paint this room white because I wanted to have the whitewashed lumpy walls of that early house repeated here in London?

The ceiling is a ceiling: flat, white, plain. It has a plaster border which is too heavy for the room and looks as if it might fall off easily. The whole building has a look of solid ugliness, but it was built cheap and is not solid at all. For instance, walls, tapped, sound hollow; the plaster, when exposed, at once starts to trickle as if the walls were of loose sand held together by wallpaper. I can hear anything that goes on over my head, where the old woman who likes to hear a bit of life lives with her husband. She is Swedish, gives Swedish lessons. She dresses prettily, and looks a dear respectable old thing. Yet she is quite mad. Her door has four heavy, specially fitted locks inside, as well as bolts and bars. If I knock she opens the door on a chain four inches long and peers through to make sure that I (or they) will not attack her. Inside is a vision of neatness and order. She spends all day cleaning and arranging. When she can't find anything more to do in her flat she posts notices on the stairs saying: 'Any person who drops rubbish on these stairs will be reported to the Authorities!' Then she visits every flat in turn (there are eight identical flats one above the other) and says confidingly: 'Of course the notice isn't meant for you.'

Her husband works for an export firm and is away a good deal. When she expects him back, she dresses as carefully as a bride and goes off to meet him, blushing. On the nights he comes back from his trips the bed creaks over my head, and I hear them giggling.

They are an orderly couple, bed at eleven every night, up every morning at nine. As for myself, my life has no outward order and I like having them up there. Sometimes, when I've worked late, I hear them getting up and I think through my sleep or half sleep: Good, the day's started, has it? And I drift back to a semi-consciousness blended with their footsteps and the rattling of cups.

Sometimes, when I sleep in the afternoons, which I do because afternoon sleep is more interesting than night sleep, she takes a nap too. I think of her and of myself lying horizontally above each other, as if we were on two shelves.

When I lie down after lunch there is nothing unplanned about it. First I must feel the inner disturbance or alertness that is due to overstimulation, or being a little sick or very tired. Then I darken the room, shut all the doors so the telephone won't wake me (though its distant ringing can be a welcome dream-progenitor) and I get into bed carefully, preserving the mood. It is these sleeps which help me with my work, telling me what to write or where I've gone wrong. And they save me from the fever of restlessness that comes from seeing too many people. I always drift off to sleep in the afternoons with the interest due to a long journey into the unknown, and the sleep is thin and extraordinary and takes me into regions hard to describe in a waking state.

But one afternoon there was no strange journey, nor was there useful information about my work. The sleep was so different from usual that for some time I thought I was awake.

I had been lying in the semidark, the curtains, of varying shades of dark blue, making a purply-moving shade. Outside it was a busy afternoon. I could hear sounds from the market underneath, and there was angry shouting, a quarrel of some

kind, a man's voice and a woman's. I was looking at the fireplace and thinking how ugly it was, wondering what sort of
person had deliberately chosen such a hideous shape of black
iron. Though of course I had painted it over. Yes, whether I
could afford it or not, I must get rid of the square bronze gas
fire and find a prettier one. I saw the bronze shape had gone;
there was a small black iron grate and a small fire in it, smoking.
The smoke was coming into the room, and my eyes were sore.

The room was different; I felt chilled and estranged from
myself as I looked. The walls had a paper whose general effect
was a dingy brown, but looking closely at it I saw a small
pattern of brownish-yellow leaves and brown stems. There
were stains on it. The ceiling was yellowish and shiny from the
smoke. There were some shreds of pinky-brown curtains at the
windows with a tear in one so that the bottom edge hung down.

I was no longer lying on the bed, but sitting by the fire across
the room, looking at the bed and at the window. Outside a shrill
quarrel went on, the voices rising up from the street. I felt cold,
I was shivering, and my eyes watered. In the little grate sat
three small lumps of shiny coal, smoking dismally. Under me
was a cushion or a folded coat, something like that. The room
seemed much larger. Yes, it was a largish room. A chest of
brown-varnished wood stood by the bed which was low, a good
foot lower than mine. There was a red army blanket stretched
across the bed's foot. The recesses on either side of the fireplace
had shallow wooden shelves down them, holding folded clothes,
old magazines, crockery, a brown teapot. These things conveyed an atmosphere of thin poverty.

I was alone in the room, though someone was next door. I
could hear sounds that made me unhappy, apprehensive. From
upstairs a laugh, hostile to me. Was the old Swedish lady
laughing? With whom? Had her husband come back suddenly?

I was desolate with a loneliness that felt it would never be
assuaged, no one would ever come to comfort me. I sat and
looked at the bed which had the cheap red blanket on it that
suggested illness, and sniffed because the smoke was tearing at
the back of my throat. I was a child, I knew that. And that there
was a war, something to do with war, war had something to do

with this dream or memory – *whose*? I came back to my own room, lying on my bed, with silence upstairs and next door. I was alone in the flat, watching my soft dark blue curtains softly moving. I was filled with misery.

I left my pretty bedroom and made myself tea; then returned to draw the curtains and let the light in. I switched on the gas heater which came up hot and red, driving the memory of cold away; and I looked behind its bronze efficiency into a grate that had not had coals in it, I knew, for years.

I have tried to dream myself back into that other room which is under this room, or beside it, or in it, or existing in someone's memory. Which war was it? Whose was the chilly poverty? And I would like to know more about the frightened little child. He (or she) must have been very small for the room to look so big. So far I have failed. Perhaps it was the quarrel outside in the street that . . . that *what*? And why?

ENGLAND VERSUS ENGLAND

'I think I'll be off,' said Charlie. 'My things are packed.' He had made sure of getting his holdall ready so that his mother wouldn't. 'But it's early,' she protested. Yet she was already knocking red hands together to rid them of water while she turned to say goodbye: she knew her son was leaving early to avoid the father. But the back door now opened and Mr Thornton came in. Charlie and his father were alike: tall, overthin, big-boned. The old miner stooped, his hair had gone into grey wisps, and his hollow cheeks were coal-pitted. The young man was still fresh, with jaunty fair hair and alert eyes. But there were scoops of strain under his eyes.

'You're alone,' said Charlie involuntarily, pleased, ready to sit down again. The old man was not alone. Three men came into view behind him in the light that fell into the yard from the door, and Charlie said quickly: 'I'm off, Dad, it's goodbye till Christmas.' They all came crowding into the little kitchen, bringing with them the spirit of facetiousness that seemed to Charlie his personal spiteful enemy, like a poltergeist always standing in wait somewhere behind his right shoulder. 'So you're back to the dreaming spires,' said one man, nodding goodbye. 'Off to t'palaces of learning,' said another. Both were smiling. There was no hostility in it, or even envy, but it shut Charlie out of his family, away from his people. The third man, adding his tribute to this, the most brilliant son of the village said: 'You'll be coming back to a right Christmas with us, then, or will you be frolicking with t'lords and t'earls you're the equal of now?'

'He'll be home for Christmas,' said the mother sharply. She turned her back on them, and dropped potatoes one by one from a paper bag into a bowl.

'For a day or so, any road,' said Charlie, in obedience to the prompting spirit. 'That's time enough to spend with t'hewers of wood and t'drawers of water.' The third man nodded, as if to say: That's right! and put back his head to let out a relieved bellow. The father and the other two men guffawed with him. Young Lennie pushed and shoved Charlie encouragingly and Charlie jostled back, while the mother nodded and smiled because of the saving horseplay. All the same, he had not been home for nearly a year, and when they stopped laughing and stood waiting for him to go, their grave eyes said they were remembering this fact.

'Sorry I've not had more time with you, son,' said Mr Thornton, 'but you know how 'tis.'

The old miner had been union secretary, was now chairman, and had spent his working life as miners' representative in a dozen capacities. When he walked through the village, men at a back door, or a woman in an apron, called: 'Just a minute, Bill,' and came after him. Every evening Mr Thornton sat in the kitchen, or in the parlour when the television was claimed by the children, giving advice about pensions, claims, work rules, allowances; filling in forms; listening to tales of trouble. Ever since Charlie could remember, Mr Thornton had been less his father than the father of the village. Now the three miners went into the parlour, and Mr Thornton laid his hand on his son's shoulder, and said: 'It's been good seeing you,' nodded, and followed them. As he shut the door he said to his wife: 'Make us a cup of tea, will you, lass?'

'There's time for a cup, Charlie,' said the mother, meaning there was no need for him to rush off now, when it was unlikely any more neighbours would come in. Charlie did not hear. He was watching her slosh dirty potatoes about under the running tap while with her free hand she reached for the kettle. He went to fetch his raincoat and his holdall listening to the nagging inner voice which he hated, but which he felt as his only protection against the spiteful enemy outside: 'I can't stand it when my father apologizes to me – he was apologizing to me for not seeing more of me. If he wasn't as he is, better than anyone else in the village, and our home the only house with real books in it, I wouldn't be at Oxford, I wouldn't have done well at school, so it cuts both ways.' The words, cut both ways, echoed uncannily in his inner ear, and he felt queasy, as if the earth he stood on was shaking. His eyes cleared on the sight of his mother, standing in front of him, her shrewd, non-judging gaze on his face. 'Eh, lad,' she said, 'you don't look any too good to me.' 'I'm all right,' he said hastily, and kissed her, adding: 'Say my piece to the girls when they come in.' He went out, with Lennie behind him.

The two youths walked in silence past fifty crammed lively brightly lit kitchens whose doors kept opening as the miners came in from the pit for their tea. They walked in silence along the front of fifty more houses. The fronts were all dark. The life of the village, even now, was in the kitchens where great fires roared all day on the cheap coal. The village had been built in the thirties by the company, now nationalized. There were two thousand houses, exactly alike, with identical patches of carefully tended front garden, and busy back yards. Nearly every house had a television aerial. From every chimney poured black smoke.

At the bus stop Charlie turned to look back at the village, now a low hollow of black, streaked and spattered with sullen wet lights. He tried to isolate the gleam from his own home, while he thought how he loved his home and how he hated the village. Everything about it offended him, yet as soon as he stepped inside his kitchen he was received into warmth. That morning he had stood on the front step and looked out on lines of grey stucco houses on either side of grey tarmac; on grey ugly lamp-posts and greyish hedges, and beyond to the grey minetip and the neat black diagram of the minehead.

He had looked, listening while the painful inner voice lectured: 'There's nothing in sight, not one object or building anywhere, that is beautiful. Everything is so ugly and mean and graceless that it should be bulldozed into the earth and out of the memory of man.' There was not even a cinema. There was a post office, and attached to it a library that had romances and war stories. There were two miners' clubs for drinking. And there was television. These were the amenities for two thousand families.

When Mr Thornton stood on his front step and looked forth

he smiled with pride and called his children to say: 'You've never seen what a miners' town can be like. You couldn't even imagine the conditions. Slums, that's what they used to be. Well, we've put an end to all that ... Yes, off you go to Doncaster, I suppose, dancing and the pictures – that's all you can think about. And you take it all for granted. Now, in our time ...'

And so when Charlie visited his home he was careful that none of his bitter criticisms reached words, for above all, he could not bear to hurt his father.

A group of young miners came along for the bus. They wore smartly shouldered suits, their caps set at angles, and scarves flung back over their shoulders. They greeted Lennie, looked to see who the stranger was, and when Lennie said: 'This is my brother,' they nodded and turned quickly to board the bus. They went upstairs, and Lennie and Charlie went to the front downstairs. Lennie looked like them, with a strong cloth cap and a jaunty scarf. He was short, stocky, strong – 'built for t'pit,' Mr Thornton said. But Lennie was in a foundry in Doncaster. No pit for him, he said. He had heard his father coughing through all the nights of his childhood, and the pit wasn't for him. But he had never said this to his father.

Lennie was twenty. He earned seventeen pounds a week, and wanted to marry a girl he had been courting for three years now. But he could not marry until the big brother was through college. The father was still on the coal face, when by rights of age he should have been on the surface, because he earned four pounds a week more on the face. The sister in the office had wanted to be a schoolteacher, but at the moment of decision all the extra money of the family had been needed for Charlie. It cost them two hundred pounds a year for his extras at Oxford. The only members of the family not making sacrifices for Charlie were the schoolgirl and the mother.

It was half an hour on the bus, and Charlie's muscles were set hard in readiness for what Lennie might say, which must be resisted. Yet he had come home thinking: Well, at least I can talk it out with Lennie, I can be honest with him.

Now Lennie said facetiously, but with an anxious loving inspection of his brother's face: 'And what for do we owe the pleasure of your company, Charlie boy? You could have knocked us all down with a feather when you said you were coming this weekend.'

Charlie said angrily: 'I got fed up with t'earls and t'dukes.'

'Eh,' said Lennie quickly, 'but you didn't need to mind *them*, they didn't mean to rile you.'

'I know they didn't.'

'Mum's right,' said Lennie, with another anxious but carefully brief glance, 'you're not looking too good. What's up?'

'What if I don't pass t'examinations,' said Charlie in a rush.

'Eh, but what is this, then? You were always first in school. You were the best of everyone. Why shouldn't you pass, then?'

'Sometimes I think I won't,' said Charlie lamely, but glad he had let the moment pass.

Lennie examined him again, this time frankly, and gave a movement like a shrug. But it was a hunching of the shoulders against a possible defeat. He sat hunched, his big hands on his knees. On his face was a small critical grin. Not critical of Charlie, not at all, but of life.

His heart beating painfully with guilt, Charlie said: 'It's not as bad as that, I'll pass.' The inner enemy remarked softly: I'll pass, then I'll get a nice pansy job in a publisher's office with the other wet-nosed little boys, or I'll be a sort of clerk. Or I'll be a teacher – I've no talent for teaching, but what's that matter? Or I'll be on the management side of industry, pushing people like Lennie around. And the joke is, Lennie's earning more than I shall for years.' The enemy behind his right shoulder began satirically tolling a bell and intoned: 'Charlie Thornton, in his third year at Oxford, was found dead in a gas-filled bed-sitting room this morning. He had been overworking. Death from natural causes.' The enemy added a loud rude raspberry and fell silent. But he was waiting: Charlie could feel him there waiting.

Lennie said: 'Seen a doctor, Charlie boy?'

'Yes. He said I should take it easy a bit. That's why I came home.'

'No point killing yourself working.'

'No, it's not serious, he just said I must take it easy.'

Lennie's face remained grave. Charlie knew that when he got home he would say to the mother: 'I think Charlie's got summat on his mind.' And his mother would say (while she stood shaking chips of potato into boiling fat): 'I expect sometimes he wonders is the grind worth it. And he sees you earning, when he isn't.' She would say, after a silence during which they exchanged careful looks: 'It must be hard for him, coming here, everything different, then off he goes, everything different again.'

'Shouldn't worry, Mum.'

'I'm not worrying. Charlie's all right.'

The inner voice inquired anxiously: 'If she's on the spot about the rest, I suppose she's right about the last bit too – *I suppose I am all right?*'

But the enemy behind his right shoulder said: 'A man's best friend is his mother, she never lets a thing pass.'

Last year he had brought Jenny down for a weekend, to satisfy the family's friendly curiosity about the posh people he knew these days. Jenny was a poor clergyman's daughter, bookish, a bit of a prig, but a nice girl. She had easily navigated the complicated currents of the weekend, while the family waited for her to put on 'side'. Afterwards Mrs Thornton had said, putting her finger on the sore spot: 'That's a right nice girl. She's a proper mother to you, and that's a fact.' The last was not a criticism of the girl, but of Charlie. Now Charlie looked with envy at Lennie's responsible profile and said to himself: Yes, he's a man. He has been for years, since he left school. Me, I'm a proper baby, and I've got two years over him.

For above everything else, Charlie was made to feel, every time he came home, that these people, his people, were serious; while he and the people with whom he would now spend his life (if he passed the examination) were not serious. He did not believe this. The inner didactic voice made short work of any such idea. The outer enemy could, and did, parody it in a hundred ways. His family did not believe it, they were proud of him. Yet Charlie felt it in everything they said and did. They protected him. They sheltered him. And above all, they still paid for him. At his age, his father had been working in the pit for eight years.

Lennie would be married next year. He already talked of a family. He, Charlie (if he passed the examination), would be running around licking people's arses to get a job, Bachelor of Arts, Oxford, and a drug on the market.

They had reached Doncaster. It was raining. Soon they would pass where Doreen, Lennie's girl, worked. 'You'd better get off here,' Charlie said. 'You'll have all that drag back through the wet.' 'No, s'all right, I'll come with you to the station.'

There were another five minutes to go. 'I don't think it's right, the way you get at Mum,' Lennie said, at last coming to the point.

'But I haven't said a bloody word,' said Charlie, switching without having intended it into his other voice, the middle-class voice which he was careful never to use with his family except in joke. Lennie gave him a glance of surprise and reproach and said: 'All the same. She feels it.'

'But it's bloody ridiculous.' Charlie's voice was rising. 'She stands in that kitchen all day, pandering to our every whim, when she's not doing housework or making a hundred trips a day with that bloody coal . . .' In the Christmas holidays, when Charlie had visited home last, he had fixed up a bucket on the frame of an old pram to ease his mother's work. This morning he had seen the contrivance collapsed and full of rainwater in the back yard. After breakfast Lennie and Charlie had sat at the table in their shirt-sleeves watching their mother. The door was open into the back yard. Mrs Thornton carried a shovel whose blade was nine inches by ten, and was walking back and forth from the coalhole in the yard, through the kitchen, into the parlour. On each inward journey, a small clump of coal balanced on the shovel. Charlie counted that his mother walked from the coalhole to the kitchen fire and the parlour fire thirty-six times. She walked steadily, the shovel in front, held like a spear in both hands, and her face frowned with purpose. Charlie had dropped his head on to his arms and laughed soundlessly until he felt Lennie's warning gaze and stopped the heave of his shoulders. After a moment he had sat up, straight-faced. Lennie said: 'Why do you get at Mum, then?' Charlie said: 'But I haven't said owt.' 'No, but she's getting riled. You always show what you think, Charlie boy.' As Charlie did not respond to his appeal – for far more than present charity – Lennie went on: 'You can't teach an old dog new tricks.' 'Old! She's not fifty!'

Now Charlie said, continuing the early conversation: 'She goes on as if she were an old woman. She wears herself out with nothing – she could get through all the work she has in a couple of hours if she organized herself. Or if just for once she told us where to get off.'

'What'd she do with herself then?'

'Do? Well, she could do something for herself. Read. Or see friends. Or something.'

'She feels it. Last time you went off she cried.'

'She *what*?' Charlie's guilt almost overpowered him, but the inner didactic voice switched on in time and he spoke through it: 'What right have we to treat her like a bloody servant? Betty likes her food this way and that way, and Dad won't eat this and that, and she stands there and humours the lot of us – like a servant.'

'And who was it last night said he wouldn't have fat on his meat and changed it for hers?' said Lennie smiling, but full of reproach.

'Oh, I'm just as bad as the rest of you,' said Charlie, sounding false. 'It makes me wild to see it,' he said, sounding sincere. Didactically he said: 'All the women in the village – they take it for granted. If someone organized them so that they had half a day to themselves sometimes, they'd think they were being insulted – they can't stop working. Just look at Mum, then. She comes into Doncaster to wrap sweets two or three times a week – well, she actually loses money on it, by the time she's paid bus fares. I said to her, "You're actually losing money on it," and she said: "I like to get out and see a bit of life." A bit of life! Wrapping sweets in a bloody factory. Why can't she just come into town of an evening and have a bit of fun without feeling she has to pay for it by wrapping sweets, sweated bloody labour? And she actually loses on it. It doesn't make sense. They're human beings, aren't they? Not just . . .'

'Not just what?' asked Lennie angrily. He had listened to Charlie's tirade, his mouth setting harder, his eyes narrowing. 'Here's the station,' he said in relief. They waited for the young miners to clatter down and off before going forward themselves. 'I'll come with you to your stop,' said Charlie; and they crossed the dark, shiny, grimy street to the opposite stop for the bus which would take Lennie back to Doreen.

'It's no good thinking we're going to change, Charlie boy.'

'Who said change?' said Charlie excitedly; but the bus had come, and Lennie was already swinging on to the back. 'If you're in trouble just write and say,' said Lennie, and the bell pinged and his face vanished as the lit bus was absorbed by the light-streaked drizzling darkness.

There was half an hour before the London train. Charlie stood with the rain on his shoulders, his hands in his pockets, wondering whether to go after his brother and explain – what? He bolted across the street to the pub near the station. It was run by an Irishman who knew him and Lennie. The place was still empty, being just after opening time.

'It's you then,' said Mike, drawing him a pint of bitter without asking. 'Yes, it's me,' said Charlie, swinging himself up on to a stool.

'And what's in the great world of learning?'

'Oh Jesus, *no*!' said Charlie. The Irishman blinked, and Charlie said quickly: 'What have you gone and tarted this place up for?'

The pub had been panelled in dark wood. It was ugly and comforting. Now it had half a dozen bright wallpapers and areas of shining paint, and Charlie's stomach moved again, light filled his eyes, and he set his elbows hard down for support, and put his chin on his two fists.

'The youngsters like it,' said the Irishman. 'But we've left the bar next door as it was for the old ones.'

'You should have a sign up: Age This Way,' said Charlie. 'I'd have known where to go.' He carefully lifted his head off

his fists, narrowing his eyes to exclude the battling colours of
the wallpapers, the shine of the paint.

'You look bad,' said the Irishman. He was a small, round,
alcoholically cheerful man who, like Charlie, had two voices.
For the enemy – that is, all the English whom he did not regard
as a friend, which meant people who were not regulars – he put
on an exaggerated brogue which was bound, if he persisted, to
lead to the political arguments he delighted in. For friends like
Charlie he didn't trouble himself. He now said: 'All work and
no play.'

'That's right,' said Charlie. 'I went to the doctor. He gave me
a tonic and said I am fundamentally sound in wind and limb.
"You are sound in wind and limb," he said,' said Charlie,
parodying an upper-class English voice for the Irishman's
pleasure.

Mike winked, acknowledging the jest, while his professionally humorous face remained serious. 'You can't burn the
candle at both ends,' he said in earnest warning.

Charlie laughed out. 'That's what the doctor said. You can't
burn the candle at both ends, he said.'

This time, when the stool he sat on, and the floor beneath the
stool, moved away from him, and the glittering ceiling dipped
and swung, his eyes went dark and stayed dark. He shut them
and gripped the counter tight. With his eyes still shut he said
facetiously: 'It's the clash of cultures, that's what it is. It makes
me light-headed.' He opened his eyes and saw from the Irishman's face that he had not said these words aloud.

He said aloud: 'Actually the doctor was all right, he meant
well. But Mike, I'm not going to make it, I'm going to fail.'

'Well, it won't be the end of the world.'

'*Jesus.* That's what I like about you, Mike, you take a broad
view of life.'

'I'll be back,' said Mike, going to serve a customer.

A week ago Charlie had gone to the doctor with a cyclostyled
leaflet in his hand. It was called 'A Report Into the Increased
Incidence of Breakdown Among Undergraduates'. He had
underlined the words:

Young men from working-class and lower-middle-class families on scholarships are particularly vulnerable. For them, the gaining of a degree is obviously crucial. In addition they are under the continuous strain of adapting themselves to middle-class mores that are foreign to them. They are victims of a clash of standards, a clash of cultures, divided loyalties.

The doctor, a young man of about thirty, provided by the college authorities as a sort of father figure to advise on work problems, personal problems and (as the satirical alter ego took pleasure in pointing out) on clash-of-culture problems, glanced once at the pamphlet and handed it back. He had written it. As, of course, Charlie had known. 'When are your examinations?' he asked. *Getting to the root of the matter, just like Mum,* remarked the malevolent voice from behind Charlie's shoulder.

'I've got five months, doctor, and I can't work and I can't sleep.'

'For how long?'

'It's been coming on gradually.' *Ever since I was born,* said the enemy.

'I can give you sedatives and sleeping pills, of course, but that's not going to touch what's really wrong.'

Which is, all this unnatural mixing of the classes. Doesn't do, you know. People should know their place and stick to it. 'I'd like some sleep pills, all the same.'

'Have you got a girl?'

'Two.'

The doctor paid out an allowance of man-of-the-world sympathy, then shut off his smile and said: 'Perhaps you'd be better with one?'

Which, my mum figure, or my lovely bit of sex? 'Perhaps I would, at that.'

'I could arrange for you to have some talks with a psychiatrist – well, not if you don't want,' he said hastily, for the alter ego had exploded through Charlie's lips in a horselaugh and: 'What can the trick cyclist tell me I don't know?' He roared with laughter, flinging his legs up; and an ashtray went circling around the room on its rim. Charlie laughed, watched the ashtray, and thought: There, I knew all the time it was a poltergeist sitting there behind my shoulder. I swear I never touched that damned ashtray.

The doctor waited until it circled near him, stopped it with his foot, picked it up, laid it back on the desk. 'It's no point your going to him if you feel like that.'

All avenues explored, all roads charted.

'Well now, let's see, have you been to see your family recently?'

'Last Christmas. No, doctor, it's not because I don't want to, it's because I can't work there.' *You try working in an atmosphere of trade union meetings and the telly and the pictures in Doncaster. You try it, doc. And besides all my energies go into not upsetting them. Because I do upset them. My dear doc, when we scholarship boys jump our class, it's not we who suffer, it's our families. We are an expense, doc. And besides – write a thesis, I'd like to read it . . . Call it: Long-term effects on working-class or lower-middle-class family of a scholarship child whose existence is a perpetual reminder that they are nothing but ignorant non-cultured clods. How's that for a thesis, doc? Why, I do believe I could write it myself.*

'If I were you, I'd go home for a few days. Don't try to work at all. Go to the pictures. Sleep and eat and let them fuss over you. Get this prescription made up and come and see me when you get back.'

'Thanks, doc, I will.' *You mean well.*

The Irishman came back to find Charlie spinning a penny, so intent on this game that he did not see him. First he spun it with his right hand, anticlockwise, then with his left, clockwise. The right hand represented his jeering alter ego. The left hand was the didactic and rational voice. The left hand was able to keep the coin in a glittering spin for much longer than the right.

'You ambidextrous?'

'Yes, always was.'

The Irishman watched the boy's frowning, teeth-clenched concentration for a while, then removed the untouched beer and poured him a double whisky. 'You drink that and get on the train and sleep.'

'Thanks, Mike. Thanks.'

'That was a nice girl you had with you last time.'

'I've quarrelled with her. Or rather, she's given me the boot. And quite right too.'

After the visit to the doctor Charlie had gone straight to Jenny. He had guyed the interview while she sat, gravely listening. Then he had given her his favourite lecture on the crass and unalterable insensibility of anybody anywhere born middle-class. No one but Jenny ever heard this lecture. She said at last: 'You *should* go and see a psychiatrist. No, don't you see, it's not fair.'

'Who to, me?'

'No, me. What's the use of shouting at me all the time? You should be saying these things to him.'

'*What?*'

'Well, surely you can see that. You spend all your time lecturing me. You make use of me, Charles.' (She always called him Charles.)

What she was really saying was: 'You should be making love to me, not lecturing me.' Charlie did not really like making love to Jenny. He forced himself when her increasingly tart and accusing manner reminded him that he ought to. He had another girl, whom he disliked, a tall crisp middle-class girl called Sally. She called him, mocking: Charlie boy. When he had slammed out of Jenny's room, he had gone to Sally and fought his way into her bed. Every act of sex with Sally was a slow, cold subjugation of her by him. That night he had said, when she lay at last, submissive, beneath him: 'Horny-handed son of toil wins by his unquenched virility beautiful daughter of the moneyed classes. And doesn't she love it.'

'Oh yes I do, Charlie boy.'

'I'm nothing but a bloody sex symbol.'

'Well,' she murmured, already self-possessed, freeing herself, 'that's all I am to you.' She added defiantly, showing that she did care, and that it was Charlie's fault: 'And I couldn't care less.'

'Dear Sally, what I like about you is your beautiful honesty.'

'Is that what you like about me? I thought it was the thrill of beating me down.'

Charlie said to the Irishman: 'I've quarrelled with everyone I know in the last weeks.'

'Quarrelled with your family too?'

'*No*,' he said, appalled, while the room again swung around him. 'Good Lord no,' he said in a different tone – grateful. He added savagely: 'How could I? I can never say anything to them I really think.' He looked at Mike to see if he had actually said these words aloud. He had, because now Mike said: 'So you know how I feel. I've lived thirty years in this mucking country, and if you arrogant sods knew what I'm thinking half the time . . .'

'Liar. You say whatever you think, from Cromwell to the Black and Tans and Casement. You never let up. But it's not hurting yourself to say it.'

'Yourself, is it?'

'Yes. But it's all insane. Do you realize how insane it all is, Mike? There's my father. Pillar of the working class. Labour Party, trade union, the lot. But I've been watching my tongue not to say I spent last term campaigning about – he takes it for granted even *now* that the British should push the wogs around.'

'You're a great nation,' said the Irishman. 'But it's not your personal fault, so drink up and have another.'

Charlie drank his first Scotch, and drew the second glass towards him. 'Don't you see what I mean?' he said, his voice rising excitedly. 'Don't you see that it's all *insane*? There's my mother, her sister is ill and it looks as if she'll die. There are two kids, and my mother'll take them both. They're nippers, three and four, it's like starting a family all over again. She thinks nothing of it. If someone's in trouble, she's the mug, every time. But there she sits and says: "Those juvenile offenders ought to be flogged until they are senseless." She read it in the papers and so she says it. She said it to me and I kept my mouth shut. And they're all alike.'

'Yes, but you're not going to change it, Charlie, so drink up.'

A man standing a few feet down the bar had a paper sticking out of his pocket. Mike said to him: 'Mind if I borrow your paper for the winners, sir?'

'Help yourself.'

Mike turned the paper over to the back page. 'I had five quid on today,' he said. 'Lost it. Lovely bit of horseflesh, but I lost it.'

'Wait,' said Charlie excitedly, straightening the paper so he could see the front page. WARDROBE MURDERER GETS SECOND CHANCE, it said. 'See that?' said Charlie. 'The Home Secretary says he can have another chance, they can review the case, he says.'

The Irishman read, cold-faced. 'So he does,' he said.

'Well, I mean to say, there's some decency left, then. I mean if the case can be reviewed it shows they do *care* about something at least.'

'I don't see it your way at all. It's England versus England, that's all. Fair play all round, but they'll hang the poor sod on the day appointed as usual.' He turned the newspaper and studied the race news.

Charlie waited for his eyes to clear, held himself steady with one hand flat on the counter, and drank his second double. He pushed over a pound note, remembering it had to last three days, and that now he had quarrelled with Jenny there was no place for him to stay in London.

'No, it's on me,' said Mike. 'I asked you. It's been a pleasure seeing you, Charlie. And don't take the sins of the world on your personal shoulders, lad, because that doesn't do anyone any good, does it, now?'

'See you at Christmas, Mike, and thanks.'

He walked carefully out into the rain. There was no solitude to be had on the train that night, so he chose a compartment with one person in it, and settled himself in a corner before looking to see who it was he had with him. It was a girl. He saw then that she was pretty, and then that she was upper-class. Another Sally, he thought, sensing danger, seeing the cool, self-sufficient little face. Hey, there, Charlie, he said to himself, keep yourself in order, or you've had it. He carefully located himself: *he*, Charlie, was now a warm, whisky-comforted belly, already a little sick. Close above it, like a silent loudspeaker, was the source of the hectoring voice. Behind his shoulder waited his grinning familiar. *He must keep them all apart.* He tested the didactic voice: It's not her fault, poor bitch, victim of the class system, she can't help she sees everyone under her like dirt ... But the alcohol was working strongly and meanwhile his familiar was calculating: She's had a good look, but can't make me out. My clothes are right, my haircut's on the line, but there's something that makes her wonder. She's waiting for me to speak, then she'll make up her mind. Well, first I'll get her, and then I'll speak.

He caught her eyes and signalled an invitation, but it was an aggressive invitation, to make it as hard for her as he could. After a bit, she smiled at him. Then he roughened his speech to the point of unintelligibility and said: ' 'Appen you'd like t'window up? What wi' t'rain and t'wind and all.'

'What?' she said sharply, her face lengthening into such a comical frankness of shock that he laughed out, and afterwards inquired impeccably: 'Actually it is rather cold, isn't it? Wouldn't you like to have the window up?' She picked up a magazine and shut him out, while he watched, grinning, the blood creep up from under her neat collar to her hairline.

The door slid back; two people came in. They were a man and his wife, both small, crumpled in face and flesh, and dressed in their best for London. There was a fuss and a heaving of suitcases and murmured apologies because of the two superior young people. Then the woman, having settled herself in a corner, looked steadily at Charlie, while he thought: Deep calls to deep, *she* knows who I am all right, she's not foxed by the trimmings. He was right, because soon she said familiarly: 'Would you put the window up for me, lad? It's a rare cold night and no mistake.'

Charlie put up the window, not looking at the girl, who was hiding behind the magazine. Now the woman smiled, and the man smiled too, because of her ease with the youth.

'You comfortable like that, father?' she asked.

'Fair enough,' said the husband on the stoical note of the confirmed grumbler.

'Put your feet up beside me, any road.'

'But I'm all right, lass,' he said bravely. Then, making a favour of it, he loosened his laces, eased his feet inside too-new shoes, and set them on the seat beside his wife.

She, for her part, was removing her hat. It was of shapeless grey felt, with a pink rose at the front. Charlie's mother owned just such a badge of respectability, renewed every year or so at the sales. Hers was always bluish felt, with a bit of ribbon or coarse net, and she would rather be seen dead than without it in public.

The woman sat fingering her hair, which was thin and greying. For some reason, the sight of her clean pinkish scalp shining through the grey wisps made Charlie wild with anger. He was taken by surprise, and again summoned himself to himself, making the didactic voice lecture: 'The working woman of these islands enjoys a position in the family superior to that of the middle-class woman, etc., etc., etc.' This was an article he had read recently, and he continued to recite from it, until he realized the voice had become an open sneer, and was saying: 'Not only is she the emotional bulwark of the family, but she is frequently the breadwinner as well, such as wrapping sweets at night, sweated labour for pleasure, anything to get out of the happy home for a few hours.'

The fusion of the two voices, the nagging inside voice, and the jeer from the dangerous force outside, terrified Charlie, and he told himself hastily: 'You're drunk, that's all, now keep your mouth shut, for God's sake.'

The woman was asking him: 'Are you feeling all right?'

'Yes, I'm all right,' he said carefully.

'Going all the way to London?'

'Yes, I'm going all the way to London.'

'It's a long drag.'

'Yes, it's a long drag.'

At this echoing dialogue, the girl lowered her magazine to give him a sharp contemptuous look, up and down. Her face was now smoothly pink, and her small pink mouth was judging.

'You have a mouth like a rosebud,' said Charlie, listening horrified to these words emerging from him.

The girl jerked up the magazine. The man looked sharply at Charlie, to see if he had heard aright, and then at his wife, for guidance. The wife looked doubtfully at Charlie, who offered her a slow desperate wink. She accepted it, and nodded at her husband: boys will be boys. They both glanced warily at the shining face of the magazine.

'We're on our way to London too,' said the woman.

'So you're on your way to London.'

Stop it, he told himself. He felt a foolish slack grin on his face, and his tongue was thickening in his mouth. He shut his eyes, trying to summon Charlie to his aid, but his stomach was rolling, warm and sick. He lit a cigarette for support, watching his hands at work. 'Lily-handed son of learning wants a manicure badly,' commented a soft voice in his ear; and he saw the cigarette poised in a parody of a cad's gesture between displayed nicotined fingers. Charlie, smoking with poise, sat preserving a polite, sarcastic smile.

He was in the grip of terror. He was afraid he might slide off the seat. He could no longer help himself.

'London's a big place, for strangers,' said the woman.

'But it makes a nice change,' said Charlie, trying hard.

The woman, delighted that a real conversation was at last under way, settled her shabby old head against a leather bulge, and said: 'Yes, it does make a nice change.' The shine on the leather confused Charlie's eyes; he glanced over at the magazine, but its glitter, too, seemed to invade his pupils. He looked at the dirty floor, and said: 'It's good for people to get a change now and then.'

'Yes, that's what I tell my husband, don't I, father? It's good for us to get away, now and then. We have a married daughter in Streatham.'

'It's a great thing, family ties.'

'Yes, but it's a drag,' said the man. 'Say what you like, but it is. After all, I mean, when all is said and done.' He paused, his head on one side, with a debating look, waiting for Charlie to take it up.

Charlie said: 'There's no denying it, say what you like, I mean, there's no doubt about *that*.' And he looked interestedly at the man for his reply.

The woman said: 'Yes, but the way I look at it, you've got to get *out* of yourself sometimes, look at it that way.'

'It's all very well,' said the husband, on a satisfied but grumbling note, 'but if you're going to do that, well, for a start-off, it's an expense.'

'If you don't throw a good penny after a bad one,' said Charlie judiciously, 'I mean, what's the point?'

'Yes, that's it,' said the woman excitedly, her old face animated. 'That's what I say to father, what's the point if you don't sometimes let yourself go?'

'I mean, life's bad enough as it is,' said Charlie, watching the magazine slowly lower itself. It was laid precisely on the seat. The girl now sat, two small brown-gloved hands in a ginger-tweeded lap, staring him out. Her blue eyes glinted into his, and he looked quickly away.

'Well, I can see that right enough,' said the man, 'but there again, you've got to know where to stop.'

'That's right,' said Charlie, 'you're dead right.'

'I know it's all right for some,' said the man, 'I know that, but if you're going to do that, you've got to consider. That's what I think.'

'But father, you know you enjoy it, once you're there and Joyce has settled you in your own corner with your own chair and your cup to yourself.'

'Ah,' said the man, nodding heavily, 'but it's not as easy as that, now, is it? Well, I mean, that stands to reason.'

'Ah,' said Charlie, shaking his head, feeling it roll heavily in the socket of his neck, 'but if you're going to consider at all, then what's the point? I mean, what I think is, for a start-off, there's no doubt about it.'

The woman hesitated, started to say something, but let her

small bright eyes falter away. She was beginning to colour.

Charlie went on compulsively, his head turning like a clock-work man's: 'It's what you're used to, that's what I say, well I mean. *Well*, and there's another thing, when all is said and done, and after all, if you're going to take one thing with another . . .'

'Stop it,' said the girl, in a sharp high voice.

'It's a question of principle,' said Charlie, but his head had stopped rolling and his eyes had focused.

'If you don't stop I'm going to call the guard and have you put in another compartment,' said the girl. To the old people she said in a righteous scandalized voice: 'Can't you see he's laughing at you? Can't you see?' She lifted the magazine again.

The old people looked suspiciously at Charlie, dubiously at each other. The woman's face was very pink and her eyes bright and hot.

'I think I am going to get forty winks,' said the man, with general hostility. He settled his feet, put his head back, and closed his eyes.

Charlie said: 'Excuse me,' and scrambled his way to the corridor over the legs of the man, then the legs of the woman, muttering: 'Excuse me, excuse me, I'm sorry.'

He stood in the corridor, his back jolting slightly against the shifting wood of the compartment's sides. His eyes were shut, his tears running. Words, no longer articulate, muttered and jumbled somewhere inside him, a stream of frightened pro-testing phrases.

Wood slid against wood close to his ear, and he heard the softness of clothed flesh on wood.

'If it's that bloody little bint I'll kill her,' said a voice, small and quiet, from his diaphragm.

He opened his murderous eyes on the woman. She looked concerned.

'I'm sorry,' he said, stiff and sullen, 'I'm sorry, I didn't mean . . .'

'It's all right,' she said, and laid her two red hands on his crossed quivering forearms. She took his two wrists, and laid his arms gently down by his sides. 'Don't take on,' she said, 'it's all right, it's all right, son.'

The tense rejection of his flesh caused her to take a step back from him. But there she stood her ground and said: 'Now look, son, there's no point taking on like that, well, is there? I mean to say, you've got to take the rough with the smooth, and there's no other way of looking at it.'

She waited, facing him, troubled but sure of herself.

After a while Charlie said: 'Yes, I suppose you're right.'

She nodded and smiled, and went back into the compartment. After a moment, Charlie followed her.

TWO POTTERS

I have only known one potter in this country, Mary Tawnish, and she lives out of London in a village where her husband is a schoolteacher. She seldom comes to town, and I seldom leave it, so we write.

The making of pots is not a thing I often think of, so when I dreamed about the old potter it was natural to think of Mary. But it was difficult to tell her: there are two kinds of humanity, those who dream and those who don't, and both tend to despise, or to tolerate, the other. Mary Tawnish says, when others relate their dreams: 'I've never had a dream in my life.' And adds, to soften or placate: 'At least, I don't remember. They say it's a question of remembering?'

I would have guessed her to be a person who would dream a good deal, I don't know why.

A tall woman, and rather large, she has bright brown clustering hair, and brown eyes that give the impression of light, though not from their surface: it is not a 'bright' or 'brilliant' glance. She looks at you, smiling or not, but always calm, and there is an impression of light, which seems caught in the structure of colour in the iris, so sometimes her eyes look yellow, set off by smooth brown eyebrows.

A large, slow-moving woman, with large white slow hands. And a silent one – she is a listener.

Her life has been a series of dramas: a childhood on the move with erratic parents, a bad first marriage, a child that died, lovers, but none lasting; then a second marriage to William Tawnish who teaches physics and biology. He is a quick, biting, bitter little man with whom she has three half-grown children.

More than once I have told her story, without comment, in order to observe the silent judgment: Another misfit, another unhappy soul, only to see the judger confounded on meeting her, for there was never a woman less fitted by nature for

discord or miseries. Or so it would seem. So it seems she feels
herself, for she disapproves of other people's collisions with
themselves, just as if her own life had nothing to do with her.

The first dream about the potter was simple and short. Once
upon a time ... there was a village or a settlement, not in
England, that was certain, for the scene was of a baked red-dust
bareness. Low rectangular structures, of simple baked mud, also
reddish-brown, were set evenly on the baked soil, yet because
some were roofless and others in the process of crumbling, and
others half built, there was nothing finished or formed about
this place. And for leagues and leagues, in all directions, the
great plain, of reddish earth, and in the middle of the plain, the
settlement that looked as if it were hastily moulded by a great
hand out of wet clay, allowed to dry, and left there. It seemed
uninhabited, but in an empty space among the huts, all by
himself, working away on a primitive potter's wheel turned by
foot, was an old man. He wore a garment of coarse sacking over
yellowish and dusty limbs. One bare foot was set in the dust
near me, the cracked toes spread and curled. He had a bit of
yellow straw stuck in close grizzling hair.

When I woke from this dream I was rested and excited, in
spite of the great dried-up plain and the empty settlement one
precarious stage from the dust. In the end I sat down and wrote
to Mary Tawnish, although I could hear her flat comment very
clearly: Well, that's interesting. Our letters are usually of the
kind known as 'keeping in touch'. First I inquired about her
children, and about William, and then I told the dream: 'For
some reason I thought of you. I did know a man who made pots
in Africa. The farmer he worked for discovered he had a talent
for potmaking (it seemed his tribe were potters by tradition)
because when they made bricks for the farm, this man, Elija,
slipped little dishes and bowls into the kiln to bake with the
bricks. The farmer used to pay him a couple of shillings a week
extra, and sold the dishes to a dealer in the city. He made
simple things, not like yours. He had no wheel, of course. He
didn't use colour. His things were a darkish yellow, because of
the kind of soil on that farm. A bit monotonous after a bit. And
they broke easily. If you come up to London give me a ring ...'

She didn't come, but soon I had a letter with a postscript: What an interesting dream, thanks so much for telling me.

I dreamed about the old potter again. There was the great, flat, dust-beaten reddish plain, ringed by very distant blue-hazed mountains, so far away they were like mirages, or clouds, or low-lying smoke. There was the settlement. And there the old potter, sitting on one of his own upturned pots, one foot set firmly in the dust, and the other moving the wheel; one palm shaping the clay, the other shedding water which glittered in the low sullen glare in flashes of moving light on its way to the turning wet clay. He was extremely old, his eyes faded and of the same deceiving blue as the mountains. All around him, drying in rows on a thin scattering of yellow straw, were pots of different sizes. They were all round. The huts were rectangular, the pots round. I looked at these two different manifestations of the earth, separated by shape; and then through a gap in the huts to the plain. No one in sight. It seemed no one lived there. Yet there sat the old man, with the hundreds of pots and dishes drying in rows on the straw, dipping his hand into an enormous jar of water and scattering drops that smelled sweet as they hit the dust and pitted it.

Again I thought of Mary. But they had nothing in common, that poor old potter who had no one to buy his work, and Mary who sold her strange coloured bowls and jugs to the big shops in London. I wondered what the old potter would think of Mary's work – particularly what he'd think of a square flat dish I'd bought from her, coloured a greenish-yellow. The square had, as it were, slipped out of whack, and the surface is rough, with finger marks left showing. I serve cheese on it. The old man's jars were for millet, I knew that, or for soured milk.

I wrote and told Mary the second dream, thinking: Well, if it bores or irritates her, it's too bad. This time she rang me up. She wanted me to go down to one of the shops which had been slow in making a new order. Weren't her things selling? she wanted to know. She added she was getting a fellow feeling for the old potter, he didn't have any customers either, from the size of his stock. But it turned out that the shop had sold all Mary's things, and had simply forgotten to order more.

I waited, with patient excitement, for the next instalment, or unfolding, of the dream.

The settlement was now populated, indeed, teeming, and it was much bigger. The low flat rooms of dull earth had spread over an area of some miles. They were not separated now, but linked. I walked through a system of these rooms. They were roughly the same size, but set at all angles to each other so that, standing in one, it might have one, two, three doors, leading to a corresponding number of mud rooms. I walked for something like half a mile through low dark rooms without once needing to cross a roofless space, and when I emerged in the daylight, there was the potter, and beyond him a marketplace. But a poor one. From out of his great jars, women, wearing the same sort of yellowish sacking as he, sold grain and milk to dusty, small-ish, rather listless people. The potter worked on, under heavy sunlight, with his rows and rows of clay vessels drying on the glinting yellow straw. A very small boy crouched by him, watching every movement he made. I saw how the water shaken from the old fingers on the whirling pot flew past it and spattered the small intent poverty-shaped face with its nar-rowed watching eyes. But the face received the water unflinch-ing, probably unnoticed.

Beyond the settlement stretched the plain. Beyond that, the thin, illusory mountains. Over the red flat plain drifted small shadows: they were from great birds wheeling and banking and turning.

I wrote to Mary and she wrote back that she was glad the old man had some customers at last, she had been worried about him. As for her, she thought it was time he used some colour, all that red dust was depressing. She said she could see the settle-ment was short of water, since I hadn't mentioned a well, let alone a river, only the potter's great brimming jar which reflected the blue sky, the sun, the great birds. Wasn't a diet of milk and millet bad for people? Here she broke off to say she supposed I couldn't help all this, it was my nature, and 'Apropos, isn't it time your poor village had a storyteller at least? How bored the poor things must be!'

I wrote back to say I was not responsible for this settlement, and whereas if I had my way, it would be set in groves of fruit trees and surrounded by whitening corn fields, with a river full of splashing brown children, I couldn't help it, that's how things were in this place, wherever it was.

One day in a shop I saw a shelf of her work and noticed that some of them were of smooth, dully shining brown, like polished skin – jars, and flat round plates. Our village potter would have known these, nothing to surprise him here. All the same, there was a difference between Mary's consciously simple vessels, and the simplicity of the old potter. I looked at them and thought: Well, my dear, that's not going to get you very far ... But I would have found it hard to say exactly what I meant, and in fact I bought a plate and a jar, and they gave me great pleasure, thinking of Mary and the old potter linked in them, between my hands.

Quite a long time passed. When I dreamed again all the plain was populated. The mountains had come closer in, reaching up tall and blue into blue sky, circumscribing the plain. The settlements, looked at from the height of the mountaintops, seemed like patches of slightly raised surface on the plain. I understood their nature and substance: a slight raising of the dust here and there, like the frail patterning of raindrops hitting dry dust, pitting it, then the sun coming out swiftly to dry the dust. The resulting tiny fragile patterned crust of dried dust – that gives, as near as I can, the feeling the settlements gave me, viewed from the mountains. Except that the raised dried crusts were patterned in rectangles. I could see the tiny patternings all over the plain. I let myself down from the mountains, through the great birds that wheeled and floated, and descended to the settlement I knew. There sat the potter, the clay curving under his left hand as he flicked water over it from his right. It was all going on as usual – I was reassured by his being there, creating his pots. Nothing much had changed, though so much time had passed. The low flat monotonous dwellings were the same, though they had crumbled to dust and raised themselves from it a hundred times since I had been here last. No green yet, no river. A scum-covered creek had goats grazing beside it, and the millet grew in straggly patches, flattened and brown from drought. In the marketplace were pinkish fruits, lying in heaps by the soft piles of millet, on woven straw mats. I didn't know the fruit: it was small, about plum-size, smooth-skinned, and I felt it had a sharp pulpy taste. Pinky-yellow skins lay scattered in the dust. A man passed me, with a low slinking movement of the hips, holding his sacklike garment in position at his side with the pressure of an elbow, staring in front of him over the pink fruit which he pressed against sharp yellow teeth.

I wrote and told Mary the plain was more populated, but that things hadn't improved much, except for the fruit. But it was astringent, I wouldn't care for it myself.

She wrote back to say she was glad she slept so soundly, she would find such dreams depressing.

I said there was nothing depressing about it. I entered the dream with pleasure, as if listening to a storyteller say: Once upon a time ...

But the next was discouraging, I woke depressed. I stood by the old potter in the marketplace, and for once his hands were still, the wheel at rest. His eyes followed the movements of the people buying and selling, and his mouth was bitter. Beside him, his vessels stood in rows on the warm glinting straw. From time to time a woman came picking her way along the rows, bending to narrow her eyes at the pots. Then she chose one, dropped a coin in the potter's hand, and bore it off over her shoulder.

I was inside the potter's mind and I knew what he was thinking. He said: 'Just once, Lord, just once, just once!' He put his hand down into a patch of hot shade under the wheel and lifted on his palm a small clay rabbit which he held out to the ground. He sat motionless, looking at the sky, then at the rabbit praying: 'Please, Lord, just once.' But nothing happened.

I wrote to Mary that the old man was tired with long centuries of making pots whose life was so short: the litter of broken pots under the settlement had raised its level twenty feet by now, and every pot had come off his wheel. He wanted God to breathe life into his clay rabbit. He had hoped to see it lift up its long red-veined ears, to feel its furry feet on his palm,

L

and watch it hop down and off among the great earthenware
pots, sniffing at them and twitching its ears – a live thing
among the forms of clay.

Mary said the old man was getting above himself. She said
further: 'Why a *rabbit*? I simply don't *see* a rabbit. What use
would a rabbit be? Do you realize that apart from goats (you
say they have milk), and those vultures overhead, they have no
animals at all? Wouldn't a cow be better than a rabbit?'

I wrote: 'I can't do anything about that place when I'm
dreaming it, but when I'm awake, why not? Right then, the
rabbit hopped off the old man's hand into the dust. It sat
twitching its nose and throbbing all over, the way rabbits do.
Then it sprang slowly off and began nibbling at the straw,
while the old man wept with happiness. Now what have you to
say? If I say there was a rabbit, a rabbit there was. Besides, that
poor old man deserves one, after so long. God could have done
so much, it wouldn't have cost Him anything.'

I had no reply to that letter, and I stopped dreaming about
the settlement. I knew it was because of my effrontery in creating that rabbit, inserting myself into the story. Very well, then
... I wrote to Mary: 'I've been thinking: suppose it had been
you who'd dreamed about the potter – all right, all right, just
suppose it. Now. Next morning you sat at the breakfast table,
your William at one end, and the children between eating
cornflakes and drinking milk. You were rather silent. (Of
course you usually are.) You looked at your husband and you
thought: What on earth would he say if I told him what I'm
going to do? You said nothing, presiding at the table; then you
sent the children off to school, and your husband to his classes.
Then you were alone and when you'd washed the dishes and
put them away, you went secretly into the stone-floored room
where your wheel and the kiln are, and you took some clay and
you made a small rabbit and you set it on a high shelf behind
some finished vases to dry. You didn't want anyone to see that
rabbit. One day, a week later, when it was dry, you waited until
your family was out of the house, then you put your rabbit on
your palm, and you went into a field, and you knelt down and
held the rabbit out to the grass, and you waited. You didn't

pray, because you don't believe in God, but you wouldn't have been in the least surprised if that rabbit's nose had started to twitch and its long soft ears stood up . . .'

Mary wrote: 'There aren't any rabbits any more, had you forgotten myxomatosis? Actually I did make some small rabbits recently, for the children, in blue and green glaze, because it occurred to me the two youngest haven't seen a rabbit out of a picture book. Still, they're coming back in some parts, I hear. The farmers will be angry.'

I wrote: 'Yes, I had forgotten. Well then . . . sometimes at evening, when you walk in the fields, you think: How nice to see a rabbit lift his paws and look at us. You remember the rotting little corpses of a few years back. You think: *I'll try again.* Meantime, you're nervous of what William will say, he's such a rationalist. Well of course, so are we, but he wouldn't even play a little. I may be wrong, but I think you're afraid of William catching you out, and you are careful not to be caught. One sunny morning you take it out on to the field and . . . all right, all right then, it *doesn't* hop away. You can't decide whether to lay your clay rabbit down among the warm grasses (it's a sunny day) and let it crumble back into the earth, or whether to bake it in your kiln. You haven't baked it, it's even rather damp still: the old potter's rabbit was wet, just before he held it out into the sun he sprinkled water on it, I saw him.

'Later you decide to tell your husband. Out of curiosity? The children are in the garden, you can hear their voices, and William sits opposite you reading the newspaper. You have a crazy impulse to say: I'm going to take my rabbit into the field tonight and pray for God to breathe life into it, a field without rabbits is empty. Instead you say: "William, I had a dream last night . . ." First he frowns, a quick frown, then he turns those small quick sandy-lashed intelligent eyes on you, taking it all in. To your surprise, instead of saying: "I don't remember your ever dreaming," he says: "Mary, I didn't know you disapproved of the farmers killing off their rabbits." You say: "I didn't disapprove. I'd have done the same, I suppose." The fact that he's not reacted with sarcasm or impatience, as he might very well, makes you feel guilty when you lift the clay rabbit down, take it out to a field and set it in a hedge, its nose pointing out towards some fresh grass. That night William says, casual: "You'll be glad to hear the rabbits are back. Basil Smith shot one in his field – the first for eight years, he says. Well, I'm glad myself, I've missed the little beggars." You are delighted. You slip secretly into a cold misty moonlight and you run to the hedge and of course the rabbit is gone. You stand, clutching your thick green stole around you, because it's cold, shivering, but delighted, delighted! Though you know quite well one of your children, or someone else's child, has slipped along this hedge, seen the rabbit, and taken it off to play with.'

Mary wrote: 'Oh all right, if you say so, so it is. But I must tell you, if you are interested in *facts*, that the only thing that has happened is that Dennis (the middle one) put his blue rabbit out in a hedge for a joke near the Smith's gate, and Basil Smith shot it to smithereens one dusk thinking it was real. He used to lose a small fortune every year to rabbits, he didn't think it was a funny joke at all. Anyway, why don't you come down for a weekend?'

The Tawnishes live in an old farmhouse on the edge of the village. There is a great garden, with fruit trees, roses – everything. The big house and the three boys mean a lot of work, but Mary spends all the time she can in the shed that used to be a dairy where she pots. I arrived to find them in the kitchen, having lunch. Mary nodded to me to sit down. William was in conflict with the middle boy, Dennis, who was, as the other two boys kept saying, 'showing off'. Or rather, he was in that torment of writhing self-consciousness that afflicts small boys sometimes, rolling his eyes while he stuttered and wriggled, his whole sandy freckled person scarlet and miserable.

'Well I did I did I did I did I did . . .' He paused for breath, his eyes popping, and his older brother chanted: 'No you didn't, you didn't, you didn't.'

'Yes I did I did I did I did . . .'

And the father said, brisk but irritated: 'Now then, Dennis, use your loaf, you couldn't have, because it is obvious you have *not*.'

'But I did I did I did I did . . .'

'Well, then, you had better go out of the room until you come to your senses and are fit company for rational people,' said his father, triumphantly in the right.

The child choked on his battling breath, and ran howling out into the garden. Where, after a minute, the older boy followed, ostensibly to control him.

'He did what?' I asked.

'Who knows?' said Mary. There she sat, at the head of the table, bright-eyed and smiling, serving apple pie and custard, a dark changeling in the middle of her gingery, freckled family.

Her husband said, brisk: 'What do you mean, who knows? You know quite well.'

'It's his battle with Basil Smith,' said Mary to me. 'Ever since Basil Smith shot at his blue rabbit and broke it, there's been evil feeling on both sides. Dennis claims that he set fire to the Smith farmhouse last night.'

'*What?*'

Mary pointed through a low window, where the Smith's house showed, two fields away, like a picture in a frame.

William said: 'He's hysterical and he's got to stop it.'

'Well,' said Mary, 'if Basil shot my blue rabbit I'd want to burn his house down too. It seems quite reasonable to me.'

William let out an exclamation of rage; checked himself because of my presence, shot fiery glances all round, and went out, taking the youngest boy with him.

'Well,' said Mary. 'Well . . .' She smiled. 'Come into the pottery, I've got something to show you.' She went ahead along a stone passage, a tall, lazy-moving woman, her bright brown hair catching the light. As we passed an open window, there was a fearful row of shrieks, yells, blows; and we saw the three boys rolling and tussling in the grass, while William danced futilely around them shouting: 'Stop it, stop it at once.' Their mother proceeded, apparently uninterested, into the potting room.

This held the potting apparatus, and a great many jars, plates, and jugs of all colours and kinds ranged on shelves. She lifted down a creature from a high shelf, and set it before me. Then she left it with me, while she bent to attend to the kiln.

It was yellowish-brown, a sort of rabbit or hare, but with ears like neither – narrower, sharp, short, like the pointed unfolding shoots of a plant. It had a muzzle more like a dog's than a rabbit's; it looked as if it did not eat grass – perhaps insects and beetles? Yellowish eyes were set on the front of its head. Its hind legs were less powerful than a rabbit's, or hare's; and I saw its talents were for concealment, not for escaping enemies in great pistoning leaps. It rested on short, stubby hind legs, with front paws held up in a queer, twisted, almost affected posture, head turned to one side, and ears furled around each other. It looked as if it had been wound up like a spring, and had half unwound. It looked like a strangely shaped rock, or like the harsh twisted plants that sometimes grow on rocks.

Mary came back and stood by me, her head slightly on one side, with her characteristic small patient smile that nevertheless held a sweet concealed exasperation.

'Well,' she said, 'there it is.'

I hesitated, because it was not the creature I had seen on the old potter's palm.

'What was an English rabbit doing there at all?' she asked.

'I didn't say it was an English rabbit.'

But of course, she was right: this animal was far more in keeping with the dried mud houses, the dusty plain, than the pretty furry rabbit I had dreamed.

I smiled at Mary, because she was humouring me, as she humoured her husband and her children. For some reason I thought of her first husband and her lovers, two of whom I had known. At moments of painful crisis, or at parting, had she stood thus – a calm, pretty woman, smiling her sweetly satirical smile, as if to say: 'Well, make a fuss if you like, it's got nothing at all to do with me'? If so, I'm surprised that one of them didn't murder her.

'Well,' I said at last, 'thanks. Can I take this thing, whatever it is?'

'Of course. I made it for you. You must admit, it may not be pretty, but it's more likely to be *true*.'

I accepted this, as I had to; and I said: 'Well, thanks for coming down to our level long enough to play games with us.'

At which there was a flash of yellow light from her luminous eyes, while her face remained grave, as if amusement, or acknowledgment of the *truth*, could only be focused in her thus, through a change of light in her irises.

A few minutes later, the three boys and the father came round this part of the house in a whirlwind of quarrelling energy. The aggrieved Dennis was in tears, and the father almost beside himself. Mary, who until now had remained apart from it all, gave an exclamation, slipped on a coat, and said: 'I can't stand this. I'm going to talk to Basil Smith.'

She went out, and I watched her cross the fields to the other house.

Meanwhile Dennis, scarlet and suffering, came into the pottery in search of his mother. He whirled about, looking for her, then grabbed my creature, said: 'Is that for me?' snatched it possessively to him when I said: 'No, it's for me,' set it down when I told him to, and stood breathing like a furnace, his freckles like tea leaves against his skin.

'Your mother's gone to see Mr Smith,' I said.

'He shot my rabbit,' he said.

'It wasn't a real rabbit.'

'But he thought it was a real rabbit.'

'Yes, but you knew he would think so, and that he'd shoot at it.'

'He killed it!'

'You wanted him to!'

At which he let out a scream and danced up and down like a mad boy, shouting: 'I didn't I didn't I didn't I didn't . . .'

His father, entering on this scene, grabbed him by his flailing arms, fought the child into a position of tensed stillness, and held him there, saying, in a frenzy of incredulous common sense: 'I've-never-in-my-life-heard-such-lunacy!'

Now Mary came in, accompanied by Mr Smith, a large, fair, youngish man, with a sweet open face, which was uncomfortable now, because of what he had agreed to do.

'Let that child go,' said Mary to her husband. Dennis dropped to the floor, rolled over, and lay face down, heaving with sobs.

'Call the others!'

Resignation itself, William went to the window, and shouted: 'Harry, John, Harry, John, come here at once, your mother wants you.' He then stood, with folded arms, a defeated philosopher, grinning angrily while the two other children came in and stood waiting by the door.

'Now,' said Mary. 'Get up, Dennis.'

Dennis got up, his face battered with suffering, and looked with hope towards his mother.

Mary looked at Basil Smith.

Who said, careful to get the words right: 'I am very sorry that I killed your rabbit.'

The father let out a sharp outraged breath, but kept quiet at a glance from his wife.

The chest of Dennis swelled and sank – in one moment there would be a storm of tears.

'Dennis,' said Mary, 'say after me: Mr Smith, I'm very sorry I set fire to your house.'

Dennis said in a rush, to get it out in time: 'Mr Smith I'm very sorry I set fire to your ... to your ... to your ...' He sniffed and heaved, and Mary said firmly: '*House*, Dennis.'

'House,' said Dennis, in a wail. He then rushed at his mother, buried his head in her waist, and stood howling and wrestling, while she laid large hands on his ginger head and smiled over it at Mr Basil Smith.

'Dear God,' said her husband, letting his folded arms drop dramatically, now the ridiculous play was over. 'Come and have a drink, Basil.'

The men went off. The two other children stood silent and abashed, because of the force of Dennis's emotion, for which they clearly felt partly responsible. Then they slipped out to play. The house was tranquil again, save for Dennis's quietening sobs. Soon Mary took the boy up to his room to sleep it off. I stayed in the great, stone-floored pottery, looking at my strange twisted animal, and the blues and greens of Mary's work all around the walls.

Supper was early and soon over. The boys were silent, Dennis too limp to eat. Bed was prescribed for everyone. William kept looking at his wife, his mouth set under his ginger moustache, and he could positively be heard thinking: Filling them full of this nonsense while I try to bring them up reasonable human beings! But she avoided his eyes, and sat calm and remote, serving mashed potatoes and brown stew. It was only when we had finished the washing up that she smiled at him — her sweet, amused smile. It was clear they needed to be alone. I said I wanted an early night and left them: he had gone to touch her before I was out of the room.

Next day, a warm summer Sunday, everyone was relaxed, the old house peaceful. I left that evening, with my clay creature, and Mary said smiling, humouring me: 'Let me know how things go on with your place, wherever it is.' But I had her beautiful animal in my suitcase, so I did not mind being humoured.

That night, at home, I went into the marketplace, and up to the old potter who stilled his wheel when he saw me coming. The small boy lifted his frowning attentive eyes from the potter's hand and smiled at me. I held out Mary's creature. The old man took it, screwed up his eyes to examine it, nodded. He held it in his left hand, scattered water on it with his right, held his palm down towards the littered dust, and the creature jumped off it and away, with quick, jerky movements, not stopping until it was through the huts, clear of the settlement, and against a small outcrop of jagged brown rocks where it raised its front paws and froze in the posture Mary had created for it. Overhead an eagle or a hawk floated by, looked down, but failed to see Mary's creature, and floated on, up and away into the great blue spaces over the flat dry plain to the mountains. I heard the wheel creak; the old man was back at work. The small boy crouched, watching, and the water flung by the potter's right hand sprayed the bowl he was making and the child's face, in a beautiful curving spray of glittering light.

BETWEEN MEN

The chair facing the door was covered in coffee-brown satin. Maureen Jeffries wore dark brown silk tights and a white ruffled shirt. She would look a delectable morsel in the great winged chair. No sooner was she arranged in it, however, than she got out again (with a pathetic smile of which she was certainly unconscious) and sat less dramatically in the corner of a yellow settee. Here she remained some minutes, thinking that after all, her letter of invitation had said, jocularly (she was aware the phrase had an arch quality she did not altogether like): 'Come and meet the new me!'

What was new was her hairstyle, that she was a stone lighter in weight, that she had been dowered afresh by nature (a word she was fond of) with delicacy of complexion. There was no doubt all this would be better displayed in the big brown chair: she made the change back again.

The second time she removed herself to the yellow settee was out of decency, a genuine calculation of kindness. To ask Peggy Bayley to visit her at all *was* brave of her, she had needed to swallow pride. But Peggy would not be able to compete with the ruffled lace shirt and all that it set off, and while this would be so precisely because of her advantages – that she was married, comfortably, to Professor Bayley (whose mistress she, Maureen, had been for four years) – nevertheless there was no need to rub in her, Maureen's, renewed and indeed incredible attractiveness, even though it had been announced by the words: *the new me.*

Besides, her attractiveness was all that she, Maureen, had to face the world with again, and why not display it to the wife of Professor Bayley, who had not married herself, but had married Peggy instead? Though (she whispered it to herself, fierce and bitter) if she had tricked Tom Bayley into it, put pressure on

him, as Peggy had, no doubt she would be Mrs Bayley . . . She
would go back to the brown chair.

But if *she* had tricked Tom into it, then it would have served
her right, as it certainly served Peggy right, if from the start of
this marriage Tom Bayley had insisted on a second, bachelor
flat into which she, Maureen, was never allowed to go, just as
Peggy was not. She, Maureen, would have refused marriage on
such terms, she must give herself credit for that; in fact, her
insistence on fidelity from Tom, a natural philanderer, was
doubtless the reason for his leaving her for Peggy. So on the
whole she did not really envy Peggy, who had achieved marriage when she was already nearly forty with the eminent and
attractive professor at the price of knowing from the start she
would not be the only woman in his life; and knowing, more-
over, she had achieved marriage by the oldest trick in the
world . . .

At this point Maureen left the brown chair for the third time,
found the yellow settee obvious, and sat on the floor, in the grip
of self-disgust. She was viewing the deterioration of her character, even while she was unable to stop the flow of her bitter
thoughts about Peggy. Viewing herself clear-sightedly had, in
fact, been as much her occupation for the last six months of
semi-retreat as losing a stone and regaining her beauty.

Which she had: she was thirty-nine and she had never been
more attractive. The tomboy who had left home in Iowa for the
freedoms of New York had been lovely, as every fairly endowed young girl is lovely, but what she was now was the
product of twenty years of work on herself. And other people's
work too . . . She was a small, round, white-skinned, big-
brown-eyed black-haired beauty, but her sympathy, her softness, her magnetism were the creation of the loves of a dozen
intelligent men. No, she did not envy her eighteen-year-old self
at all. But she did envy, envied every day more bitterly, that
young girl's genuine independence, largeness, scope, and courage.

It had been six months ago when her most recent – and, she
had hoped, her final – lover, Jack Boles, had left her, and left

her in pieces, that it had occurred to her that twenty – indeed, only ten – years ago *she* had discarded lovers, *she* had been the one to say, as Jack had said – embarrassed and guilty, but not more than he could easily come to terms with – 'I'm sorry, forgive me, I'm off.' And, and this was the point, she had never calculated the consequences to herself, had taken money from no man, save what she considered she had earned, had remained herself always. (In her time with Jack she had expressed opinions not her own to please him: he was a man who disliked women disagreeing with him.) Above all, she had never given a moment's thought to what people might say. But when Jack threw her over, after an affair which was publicized through the newspapers for months ('Famous film director shares flat in Cannes with the painter Maureen Jeffries') she had thought first of all: I'll be a laughing stock. She had told everyone, with reason, that he would marry her. Then she thought: But he stayed with me less than a year, no one has got tired of me before so quickly. Then: the woman he has thrown me over for is not a patch on me, and she can't even cook. Then back again to the beginning: People must be laughing at me.

Self-contempt poisoned her, particularly as she was unable to let Jack go, but pursued him with telephone calls, letters, reproaches, reminders that he had promised marriage. She spoke of what she had given him, did everything in fact that she despised most in women. Above all, she had not left this flat whose rent he had recently paid for five years. What it amounted to was, he was buying her off with the lease of this flat.

And instead of walking right out of it with her clothes (she was surely entitled to those?) she was still here, making herself beautiful and fighting down terror.

At eighteen, leaving her father's house (he was a post-office clerk), she had had her sex and her courage. Not beauty. For like many other professional beauties, women who spend their lives with men, she was not beautiful at all. What she had was a focused sex, her whole being aware and sharpened by sex, that made her seem beautiful. Now, twenty years later, after being the mistress of eleven men, all of them eminent or at least potentially eminent, she had her sex, and her courage. *But* – since she had never put her own talent, painting, first; but always the career of whichever man she was living with, and out of an instinct of generosity which was probably the best thing in her – she now could not earn a living. At least, not in the style she had been used to.

Since she had left home she had devoted her talents, her warmth, her imagination to an art teacher (her first lover), two actors (then unknown, now world-famous), a choreographer; a writer; another writer; then, crossing the Atlantic to Europe, a film director (Italy), an actor (France), a writer (London), Professor Tom Bayley (London), Jack Boles, film director (London). Who could say how much of her offered self, her continually poured-forth devotion to their work, was responsible for their success? (As she demanded of herself fiercely, weeping, in the dark hours.)

She now had left her sympathy, her charm, her talents for dress and decor, a minor talent for painting (which did not mean she was not a discriminating critic of other people's work), the fact she was a perfect cook, and her abilities in bed, which she knew were outstanding.

And the moment she stepped out of this flat, she would step out, also, of the world of international money and prestige. To what? Her father, now living in a rooming house in Chicago? No, her only hope was to find another man as eminent and lustrous as the others; for she could no longer afford the unknown geniuses, the potential artists. This is what she was waiting for, and why she remained in the luxurious flat, which must serve as a base; and why she despised herself so painfully; and why she had invited Peggy Bayley to visit her. One: she needed to bolster herself up by seeing this woman, whose career (as the mistress of well-known men) had been similar to hers, and who was now well married. Second: she was going to ask her help. She had gone carefully through the list of her ex-lovers, written to three, and drawn three friendly but unhelpful letters. She had remained, officially, a 'friend' of Tom Bayley; but she knew better than to offend his wife by approaching him except with her approval. She would ask Peggy to ask Tom to use his influence to get her a job of the kind that would enable her to meet the right sort of man.

When the doorbell rang, and she had answered it, she went hastily to the big brown chair, this time out of bravado, even honesty. She was appealing to the wife of a man whose very publicized mistress she had been; and she did not wish to soften the difficulties of it by looking less attractive than she could; even though Peggy would enter with nothing left of her own beauty; for three years of marriage with Professor Bayley had turned her into a sensible, good-looking woman, the sleek feline quality gone that had led *her* from Cape Town to Europe as a minor actress, which career she had given up, quite rightly, for the one she was born for.

But Peggy Bayley entered, as it were, four years back: if Maureen was small, delicate, luscious, then Peggy's mode was to be a siren: Maureen jerked herself up, saw Peggy push pale hair off a brown cheek with a white ringed hand and slide her a green-eyed mocking smile. She involuntarily exclaimed: 'Tom's ditched you!'

Peggy laughed – her voice, like Maureen's, was the husky voice of the sex-woman – and said: 'How did you guess!' At which she turned, her hips angled in a mannequin's pose, letting her gold hair fall over her face, showing off a straight green linen dress that owed everything to a newly provocative body. Not a trace left of the sensible healthy housewife of the last three years: she, like Maureen, was once again focused behind her sexuality, poised on it, vibrating with it.

She said: 'We both of us *look* very much the better for being ditched!'

Now, with every consciousness of how she looked, she appropriated the yellow settee in a coil of femininity, and said: 'Give me a drink and don't look so surprised. After all, I suppose I could have seen it coming?' This was a query addressed to – a fellow conspirator? No. Victim? No. Fellow artisan – yes. Maureen realized that the only-just-under-the-surface hostility that had characterized their meetings when Peggy was with Tom Bayley had vanished entirely. But she was not altogether happy yet about this flow of comradeship. Frowning, she got out of the brown satin chair, a cigarette clumsy between her lips. She remembered that the frown and the dangling cigarette belonged to the condition of *a woman sure of a man*; her instincts were, then, to lie to Peggy, and precisely because she did not like to admit, even now, long after the fact, just how badly she was alone? She poured large brandies, and asked: 'Who did he leave you for?'

Peggy said: 'I left him,' and kept her green eyes steady on Maureen's face to make her accept it, despite the incredulity she saw there.

'No, really, it's true – of course there were women all the time, that's why he insisted on the hidey-hole in Chelsea . . .' Maureen definitely smiled now, to remind her of how often she had *not* acknowledged the reason for the hidey-hole. It had been 'Bill's study, where he can get away from dreary domesticity'. Peggy accepted the reminder with a small honest smile that nevertheless had impatience: 'Well of course I told lies and played little games, don't we all?' – that's what the smile said; and Maureen's dislike of herself made her say aloud, so as to put an end to her silent rancorous criticism of Peggy: 'Well, all right then. But you did force him to marry you.' She had taken three large gulps of brandy. Whereas she had drunk far too much in the months after Jack had left her, during the last weeks her diet had forbidden her alcohol, and she was out of practice. She felt herself already getting tight, and she said: 'If I'm going to get tight, then you've got to too.'

'I was drunk every day and night for two months,' said Peggy, again with the level green look. 'But you can't drink if you want to keep pretty.'

Maureen went back to the brown chair, looked at Peggy through coiling blue smoke, and said: 'I was drunk all the time for – it was ages. It was disgusting. I couldn't stop.'

Peggy said: 'Well all right, we've finished with that. But the point was, not the other women – we discussed his character thoroughly when we married and . . .' Here she stopped to acknowledge Maureen's rather sour smile, and said: 'It's part of our role, isn't it, to thoroughly discuss their characters?' At this, both women's eyes filled with tears, which both blinked away. Another barrier had gone down.

Peggy said: 'I came here to show myself off, because of your boasting little letter – I've been watching you patronize me since I married Tom, being dull and ordinary – I wanted *you* to see the new me! ... God knows why one loses one's sex when one's settled with a man.'

They both giggled suddenly, rolling over, Peggy on her yellow linen, Maureen on her glossy brown. Then at the same moment, they had to fight back the tears.

'No,' said Maureen, sitting up, 'I'm not going to cry, oh no! I've stopped crying, there's not the slightest point.'

'Then let's have some more to drink,' and Peggy handed over her glass.

They were both tight, already; since both were in any case on the edge of themselves with fasting.

Maureen half filled both glasses wtih brandy, and asked: 'Did you really leave him?'

'Yes.'

'Then you've got better reason to like yourself than I have. I fought, and I made scenes, and when I think of it now ...' She took a brandy gulp, looked around the expensive room, and said: 'And I'm still living on him now and that's what's so horrible.'

'Well, don't cry, dear,' said Peggy. The brandy was slurring her, making her indolent. The *dear* made Maureen shrink. It was the meaningless word of the theatre and film people, which was all right, even enjoyable, with the theatre and film people, but it was only one step from ...

'*Don't*,' said Maureen, sharp. Peggy widened her long green eyes in a 'charming' way, then let them narrow into the honesty of her real nature, and laughed.

'I see your point,' she said. 'Well, we'd better face it, hadn't we? We're not so far off, are we?'

'*Yes*,' said Maureen. 'I've been thinking it out. If we had married them, that marriage certificate, you know, well then, we'd have felt quite all right to take money, in return for everything, everything, everything!' She put her face down and sobbed.

'Shut up,' said Peggy. But it sounded because of her tightness like 'Shhrrrp.'

'No,' said Maureen, sitting up and sniffing. 'It's true. I've never taken money – I mean I've never taken anything more than housekeeping money and presents of clothes – have you?' Peggy was not looking at her, so she went on: 'All right, but I'll take a guess that Tom Bayley's the first man you've taken a settlement from, or alimony – isn't that so? And that's because you were married to him.'

'I suppose so. I told myself I wouldn't but I have.'

'And you don't really feel bad about it, just because of that marriage certificate?'

Peggy turned her glass round and round between long soft fingers and at length nodded: I suppose so.

'Yes. Of course. And all the fun we've both made about that marriage certificate in our time. But the point is, taking money when you're married doesn't make you *feel* like a tart. With all the men I've been with, I've always had to argue with myself, I've said, Well, how much would he have to pay for what I do for him – the cooking and the housekeeping and the interior decoration and the advice? A fortune! So there's no need for me to feel badly about living in his flat and taking clothes. But I did feel bad, always. But if Jack had married me, living in this bloody flat of his wouldn't make me feel like a bloody tart.' She burst into savage angry tears, stopped herself, breathed deeply, and sat silent, breathing deep. Then she got up, refilled her glass and Peggy's, and sat down. The two women sat in silence, until at last Maureen said: 'Why did you leave him?'

'When he married me we both thought I was pregnant . . . no, it's true. I know what you and everyone else said, but it was true. I had no periods for three months, and then I was very ill, they said it was a miscarriage.'

'He wants children?'

'Didn't he with you?'

'No.'

'Then he's changed. He wants them badly.'

'Jack wouldn't hear of children, wouldn't hear of them, but that little bitch he's ditched me for ... I hear you're great friends with them?' She meant Jack and the girl for whom she was thrown over.

Peggy said: 'Jack is a great friend of Tom's.' This was very dry, and Maureen said: 'Yes. Yes! All Jack's friends – I cooked for them, I entertained them, but do you know not one of them has even rung me up since he left me? They were *his* friends, not mine.'

'Exactly. Since I left Tom I haven't seen either Jack or his new girl. They visit Tom.'

'I suppose one of Tom's girls got pregnant?'

'Yes. He came to me and told me. I knew what I was supposed to do, and I did it. I said: Right, you can have your divorce.'

'Then you've got your self-respect, at least.'

Peggy turned her glass round, looking into it; it slopped over on to the yellow linen. Both women watched the orange stain spread, without moving, in an aesthetic interest.

'No, I haven't,' said Peggy. 'Because I said: "You can have your divorce, but you've got to give me so much money, or else I'll sue you for infidelity – I've got the evidence a thousand times over." '

'How much?'

Peggy coloured, took a gulp of brandy and said: 'I'm going to get forty pounds a month alimony. It's a lot for him – he's a professor, not a film director.'

'He can't afford it?'

'No. He told me he must give up his hidey-hole. I said: "Too bad." '

'What's she like?'

'Twenty-seven. An art student. She's pretty and sweet and dumb.'

'But she's pregnant.'

'Yes.'

'You've never had a baby?'

'No. But I've had several abortions and miscarriages.'

The two women looked frankly at each other, their faces bitter.

'Yes,' said Maureen. 'I've had five abortions and one of them was by one of those old women. I don't even use anything, and I don't get pregnant ... How did you like Jack's new girl?'

'I liked her,' said Peggy, apologetically.

'She's an intellectual,' said Maureen: it sounded like 'inteleshual'.

'Yes.'

'Ever so bright and well-informed.' Maureen battled a while with her better self, won the battle, and said: 'But *why*? She's attractive, but she's such a schoolgirl, she's a nice bright clever little schoolgirl with nice bright clever little clothes.'

Peggy said: 'Stop it. Stop it at once.'

'Yes,' said Maureen. But she added, out of her agonized depths: 'And she can't even cook!'

And now Peggy laughed, flinging herself back and spilling more brandy from her drunken hand. After a while, Maureen laughed too.

Peggy said: 'I was thinking, how many times have wives and mistresses said about us: Peggy's such a bore, Maureen's so obvious.'

'I can hear them: of course they're very pretty, and of course they can dress well, and they're marvellous cooks, and I suppose they're good in bed, but what have they *got*?'

'Stop it,' said Peggy.

Both women were now drunk. It was getting late. The room was full of shadow, its white walls fading into blue heights; the glossy chairs, tables, rugs, sending out deep gleams of light.

'Shall I turn on the light?'

'Not yet.' Peggy now got up herself to refill her glass. She said: 'I hope she has the sense not to throw up her job.'

'Who, Jack's red-headed bitch?'

'Who else? Tom's girl is all right, she's actually pregnant.'

'You're right. But I bet she does, I bet Jack's trying to make her give it up.'

'I know he is. Just before I left Tom – before he threw me

over – your Jack and she were over to dinner. Jack was getting at her for her column, he was sniping at her all evening – he said it was a left-wing society hostess's view of politics. A left-wing bird's-eye view, he said.'

'He hated me painting,' said Maureen. 'Every time I said I wanted a morning to paint, he made gibes about Sunday painters. I'd serve him his breakfast, and go up to the studio – well, it's the spare room really. First he'd shout up funny cracks, then he'd come up and say he was hungry. He'd start being hungry at eleven in the morning. Then if I didn't come down and cook, he'd make love. Then we'd talk about his work. We'd talk about his bloody films all day and half the night . . .' Maureen's voice broke into a wail: 'It's all so unfair, so unfair, so unfair . . . they were all like that. I'm not saying I'd have been a great painter, but I might have been something. Something of my own . . . Not one of those men did anything but make fun, or patronize me . . . all of them, in one way or another. And of course, one always gives in, because one cares more for . . .'

Peggy who had been half asleep, drooping over her settee, sat up and said: 'Stop it, Maureen. What's the good of it?'

'But it's true. I've spent twenty years of my life, eighteen hours a day, bolstering up some man's ambition. Well, isn't it true?'

'It's true, but stop it. We chose it.'

'Yes. And if that silly red-haired bitch gives up her job, she'll get what she deserves.'

'She'll be where we are.'

'But Jack says he's going to marry her.'

'Tom married me.'

'He was intrigued by that clever little red-headed mind of hers. All those bright remarks about politics. But now he's doing everything he can to stop her column. Not that it would be any loss to the nation, but she'd better watch out, oh yes, she had . . .' Maureen weaved her brandy glass back and forth in front of hypnotized eyes.

'Which is the other reason I came to see you.'

'You didn't come to see the new me?'

'It's the same thing.'

'Well?'

'How much money have you got?'

'Nothing.'

'How long is the lease for this flat?' Maureen held up the fingers of one hand. 'Five years? Then sell the lease.'

'Oh I couldn't.'

'Oh yes you could. It would bring you in about two thousand, I reckon. We could take a flat somewhere less expensive.'

'*We* could?'

'And I've got forty pounds a month. Well, then.'

'Well then what?' Maureen was lying practically flat in the big chair, her white lace shirt ruffled up around her breasts, so that a slim brown waist and diaphragm showed above the tight brown trousers. She held her brandy glass in front of her eyes and moved it back and forth, watching the amber liquid slopping in the glass. From time to time the brandy fell on her brown stomach flesh and she giggled.

Peggy said: 'If we don't do something, I've got to go back to my parents in Oudtshoorn – they're ostrich farmers. I was the bright girl that escaped. Well, I'll never make an actress. So I'll be back living out my life among the sugar-bushes and the ostriches. And where will you be?'

'Ditto, ditto.' Maureen now wriggled her soft brown head sideways and let brandy drip into her open mouth.

'We're going to open a dress shop. If there's one thing we both really understand, it's how to dress.'

'Good idea.'

'What city would you fancy?'

'I fancy Paris.'

'We couldn't compete in Paris.'

'No, can't compete in ... how about Rome? I've got three ex-lovers in Rome.'

'They're not much good when it comes to trouble.'

'No good at all.'

'Better stay in London.'

'Better stay in London. Like another drink?'

'Yes. Yesssh.'

'I'lll get-get-itit.'

'Next time, we musn't go to bed without the marriage shertificate.'

'A likely shtory.'

'But it's against my prinshiples, bargaining.'

'Oh I know, I know.'

'Yesh.'

'Perhaps we'd better be leshbians, what do you think?'

Peggy got up, with difficulty, came to Maureen, and put her hand on Maureen's bare diaphragm. 'Doesh that do anything for you?'

'Not a thing.'

'I fanshy men myself,' said Peggy, returning to her settee, where she sat with a bump, spilling liquor.

'Me too and a fat lot of good it duz ush.'

'Next time, we don't give up our jobs, we stick with the dress shop.'

'Yessh . . .'

A pause. Then Peggy sat up, and focused. She was pervaded by an immense earnestness. 'Listen,' she said. 'No, damn it, lishen, that's what I mean to shay all the time, I really mean it.'

'I do too.'

'No. No giving it up the firsht time a m-m-man appearsh. Damn it, I'm drunk, but I mean it . . . No, Maureen, I'm not going to shtart a dresh shop unless that's undershtood from the shtart. We musht we *musht* agree to that, work firsht, or elshe, or *else* you know where we're going to end up.' Peggy brought out the last in a rush, and lay back, satisfied.

Maureen now sat up, earnest, trying to control her tongue: 'But . . . what . . . we are both *good* at, itsh, it's bolshtering up some damned genus, genius.'

'Not any more. Oh no. You've got to *promish* me, Maureen, promish me, or *elshe* . . .'

'All right, I promish.'

'Good.'

'Have another drink?'

'Lovely brandy, lovely lovely lovely blandy.'

'Lovely brandy . . .'

TO ROOM NINETEEN

This is a story, I suppose, about a failure in intelligence: the Rawlingses' marriage was grounded in intelligence.

They were older when they married than most of their married friends: in their well-seasoned late twenties. Both had had a number of affairs, sweet rather than bitter; and when they fell in love – for they did fall in love – had known each other for some time. They joked that they had saved each other 'for the real thing'. That they had waited so long (but not too long) for this real thing was to them a proof of their sensible discrimination. A good many of their friends had married young, and now (they felt) probably regretted lost opportunities; while others, still unmarried, seemed to them arid, self-doubting, and likely to make desperate or romantic marriages.

Not only they, but others, felt they were well matched: their friends' delight was an additional proof of their happiness. They had played the same roles, male and female, in this group or set, if such a wide, loosely connected, constantly changing constellation of people could be called a set. They had both become, by virtue of their moderation, their humour, and their abstinence from painful experience people to whom others came for advice. They could be, and were, relied on. It was one of those cases of a man and a woman linking themselves whom no one else had ever thought of linking, probably because of their similarities. But then everyone exclaimed: Of course! How right! How was it we never thought of it before!

And so they married amid general rejoicing, and because of their foresight and their sense for what was probable, nothing was a surprise to them.

Both had well-paid jobs. Matthew was a sub-editor on a large London newspaper, and Susan worked in an advertising firm. He was not the stuff of which editors or publicized journalists are made, but he was much more than 'a sub-editor', being one of the essential background people who in fact steady, inspire and make possible the people in the limelight. He was content with this position. Susan had a talent for commercial drawing. She was humorous about the advertisements she was responsible for, but she did not feel strongly about them one way or the other.

Both, before they married, had had pleasant flats, but they felt it unwise to base a marriage on either flat, because it might seem like a submission of personality on the part of the one whose flat it was not. They moved into a new flat in South Kensington on the clear understanding that when their marriage had settled down (a process they knew would not take long, and was in fact more a humorous concession to popular wisdom than what was due to themselves) they would buy a house and start a family.

And this is what happened. They lived in their charming flat for two years, giving parties and going to them, being a popular young married couple, and then Susan became pregnant, she gave up her job, and they bought a house in Richmond. It was typical of this couple that they had a son first, then a daughter, then twins, son and daughter. Everything right, appropriate, and what everyone would wish for, if they could choose. But people did feel these two had chosen; this balanced and sensible family was no more than what was due to them because of their infallible sense for *choosing* right.

And so they lived with their four children in their gardened house in Richmond and were happy. They had everything they had wanted and had planned for.

And yet . . .

Well, even this was expected, that there must be a certain flatness . . .

Yes, yes, of course, it was natural they sometimes felt like this. Like what?

Their life seemed to be like a snake biting its tail. Matthew's job for the sake of Susan, children, house, and garden – which caravanserai needed a well-paid job to maintain it. And Susan's practical intelligence for the sake of Matthew, the children, the house and the garden – which unit would have collapsed in a week without her.

But there was no point about which either could say: 'For the sake of *this* is all the rest.' Children? But children can't be a centre of life and a reason for being. They can be a thousand things that are delightful, interesting, satisfying, but they can't be a wellspring to live from. Or they shouldn't be. Susan and Matthew knew that well enough.

Matthew's job? Ridiculous. It was an interesting job, but scarcely a reason for living. Matthew took pride in doing it well; but he could hardly be expected to be proud of the newspaper: the newspaper he read, *his* newspaper, was not the one he worked for.

Their love for each other? Well, that was nearest it. If this wasn't a centre, what was? Yes, it was around this point, their love, that the whole extraordinary structure revolved. For extraordinary it certainly was. Both Susan and Matthew had moments of thinking so, of looking in secret disbelief at this thing they had created: marriage, four children, big house, garden, charwomen, friends, cars . . . and this *thing*, this entity, all of it had come into existence, been blown into being out of nowhere, because Susan loved Matthew and Matthew loved Susan. Extraordinary. So that was the central point, the wellspring.

And if one felt that it simply was not strong enough, important enough, to support it all, well whose fault was that? Certainly neither Susan's nor Matthew's. It was in the nature of things. And they sensibly blamed neither themselves nor each other.

On the contrary, they used their intelligence to preserve what they had created from a painful and explosive world: they looked around them, and took lessons. All around them, marriages collapsing, or breaking, or rubbing along (even worse, they felt). They must not make the same mistakes, they must not.

They had avoided the pitfall so many of their friends had fallen into – of buying a house in the country *for the sake of the children*; so that the husband became a weekend husband, a weekend father, and the wife always careful not to ask what went on in the town flat which they called (in joke) a bachelor flat. No, Matthew was a full-time husband, a full-time father, and at nights, in the big married bed in the big married bedroom (which had an attractive view of the river) they lay beside each other talking and he told her about his day, and what he had done, and whom he had met; and she told him about her day (not as interesting, but that was not her fault) for both knew of the hidden resentments and deprivations of the woman who has lived her own life – and above all, has earned her own living – and is now dependent on a husband for outside interests and money.

Nor did Susan make the mistake of taking a job for the sake of her independence, which she might very well have done, since her old firm, missing her qualities of humour, balance, and sense, invited her often to go back. Children needed their mother to a certain age, that both parents knew and agreed on; and when these four healthy wisely brought-up children were of the right age, Susan would work again, because she knew, and so did he, what happened to women of fifty at the height of their energy and ability, with grown-up children who no longer needed their full devotion.

So here was this couple, testing their marriage, looking after it, treating it like a small boat full of helpless people in a very stormy sea. Well, of course, so it was ... The storms of the world were bad, but not too close – which is not to say they were selfishly felt: Susan and Matthew were both well-informed and responsible people. And the inner storms and quicksands were understood and charted. So everything was all right. Everything was in order. Yes, things were under control.

So what did it matter if they felt dry, flat? People like themselves, fed on a hundred books (psychological, anthropological, sociological) could scarcely be unprepared for the dry, controlled wistfulness which is the distinguishing mark of the intelligent marriage. Two people, endowed with education, with discrimination, with judgment, linked together voluntarily from their will to be happy together and to be of use to others –

one sees them everywhere, one knows them, one even is that thing oneself: sadness because so much is after all so little. These two, unsurprised, turned towards each other with even more courtesy and gentle love: this was life, that two people, no matter how carefully chosen, could not be everything to each other. In fact, even to say so, to think in such a way, was banal, they were ashamed to do it.

It was banal, too, when one night Matthew came home late and confessed he had been to a party, taken a girl home and slept with her. Susan forgave him, of course. Except that forgiveness is hardly the word. Understanding, yes. But if you understand something, you don't forgive it, you are the thing itself: forgiveness is for what you *don't* understand. Nor had he *confessed* – what sort of word is that?

The whole thing was not important. After all, years ago they had joked: Of course I'm not going to be faithful to you, no one can be faithful to one other person for a whole lifetime. (And there was the word *faithful* – stupid, all these words, stupid, belonging to a savage old world.) But the incident left both of them irritable. Strange, but they were both bad-tempered, annoyed. There was something unassimilable about it.

Making love splendidly after he had come home that night, both had felt that the idea that Myra Jenkins, a pretty girl met at a party, could be even relevant was ridiculous. They had loved each other for over a decade, would love each other for years more. Who, then, was Myra Jenkins?

Except, thought Susan, unaccountably bad-tempered, she was (is?) the first. In ten years. So either the ten years' fidelity was not important, or she isn't. (No, no, there is something wrong with this way of thinking, there must be.) But if she isn't important, presumably it wasn't important either when Matthew and I first went to bed with each other that afternoon whose delight even now (like a very long shadow at sundown) lays a long, wand-like finger over us. (Why did I say sundown?) Well, if what we felt that afternoon was not important, nothing is important, because if it hadn't been for what we felt, we wouldn't be Mr and Mrs Rawlings with four children, etc., etc. The whole thing is *absurd* – for him to have come home and told me was absurd. For him not to have told me was absurd. For me to care, or for that matter not to care, is absurd . . . and who is Myra Jenkins? Why, no one at all.

There was only one thing to do, and of course these sensible people did it: they put the thing behind them, and consciously, knowing what they were doing, moved forward into a different phase of their marriage, giving thanks for past good fortune as they did so.

For it was inevitable that the handsome, blond, attractive, manly man, Matthew Rawlings, should be at times tempted (oh, what a word!) by the attractive girls at parties she could not attend because of the four children; and that sometimes he would succumb (a word even more repulsive, if possible) and that she, a good-looking woman in the big well-tended garden at Richmond, would sometimes be pierced as by an arrow from the sky with bitterness. Except that bitterness was not in order, it was out of court. Did the casual girls touch the marriage? They did not. Rather it was they who knew defeat because of the handsome Matthew Rawlings's marriage body and soul to Susan Rawlings.

In that case why did Susan feel (though luckily not for longer than a few seconds at a time) as if life had become a desert, and that nothing mattered, and that her children were not her own?

Meanwhile her intelligence continued to assert that all was well. What if her Matthew did have an occasional sweet afternoon, the odd affair? For she knew quite well, except in her moments of aridity, that they were very happy, that the affairs were not important.

Perhaps that was the trouble? It was in the nature of things that the adventures and delights could no longer be hers, because of the four children and the big house that needed so much attention. But perhaps she was secretly wishing, and even knowing that she did, that the wildness and the beauty could be his. But he was married to her. She was married to him. They were married inextricably. And therefore the gods could not strike him with the real magic, not really. Well, was it Susan's fault that after he came home from an adventure he looked harassed rather than fulfilled? (In fact, that was how she knew he had been *unfaithful*, because of his sullen air, and his glances at her, similar to hers at him: What is it that I share with this person that shields all delight from me?) But none of it by anybody's fault. (But what did they feel ought to be somebody's fault?) Nobody's fault, nothing to be at fault, no one to blame, no one to offer or to take it ... and nothing wrong, either, except that Matthew never was really struck, as he wanted to be, by joy; and that Susan was more and more often threatened by emptiness. (It was usually in the garden that she was invaded by this feeling: she was coming to avoid the garden, unless the children or Matthew were with her.) There was no need to use the dramatic words, unfaithful, forgive, and the rest: intelligence forbade them. Intelligence barred, too, quarrelling, sulking, anger, silences of withdrawal, accusations and tears. Above all, intelligence forbids tears.

A high price has to be paid for the happy marriage with the four healthy children in the large white gardened house.

And they were paying it, willingly, knowing what they were doing. When they lay side by side or breast to breast in the big civilized bedroom overlooking the wild sullied river, they laughed, often, for no particular reason; but they knew it was really because of these two small people, Susan and Matthew, supporting such an edifice on their intelligent love. The laugh comforted them; it saved them both, though from what, they did not know.

They were now both fortyish. The older children, boy and girl, were ten and eight, at school. The twins, six, were still at home. Susan did not have nurses or girls to help her: childhood is short; and she did not regret the hard work. Often enough she was bored, since small children can be boring; she was often very tired; but she regretted nothing. In another decade, she would turn herself back into being a woman with a life of her own.

Soon the twins would go to school, and they would be away from home from nine until four. These hours, so Susan saw it, would be the preparation for her own slow emancipation away from the role of hub-of-the-family into woman-with-her-own-life. She was already planning for the hours of freedom when all the children would be 'off her hands'. That was the phrase used by Matthew and by Susan and by their friends, for the moment when the youngest child went off to school. 'They'll be off your hands, darling Susan, and you'll have time to yourself.' So said Matthew, the intelligent husband, who had often enough commended and consoled Susan, standing by her in spirit during the years when her soul was not her own, as she said, but her children's.

What it amounted to was that Susan saw herself as she had been at twenty-eight, unmarried; and then again somewhere about fifty, blossoming from the root of what she had been twenty years before. As if the essential Susan were in abeyance, as if she were in cold storage. Matthew said something like this to Susan one night: and she agreed that it was true – she did feel something like that. What, then, was this essential Susan? She did not know. Put like that it sounded ridiculous, and she did not really feel it. Anyway, they had a long discussion about the whole thing before going off to sleep in each other's arms.

So the twins went off to their school, two bright affectionate children who had no problems about it, since their older brother and sister had trodden this path so successfully before them. And now Susan was going to be alone in the big house, every day of the school term, except for the daily woman who came in to clean.

It was now, for the first time in this marriage, that something happened which neither of them had foreseen.

This is what happened. She returned, at nine-thirty, from taking the twins to the school by car, looking forward to seven blissful hours of freedom. On the first morning she was simply restless, worrying about the twins 'naturally enough' since this was their first day away at school. She was hardly able to contain herself until they came back. Which they did happily, excited by the world of school, looking forward to the next day. And the next day Susan took them, dropped them, came back, and found herself reluctant to enter her big and beautiful home because it was as if something was waiting for her there that she did not wish to confront. Sensibly, however, she parked the car in the garage, entered the house, spoke to Mrs Parkes the daily woman about her duties, and went up to her bedroom. She was possessed by a fever which drove her out again, downstairs, into the kitchen, where Mrs Parkes was making cake and did not need her, and into the garden. There she sat on a bench, and tried to calm herself, looking at trees, at a brown glimpse of the river. But she was filled with tension, like a panic: as if an enemy was in the garden with her. She spoke to herself severely, thus: All this is quite natural. First, I spent twelve years of my adult life working, *living my own life*. Then I married, and from the moment I became pregnant for the first time I signed myself over, so to speak, to other people. To the children. Not for one moment in twelve years have I been alone, had time to myself. So now I have to learn to be myself again. That's all.

And she went indoors to help Mrs Parkes cook and clean, and found some sewing to do for the children. She kept herself occupied every day. At the end of the first term she understood she felt two contrary emotions. First: secret astonishment and dismay that during those weeks when the house was empty of children she had in fact been more occupied (had been careful to keep herself occupied) than ever she had been when the children were around her needing her continual attention. Second: that now she knew the house would be full of them, and for five weeks, she resented the fact she would never be alone. She was already looking back at those hours of sewing, cooking (but by herself), as at a lost freedom which would not be hers for five long weeks. And the two months of term which would succeed the five weeks stretched alluringly open to her – freedom. But what freedom – when in fact she had been so careful *not* to be free of small duties during the last weeks? She looked at herself, Susan Rawlings, sitting in a big chair by the window in the bedroom, sewing shirts or dresses, which she might just as well have bought. She saw herself making cakes for hours at a time in the big family kitchen: yet usually she bought cakes. What she saw was a woman alone, that was true, but she had not felt alone. For instance, Mrs Parkes was always somewhere in the house. And she did not like being in the

garden at all, because of the closeness there of the enemy –
irritation, restlessness, emptiness, whatever it was, which keeping her hands occupied made less dangerous for some reason.

Susan did not tell Matthew of these thoughts. They were not
sensible. She did not recognize herself in them. What should
she say to her dear friend and husband Matthew? 'When I go
into the garden, that is, if the children are not there, I feel as if
there is an enemy there waiting to invade me.' 'What enemy,
Susan darling?' 'Well I don't know, really . . .' 'Perhaps you
should see a doctor?'

No, clearly this conversation should not take place. The holidays began and Susan welcomed them. Four children, lively,
energetic, intelligent, demanding: she was never, not for a
moment of her day, alone. If she was in a room, they would be
in the next room, or waiting for her to do something for them;
or it would soon be time for lunch or tea, or to take one of them
to the dentist. Something to do: five weeks of it, thank goodness.

On the fourth day of these so welcome holidays, she found
she was storming with anger at the twins, two shrinking beautiful children who (and this is what checked her) stood hand in
hand looking at her with sheer dismayed disbelief. This was
their calm mother, shouting at them. And what for? They had
come to her with some game, some bit of nonsense. They looked
at each other, moved closer for support, and went off hand in
hand, leaving Susan holding on to the windowsill of the living
room, breathing deep, feeling sick. She went to lie down, telling
the older children she had a headache. She heard the boy Harry
telling the little ones: 'It's all right, Mother's got a headache.'
She heard that *It's all right* with pain.

That night she said to her husband: 'Today I shouted at the
twins, quite unfairly.' She sounded miserable, and he said
gently: 'Well, what of it?'

'It's more of an adjustment than I thought, their going to
school.'

'But Susie, Susie darling . . .' For she was crouched weeping
on the bed. He comforted her: 'Susan, what is all this about?
You shouted at them? What of it? If you shouted at them fifty
times a day it wouldn't be more than the little devils deserve.'

But she wouldn't laugh. She wept. Soon he comforted her with his body. She became calm. Calm, she wondered what was wrong with her, and why she should mind so much that she might, just once, have behaved unjustly with the children. What did it matter? They had forgotten it all long ago: Mother had a headache and everything was all right.

It was a long time later that Susan understood that that night, when she had wept and Matthew had driven the misery out of her with his big solid body, was the last time, ever in their married life, that they had been – to use their mutual language – with each other. And even that was a lie, because she had not told him of her real fears at all.

The five weeks passed, and Susan was in control of herself, and good and kind, and she looked forward to the holidays with a mixture of fear and longing. She did not know what to expect. She took the twins off to school (the elder children took themselves to school) and she returned to the house determined to face the enemy wherever he was, in the house, or the garden or – where?

She was again restless, she was possessed by restlessness. She cooked and sewed and worked as before, day after day, while Mrs Parkes remonstrated: 'Mrs Rawlings, what's the need for it? I can do that, it's what you pay me for.'

And it was so irrational that she checked herself. She would put the car into the garage, go up to her bedroom, and sit, hands in her lap, forcing herself to be quiet. She listened to Mrs Parkes moving around the house. She looked out into the garden and saw the branches shake the trees. She sat defeating the enemy, restlessness. Emptiness. She ought to be thinking about her life, about herself. But she did not. Or perhaps she could not. As soon as she forced her mind to think about Susan (for what else did she want to be alone for?) it skipped off to thoughts of butter or school clothes. Or it thought of Mrs Parkes. She realized that she sat listening for the movements of the cleaning woman, following her every turn, bend, thought. She followed her in her mind from kitchen to bathroom, from table to oven, and it was as if the duster, the cleaning cloth, the saucepan, were in her own hand. She would hear herself saying:

No, not like that, don't put that there . . . Yet she did not give a damn what Mrs Parkes did, or if she did it at all. Yet she could not prevent herself from being conscious of her, every minute. Yes, this was what was wrong with her: she needed, when she was alone, to be really alone, with no one near. She could not endure the knowledge that in ten minutes or in half an hour Mrs Parkes would call up the stairs: 'Mrs Rawlings, there's no silver polish. Madam, we're out of flour.'

So she left the house and went to sit in the garden where she was screened from the house by trees. She waited for the demon to appear and claim her, but he did not.

She was keeping him off, because she had not, after all, come to an end of arranging herself.

She was planning how to be somewhere where Mrs Parkes would not come after her with a cup of tea, or a demand to be allowed to telephone (always irritating since Susan did not care who she telephoned or how often), or just a nice talk about something. Yes, she needed a place, or a state of affairs, where it would not be necessary to keep reminding herself: In ten minutes I must telephone Matthew about . . . and at half past three I must leave early for the children because the car needs cleaning. And at ten o'clock tomorrow I must remember . . . She was possessed with resentment that the seven hours of freedom in every day (during weekdays in the school term) were not free, that never, not for one second, ever, was she free from the pressure of time, from having to remember this or that. She could never forget herself; never really let herself go into forgetfulness.

Resentment. It was poisoning her. (She looked at this emotion and thought it was absurd. Yet she felt it.) She was a prisoner. (She looked at this thought too, and it was no good telling herself it was a ridiculous one.) She must tell Matthew – but what? She was filled with emotions that were utterly ridiculous, that she despised, yet that nevertheless she was feeling so strongly she could not shake them off.

The school holidays came round, and this time they were for nearly two months, and she behaved with a conscious controlled decency that nearly drove her crazy. She would lock herself in the bathroom, and sit on the edge of the bath, breathing deep, trying to let go into some kind of calm. Or she went up into the spare room, usually empty, where no one would expect her to be. She heard the children calling 'Mother, Mother', and kept silent, feeling guilty. Or she went to the very end of the garden, by herself, and looked at the slow-moving brown river; she looked at the river and closed her eyes and breathed slow and deep, taking it into her being, into her veins.

Then she returned to the family, wife and mother, smiling and responsible, feeling as if the pressure of these people – four lively children and her husband – were a painful pressure on the surface of her skin, a hand pressing on her brain. She did not once break down into irritation during these holidays, but it was like living out a prison sentence, and when the children went back to school, she sat on a white stone seat near the flowing river, and she thought: It is not even a year since the twins went to school since *they were off my hands* (What on earth did I think I meant when I used that stupid phrase?) and yet I'm a different person. I'm simply not myself. I don't understand it.

Yet she had to understand it. For she knew that this structure – big white house, on which the mortgage still cost four hundred a year, a husband, so good and kind and insightful, four children, all doing so nicely, and the garden where she sat, and Mrs Parkes the cleaning woman – all this depended on her, and yet she could not understand why, or even what it was she contributed to it.

She said to Matthew in their bedroom: 'I think there must be something wrong with me.'

And he said: 'Surely not, Susan? You look marvellous – you're as lovely as ever.'

She looked at the handsome blond man, with his clear, intelligent, blue-eyed face, and thought: Why is it I can't tell him? Why not? And she said: 'I need to be alone more than I am.'

At which he swung his slow blue gaze at her, and she saw what she had been dreading: Incredulity. Disbelief. And fear. An incredulous blue stare from a stranger who was her husband, as close to her as her own breath.

He said: 'But the children are at school and off your hands.'

She said to herself: I've got to force myself to say: Yes, but do you realize that I never feel free? There's never a moment I can say to myself: There's nothing I have to remind myself about, nothing I have to do in half an hour, or an hour, or two hours . . .

But she said: 'I don't feel well.'

He said: 'Perhaps you need a holiday.'

She said, appalled: 'But not without you, surely?' For she could not imagine herself going off without him. Yet that was what he meant. Seeing her face, he laughed, and opened his arms, and she went into them, thinking: Yes, yes, but why can't I say it? And what is it I have to say?

She tried to tell him, about never being free. And he listened and said: 'But Susan, what sort of freedom can you possibly want – short of being dead! Am I ever free? I go to the office, and I have to be there at ten – all right, half past ten, sometimes. And I have to do this or that, don't I? Then I've got to come home at a certain time – I don't mean it, you know I don't – but if I'm not going to be back home at six I telephone you. When can I ever say to myself: I have nothing to be responsible for in the next six hours?'

Susan, hearing this, was remorseful. Because it was true. The good marriage, the house, the children, depended just as much on his voluntary bondage as it did on hers. But why did he not feel bound? Why didn't he chafe and become restless? No, there was something really wrong with her and this proved it.

And that word *bondage* – why had she used it? She had never felt marriage, or the children, as bondage. Neither had he, or surely they wouldn't be together lying in each other's arms content after twelve years of marriage.

No, her state (whatever it was) was irrelevant, nothing to do with her real good life with her family. She had to accept the fact that, after all, she was an irrational person and to live with it. Some people had to live with crippled arms, or stammers, or being deaf. She would have to live knowing she was subject to a state of mind she could not own.

Nevertheless, as a result of this conversation with her husband, there was a new regime next holidays.

The spare room at the top of the house now had a cardboard sign saying: PRIVATE! DO NOT DISTURB! on it. (This sign had been drawn in coloured chalks by the children, after a discussion between the parents in which it was decided that was psychologically the right thing.) The family and Mrs Parkes knew this was 'Mother's Room' and that she was entitled to her privacy. Many serious conversations took place between Matthew and the children about not taking Mother for granted. Susan overheard the first, between father and Harry, the older boy, and was surprised at her irritation over it. Surely she could have a room somewhere in that big house and retire into it without such a fuss being made? Without it being so solemnly discussed? Why couldn't she simply have announced: 'I'm going to fit out the little top room for myself, and when I'm in it I'm not to be disturbed for anything short of fire'? Just that, and finished; instead of long earnest discussions. When she heard Harry and Matthew explaining it to the twins with Mrs Parkes coming in — 'Yes, well, a family sometimes gets on top of a woman' — she had to go right away to the bottom of the garden until the devils of exasperation had finished their dance in her blood.

But now there was a room, and she could go there when she liked, she used it seldom: she felt even more caged there than in her bedroom. One day she had gone up there after a lunch for ten children she had cooked and served because Mrs Parkes was not there, and had sat alone for a while looking into the garden. She saw the children stream out from the kitchen and stand looking up at the window where she sat behind the curtains. They were all — her children and their friends — discussing Mother's Room. A few minutes later, the chase of children in some game came pounding up the stairs, but ended as abruptly as if they had fallen over a ravine, so sudden was the silence. They had remembered she was there, and had gone silent in a great gale of 'Hush! Shhhhh! Quiet, you'll disturb her . . .' And they went tiptoeing downstairs like criminal conspirators. When she came down to make tea for them, they all apologized.

The twins put their arms around her, from front and back, making a human cage of loving limbs, and promised it would never occur again. 'We forgot, Mummy, we forgot all about it!'

What it amounted to was that Mother's Room, and her need for privacy, had become a valuable lesson in respect for other people's rights. Quite soon Susan was going up to the room only because it was a lesson it was a pity to drop. Then she took sewing up there, and the children and Mrs Parkes came in and out: it had become another family room.

She sighed, and smiled, and resigned herself – she made jokes at her own expense with Matthew over the room. That is, she did from the self she liked, she respected. But at the same time, something inside her howled with impatience, with rage . . . And she was frightened. One day she found herself kneeling by her bed and praying: 'Dear God, keep it away from me, keep him away from me.' She meant the devil, for she now thought of it, not caring if she were irrational, as some sort of demon. She imagined him, or it, as a youngish man, or perhaps a middle-aged man pretending to be young. Or a man young-looking from immaturity? At any rate, she saw the young-looking face which, when she drew closer, had dry lines about mouth and eyes. He was thinnish, meagre in build. And he had a reddish complexion, and ginger hair. That was he – a gingery, energetic man, and he wore a reddish hairy jacket, unpleasant to the touch.

Well, one day she saw him. She was standing at the bottom of the garden, watching the river ebb past, when she raised her eyes and saw this person, or being, sitting on the white stone bench. He was looking at her, and grinning. In his hand was a long crooked stick, which he had picked off the ground, or broken off the tree above him. He was absent-mindedly, out of an absent-minded or freakish impulse of spite, using the stick to stir around in the coils of a blindworm or a grass snake (or some kind of snake-like creature: it was whitish and unhealthy to look at, unpleasant). The snake was twisting about, flinging its coils from side to side in a kind of dance of protest against the teasing prodding stick.

Susan looked at him thinking: Who is the stranger? What is he doing in our garden? Then she recognized the man around whom her terrors had crystallized. As she did so, he vanished. She made herself walk over to the bench. A shadow from a branch lay across thin emerald grass, moving jerkily over its roughness, and she could see why she had taken it for a snake, lashing and twisting. She went back to the house thinking: Right, then, so I've seen him with my own eyes, so I'm not crazy after all – there *is* a danger because I've seen him. He is lurking in the garden and sometimes even in the house, and he wants *to get into me and to take me over.*

She dreamed of having a room or a place, anywhere, where she could go and sit, by herself, no one knowing where she was.

Once, near Victoria, she found herself outside a news agent that had Rooms to Let advertised. She decided to rent a room, telling no one. Sometimes she could take the train in from Richmond and sit alone in it for an hour or two. Yet how could she? A room would cost three or four pounds a week, and she earned no money, and how could she explain to Matthew that she needed such a sum? What for? It did not occur to her that she was taking it for granted she wasn't going to tell him about the room.

Well, it was out of the question, having a room; yet she knew she must.

One day, when a school term was well established, and none of the children had measles or other ailments, and everything seemed in order, she did the shopping early, explained to Mrs Parkes she was meeting an old school friend, took the train to Victoria, searched until she found a small quiet hotel, and asked for a room for the day. They did not let rooms by the day, the manageress said, looking doubtful, since Susan so obviously was not the kind of woman who needed a room for unrespectable reasons. Susan made a long explanation about not being well, being unable to shop without frequent rests for lying down. At last she was allowed to rent the room provided she paid a full night's price for it. She was taken up by the manageress and a maid, both concerned over the state of her health ... which must be pretty bad if, living at Richmond (she had signed her name and address in the register), she needed a shelter at Victoria.

The room was ordinary and anonymous, and was just what Susan needed. She put a shilling in the gas fire, and sat, eyes shut, in a dingy armchair with her back to a dingy window. She was alone. She was alone. She was alone. She could feel pressures lifting off her. First the sounds of traffic came very loud; then they seemed to vanish; she might even have slept a little. A knock on the door: it was Miss Townsend the manageress, bringing her a cup of tea with her own hands, so concerned was she over Susan's long silence and possible illness.

Miss Townsend was a lonely woman of fifty, running this hotel with all the rectitude expected of her, and she sensed in Susan the possibility of understanding companionship. She stayed to talk. Susan found herself in the middle of a fantastic story about her illness, which got more and more improbable as she tried to make it tally with the large house at Richmond, well-off husband, and four children. Suppose she said instead: Miss Townsend, I'm here in your hotel because I need to be alone for a few hours, above all *alone and with no one knowing where I am*. She said it mentally, and saw, mentally, the look that would inevitably come on Miss Townsend's elderly maiden's face. 'Miss Townsend, my four children and my husband are driving me insane, do you understand that? Yes, I can see from the gleam of hysteria in your eyes that comes from loneliness controlled but only just contained that I've got everything in the world you've ever longed for. Well, Miss Townsend, I don't want any of it. You can have it, Miss Townsend. I wish I was absolutely alone in the world, like you. Miss Townsend, I'm besieged by seven devils, Miss Townsend, Miss Townsend, let me stay here in your hotel where the devil can't get me . . .' Instead of saying all this, she described her anaemia, agreed to try Miss Townsend's remedy for it, which was raw liver, minced, between whole-meal bread, and said yes, perhaps it would be better if she stayed at home and let a friend do shopping for her. She paid her bill and left the hotel, defeated.

At home Mrs Parkes said she didn't really like it, no, not

really, when Mrs Rawlings was away from nine in the morning until five. The teacher had telephoned from school to say Joan's teeth were paining her, and she hadn't known what to say; and what was she to make for the children's tea, Mrs Rawlings hadn't said.

All this was nonsense, of course. Mrs Parkes's complaint was that Susan had withdrawn herself spiritually, leaving the burden of the big house on her.

Susan looked back at her day of 'freedom' which had resulted in her becoming a friend to the lonely Miss Townsend, and in Mrs Parkes's remonstrances. Yet she remembered the short blissful hour of being alone, really alone. She was determined to arrange her life, no matter what it cost, so that she could have that solitude more often. An absolute solitude, where no one knew her or cared about her.

But how? She thought of saying to her old employer: I want you to back me up in a story with Matthew that I am doing part-time work for you. The truth is that ... but she would have to tell him a lie too, and which lie? She could not say: I want to sit by myself three or four times a week in a rented room. And besides, he knew Matthew, and she could not really ask him to tell lies on her behalf, apart from his being bound to think it meant a lover.

Suppose she really took a part-time job, which she could get through fast and efficiently, leaving time for herself. What job? Addressing envelopes? Canvassing?

And there was Mrs Parkes, working widow, who knew exactly what she was prepared to give to the house, who knew by instinct when her mistress withdrew in spirit from her responsibilities. Mrs Parkes was one of the servers of this world, but she needed someone to serve. She had to have Mrs Rawlings, her madam, at the top of the house or in the garden, so that she could come and get support from her: 'Yes, the bread's not what it was when I was a girl ... Yes, Harry's got a wonderful appetite, I wonder where he puts it all ... Yes, it's lucky the twins are so much of a size, they can wear each other's shoes, that's a saving in these hard times ... Yes, the cherry jam from Switzerland is not a patch on the jam from Poland,

and three times the price . . .' And so on. That sort of talk Mrs Parkes must have, every day, or she would leave, not knowing herself why she left.

Susan Rawlings, thinking these thoughts, found that she was prowling through the great thicketed garden like a wild cat: she was walking up the stairs, down the stairs, through the rooms, into the garden, along the brown running river, back, up through the house, down again . . . It was a wonder Mrs Parkes did not think it strange. But on the contrary, Mrs Rawlings could do what she liked, she could stand on her head if she wanted, provided she was *there*. Susan Rawlings prowled and muttered through her house, hating Mrs Parkes, hating poor Miss Townsend, dreaming of her hour of solitude in the dingy respectability of Miss Townsend's hotel bedroom, and she knew quite well she was mad. Yes, she was mad.

She said to Matthew that she must have a holiday. Matthew agreed with her. This was not as things had been once – how they had talked in each other's arms in the marriage bed. He had, she knew, diagnosed her finally as *unreasonable*. She had become someone outside himself that he had to manage. They were living side by side in this house like two tolerably friendly strangers.

Having told Mrs Parkes, or rather, asked for her permission, she went off on a walking holiday in Wales. She chose the remotest place she knew of. Every morning the children telephoned her before they went off to school, to encourage and support her, just as they had over Mother's Room. Every evening she telephoned them, spoke to each child in turn, and then to Matthew. Mrs Parkes, given permission to telephone for instructions or advice, did so every day at lunchtime. When, as happened three times, Mrs Rawlings was out on the mountainside, Mrs Parkes asked that she should ring back at such and such a time, for she would not be happy in what she was doing without Mrs Rawlings's blessing.

Susan prowled over wild country with the telephone wire holding her to her duty like a leash. The next time she must telephone, or wait to be telephoned, nailed her to her cross. The mountains themselves seemed trammelled by her unfreedom.

Everywhere on the mountains, where she met no one at all, from breakfast time to dusk, excepting sheep, or a shepherd, she came face to face with her own craziness which might attack her in the broadest valleys, so that they seemed too small; or on a mountain-top from which she could see a hundred other mountains and valleys, so that they seemed too low, too small, with the sky pressing down too close. She would stand gazing at a hillside brilliant with ferns and bracken, jewelled with running water, and see nothing but her devil, who lifted inhuman eyes at her from where he leaned negligently on a rock, switching at his ugly yellow boots with a leafy twig.

She returned to her home and family, with the Welsh emptiness at the back of her mind like a promise of freedom.

She told her husband she wanted to have an *au pair* girl.

They were in their bedroom, it was late at night, the children slept. He sat, shirted and slippered, in a chair by the window, looking out. She sat brushing her hair and watching him in the mirror. A time-hallowed scene in the connubial bedroom. He said nothing, while she heard the arguments coming into his mind, only to be rejected because every one was *reasonable*.

'It seems strange to get one now, after all, the children are in school most of the day. Surely the time for you to have help was when you were stuck with them day and night. Why don't you ask Mrs Parkes to cook for you? She's even offered to – I can understand if you are tired of cooking for six people. But you know that an *au pair* girl means all kinds of problems, it's not like having an ordinary char in during the day . . .'

Finally he said carefully: 'Are you thinking of going back to work?'

'No,' she said, 'no, not really.' She made herself sound vague, rather stupid. She went on brushing her black hair and peering at herself so as to be oblivious of the short uneasy glances her Matthew kept giving her. 'Do you think we can't afford it?' she went on vaguely, not at all the old efficient Susan who knew exactly what they could afford.

'It's not that,' he said, looking out of the window at dark trees, so as not to look at her. Meanwhile she examined a round, candid, pleasant face with clear dark brows and clear grey eyes.

A sensible face. She brushed thick healthy black hair and thought: Yet that's the reflection of a madwoman. How very strange! Much more to the point if what looked back at me was the gingery green-eyed demon with his dry meagre smile ... Why wasn't Matthew agreeing? After all, what else could he do? She was breaking her part of the bargain and there was no way of forcing her to keep it: that her spirit, her soul, should live in this house, so that the people in it could grow like plants in water, and Mrs Parkes remain content in their service. In return for this, he would be a good loving husband, and responsible towards the children. Well, nothing like this had been true of either of them for a long time. He did his duty, perfunctorily; she did not even pretend to do hers. And he had become like other husbands, with his real life in his work and the people he met there, and very likely a serious affair. All this was her fault.

At last he drew heavy curtains, blotting out the trees, and turned to force her attention: 'Susan, are you really sure we need a girl?' But she would not meet his appeal at all. She was running the brush over her hair again and again, lifting fine black clouds in a small hiss of electricity. She was peering in and smiling as if she were amused at the clinging hissing hair that followed the brush.

'Yes, I think it would be a good idea on the whole,' she said, with the cunning of a madwoman evading the real point.

In the mirror she could see her Matthew lying on his back, his hands behind his head, staring upwards, his face sad and hard. She felt her heart (the old heart of Susan Rawlings) soften and call out to him. But she set it to be indifferent.

He said: 'Susan, the children?' It was an appeal that *almost* reached her. He opened his arms, lifting them from where they had lain by his sides, palms up, empty. She had only to run across and fling herself into them, on to his hard, warm chest, and melt into herself, into Susan. But she could not. She would not see his lifted arms. She said vaguely: 'Well, surely it'll be even better for them? We'll get a French or a German girl and they'll learn the language.'

In the dark she lay beside him, feeling frozen, a stranger. She felt as if Susan had been spirited away. She disliked very much this woman who lay here, cold and indifferent beside a suffering man, but she could not change her.

Next morning she set about getting a girl, and very soon came Sophie Traub from Hamburg, a girl of twenty, laughing, healthy, blue-eyed, intending to learn English. Indeed, she already spoke a good deal. In return for a room – 'Mother's Room' – and her food, she undertook to do some light cooking, and to be with the children when Mrs Rawlings asked. She was an intelligent girl and understood perfectly what was needed. Susan said: 'I go off sometimes, for the morning or for the day – well, sometimes the children run home from school, or they ring up, or a teacher rings up. I should be here, really. And there's the daily woman . . .' And Sophie laughed her deep fruity *Fräulein's* laugh, showed her fine white teeth and her dimples, and said: 'You want some person to play mistress of the house sometimes, not so?'

'Yes, that is just so,' said Susan, a bit dry, despite herself, thinking in secret fear how easy it was, how much nearer to the end she was than she thought. Healthy Fräulein Traub's instant understanding of their position proved this to be true.

The *au pair* girl, because of her own common sense, or (as Susan said to herself with her new inward shudder) because she had been *chosen* so well by Susan, was a success with everyone, the children liking her, Mrs Parkes forgetting almost at once that she was German, and Matthew finding her 'nice to have around the house'. For he was now taking things as they came, from the surface of life, withdrawn both as a husband and a father from the household.

One day Susan saw how Sophie and Mrs Parkes were talking and laughing in the kitchen, and she announced that she would be away until teatime. She knew exactly where to go and what she must look for. She took the District Line to South Kensington, changed to the Circle, got off at Paddington, and walked around looking at the smaller hotels until she was satisfied with one which had FRED'S HOTEL painted on windowpanes that needed cleaning. The façade was a faded shiny yellow, like unhealthy skin. A door at the end of a passage said she must knock; she did, and Fred appeared. He was not at all attractive, not in any way, being fattish, and run-down, and wearing a tasteless striped suit. He had small sharp eyes in a white creased face, and was quite prepared to let Mrs Jones (she chose the farcical name deliberately, staring him out) have a room three days a week from ten until six. Provided of course that she paid in advance each time she came? Susan produced fifteen shillings (no price had been set by him) and held it out, still fixing him with a bold unblinking challenge she had not known until then she could use at will. Looking at her still, he took up a ten-shilling note from her palm between thumb and forefinger, fingered it; then shuffled up two half crowns, held out his own palm with these bits of money displayed thereon, and let his gaze lower broodingly at them. They were standing in the passage, a red-shaded light above, bare boards beneath, and a strong smell of floor polish rising about them. He shot his gaze up at her over the still-extended palm, and smiled as if to say: What do you take me for? 'I shan't,' said Susan, 'be using this room for the purposes of making money.' He still waited. She added another five shillings, at which he nodded and said: 'You pay, and I ask no questions.' 'Good,' said Susan. He now went past her to the stairs, and there waited a moment: the light from the street door being in her eyes, she lost sight of him momentarily. Then she saw a sober-suited, white-faced, white-balding little man trotting up the stairs like a waiter, and she went after him. They proceeded in utter silence up the stairs of this house where no questions were asked – Fred's Hotel, which could afford the freedom for its visitors that poor Miss Townsend's hotel could not. The room was hideous. It had a single window, with thin green brocade curtains, a three-quarter bed that had a cheap green satin bedspread on it, a fireplace with a gas fire and a shilling meter by it, a chest of drawers, and a green wicker armchair.

'Thank you,' said Susan, knowing that Fred (if this was Fred, and not George, or Herbert or Charlie) was looking at her, not so much with curiosity, an emotion he would not own to, for professional reasons, but with a philosophical sense of what was appropriate. Having taken her money and shown her up and agreed to everything, he was clearly disapproving of her for coming here. She did not belong here at all, so his look said. (But she knew, already, how very much she did belong: the room had been waiting for her to join it.) 'Would you have me called at five o'clock, please?' and he nodded and went downstairs.

It was twelve in the morning. She was free. She sat in the armchair, she simply sat, she closed her eyes and sat and let herself be alone. She was alone and no one knew where she was. When a knock came on the door she was annoyed, and prepared to show it: but it was Fred himself, it was five o'clock and he was calling her as ordered. He flicked his sharp little eyes over the room – bed, first. It was undisturbed. She might never have been in the room at all. She thanked him, said she would be returning the day after tomorrow, and left. She was back home in time to cook supper, to put the children to bed, to cook a second supper for her husband and herself later. And to welcome Sophie back from the pictures where she had gone with a friend. All these things she did cheerfully, willingly. But she was thinking all the time of the hotel room, she was longing for it with her whole being.

Three times a week. She arrived promptly at ten, looked Fred in the eyes, gave him twenty shillings, followed him up the stairs, went into the room, and shut the door on him with gentle firmness. For Fred, disapproving of her being here at all, was quite ready to let friendship, or at least acquaintanceship, follow his disapproval, if only she would let him. But he was content to go off on her dismissing nod with the twenty shillings in his hand.

She sat in the armchair and shut her eyes.

What did she *do* in the room? Why, nothing at all. From the chair, when it had rested her, she went to the window, stretching her arms, smiling, treasuring her anonymity, to look out. She was no longer Susan Rawlings, mother of four, wife of Matthew, employer of Mrs Parkes and of Sophie Traub, with these and those relations with friends, schoolteachers, tradesmen. She no longer was mistress of the big white house and garden, owning clothes suitable for this and that activity or occasion. She was Mrs Jones, and she was alone, and she had no past and no future. Here I am, she thought, after all these years of being married and having children and playing those roles of responsibility – and I'm just the same. Yet there have been times I thought that nothing existed of me except the roles that went with being Mrs Matthew Rawlings. Yes, here I am, and if I never saw any of my family again, here I would still be ... how very strange that is! And she leaned on the sill, and looked into the street, loving the men and women who passed, because she did not know them. She looked at the downtrodden buildings over the street, and at the sky, wet and dingy, or sometimes blue, and she felt she had never seen buildings or sky before. And then she went back to the chair, empty, her mind a blank. Sometimes she talked aloud, saying nothing – an exclamation, meaningless, followed by a comment about the floral pattern on the thin rug, or a stain on the green satin coverlet. For the most part, she wool-gathered – what word is there for it? – brooded, wandered, simply went dark, feeling emptiness run deliciously through her veins, like the movement of her blood.

This room had become more her own than the house she lived in. One morning she found Fred taking her a flight higher than usual. She stopped, refusing to go up, and demanded her usual room, Number 19. 'Well, you'll have to wait half an hour then,' he said. Willingly she descended to the dark disinfectant-smelling hall, and sat waiting until the two, man and woman, came down the stairs, giving her swift indifferent glances before they hurried out into the street, separating at the door. She went up to the room, *her* room, which they had just vacated. It was no less hers, though the windows were set wide open, and a maid was straightening the bed as she came in.

After these days of solitude, it was both easy to play her part as mother and wife, and difficult – because it was so easy: she felt an impostor. She felt as if her shell moved here, with her family, answering to Mummy, Mother, Susan, Mrs Rawlings. She was surprised no one saw through her, that she wasn't turned out of doors, as a fake. On the contrary, it seemed the children loved her more; Matthew and she 'got on' pleasantly, and Mrs Parkes was happy in her work under (for the most

part, it must be confessed) Sophie Traub. At night she lay
beside her husband, and they made love again, apparently just
as they used to, when they were really married. But she, Susan,
or the being who answered so readily and improbably to the
name of Susan, was not there: she was in Fred's Hotel, in
Paddington, waiting for the easing hours of solitude to begin.

Soon she made a new arrangement with Fred and with
Sophie. It was for five days a week. As for the money, five
pounds, she simply asked Matthew for it. She saw that she was
not even frightened he might ask what for: he would give it to
her, she knew that, and yet it was terrifying it could be so, for
this close couple, these partners, had once known the desti-
nation of every shilling they must spend. He agreed to give her
five pounds a week. She asked for just so much, not a penny
more. He sounded indifferent about it. It was as if he were
paying her, she thought: *paying her off* – yes, that was it.
Terror came back for a moment, when she understood this, but
she stilled it: things had gone too far for that. Now, every week,
on Sunday nights, he gave her five pounds, turning away from
her before their eyes could meet on the transaction. As for
Sophie Traub, she was to be somewhere in or near the house
until six at night, after which she was free. She was not to cook,
or to clean, she was simply to be there. So she gardened or
sewed, and asked friends in, being a person who was bound to
have a lot of friends. If the children were sick, she nursed them.
If teachers telephoned, she answered them sensibly. For the
five daytimes in the school week, she was altogether the mistress of the house.

One night in the bedroom, Matthew asked: 'Susan, I don't
want to interfere – don't think that, please – but are you sure
you are well?'

She was brushing her hair at the mirror. She made two more
strokes on either side of her head, before she replied: 'Yes, dear,
I am sure I am well.'

He was again lying on his back, his big blond head on his
hands, his elbows angled up and part-concealing his face. He
said: 'Then Susan, I have to ask you this question, though you
must understand, I'm not putting any sort of pressure on you.'

(Susan heard the word pressure with dismay, because this was inevitable, of course she could not go on like this.) 'Are things going to go on like this?'

'Well,' she said, going vague and bright and idiotic again, so as to escape: 'Well, I don't see why not.'

He was jerking his elbows up and down, in annoyance or in pain, and, looking at him, she saw he had got thin, even gaunt; and restless angry movements were not what she remembered of him. He said: 'Do you want a divorce, is that it?'

At this, Susan only with the greatest difficulty stopped herself from laughing: she could hear the bright bubbling laughter she *would* have emitted, had she let herself. He could only mean one thing: she had a lover, and that was why she spent her days in London, as lost to him as if she had vanished to another continent.

Then the small panic set in again: she understood that he hoped she did have a lover, he was begging her to say so, because otherwise it would be too terrifying.

She thought this out, as she brushed her hair, watching the fine black stuff fly up to make its little clouds of electricity, hiss, hiss, hiss. Behind her head, across the room, was a blue wall. She realized she was absorbed in watching the black hair making shapes against the blue. She should be answering him. 'Do *you* want a divorce, Matthew?'

He said: 'That surely isn't the point, is it?'

'You brought it up, I didn't,' she said, brightly, suppressing meaningless tinkling laughter.

Next day she asked Fred: 'Have inquiries been made for me?'

He hesitated, and she said: 'I've been coming here a year now. I've made no trouble, and you've been paid every day. I have a right to be told.'

'As a matter of fact, Mrs Jones, a man did come asking.'

'A man from a detective agency?'

'Well, he could have been, couldn't he?'

'I was asking you . . . well, what did you tell him?'

'I told him a Mrs Jones came every weekday from ten until five or six and stayed in Number 19 by herself.'

'Describing me?'

'Well, Mrs Jones, I had no alternative. Put yourself in my place.'

'By rights I should deduct what that man gave you for the information.'

He raised shocked eyes: she was not the sort of person to make jokes like this! Then he chose to laugh: a pinkish wet slit appeared across his white crinkled face: his eyes positively begged her to laugh, otherwise he might lose some money. She remained grave, looking at him.

He stopped laughing and said: 'You want to go up now?' – returning to the familiarity, the comradeship, of the country where no questions are asked, on which (and he knew it) she depended completely.

She went up to sit in her wicker chair. But it was not the same. Her husband had searched her out. (The world had searched her out.) The pressures were on her. She was here with his connivance. He might walk in at any moment, here, into Room 19. She imagined the report from the detective agency: 'A woman calling herself Mrs Jones, fitting the description of your wife (etc., etc., etc.), stays alone all day in Room No. 19. She insists on this room, waits for it if it is engaged. As far as the proprietor knows, she receives no visitors there, male or female.' A report something on these lines, Matthew must have received.

Well of course he was right: things couldn't go on like this. He had put an end to it all simply by sending the detective after her.

She tried to shrink herself back into the shelter of the room, a snail pecked out of its shell and trying to squirm back. But the peace of the room had gone. She was trying consciously to revive it, trying to let go into the dark creative trance (or whatever it was) that she had found there. It was no use, yet she craved for it, she was as ill as a suddenly deprived addict.

Several times she returned to the room, to look for herself there, but instead she found the unnamed spirit of restlessness, a prickling fevered hunger for movement, an irritable self-consciousness that made her brain feel as if it had coloured lights going on and off inside it. Instead of the soft dark that had been the room's air, were now waiting for her demons that made her dash blindly about, muttering words of hate; she was impelling herself from point to point like a moth dashing itself against a windowpane, sliding to the bottom, fluttering off on broken wings, then crashing into the invisible barrier again. And again and again. Soon she was exhausted, and she told Fred that for a while she would not be needing the room, she was going on holiday. Home she went, to the big white house by the river. The middle of a weekday, and she felt guilty at returning to her own home when not expected. She stood unseen, looking in at the kitchen window. Mrs Parkes, wearing a discarded floral overall of Susan's, was stooping to slide something into the oven. Sophie, arms folded, was leaning her back against a cupboard and laughing at some joke made by a girl not seen before by Susan – a dark foreign girl, Sophie's visitor. In an armchair Molly, one of the twins, lay curled, sucking her thumb and watching the grownups. She must have some sickness, to be kept from school. The child's listless face, the dark circles under her eyes, hurt Susan: Molly was looking at the three grownups working and talking in exactly the same way Susan looked at the four through the kitchen window: she was remote, shut off from them.

But then, just as Susan imagined herself going in, picking up the little girl, and sitting in an armchair with her, stroking her probably heated forehead, Sophie did just that: she had been standing on one leg, the other knee flexed, its foot set against the wall. Now she let her foot in its ribbon-tied red shoe slide down the wall, stood solid on two feet, clapping her hands before and behind her, and sang a couple of lines in German, so that the child lifted her heavy eyes at her and began to smile. Then she walked, or rather skipped, over to the child, swung her up, and let her fall into her lap at the same moment she sat herself. She said: 'Hopla! Hopla! Molly . . .' and began stroking the dark untidy young head that Molly laid on her shoulder for comfort.

Well . . . Susan blinked the tears of farewell out of her eyes, and went quietly up the house to her bedroom. There she sat looking at the river through the trees. She felt at peace, but in a way that was new to her. She had no desire to move, to talk, to do anything at all. The devils that had haunted the house, the garden, were not there; but she knew it was because her soul was in Room 19 in Fred's Hotel; she was not really here at all. It was a sensation that should have been frightening: to sit at her own bedroom window, listening to Sophie's rich young voice sing German nursery songs to her child, listening to Mrs Parkes clatter and move below, and to know that all this had nothing to do with her: she was already out of it.

Later, she made herself go down and say she was home: it was unfair to be here unannounced. She took lunch with Mrs Parkes, Sophie, Sophie's Italian friend Maria, and her daughter Molly, and felt like a visitor.

A few days later, at bedtime, Matthew said: 'Here's your five pounds,' and pushed them over to her. Yet he must have known she had not been leaving the house at all.

She shook her head, gave it back to him, and said, in explanation, not in accusation: 'As soon as you knew where I was, there was no point.'

He nodded, not looking at her. He was turned away from her: thinking, she knew, how best to handle this wife who terrified him.

He said: 'I wasn't trying to . . . it's just that I was worried.'

'Yes I know.'

'I must confess that I was beginning to wonder . . .'

'You thought I had a lover?'

'Yes, I am afraid I did.'

She knew that he wished she had. She sat wondering how to say: 'For a year now I've been spending all my days in a very sordid hotel room. It's the place where I'm happy. In fact, without it I don't exist.' She heard herself saying this, and understood how terrified he was that she might. So instead she said: 'Well, perhaps you're not far wrong.'

Probably Matthew would think the hotel proprietor lied: he would want to think so.

'Well,' he said, and she could hear his voice spring up, so to speak, with relief: 'In that case I must confess I've got a bit of an affair on myself.'

She said, detached and interested: 'Really? Who is she?' and saw Matthew's startled look because of this reaction.

'It's Phil. Phil Hunt.'

She had known Phil Hunt well in the old unmarried days. She was thinking: No, she won't do, she's too neurotic and difficult. She's never been happy yet. Sophie's much better: Well Matthew will see that himself, as sensible as he is.

This line of thought went on in silence, while she said aloud: 'It's no point telling you about mine, because you don't know him.'

Quick, quick, invent, she thought. Remember how you invented all that nonsense for Miss Townsend.

She began slowly, careful not to contradict herself: 'His name is Michael' – (*Michael What?*) – 'Michael Plant.' (What a silly name!) 'He's rather like you – in looks, I mean.' And indeed, she could imagine herself being touched by no one but Matthew himself. 'He's a publisher.' (Really? Why?) 'He's got a wife already and two children.'

She brought out this fantasy, proud of herself.

Matthew said: 'Are you two thinking of marrying?'

She said, before she could stop herself: 'Good God, *no*!'

She realized, if Matthew wanted to marry Phil Hunt, that this was too emphatic, but apparently it was all right, for his voice sounded relieved as he said: 'It is a bit impossible to imagine oneself married to anyone else, isn't it?' With which he pulled her to him, so that her head lay on his shoulder. She turned her face into the dark of his flesh, and listened to the blood pounding through her ears saying: I am alone, I am alone, I am alone.

In the morning Susan lay in bed while he dressed.

He had been thinking things out in the night, because now he said: 'Susan, why don't we make a foursome?'

Of course, she said to herself, of course he would be bound to say that. If one is sensible, if one is reasonable, if one never allows oneself a base thought or an envious emotion, naturally one says: Let's make a foursome!

'Why not?' she said.

'We could all meet for lunch. I mean, it's ridiculous, you sneaking off to filthy hotels, and me staying late at the office, and all the lies everyone has to tell.'

What on earth did I say his name was? – she panicked, then said: 'I think it's a good idea, but Michael is away at the moment. When he comes back though – and I'm sure you two would like each other.'

'He's away, is he? So that's why you've been . . .' Her husband put his hand to the knot of his tie in a gesture of male coquetry she would not before have associated with him; and he bent to kiss her cheek with the expression that goes with the words: Oh you naughty little puss! And she felt its answering look, naughty and coy, come on to her face.

Inside she was dissolving in horror at them both, at how far they had both sunk from honesty of emotion.

So now she was saddled with a lover, and he had a mistress! How ordinary, how reassuring, how jolly! And now they would make a foursome of it, and go about to theatres and restaurants. After all, the Rawlingses could well afford that sort of thing, and presumably the publisher Michael Plant could afford to do himself and his mistress quite well. No, there was nothing to stop the four of them developing the most intricate relationship of civilized tolerance, all enveloped in a charming afterglow of autumnal passion. Perhaps they would all go off on holidays together? She had known people who did. Or perhaps Matthew would draw the line there? Why should he, though, if he was capable of talking about 'foursomes' at all?

She lay in the empty bedroom, listening to the car drive off with Matthew in it, off to work. Then she heard the children clattering off to school to the accompaniment of Sophie's cheerfully ringing voice. She slid down into the hollow of the bed, for shelter against her own irrelevance. And she stretched out her hand to the hollow where her husband's body had lain, but found no comfort there: he was not her husband. She curled herself up in a small tight ball under the clothes: she could stay here all day, all week, indeed, all her life.

But in a few days she must produce Michael Plant, and – but how? She must presumably find some agreeable man prepared to impersonate a publisher called Michael Plant. And in return for which she would – what? Well, for one thing they would make love. The idea made her want to cry with sheer exhaustion. Oh no, she had finished with all that – the proof of it was that the words 'make love', or even imagining it, trying hard to revive no more than the pleasures of sensuality, let alone affection, or love, made her want to run away and hide from the sheer effort of the thing . . . Good Lord, why make love at all? Why make love with anyone? Or if you are going to make love, what does it matter who with? Why shouldn't she simply walk into the street, pick up a man and have a roaring sexual affair with him? Why not? Or even with Fred? What difference did it make?

But she had let herself in for it – an interminable stretch of time with a lover, called Michael, as part of a gallant civilized foursome. Well, she could not, and would not.

She got up, dressed, went down to find Mrs Parkes, and asked her for the loan of a pound, since Matthew, she said, had forgotten to leave her money. She exchanged with Mrs Parkes variations on the theme that husbands are all the same, they don't think, and without saying a word to Sophie, whose voice could be heard upstairs from the telephone, walked to the underground, travelled to South Kensington, changed to the Inner Circle, got out at Paddington, and walked to Fred's Hotel. There she told Fred that she wasn't going on holiday after all, she needed the room. She would have to wait an hour, Fred said. She went to a busy tearoom-cum-restaurant around the corner, and sat watching the people flow in and out the door that kept swinging open and shut, watched them mingle and merge and separate, felt her being flow into them, into their movement. When the hour was up she left a half crown for her pot of tea, and left the place without looking back at it, just as she had left her house, the big, beautiful white house, without another look, but silently dedicating it to Sophie. She returned to Fred, received the key of No. 19, now free, and ascended the grimy stairs slowly, letting floor after floor fall away below her, keeping her eyes lifted, so that floor after floor descended jerkily to her level of vision, and fell away out of sight.

No. 19 was the same. She saw everything with an acute, narrow, checking glance: the cheap shine of the satin spread, which had been replaced carelessly after the two bodies had finished their convulsions under it; a trace of powder on the glass that topped the chest of drawers; an intense green shade in a fold of the curtain. She stood at the window, looking down, watching people pass and pass and pass until her mind went dark from the constant movement. Then she sat in the wicker chair, letting herself go slack. But she had to be careful, because she did not want, today, to be surprised by Fred's knock at five o'clock.

The demons were not here. They had gone forever, because she was buying her freedom from them. She was slipping already into the dark fructifying dream that seemed to caress her inwardly, like the movement of her blood . . . but she had to think about Matthew first. Should she write a letter for the coroner? But what should she say? She would like to leave him with the look on his face she had seen this morning – banal, admittedly, but at least confidently healthy. Well, that was impossible, one did not look like that with a wife dead from suicide. But how to leave him believing she was dying because of a man – because of the fascinating publisher Michael Plant? Oh, how ridiculous! How absurd! How humiliating! But she decided not to trouble about it, simply not to think about the living. If he wanted to believe she had a lover, he would believe it. And he *did* want to believe it. Even when he had found out that there was no publisher in London called Michael Plant, he would think: Oh poor Susan, she was afraid to give me his real name.

And what did it matter whether he married Phil Hunt or Sophie? Though it ought to be Sophie who was already the mother of those children . . . and what hypocrisy to sit here worrying about the children, when she was going to leave them because she had not got the energy to stay.

She had about four hours. She spent them delightfully, darkly, sweetly, letting herself slide gently, gently, to the edge of the river. Then, with hardly a break in her consciousness, she got up, pushed the thin rug against the door, made sure the windows were tight shut, put two shillings in the meter, and turned on the gas. For the first time since she had been in the room she lay on the hard bed that smelled stale, that smelled of sweat and sex.

She lay on her back on the green satin cover, but her legs were chilly. She got up, found a blanket folded into the bottom of the chest of drawers, and carefully covered her legs with it. She was quite content lying there, listening to the faint soft hiss of the gas that poured into the room, into her lungs, into her brain, as she drifted off into the dark river.

MARTHA QUEST
Book One in the *Children of Violence* series

Martha is a young girl living on a farm in Africa, feeling her way through the torments of adolescence and early womanhood to marriage. She is a romantic idealist in revolt against the puritan snobbery of her parents, trying to live life to the full with every nerve, emotion and instinct bared to experience. For her this is a time of solitary reading, daydreams, dancing – and the first disturbing encounters with sex.

'Extraordinarily impressive'
New York Times

£1.25

A PROPER MARRIAGE
Book Two in the *Children of Violence* series

The war clouds are gathering over Europe, and for Martha Quest, the first passionate flush of marriage is beginning to fade. Sensuality becomes dulled by habit, marriage becomes motherhood, and, with the outbreak of war, Martha's political consciousness begins to dawn. The barriers between her and the frightening world outside finally dissolve.

'Strength . . . sobriety . . . integrity . . . Mrs Lessing knows just what she is doing and a real, densely imagined, completely credible world emerges'
John Wain

£1.25

A RIPPLE FROM THE STORM
Book Three in the *Children of Violence* series

The outstanding continuation of the story of Martha Quest, Doris Lessing's most brilliantly portrayed representative of modern womanhood – passionate, wilful, uneasy in her emancipation. As the reader follows Martha through her emotional entanglements and her deepening involvement with politics, a magnificent panorama of 20th century life emerges, compassionate yet uncompromising in the fierce integrity of the author's vision.

'Not even Osborne or Amis can have much to teach author Doris Lessing'
Time

95p

LANDLOCKED
Book Four in the *Children of Violence* series

The whole world seems to have the post-war blues in the aftermath of World War II, and Martha Quest is no exception. Increasingly disillusioned with the Communist faith she once so fervently embraced, tiring of her neurotic lover Thomas, Martha embodies the plight of liberated 20th century womanhood. Doris Lessing portrays Martha and her crumbling world with an insight and compassion unmatched by any other living author.

'She never puts a foot wrong . . . for sheer poise I don't think there's been an author to touch her since Jane Austen'
John Wain, *The Observer*

£1.25

THE FOUR-GATED CITY
Book Five in the *Children of Violence* series

The Four-Gated City is the concluding volume in Doris Lessing's epic novel-sequence. It gives us Martha Quest in the Britain of the CND marches, 'Swinging' London, permissiveness and maybe social anarchy. But the author is not content to leave us there – we are taken a few years forward into a post-third-world-war world where the mutated fruits of humanity's stupidity are beginning to show their eerie presence.

'Staggering'
New York Times

'A powerful, prophetic, mysterious work, a truly extraordinary novel'
Saturday Review

'A brilliant and disturbing book'
The Times

'The supreme achievement of a writer whom I regard as quite simply beyond my – or anyone else's – criticism'
Mervyn Jones, *Tribune*

£1.50

THE GOLDEN NOTEBOOK

Somewhere between emancipation and liberation were Free Women – women without husbands following marital collapse. *The Golden Notebook* is a story of Free Women, and has been variously seen as the 'bible' of Women's Liberation, as a political tract and as a story of mental breakdown. It is a book in which men and women will go on finding themselves and their battles for generations.

'One of the most serious, intelligent and honest writers of the whole post-war generation'
Sunday Times

£1.95